"He's Dead, Em."

"We don't have proof of that," I said. "We never found a body. He had funds. He's got the wits to survive."

Brian shrugged.

I went up to my office to think this out. I'd been retreating too long. I needed to press an attack. But I couldn't find an enemy, and my fighting skills were theoretical at best. What did I have going for me?

The love of a good man. A more than passing familiarity with the local constabulary. A kickass collection of reference material. Degrees with honors from a couple of prestigious universities. Tenure.

There you go. That's a lot right there.

I had brains, but Tony was at least my match. Probably a lot smarter. And he had an agenda, which now looked like it had been planned over the past four years.

Hells bells, *chica*. You're starting to make me scared.

And I have absolutely no idea what to do about it.

"Dana Cameron knows archaeology inside and out . . . and knows how to tell a rip-snorting good mystery."
Edgar® Award-winning author Aaron Elkins

The Emma Fielding Mysteries
by Dana Cameron

DANA CAMERON

ASHES AND BONES

AN EMMA FIELDING MYSTERY

WITHDRAWN

AVON BOOKS
An Imprint of HarperCollins*Publishers*

AVON BOOKS
An Imprint of HarperCollins*Publishers*
10 East 53rd Street
New York, New York 10022-5299

Copyright © 2006 by Dana Cameron
ISBN-13: 978-0-06-055467-5
ISBN-10: 0-06-055467-3
www.avonmystery.com

First Avon Books paperback printing: August 2006

Avon Trademark Reg. U.S. Pat. Off. and in Other Countries, Marca Registrada, Hecho en U.S.A.
HarperCollins® is a registered trademark of HarperCollins Publishers Inc.

Printed in the U.S.A.

10 9 8 7 6 5 4 3 2 1

To the friends who are always there, through thick and thin, reprints and revising: Beth, Ann, Pam & Pete, Anne & Jonathan, Toni & Steve, Dan, the Buffybuds, the Femmes Fatales, the Teabuds, and particularly, Mr. G.

Acknowledgments

I'D LIKE TO THANK THE FOLLOWING, ALL OF WHOM contributed to this book: Ann Barbier, Pam Crane, James Goodwin, Beth Krueger, Peter Morrison, Anne Wilder, my agent Kit Ward, my editor Sarah Durand, Eileen Dreyer, Dan Hale, Steve Kelner, D.P. Lyle, M.D., Donna Andrews, Lois Reibach, and Suzi Thurmond. Many folks in beautiful downtown Beverly, Massachusetts also helped out: the gang at the Atomic Café, the folks at the Beverly Post Office, Karen and David at Barter Brothers, Inc. Flowers–Gifts, and J.G.M. Numismatics.

ASHES AND
BONES

Chapter 1

I SAT ON THE ROCK BY THE EDGE OF THE REDDISH clay path, watching the Aqua Velva water churning on the toothy black rocks below. The sharp salt air was tempered with the heavy freshness of the nearby forest, and that kept the bright sunshine from being excessively hot. Seabirds, not so different from the sandpipers and seagulls I was used to, wheeled and played on the updrafts far beneath me, while still being an easy hundred feet above the water. It would only take a subtle shift of weight, merely straightening my legs at the hip, and I would slide from my narrow perch and finally find out if all those falling nightmares I'd been having lived up to the real thing. Even if I didn't hit one of those eager rocks, the impact on the water probably would break my back. I wondered if I would crash into one of the seabirds on the way down or if they would flap out of the way. But because I wasn't really feeling suicidal, I allowed myself the shiver of vertigo for another moment or two, enjoying the thrill and the view, before I very carefully got up and picked my way back down to the picnic spot that Brian had chosen.

Pity about the morbidity, I thought disinterestedly, particularly when things were so perfect.

I'm in what most people would call paradise, which on Earth is known as Kauai, with the man I love. I have everything I've always wanted: a tenured position, books with my name on the cover, plenty of students, hot sites to work on, and a livable if unfinished house, a genuine vacation, and I am about as much fun as a cold slate gravestone.

As a polite person, against my will I have developed into something of an adequate liar over the years, so convinced myself that I wasn't spoiling my husband Brian's vacation. He has a naturally happy disposition, particularly when the weather is warm; the booze, sex, idleness, and great food were a significant bonus. As far as our first real vacation since our honeymoon—a vacation that wasn't wrapped around a conference or research trip—it was a smashing success.

The fact that I was miserable, however, was unrelated.

I found my way down the slope and crossed the sand along the water. The beach was nearly empty, not because it was a Thursday but because we'd outlasted the other tourists and the beach wasn't any good for surfers. We could almost imagine that it was ours alone.

Physically, I felt great. I'd been catching up on my sleep. I had lost a little weight, but chalked it up to a stressful semester. No archaeologist field tan, elbow to fingers, here. I'd been super careful about the sun and could actually boast of having a tan that extended everywhere my bikini didn't, and Brian claimed the freckles that came automatically with my dark red hair were cute. The bags under my eyes had faded and most of my bruises from my Krav Maga training were gone. I'd had just enough fieldwork before coming out so that my muscles were tolerably toned and I didn't have the professorial slouch that seemed to settle in from October to May.

About twenty feet away from Brian and our towels, I remembered what was missing. I carefully smiled and waved at him. His dark brown hair was mussed from the wind and flaking out; his honey skin was glowing from the sun.

"You should have gone up," I said, sitting down. "The view was great. I could see whales way out there."

"All the views are great," he said. "Here, I've got warm sand under my butt."

"To each his own," I said. I ate the last of the mango in my fruit salad. I then flopped over on my stomach and closed my eyes. There were palm fronds rattling, and small waves endlessly lapping at the beach. The heat from the sand, eggshell white, was lulling.

"Em. You've been sleeping an awful lot lately."

His voice was tight, the sentiment came out of nowhere. Crap. I dodged it. "Since when are you opposed to napping, Lazy Boy?"

"This is something else. I mean, ever since school got out, you've either been going full tilt or you've been asleep. Here, it's been worse."

The sun turned the insides of my eyelids red and it was too bright. I turned my head to the other side, shaded my eyes, and watched the little crabs scuttling sideways just a foot away.

"Em?"

"It's called a vacation, Bri, or had you forgotten whose idea this was?" I sounded a lot bitchier than I meant to, but he was the one picking a fight.

There was a long sigh, and I thought he was giving it up. Then he said, "Em. The fingerprints weren't Tony's."

"What fingerprints?" I was so nearly asleep, if he could just not raise his voice or anything, I'd be off in a few moments . . .

"Don't be like that. The fingerprints on the postcard. The postcard that you got back in January, the one that could have come from your disgruntled student or even a few people who might be upset that you got them arrested. It couldn't be from Tony Markham. Tony's dead."

"Whatever." I shouldn't have answered; I was awake now. He'd pushed too many buttons in one go.

"You know, I was fine when there was still a possibility that Tony was alive, that he'd sent that card. But the police—your friend, Detective Bader—said that the prints weren't his, weren't a match for any they had in the . . . whatdoyoucallit."

"The AFIS database. Automated Fingerprint Identification System."

"Right. And the handwriting was similar, but not a real match, and there wasn't even enough to be conclusive. You saw that yourself, right?"

I didn't answer. Tony Markham was once a colleague of mine at Caldwell College in Maine, an archaeologist like myself. He'd happened onto a couple of petty criminals, people responsible for, among others, the death of my dear friend Pauline Westlake, and found himself intrigued by the possibilities that life outside the law offered. Something about his first murder awakened a diabolical spark in him, and although the authorities believed that Tony was dead—lost at sea during a hurricane—I had never been convinced. Tony was too wily to die so easily.

"But the fingerprints, that *is* conclusive," Brian continued. "I think we need to just chalk it up to a bad prank. You did everything you could."

"Everything I could? I went to Detective Bader, asked a favor. What else could I do?"

I could hear him as he sat up now, quite serious. "Worry, apparently. I don't know why you're letting this get to you so bad. You've been so depressed—"

I sat up, too. "I have not."

He fished out my sandwich, which I'd only nibbled, and began to tear it up, then threw it to the birds. "Looks pretty textbook to me. I mean, shit, half the guys in the lab down the hall work on developing antidepressants. I'm not entirely thick."

I ignored him; he wasn't thick, but neither did being a chemist qualify him as a psychiatrist. "Don't. You shouldn't feed them."

at a well-respected college. Our marriage had
not only graduate school and our first angst-ridden
hes, but house hunting and, recently, jointly owned
ite my earlier mood, Brian and I were still good for
r. I had my health, friends, happiness, and hell, we
enough money to begin renovating said house with
ofessionals.

which was great, but it made me really, really

g can be a great way of keeping life in order, but
pens when you get what you've been working for
fe? What do you do then? If you are single-minded,
ist determined, this can be quite unnerving.

arrange for new excavation and research projects,
esign new classes, take part in other professional
it's all a little too familiar now; and even if it isn't
there wouldn't be the same thrill of anxiety that ac-
es fresh endeavors because I know I have the skills
them.

me wondering: What was next, existentially
?

lled up into the crowded hotel parking lot, just in
mai tai hour, which by mutual agreement, was at
our earlier than at home. Usually a bourbon or beer
lf, I now found myself addicted to a complicated
k with a pink orchid floating on top. While I knew
e flowers were nothing out of the ordinary here—
ned to be like forsythia in the yards here—I still, in
New England heart, couldn't believe that people
ds on drinks. That was the coolest, most decadent
r.

m didn't hurt either.

ed up the stairs, ready to wash off, and change for
his was a trick for me; even at my most casual, I
't been able to shed my Connecticut upbringing
iedly Atlantic attitude. Everywhere I went, even in
a skirt, I felt overdressed. Brian, raised in San

"Fine." He stuffed the other half of the sandwich back
into the bag and dusted the crumbs from his hands. "Okay,
maybe some of this is still fallout from last semester, and the
plagiarism thing and all. That really wore you out. But I
think it's Tony. It's like you've got some kind of morbid
crush on him. It's kinda freaking me out and I don't think it's
healthy for you."

"That's ridiculous!" I ignored the fact I'd used "morbid"
myself ten minutes ago.

"It's like you *want* him to be back. The way you obsess
about it."

"I do *not* obsess. I just try not to think about it. I mean, after all, Tony's dead, right?"

"And for some reason, you won't believe it. It was a postcard, Emma, that's all. And you're building some kind of
fantasy around it."

It wasn't just the postcard that had only my name and the
lone word "soon" on it, I thought. It was someone introduc-
ing himself to my revolting ex-boyfriend as Billy Griggs and
asking after me. I'd watched Billy die, shot by Tony, almost
exactly four years ago this month. It was the lack of a body;
Tony had sailed off into a hurricane that he couldn't have
survived, yet there was no wreckage. It was the lily-of-the-
valley pips anonymously sent to me two years ago: Tony had
killed another man using lily of the valley.

I'd looked up the meaning of lily of the valley according
to the "language of flowers" and found that it represented
sweetness. It also represented humility, which worried me.
In a twisted way, I was convinced that Tony held me responsible for interrupting his scheme and that, with these new
"messages," he was coming back for me.

Tony had been brilliantly manipulative—he'd come close
to making me believe that I was responsible for my friend
Pauline's death—and the farther he moved away from his
old life, the more his deeds escalated in evil and violence.

So I didn't think it was a fantasy. I just don't believe in
that many coincidences.

Brian sighed, studied the sand that he'd scooped into a pile in front of him. "Look, even if someone else is behind this, fine, it's important to be careful about that sort of thing. I want you to be careful. And if they're smart enough to dig around and find out about your . . . history with Tony and Pauline's murder out at Penitence Point, and make something of that, then yes, we should be cautious. But we've told the police at home in Massachusetts, we've warned the Maine cops at Caldwell College, so if it *is* someone on campus, they'll be aware of it. I just don't know why you need to keep dwelling on this."

I shrugged. "First I'm sleeping too much, then I'm dwelling. Make up your mind." I got the tone just right that time, just the right balance of humor and reconciliation. I wasn't sold, but I was tired of arguing.

"You know what I mean." He hesitated, then said, "You know, you could see someone about it."

I stared out at the water; the sun was heading for the horizon. "About what? I'm fine. You're the one who seems to be obsessed with something."

"I mean, maybe it's some kind of post-traumatic stress disorder, reawakened by the postcard. Maybe it's some old fears that you haven't quite uprooted, yet. Or maybe it's last semester."

I thought about that. If I didn't entirely believe Brian's reasoning, it did make a certain kind of sense. I could certainly use it to make the present disagreement go away. "I don't think it's that bad, Brian. I mean, I suppose I've been feeling a little flaky lately, but I just figured it was unwinding after the end of semester and, you know, working through some stress. It actually takes time to get used to being on vacation, too, and I don't think jetlag does anyone any favors."

He reached for my hand. "I'm just asking you to maybe think about what I'm saying. Okay, babe? I don't want to ruin our vacation, but if something doesn't seem right with you, I want to deal with it, you know? I'm concerned, that's all."

"I know. And I don't want to be a [ ] when we get there tomorrow. I'm look[ ] them."

"Me too. You should hear what Ma s[ ] cook for dinner." The way to Brian's he[ ] through his stomach.

I smiled, with genuine warmth this t[ ] great. "I can't wait." I flipped over onto[ ] picked up my beach reading, a popular a[ ] noted forensic anthropologist.

The drive back to the hotel, like every driv[ ] Kauai, was a revelation. In New England[ ] turning, twisting roads, but the variation of [ ] such relatively short distances, was enough t[ ] ing every minute. Around every turn was an[ ] view of sand or trees or water that simply [ ] amidst it all was the completely recognizab[ ] coffee shops, supermarkets, and fast food pl[ ] have been uprooted from anywhere on the[ ] plopped down here. I avoided chains as f[ ] home, trying to support small local busines[ ] went into at least one while traveling anyw[ ] was fascinating to see the variations even w[ ] ifices. Walk into a drugstore and instead [ ] Halen tapes, Red Sox gear, and maple ca[ ] Kamakawiwo'ole CDs, beach mats, and [ ] in front, along with macadamia nuts in ev[ ] home, around here the nuts were so cor[ ] think they grew on trees, I thought with [ ]

The ride back did exactly what the w[ ] had been designed to do: give me a bre[ ] teries, make me count my blessings. I'[ ] my life that I couldn't have imagined a[ ] or ten years ago, even though I'd been [ ] was a kid. The holy grail of job securi[ ]

Diego, had a lot easier time finding the right mode: shorts, aloha or polo shirt, sandals. I fiddled, finding my key card, with Brian crowding behind me chanting the gimme-a-mai-tai song, and we burst into the room giggling. I pulled up short when I saw the long white box on the bed.

"Hey, what's that?" I said, rushing over to look at it. "Flowers?"

Brian looked as surprised as I. "Don't ask me. What's it say?"

He also had a better poker face than I did. "As if you didn't know. It has my name on it, silly."

Brian was still not smiling. "Seriously, Em, it's not from me."

"Then who?" I opened the card.

He held his hands up. "Gonna have to read the card, porkchop."

" 'Miss me yet?' " I looked up, confused. "Huh?"

"There's no name?"

"No." I got the box open and paused. In a land where flowers were abundant, fleshy, exotically improbable, and elegant, these stood out as all too familiar, gorgeous, but in a rustic sort of way. A New England sort of way. And in a tiny focal point, in front of the bouquet of asters, lupines, daisies, and bachelor's buttons, was a knot of lilies of the valley.

Chapter 2

WHAT THE HELL?" I STARTED TO TREMBLE.
Brian leaned over me, trying to read, his hand on my shoulder. "Em, chill. It's just flowers. There's no signature on the card?"

I shrugged his hand off. "No. I told you, no."

He looked at me, and I could see in that instant that look in his eyes, not often seen, that indicated he thought I'd checked out. That my opinion was not to be completely trusted because of hormones, or fatigue, or depression, or personal involvement, or whatever. Everyone's significant other has that look, tinged with annoyance or frustration or dismissal. But it was my own personal vision of hell: not being taken seriously by the one person in the world who should trust me entirely.

And I was too tired to argue it now, so soon after our earlier discussion. As much as I knew I was right, in spite of whatever evidence. I shrugged. "Weird, huh?"

I'd backed off too soon; Brian looked suspicious.

"I'm going to have a look through it anyway, see if there's anything else that might tell me where it's from. And I'll call the desk. Maybe they know what's going on."

"Sure, that sounds like a reasonable plan. I'm going to grab the shower; I'm starting to smell pretty ripe."

I couldn't tell whether Brian was just dodging the issue—now he was backing off too quickly. "Go ahead." At least if he was in the shower, I could paw through the flowers to my heart's content, with no weird looks following me.

I called down to the desk: Yes, they were left there; yes, they'd come from a local vendor, very reputable, with the usual delivery guy. I thanked them, called the florist. They were glad that I liked the flowers, a special order; no, they couldn't legally tell me who sent them. I pressed; they demurred again, politely, firmly.

After I took a picture of the flowers, I threw them out. Then I showered and we went down to drinks. Brian very carefully didn't ask anything more about the flowers.

Late that night, I left Brian snoring gently in bed, got dressed, and quietly shut the door behind me, making my way to the beach through the abandoned paths of the silent hotel.

I'd just made it down to the sand when I saw a flash of brilliant light, then heard a huge bang. I felt a brutal punch to my stomach. I was immediately ashamed; I should have been able to block it. But I hadn't seen it coming, there was no one there, I thought in a panic, so I couldn't really be blamed for that . . .

And then I knew the truth. I'd been shot in the belly.

The pain that followed after the impact was unlike anything I'd ever experienced, as though the first blow was just the warm-up. It lasted nearly five seconds, an exquisite eternity of unbearable agony, before I felt myself distanced from it all. Then I was finally able to look down, see what the actual damage was.

It wasn't bad, not as bad as I thought; maybe I'd be all right. The thing that impressed me most was the quantity and warmth of the blood; it seemed endless. As for seeing things that I was generally happier not seeing, there was no revulsion, just curiosity. It was fascinating, really, actually being able to recognize . . . me. Kind of strange, knowing there was all this going on inside of me, like imagining another person on the inside of me. Kind of neat. I put my hands up to the ragged hole, tried to stop the flow of blood, but it was no good; the flood I could feel running down my back was even worse.

I was dying.

Sitting on the sand, in the moonlight, little birds chasing the surf, I felt okay. I could see black stains on the sand around where I sat, but at this point, the pain was a distant memory and I was vaguely satisfied that the blood was being absorbed by the sand. A convenience, really, for such a messy end. Couldn't have done that at home, I thought. Brian was right to get us to take a vacation. If it had to happen anywhere . . .

Brian! I thought, I had to . . . no, Brian was back in the room, and I couldn't get there. Couldn't even make a noise.

Still, I struggled, tried to get to my feet. But I couldn't feel them, couldn't feel my legs under my fingers, and a wave of misery washed over me. I couldn't get to Brian. Closer to hand, I remembered that I'd seen that flash of light, a long time ago, it seemed, and tried to recall the direction. No luck.

Fighting it seemed silly. Futile. Now I couldn't even hear the waves on the shore, and I would have liked that. Dying by the ocean—in advanced old age—has always been my plan, but I didn't realize you didn't get the whole package in death—sight and sound and smell.

I'd settle for what I had. I relaxed. No sense fighting the inevitable.

Everything felt very distant now, and there was so much going on with me, that there was no room for anything else. Just me and the quiet little patch of beach I was dying on.

I kept fretting that there was something missing, something I didn't do, but with a minor sort of revelation, I realized that I'd done pretty well for myself in my nearly thirty-five years of life. Even more than I hoped—and then there was Brian. We'd even made love earlier in the evening, so I felt that I'd be leaving things about as well as I could. Not a bad end, not what I'd hoped, of course, but not bad . . .

There was that one thing. That one last thing that had been eating at me.

And there was a little rush. I felt a lightness overtake me when I realized that it was no longer my responsibility. It was so far out of my hands that I felt, so far away, myself smiling. Relief, the few times I've experienced it fully in my life, really is miraculous.

I stopped fighting. I felt myself drifting off. Didn't need to close my eyes, there was so little I could see now, on the dark beach, even with the moonlight, but I did anyway. I'd pretend I was going to sleep, which was one of my favorite sensations anyway.

Not a bad way to go, not at all.

I felt . . . something. Distantly. A pulling. Something was dragging me back.

Brian.

"Emma, open your eyes! Emma, wake up, baby."

I couldn't see anything. I could barely make out the words, the fear in his voice. I tried to say, Brian, I love you, it's too late, it's okay, I'm okay with this, don't worry. The words wouldn't come.

Someone once said that the easiest way of parting was death. He was absolutely right.

Brian wouldn't stop. I found myself feeling . . . something. I found myself being pulled back enough to recognize . . . anger. If he knew what I'd have to go through, if I came back, he would never ask me to . . .

"Em, come on, sugar, it's only a dream. Wake up, okay?"

More sensations rushing back now. Dampness, but not sand. I felt the weight return to my body, the warmth of sweaty sheets, and cold air-conditioning. The wonderful bliss left me, even as I fought to hang on to it. I had been so close.

"It was just a dream, babe. You awake now?"

I could hear now, and I realized, once I opened my eyes, that I could see. I was in the hotel room, Brian was next to me, rubbing his face sleepily.

"I'm . . . just leave . . . give me a minute, would you, sweetie?" I said finally when I realized it was just a dream. I rolled over onto my knees, bunched my hands under my forehead on the pillow while I tried to recall the vanishing shreds of the dream. I was overwhelmed to find myself here. It had been so real. My heart was still pounding unbelievably.

"Come here. It's okay, it was just a dream," Brian was saying. "Come over here, cuddle."

I backed into him, felt his arm around me, and tried to make myself relax. He nuzzled the back of my neck, and was asleep again almost instantly. Crisis identified, problem solved, sleeping the sleep of the just.

I stared at the shadows that played on the walls where the moonlight peeped in through the curtains, feeling the tears run down my cheeks. I swallowed, once, twice, but the tears wouldn't stop.

It would have been so much easier if it hadn't been a dream.

The next day, we were in San Diego. Brian's folks live in Pacific Beach, a couple of blocks off Garnet (they'd carefully taught me to pronounce the accent as they did, on the second syllable), in a beautiful house with a garden stuffed with a riot of flowers. Stan was a whisker away from retiring from his building business and Betty kept claiming that she was going to leave the library every year, but she never quite made it. It was always great to see them—you could see why Brian had turned out so well—but after three days, I got bored. The beach was pretty and funky and full of characters, but I was beached out, and even a drive over to the museums of Balboa Park didn't keep me occupied for more than an afternoon.

Brian, of course, noticed, and said so as I did the breakfast dishes, sunlight spilling across the hardwood floor. "Didn't Nolan give you homework, or something?"

Nolan taught me and Brian Krav Maga, a particularly vicious form of self-defense to which I'd become addicted. "What do you mean?"

"Didn't he tell you to look up his buddy or something, while we were here?"

"He told us *both* to keep up with the training. He gave me an address and phone number, that's all. Hardly an order. So far I've seen you do . . . um, lemme see. Exactly nothing."

"I went for a walk last night. We've been for walks every night this week."

"Yeah, to get ice cream." I put a cup on the rack to dry.

Brian grinned. "Well, why don't you give him a call today? Dad wants to show me a kitchen job he's working on. Give me some pointers."

"You think you can cheer me up with homework? Boy, I must be bad off."

"I know you like your time structured, that's all."

"Fine. I'll give him a call."

Brian's father stuck his head into the kitchen and they left. After I finished the dishes, I called. The phone was answered on the first ring, but on the other end another conversation had not ended—"and so you can tell them they'll get their money when I get mine."

"Hello?" I said.

"G'day, Temple's Martial Arts," the voice said directly into the phone. "Derek Temple himself."

"My name's Emma Fielding, and my instructor—"

Mr. Temple broke in before I'd even had a chance to explain myself. "Fielding? Right. See you in an hour."

"I was wondering—"

But he'd already hung up; I was left with the vestige of an accent I thought was Australian. I didn't know how to get to the school, I didn't know what I should bring, and now I was on my own.

I had just enough time to throw all of my gear on, consult a map, and drive like a maniac to the address. I don't know why I had such a compulsion to be on time, especially after

Temple's brusque rudeness on the phone. I figure it was because he was probably Nolan's friend and he was doing me a favor. If I wasn't up to snuff, I'd get my hide tanned next time I saw Nolan at home.

It was hard to find the place, but I eventually located the correct mall; maybe it was because of where I was traveling. So many of southern California roads seemed lined with strip malls. Made me nervous, disoriented, as I was used to navigating off New England town architecture, with greens and churches and town halls to use as landmarks. We had our share of strip malls, but at least at home there was an underlying logic I understood. Besides, around here, the ocean was in the wrong place and that always screwed me up. That and when my mother-in-law, Betty, kept telling me I'd need a coat, because it was getting down below sixty-five degrees at night.

The school was a corner property, with windows along one long side that let in lots of light. The floors were lined with mats, and there were mirrors along the other long wall. I was a few minutes early and a class was still going. Intimidation wasn't the word for what I felt when I saw the students, all ten of them, dressed entirely in black with black leather hand-wraps. There were eight men, mostly in their twenties, all either with crew cuts or entirely clean-headed. Not one of them was in less than excellent physical shape, and the collective amount of ink I saw on exposed arms and necks would have made any afficionado proud. Considering the number of bases in and around San Diego, I wouldn't have been surprised if any or all of them were military. Not with the way they moved.

The two women were hardly less intimidating, for all that they were the wispy, willowy blondes that always characterize my California experiences. Both of them were just the same, perfectly proportioned size six or less, with breasts that belied the total lack of body fat and strained both credulity and their fashionably fitted shirts. Except for that, Mr. Temple's female students were just as hard as his male students.

Holy Cobra Kai.

My chances for making a good impression were dwindling, fast. I hadn't brought my regular Krav Maga gear and was wearing blue sweats with a red T-shirt with the logo of the Chandler house dig on it. I had hand wraps, and they were black, but they were the long cloth ones you use for boxing, so I looked like a sad castoff next to this streamlined class. And while I'm tall, for a woman, and in pretty good physical shape, I felt like a lumpy, bulky mass next to these chicks.

Strike one.

As unobtrusive as I'd hoped my entrance would be, I could feel the glances follow me from the floor, especially from the slight but powerful-looking man in the front of the class, who frowned slightly and nodded. I gave a brief, general smile of acknowledgment and then focused on getting my left hand wrapped up.

A door opened behind me and a voice like the last trump filled the room. "Mr. Anderson. We have a guest."

I stood up, whipped around, and saw that the wall behind me had disappeared, largely replaced by a man. My other wrap fell off the bench and rolled across the waiting area floor onto the mats, a black streamer unraveling. I expected giggles, but only saw a smirk or two. All eyes were on the man-wall behind me, and the class snapped to, bowing to what must have been Mr. Temple.

Strike two.

He was the biggest guy I had ever seen, well over six feet tall and damn near six feet wide at the shoulders; I could have sworn that his waist was no bigger than mine, and I don't know what size his rip-stop athletic pants were, but they should have been a half-size larger because his thigh muscles bulged through them. Shoot, his calf muscles were straining at the fabric. If his students were blond, then he was literally golden-haired, his hair was cut short, but was ridiculously wavy. In fact, an image came to me—unbidden and disastrously accurate—of Dudley Do-Right or a Disney hero: slab of a head, lantern jaw, brilliant teeth in two perfect rows, and, I swear, a spit curl in the middle of his forehead. He was practically a parody of himself.

He was coming toward me.

I'd stared just a second too long.

Strike three, and I hadn't even made it out onto the floor yet. Hadn't even shaken his hand.

I was done for.

"Look at that!" he boomed, and I realized that he was the one with the strong Australian accent. "Can't take her eyes off me! Poor little thing—but no wonder! Ugly cuss she trains with back East makes the ass end of a dingo look good. And he's a teeny, tiny, little man to boot."

Now there were open smiles and a few chuckles from the floor. I smiled briefly, but I could feel my jaw tightening. He was talking about Nolan, my instructor and something of a hero to me. While Nolan was certainly . . . compact of stature, he wasn't ugly. In fact, I'd come to realize that both he and his face were in remarkably good shape, considering the man made his living by doling out beatings and that he'd probably taken more than a few himself. So who did this big lug think he was talking about?

He stuck out a hand the size of a Thanksgiving turkey. "Name's Derek Temple. Mr. Temple, to you." Engulfing my hand with his own, he turned to his students. "The lucky thing is that she's come to her senses and is going to train properly, now, with *me*."

He was still smiling like he was selling toothpaste as he turned back to me, something calm and hard behind his eyes. "Lesson one: don't tense up like that. Limits your options, darling," he said near my ear.

He let my hand go and I barely kept from shaking it out. He hadn't crushed the bones or anything, just made the point, paying me back for gaping at him before.

Now I felt a grizzly-bear paw land on my shoulder, and staggered a bit under it. "While her instructor is indeed small, ugly, and unable to get women without paying for them, he is my brother, a fellow warrior with some serious skills. Once upon a time, when I was just a pup, scarcely off the teat, some accounted him even better than I. But as you all well know, there is no one fiercer or prettier than I, is there, class?"

"NO, SIR!" came the unified cry from the floor.

"No one with slyer shoots, no one with harder locks, and no one with slicker moves. But out of respect for my comrade's advanced age and our fraternal bond, we will do our best to teach this poor girl the way it's done. No one will try to take her out on a date she doesn't want to go on, no one will mess with her, because we will have given her our skills. She will leave her mark on the silly bastard, and it will be because of us."

"YES, SIR!"

"Now, we've got five minutes left, and Mr. Anderson and I are going to give you one more valuable lesson before you go back out to the cold and uncaring world."

"THANK YOU, SIR!"

"Mr. Anderson!" Temple strode out onto the floor.

"Sir!" The man who'd been leading the class before snapped to.

"You're wearing a cup, are you not?" Temple paused to look in the mirror, moved as if to make an adjustment to his hair, and then realized there was no improvement that could be made on perfection.

Anderson smelled a rat, but answered smartly. "Yes, si—"

He didn't have time to finish the word before Temple spun around, dropped, and aimed a reverse round kick at his groin. Anderson hopped back sharply, blocked the kick, then closed the space between them, light on the balls of his feet and wary.

Temple was off the floor almost as soon as his kick missed, moving in on Anderson. He faked a round kick to the side, then whipped his foot up to the side of Anderson's head; Anderson blocked it handily, and threw a nice sweep at him. He didn't quite pull it off; Temple avoided it, then moved forward with it and kicked, landing a hard blow to Anderson's stomach. Anderson went over backward, and Temple followed him down to the ground.

They got into some grappling for a few seconds, but it was clear by now that they were just playing around, showing off for the class, and trying to impress the new kid. Finally, Temple got tired of the fooling and laid a nasty-looking armbar on Anderson, who was still fighting him.

I would have been smothered by being pinned under just one of his legs, but apparently Anderson was made of sterner stuff.

"Tell me you love me," Temple bellowed good-naturedly as his second-in-command resisted him.

"Not on your life, sir," Anderson gasped. He was still trying to work his way out of the hold, but he didn't have much in the way of options open to him. He was half giggling with the futility of his task, half on the rack with the pain he was in.

"Tell me you want to go out with me," Temple insisted. He arched his back, pulling on the arm just a bit more.

"Take a flying f—arrghh!" He tapped out and instantly Temple released him. Both men were on their feet before you could say "Boo!"

"Thank you, Mr. Anderson." They slapped hands and exchanged bows. "Who can tell me what the lesson is?"

"Mr. Anderson should have taken you up on the date?" one of the guys said.

"Cheek and impudence, Watanabe, gets you thirty and thirty." Temple sounded as cheery as before, but Watanabe dropped immediately and started banging out the crunches. "Anyone else care to try?"

"Mr. Anderson anticipated trouble, even though he was with friends in a safe place," one of the women said, after a pause. "He could have been in much worse trouble, but he wasn't. He made you work for it."

"That's my girl, Mindy, and that's why you've been lucky enough to be my blushing bride, lo, these past six years. And

Mr. Anderson knows I could have handed him his ass, but we're all good friends here, aren't we? Pay attention, all the time, especially when you feel safe: The best way to deal with trouble is to avoid it." He glanced over at the floor where Watanabe was now doing the other "thirty," which were push-ups. "How are you doing, Ed?"

"Nearly . . . done . . . sir," he got out between painful exhales. Sweat glistened on his face.

"Feels good, doesn't it?"

"Oh . . . hell, yes . . . sir."

"Good on ya. The rest of you, I'll see you next time."

They bowed out and everyone came off the floor. A few of the guys stopped to introduce themselves to me, but Temple's stentorian voice rang out again. "Now, now, ladies, this isn't a frigging tea party. I've got to knock some sense into Daniel-san over there, lucky, lucky girl."

Oh my God, I thought. I hadn't made my reference to *The Karate Kid* out loud, had I? Or was this giant freak of nature also psychic?

Mindy, once she'd bowed out from the floor, turned to Temple. "Derek, I'm going to pick up the kids from my mother before I come back here for you. What do you want from the market?"

"Mindy, my love, bring me several pounds of the finest sea scallops. We shall grill them, serve them over bitter greens with a soy-sesame sauce. After dinner, I shall tuck the young ones into their wee beds, and then proceed to make you glad you were born a woman."

"Check. Scallops." Mindy rolled her eyes so I could see as she turned to leave. "Have fun," she said to me.

"Uh, thanks." I almost wished her luck herself, but hey, it was her life and I was already in deep dookie with her mate.

I got my second wrap secured around my hand, and turned to face my doom. I stopped to bow before I hit the floor; Nolan never made me do that, but I wasn't in Kansas any more, and when in Rome . . .

Pull yourself together, Em. Focus.

I reached the center of the floor and did some jumping jacks to warm up quickly, then stretched. When Mr. Temple turned back to me, I bowed to him.

He bowed back politely. To see the broad expanse of Temple's back past his shoulders reminded me of a whale Brian and I had seen in Hawaii, its massive body arcing into the water.

"Where do you need work?" he said.

"Well, right now I'm training for my green belt."

"That's not what I asked you. Where do you need work?"

"Uh . . ."

Mr. Temple covered the distance between us with two gargantuan steps. Out of habit, Mr. Anderson's example still fresh in my mind, I stepped back, needing four quick steps to maintain the distance between us.

"Okay, good. You know not to let me dictate the pace or the space. Now stay put."

He moved in, and my nervousness must have shown on my face, because he stopped. "Don't you trust me?"

Um, frankly, no. "Nolan must think you're okay."

He threw back his head and roared with laughter. I thought I could hear the windowpanes and mirrors vibrating with the noise. "Good answer. We'll take it as read that you trust old Nolan. So stay put for a second."

He circled around me, and I tensed, waiting for an attack, then relaxed again. He'd wait until I wasn't ready and then—

I felt him stop behind me and to the right, then felt a forearm slip past my throat. Before he could get the choke hold on, I slipped down and backed out of his grasp. Stumbling a little, I regained my balance and threw a round kick at his gut. He got out of the way of course, but I kept my momentum going and threw the left leg at him, too.

"Okay, not bad, not bad. Not good, but not bad, either. Good instincts, even if the moves and commitment aren't there. You need aggression, girl! Next time, tuck your chin more before you slither out of the hold; you might not escape and you don't want to let me get my arm under your chin if you can help it. Work on keeping your stance balanced as you move. And don't ever, ever turn your back on me; I know you had momentum going from your kick, but save that fancy stuff for your Boston sword*rays*. If you feel like you have enough distance to run, then run, but this close, don't give me your back. Instead, if you see you're not going to land it, just put your foot down, square up, move in, and do a side kick.

I did the move as he described it.

He frowned. "For chrissakes, chamber that kick! I've seen harder sneezes. I want explosive action!"

"More than twenty-five years in the field, I've been moving as slowly and deliberately as I could," I muttered. "Archaeologists aren't supposed to explode."

"Enough talk."

Temple walked around me several more times, sometimes slowly, sometimes quickly. I fought hard to keep from tensing up while still paying attention to what I could feel and hear around me. Suddenly I felt a blow from behind catch me squarely in the back; there was nowhere for me to go but down. I broke my fall and managed to turn my head so I didn't mash my nose and face against the mat. I rolled over and went for a kick, but Mr. Temple flicked my foot aside as if he was shooing a mosquito and, with scary speed, shot in on top of me, into the mount.

The breath left my lungs with a whoosh. Panic set in. I tried to buck my hips to throw him off me, but he was anticipating that. He simply outweighed, out-muscled me.

As he sat on my chest, he wrapped his hands around my throat—he could have used just one, it seemed—and I tried a pluck to remove them. Again, he out-muscled me. I tried to buck with the pluck again, and it still didn't work. I simply couldn't get him off me, couldn't move his hands off my throat, which now felt like it was being crushed.

What the hell was this maniac doing? I tapped the mat, signaling that he had me.

The pressure remained, choking me. "There's no tapping out on the street!" a voice said, as if from a distance.

Still I struggled. I couldn't breathe.

"Well?" the voice boomed. "What do you do now? If you weren't in the safest place on earth, you'd be halfway down a darkened alley with me by now."

I slapped at the side of his head, shoved his chin away from me. All in vain. I was starting to see spots before my eyes.

"Do you really think you're going to do anything by going at the hardest places on my skull? Go for the soft bits: ears, nose, eyes, throat."

I grabbed at one of his ears, not sure what to do. I twisted, hard. He cursed—though not because of anything I'd done to him—and leapt up. Suddenly, air rushed into my lungs. I rolled over, coughed, struggled to my knees.

"Jesus wept! What has that dozey slacker Nolan been doing? If you tried those party tricks on someone who didn't have your best interest at heart, you'd be in very, very bad shape indeed."

He loomed over me, pointing a finger like the sawed-off end of a pool cue. "Yes, you got somewhere by twisting my ear, but only after I gave you a hint. Now I'm going to teach you, so pay attention."

"Ears!" he bellowed, suddenly pretending to clap his huge paws over my ears. If he'd actually done it, he might have blown both my eardrums.

"Nose!" He hunkered down into a low base, and still holding my head, pantomimed slamming my face against the crown of his skull, above the forehead. "No sense in messing up your pretty face; bash the silly bastard's nose against your skull, and see how he likes that."

"Eyes!" Still not letting go of my head, he regained a tall posture and jabbed at my eyes with his thumbs. "Let's see how sexy he's feeling with his aqueous humor running down your thumbs."

"Throat!" He pulled back his arm and aimed a pretend strike at my throat, which was still sore from his choke hold. "And if the bastard's still walking and looking for trouble at that point, then I shall be very surprised indeed."

He made me practice the moves several times over, faster and faster. The last time, I accidentally—I think—whacked his nose against me a little too hard.

"Sorry," I said. "My hands are slip—"

A titanic roar caused traffic to slow in the street, the drivers expecting an earthquake. "Never, never say 'sorry' near me again!" My apology seemed to make Mr. Temple the angriest of anything I'd done—or not done—the whole rest of the session. "I am the instructor and am responsible for myself as well as you. Work on your control, yes, but don't pause, don't be nice, and for chrissakes, never, never apologize."

"Sor—okay."

"As if a little girly like you could mar my eternal beauty." He did turn into the mirror, just in case I'd knocked a hair out of place, but once again was satisfied. "Once more."

I performed satisfactorily this time.

"Better. Practice on your husband at home, it'll be good for him. Show him who's boss. Now, we get to the good stuff."

Exhausted already, I glanced surreptitiously at the clock. Damn, still twenty minutes left. How could an hour last so long?

"Ah, Daniel-san, that anxious to get away from me? Give me twenty and twenty of the juiciest. You will remember next time that I am the only clock you need to worry about."

I almost protested but instead got to my knees and began the push-ups. Next time? I wilted at the thought.

"Still doing girl push-ups, are we?" came the unimpressed observation from across the room.

"Well, I'm still a girl," was as much of a retort as I dared.

"Ha! Never heard that one before."

I finished the crunches, got up, shrugged out my shoulders, and waited warily for the "good stuff."

Mr. Temple pulled out a pistol and aimed it at me.

I jumped a foot in the air. "Holy shit!"

"That's one response. Can you think of a more effective one? It's black rubber, by the way." He showed me that it was only a realistic fake.

I eyed the gun nervously; it sure had looked real to me. "Uh . . . ?"

"Not even close. Listen up. The trick with guns is this: Unless the gunman actually just puts it to your head and pulls the trigger, he's interested in control, for the time being, at least. Let's go over some moves that will remove his illusions and restore your sense of control."

We went over simple moves that would get the gun away from my head from the front, the back, and the side. "And for heaven's sake, don't forget, once you get the gun away from the bastard, use it on him. Shoot him, hit him with it, mark him up, so he *never* forgets you. And then when the cops arrive, you bat your pretty eyes and say, 'Officer, I was in fear for my life.' That'll do you."

I nodded, sweat burning my eyes.

"Right, enough gun. Now, knife!" He laughed hugely, like a demented Cossack, and I felt my shoulders slump.

Chapter 3

TWO DAYS LATER, I LIMPED DOWNSTAIRS AFTER my morning shower, and collapsed in a chair in my mother-in-law's empty kitchen. "Mr. Temple, you giant bastard. I'd hate to see what would have happened if you didn't like me."

I got up, and tried stretching out my legs, bracing against the tabletop, but it didn't help. I sat down again and tried to massage the pain away, but it was no good; it was always worse the second day. "Were you trying to kill me, Derek?"

"Ah, that's something a guy can't get too much of," Brian announced as he came into the kitchen. "His wife, rubbing her thighs, moaning another man's name."

I looked up at him. "He was a maniac, I don't know what he was teaching. It was like Krav on steroids. Do me a favor. Shoot me."

"How about a cup of coffee instead?"

"God, I couldn't even make it over that far."

"He was that good, huh?" Brian poured two cups.

I looked up, all piteousness. "So good I'm practically broken. So good that if I don't go back, I'm pretty sure he'll come looking for me."

"Got another class, then?"

"Yeah. And I bet you haven't got the guts to go with me, have you?"

Brian handed me the coffee and cocked his head. "Haven't we been married long enough for you to learn that reverse psychology doesn't work with me?"

"I'm not sure. Doesn't it work on you?"

He laughed. "Okay, when is the next class?"

"This afternoon, after lunch. Late-ish."

"Can't." He didn't look disappointed, though, which took points away from him, as far as I was concerned. "I'm helping Dad with a job."

"I thought he's retired."

"Semiretired. He's finding it hard to let go."

"Well, what about me?" I pouted. "Don't you have to help me?"

"I'll help you at home." He kissed the top of my head. "Later."

I found myself actually looking forward to the lesson, and I got in a little early, the smell of the floor mats and a faint whiff of perspiration hit me as I opened the door. I was surprised to see Mr. Temple teaching a children's karate class. As I sat among the waiting parents and wrapped my hands, I watched Temple—who, even on his knees, still towered over the six-year-olds—demonstrate a punch to a tiny girl. The rest of the class, all kneeling in their miniature *gi*s, watched in a straight line opposite them. Most were attentive; one was picking his nose.

"Once more, Paula," Temple boomed. "First, give me a good yell!"

"Chi-yai!" Paula squeaked.

"Excellent! Now, do it again, this time with the punch, just like I showed you."

The little girl squeaked again, then punched Temple in the chest. While her form looked surprisingly good to me, the punch had about as much power as a kitten's. Temple rolled back as though he'd been bulldozed.

He jumped out of the backward roll and began to clap. "Let's hear it for Miss Benson! Good job!"

The kids clapped, and Paula bowed to Mr. Temple, who bowed gravely in return. She ran back to the lineup, barely able to contain her excitement. Temple bellowed a command, and the line of kids jumped smartly to their feet and bowed to him. After he bowed again, they ran to their parents, most of whom had been trying to keep straight faces during the lesson.

He saw me sitting there, a big smile on my face. "A moment while I change, Daniel-san." He straightened the obi of his gi, took two gigantic steps to the edge of the mats, and bowed out.

Children's hour, however, was over. Class wasn't so bad, though it was much the same as before, that is to say, demanding and scary. Actually, it was a bit worse, because I thought he was telling me to come for another individual lesson, but he asked me to stand in for the group class, first, then took me for an hour on my own.

There were moments where Mr. Temple thought I was being particularly dense; he called in Mr. Anderson to beat on me, while he shouted helpful comments like "For chrissakes, no! Hit him back! Harder than *that*! Are you going to ask him to prom, or are you going to send him home in a garbage bag? Get around his guard! Give me strength!"

Which is to say, it was all just ghastly.

But I was proud that I got through what seemed like twice the class and sixty times the personal attention, which meant there was no time to catch my breath while someone else got pummeled. Thing was, I knew I'd made some progress, if not in my moves, then at least in my thinking. Temple had been riding me for having no killer instinct, no plan in attacking him. I never did anything he didn't expect, he complained, and I moved like I was doing Tai Chi, when he was looking for dynamite.

The lecture went on long enough for him to notice his sneakers were untied, and without thinking, as he knelt down to tie it, I pushed him over. I regretted the action even as I was executing it, and a lot more shortly after: Temple went over, but swept my feet out from under me and was on top of me before I knew what hit me. But he helped me up and praised me to the heavens for getting out of my own head. For taking the cheap—but effective—shot.

I knew I'd be a raggedy heap when I got home, so I just focused on driving straight through the rain. I was going to have to ask for my money back. It wasn't supposed to rain in southern California, as far as I understood, but it made for an interesting experience. We'd seen tropical downpours in Hawaii, and they were neat; the play of clouds and light over the mountains—*volcanoes*! I had to keep reminding myself then. It's fascinating, and warm enough to sit on the lanai, drink a beer, and watch the show. Listen to the show, too— palm fronds rattling are very different from summer leaves shaking; they sound like Venetian blinds clattering softly against one another.

This was different. There is very little more pathetic than a palm tree in cool rain on a dreary afternoon, unless it was the local population's response, which was just as though they'd been promised a lollipop that was taken away. In spite of my own disappointment, I was able to muster up a little self-righteous smugness, hardy New Englander, I. The rain was sending them into a brown study, and wasn't doing their driving any good. I was sore, but my left index finger that had been broken four years ago, out at Penitence Point, re- ally ached with the coming storm.

I made it home in one piece and if I hadn't been so aware of the water usage situation, I would have taken a bath and not gotten out until there was no hot water left. Brian snick- ered, just out of kicking range, as I dried off but I took my revenge by demanding that he take us all to restorative cocktails and an expensive restaurant Betty had recom- mended.

* * *

Damned if Temple wasn't at our restaurant as well. I felt a rush of excitement, like when I'd see my kindergarten teacher outside the classroom.

He and Mindy were dressed in civilian clothes and looked quite normal, if you ignored the fact that, like an iceberg, a good ninety percent of Temple was hidden by table, menu, and a ferny looking plant in a container on the floor: He liked having his back to a wall, apparently. And they looked troubled, in the middle of a whispered and unhappy discussion.

Whispering was something of a difficulty for Temple, however: "—yes, things have been difficult since the second mortgage, but no one's going to take our house, I promise you—"

Mindy shushed him, before she looked up and recognized me. She waved to us, poked Derek in the side again, which jostled him enough to spill his drink.

He was drinking what looked to me suspiciously like a mango daiquiri, with full fruit garnish. His pinky, as thick as a roll of quarters, was decorously stuck out. His civilian garb was equally colorful, a maroon sports jersey with gold corporate badges, and a small horse head logo in the corner. His frown turned, as he looked up, to a slow grin spreading across his face. "Daniel-san!" he boomed.

Mindy elbowed him again.

He lowered the volume a hair. "Er, um, Emma! Do join us!"

Brian looked like he would do it, if only for the entertainment value, and his parents were staring with frank disbelief. I considered it, but it wouldn't have been fair to my in-laws. And Mindy, while still smiling, was looking too studiously polite. "No, thank you, Mr. Temple—"

"Derek, please!" he said. "No need for formalities here!"

"Thanks, uh, Derek. I wouldn't want to interrupt your date night. Enjoy your dinner."

He looked vaguely disappointed, but Mindy relaxed, and I knew I'd made the right choice.

We continued on our way to our table, in the next section of the dining room.

"Holy cow, did you see the size of him?" Brian asked in wonder. "I mean, there was just . . . acres of him!"

I gave Brian a look. "Did you think I was exaggerating?"

"Well, *yeah*. I mean, no one's as huge as you were saying."

"Except Derek."

"Yeah, except him. Jeez, the size of him!"

Something about having seen Derek gave us something else to concentrate on. There had been a detectable pall created by my fears about the flowers and Tony Markham—*and* Brian's steadfast refusal to believe the package had anything to do with him. The pall was lifting, especially when our wine came.

"I told you the one about the first time he was brought home by the police?" Stan's glasses were sitting on his forehead, and his cheeks were flushed with a half glass of Chardonnay.

Stan was presenting his traditional gift to me, on this last night of our visit: another story about Brian's childhood. Even after close to ten years, he still seemed to have an untapped supply.

"Was that the time the homecoming prank with the goat went horribly awry?" I said.

Betty shook her head. "No, the very first time was when he was twelve and decided that he could drive and took the station wagon full of kids down to the beach."

"Right, I forgot: because he was tired of lugging his surfboard down the street. Yep, I've got both of those, now that you mention it."

Brian looked at his mother and me, thought about protesting, and then gave up, hiding himself behind his menu.

Betty put her hand on mine. "What about the botanical project that I found growing in a sunny corner of the garden when he was seventeen? The one he tried to tell me was bamboo?"

"Ah, clever, trying to fool a gardener. At least he didn't try to tell you it was a tomato plant. Yep, I heard that one, too."

"What about the fire that wrecked most of one side of the garage? About age fourteen?" Stan put down the menu, getting to serious work again.

I cocked my head. "Ah, I've heard Brian's version of that, but I would give quite a lot for a corroborative version."

"Well, if you slide the wine bottle over this way . . ."

Brian, not yet resigned to his fate, tried to distract us by signaling the waitress so we could place our orders. We did, but Stan, who had just poured an inch of wine into his glass, started up again.

"It was Saturday morning and I smelled something funny coming out of the garage. Well, that was nothing unusual, because every Saturday morning something smelled bad in the garage. That was the deal: Brian got to use his chemistry stuff—I think he had about six sets put together over the years—in the garage, when we were home, so we could deal with whatever emergency might occur. Nothing too bad had happened in the past, so it was a good arrangement, and I wasn't too worried at first. But then I noticed that the smell was getting worse and there was a . . . how can I say it?"

"A lot of furtive scurrying around," Betty supplied. "With too much quiet and not enough eye contact."

"That'll do. There was scurrying and there was furtiveness, and suddenly I saw flames. The garage is under the house, so I draw the line at flames. We called the fire department, and I got the fire extinguisher out and got to work. Asked the boy whether there was anything explosive, anything that wouldn't do well with the fire extinguisher. I knew the drill. And he was sweating bullets, which was strange because this wasn't the first fire—hence the rules about when and where Dr. Frankenstein over there could play with his stuff."

Brian was resigned now, chewing his bottom lip, letting his dad tell his version of the story.

"So I was kinda curious, and the fire department showed up, and said, Hey Stan, what's Einstein getting into now, and the usual. And we got the fire out pretty quick, and it was a real mess—god-awful sooty smoke everywhere, but not too bad in the house because we put the fan in; boys will be boys, so you do the best you can, right? And they did a little poking around, which got Bri even more furtive and agitated, even though the worst of it was over and he knew I wasn't going to do anything more than yell at him for being a dope and make him help me do the repairs on the garage. Standard operating procedure, the boy knew that. So when he was getting more nervous about the firemen rummaging through the stuff, I was curious. Well, first thing we find is that there've been some *upgrades* to the chemistry set. A couple sets more have been added, without approval from the head office. Okay, nothing too bad, nothing dangerous. Then they get to a small metal cabinet and they find that there are some real chemicals, you know, those brown plastic bottles with the official warning labels and all that good stuff? That was a whole 'nother kettle of fish, things liberated from school science closet, apparently. But still, even the lieutenant said that the cabinet was only charred on the outside, and everything was actually stored pretty safe, not that anyone's going to get away without a trip to the principal's office and pay for what he used, etcetera. And still, once we found those, Brian was still doing the weasel dance, hopping from one foot to the other, like he's got to pee or something."

Stan took a sip of water, his chest heaving with silent laughter. Brian rolled his eyes and Betty looked disapproving.

"That's when I look over and there's this pair of boobs, stuck to the wall, blinking back at me."

This was the part I hadn't heard before. I looked at Brian, who just shrugged. He was grinning now, blushing a little, which was cute and sexy.

"Seems that part of the attraction of the garage was the world-class collection of girly magazines our young man kept stashed in there. Vintage of about 1960 or so, I don't know where he got them—"

"I do," Betty said. "And I spoke to the other boy's parents

about it, too. Little brat, thinking it's okay for him to leave that stuff in our house, and get Brian in trouble for it. You know I told his mother off."

"That so? Well, good one of us took care of it."

She shook Stan's arm. "You knew about this, I told you at the time!"

"Yeah? Must have slipped my mind," Stan said.

"Must have been a Padres game on," Betty retorted.

"Anyway. A two-foot stack . . ." Stan held his hand off the floor to show just how high, wheezing with laughter, tears running down his cheeks. "Fifteen years drying out in cellars and attics, and they'd caught fire and went up—poof!" Stan could barely sit up straight now, he was laughing so hard. "All in front of the fire department, the neighbors, his mother. The whole neighborhood was finding little bits of T&A floating around for days after . . ."

"All right, all right, it's not that funny," Brian said. "Dad, you're gonna choke."

Stan slapped the table, still wheezing. "It *is* that funny!"

Betty looked around nervously. "Stan, you're making a scene now," she whispered. "And you're embarrassing Emma."

"Oh, she's not. She knows boys look at girly magazines." Stan sat up, wiped his eyes, but looked at me, a little guiltily. "You're not embarrassed, are you, Emma?"

I shook my head. "Not me. Got any more good stories like that?"

"*Hell*, yes."

"No!" Brian and his mother said together. Betty continued in a lower voice. "You know the rule, Stan. One story per visit. Now stop it. Eat your shrimp."

We did manage to find other topics, and by dessert time, I'd had just enough wine to ease my sore muscles, then enough more to let me ignore them. The waitress reappeared, bearing a dangerous-looking cocktail. She set it before me.

"Excuse me, I didn't order this," I said.

"No, the big blond guy at the table in the other room sent it for you. He said to say, 'sweets to the sweet.' "

"Oh, that's, ah, nice of him. What is it?" Looked kind of like a mai tai, but I am no connoisseur of complicated drinks.

"A Suffering Bastard."

The volcanic roar of laughter from the other room rattled the plates and glasses for several blocks.

The next day, I didn't mind that our connecting flight from Chicago to Portland was delayed. No one likes to prolong a transcoastal trip, but for me, I was safely lost. No one could find me, I was off the radar: The only person I'd want to find me was softly snoring in the seat next to me and my cell phone was turned off. I did a little work updating my syllabuses ("accent on the *abuse*," is what my grandfather Oscar used to say), and then, satisfied that I was caught up, pulled out a copy of *Shamela*, and started to giggle to myself. I doubt that my family is related to this Henry Fielding, as honored as I would be to discover a connection. I just never get tired of rereading his novels on eighteenth-century society. I love the fact that he can make me laugh out loud.

I looked up to check on the status of our connection. Another half hour before we boarded. I was drawn, once again, to the infinitely fascinating parade of humanity moving past me.

I looked straight into the eyes of one man. He smiled faintly—familiarly.

I returned to my book, then I looked up again. The guy, still walking slowly, was looking back at me through the crowd. He pursed his lips, blew me a silent kiss, no smile in his eyes.

The shock that someone would do that took me by surprise. What an odd, aggressive sort of thing to do. And then it struck me.

The man I'd just seen was Tony Markham.

Chapter 4

DEAR GOD . . . I STOOD UP. BRIAN NEEDED TO SEE; I shook him. "Brian! Brian, I just saw Tony! We have to go after him!"

He sat bolt upright, grabbing for his backpack. "I'm up, I'm ready," he mumbled. Then his eyes cleared. "Is that us?"

Why didn't he get it? "Shit! No! I just saw Tony Markham!"

The wary look came into his eyes. "Em, you couldn't have—"

I craned my neck, trying to see where Tony had gone. "We have to go after him!"

"Our flight boards in about ten minutes! We're not—"

I knew then it was futile. "Watch my stuff!"

I dove into the river of people in the crowded hallway and ran after the man I'd seen. I could hear Brian call after me, but didn't care. I knew what I saw.

As I wove in and out of the bodies, as fast as I could, I tried to remember what I'd actually seen. Same height, same build, maybe a little leaner, a little more muscle, was the impression I had. His hair was colored a dark and uniform brown, no longer the white that I knew from years ago I'd expected to see. I also thought I saw a scar over Tony's left eye, one that maybe I'd given him, kicking him in the head in my attempt to escape him at the Point. Khakis and oxford-cloth shirt, navy blazer.

I couldn't see any one who looked like him, or rather, nearly every man I saw looked like the Tony I'd just seen. About half the guys traveling through O'Hare wore exactly the same thing. And at least half of them were the same description: late middle age, medium height, medium build. Every marketeer, consultant, sales rep, technical lead on the run from one city to another could have fit that description.

I ran as far, as fast as I could, trying to search each of the gates on both sides of the terminal hall as I went. Nothing. Soon I came to a crossroads, a food-and-services court, and knew I was out of luck.

I was being paged. It was just the loudspeakers, just Brian having the airline call me, summoning me back to the gate. To reality, I supposed he'd say.

With one last desperate look around, I resigned myself to failure and turned back for my gate.

Brian was humming with impatience; he had my bags as well as his own, ready to get on the plane. "Where were you? We're boarding!"

"I told you. I thought I saw Tony." I could tell how mad he was, but we didn't have time for it now. "Here," I said, reaching for my bag. "I'll take that."

"Here. Your ticket?"

"Got it." Monosyllables and half sentences aren't ever good signs in our house.

I was sweating profusely, shaking like an overloaded washer, by the time we found our seats. Brian stowed our bags without a word. Then he fastened his seat belt, crossed his arms, and went straight to sleep—he's trained himself to do this. The hum of the airplane, and the rituals of takeoff are like a trigger. Sleeping keeps him from being nervous about leaving the ground. My husband, the scientist, can't quite rationalize human flight.

It gave me a few minutes to collect myself. I was absolutely, mortally certain that I had seen Tony. A change in hair color hadn't fooled me, the business-camouflage clothing—so similar to what he used to wear back when we were both at Caldwell College—only made his face stand out. And it was the smile that finally made me twig to it. A lot of people can have superficial similarities, but facial habits, particularly smiles, are a dead giveaway. The scar supported it. So did the kiss, as far as I was concerned.

It wasn't until I'd had a few minutes to think it over that I realized the implications of what I'd seen.

I wasn't crazy. I wasn't paranoid—well, yes, I was, but for perfectly good reasons I now knew—and I wasn't wrong. I was, however, terrified. I didn't know why Tony should come back to bother with me. If I had a fortune in gold and was heading to the Caribbean, if I had literally gotten away with murder, why would I ever come back?

The plane leveled out and Brian woke up; he was frowning. "That was strange."

"Yeah, it was."

"You want to tell me what was going on?"

Okay, so we weren't on the same page as far as what actually was strange. "I told you. I saw Tony Markham. In the airport. I had to try and catch him."

"How could it be him? How would he know you'd be there, at that moment? Just like he couldn't have known where we were staying to send the flowers—"

"It was him."

His frown deepened and fixed. "Say it was Tony—"

"Brian, I know what I saw! I tried to wake you, so you could see him, too."

"You forget; I've never met the man in person. Pictures and stories only. Say it was Tony. What would you have done if you'd caught him?"

The question took me aback. It was as reasonable as it was unexpected. "I don't know. I had to follow him, at least. I probably would have caused a scene, and that would have gotten the cops to investigate, for instance."

"You almost missed our plane." Okay, so Brian wasn't convinced.

"I didn't. I wasn't even the last person on board."

"Emma, you went tearing off after . . . wait. Do you remember what happened after your grandfather died?"

"Grampa Boyce?" I knew what he was getting at, but wanted him to say it out loud.

"No, your father's father. Oscar. Do you remember what happened?"

"Remind me." I pulled out my backpack and began looking for the papers I'd put aside. Brian might slow down if he saw I had work; he wouldn't if it was just pleasure reading.

"You kept seeing him everywhere. You told me you'd see him on the street, in traffic, at the library. I don't know what the psychological phenomenon is, if you've just got someone on your mind or you've got a wish looking to be fulfilled, but I think you're looking for Tony where he isn't."

My grandfather, Oscar Fielding, was one of the dearest people in the world to me. My first and best instructor in archaeology, he literally made me what I am today. And if that includes a certain talent for archaeology, then it also includes a reinforced Fielding stubbornness, too.

Brian sighed. "I think you're just looking for trouble. I'm worried about you, Em."

"I'm worried about me, too!" I slapped my papers down on the flimsy tray. "It was Tony! He . . . dammit, he blew a kiss at me!"

Brian fiddled with the catch on his tray table. "There's no evidence—"

I could have killed Brian for discounting me so readily. Nothing could have driven me crazier. "I saw him with my own eyes!"

"Is there any problem here?"

We looked up. The cabin attendant sternly regarded us; our argument had risen above the vibration and noise of the engines and we were drawing attention to ourselves.

"No. I'm sorry," I said. I looked at Brian. "There's no problem."

He put on his headphones, cranked the CD player up, and closed his eyes.

Three hours is a very long time to try not to talk to someone.

Monday morning I saw a blue-chino-covered butt sticking out from behind the refrigerator door. It was several sizes too large to be Brian's, and I absolutely would have forbidden the crack of doom I saw lurking below where the waistband should have been.

"Who the hell are you?" I said, marching into the kitchen.

Whoever it was started and smacked his head against the inside of the refrigerator. "Aw, jeez! Now look what you made me do. Bump my head."

The butt backed out and a man unfolded himself from my refrigerator. Shaped like a pear—perhaps a bowling pin would have been more accurate—the guy was maybe fifty. His black hair was longish and unevenly cut so that elflocks stuck out from under his paint store gimme cap. Hooded sweatshirt in navy blue, work boots spattered with every color in the Sherwin-Williams rainbow.

He was chewing on an unlit cigar; one that was unraveled at the end, so that it looked as if it had exploded. All I knew about cigars, I learned from observing my colleague Dora Sarkes-Robinson. And even I knew that a good cigar didn't smell or look like that.

"Yeah, I'm real sorry. Who are you?" I asked, my head throbbing without my coffee.

"Artimus Apostolides. Call me Artie. You know, you're out of cream."

"I don't keep cream in the house. What are you doing, here, Artie?"

"Donald Keyser told me to come. So here I am. You really don't have any cream? Your coffee is kind of strong."

Ah, it was beginning to make sense. Keyser was who we thought would be doing our electrical work; he'd promised that either he or one of his people would be out to do the several jobs we needed—upgrading the electrical for the attached outbuildings so I could have my new washer and dryer out there instead of in the basement, adding the new box for the main house, some other items—as soon as possible. When we were discussing the projects with him, he'd promised us the moon. Now that we were trying to get him to do the work, he acted like we were lucky to know him. "No cream. And we were expecting you to come more than three weeks ago."

"I'm here now. It would have been a lot easier if you could have had us here last week. Saved me some trouble."

I bit back a retort, and watched him searching the counters. "Here we go, here we go." He found the sugar bowl, dumped in two heaping tablespoons of sugar and stirred, then carefully replaced the wet spoon back into the sugar bowl. I felt my teeth grinding.

"Look, Artie, are we going to do a little electrical work today? Sometime soon?"

"Sure we are. Or I am—you're not one of those kind of ladies who hover around and watch my every move, are you?"

I sighed. "Only when I'm writing the checks, Artie."

Artie nodded, satisfied, took a big slurp of coffee, and then frowned. "Oh."

"So what's up first today?" I went over to the coffeepot. It was empty, but still turned on; my headache redoubled at the sight. I flicked off the switch.

"I thought I'd just get an idea of what the job was going to be." He settled back against the countertop, and slurped some more coffee. "You've got to sort these things out carefully, don't want to have to redo anything."

I reached into the manila folder on the table. "Here's a list of what has to be done. Mr. Keyser said the work should only take about five, six days. Tops."

"I'm not going to be rushed, do a shoddy job. You wouldn't want that."

I want my coffee, you oaf, is what I want. "I don't want a shoddy job. I do want it done quickly. Do you need me to call the alarm company, let them know the power will be out?" I had already charged up cell phones and computers, pared the food down in the fridge to those that wouldn't spoil in a hurry, and taken all the other precautions. Several times, now.

"I'll let you know." He finally set his cup down, rubbed his hands, and looked around. "All right then."

Nothing. He stood there, slurped thoughtfully.

White stabbing pains behind my eyes made it difficult to be civil. "Yes?"

He sighed. "I really like a cruller or something with my coffee in the morning, don't you?"

"I really like my coffee in the morning, but I'm not getting that," I said. "You've drunk the last of it." I knew for a fact that buying coffee beans was on my list of errands today; we'd gone through the crumbs and the emergency coffee—the assorted samples, gifts, etc., that accumulated at the back of the cupboard—at this point.

"Did I? Oh. Your boyfriend there, he told me to help myself. Next time, you'll have to get downstairs a little quicker, huh?"

"Husband," I said, through gritted teeth. Couldn't figure out if "husband" was a clarification or malediction.

"Oh." He began to pore over the punch list, looking around as he did. "Box is downstairs?" he asked, without looking up.

"Yep, I'll show you," I said, eager to do anything that would get him moving.

"No, don't trouble yourself. I'll find it. You just go on about your business."

I bit back another retort, in the hopes that he was underway now.

No such luck. "So, you gonna make me knock all the time?"

"What do you mean?" All the time? Hell—that didn't sound like five or six days to me.

"I had to knock to get in today. Your boyfriend—"

"Husband."

"—let me in. Usually, people give me a key or leave the door open."

"I'm afraid that's not possible," I said. "You're going to have to knock. One of us will let you in, I promise."

He looked hurt and his mustache drooped. "You don't trust me?"

"I'm not in the habit of giving keys out to anyone." Damn, I sounded stiff; I knew I was not scoring any points with this guy, and my tone was making it worse every second. But I was also beginning to suspect that there were no secret words to get him to work. "I'll leave you to it. If you have any questions, just holler. I'll be upstairs—no, cancel that. I'm going out. I'll be back in half an hour."

My heart beat a little faster as I opened the door to Café-Nation; maybe it was just joyful anticipation of my morning fix, maybe it was just a contact high through the density of coffee molecules in the air.

"'Lo, Emma," the woman behind the counter in the blue apron greeted me. "Red Eye?"

"Lord, yes, Tina. Feed me coffee, make me human."

"Well, I can do the one; the rest is up to you. You want it here?"

"Yes—no, I guess I better get back to the house. To go, please. And a pound of beans, whole."

"Less than two minutes."

As she busied herself with the holy apparatus, I sat on a stool by the register, an earnest and grateful supplicant. I sighed, then rummaged through my wallet for my Café-

Nation card, the one that asked "Have you been CaféNated today?," and counted off how many more trips I had before I got a free drink. Not this time, but not many more to go. I'd already been through two cards since the place opened a couple of months ago.

One of the kids who worked there came in, smiled, and said hi. It took me a second to remember her name: Bell, bell . . . Isabel. Isabel had a dumbbell in a piercing over her eye. I had always thought the piercing looked painful, but maybe if I had one, it would keep me from falling asleep facedown on my students' blue books.

I smiled back; something of a feat for me, at the moment, but she had access to the coffee, and therefore my happiness. "How's the pack?" I asked Isabel.

"Oh, they're fine," she said. "Got a new picture. Wanna see?"

I nodded and she pulled out her wallet. The picture was of her three pugs: Liam, Casey, and Wee Mikey. Bulging marble black eyes and panting tongues strained to reach the camera lens. I could swear they were smiling, all linked up with their little green harnesses.

"Nice," I said. "Wee Mikey isn't so wee anymore."

"No, but that's not why we called him that, anyway."

"Oh?"

"Well, it's kinda gross, but when we've got them all harnessed up together? Everyone runs to have a pee? Mikey's aim is pretty bad. Pees all over the other guys, pees all over himself. It's a mess."

"Oh," was all I could manage.

"Charming," Tina said. She handed me my double cappuccino with an extra shot, and grinned as she measured out the bag of Columbian beans.

I handed her my card, which she stamped, and the money for the coffee; I tossed the change into the jar.

Tina looked at me a little more closely. "Here," she said, reaching under the counter and pulling out a small stick of chocolate.

"I didn't order a mocha," I said.

"No, but you look like you could use the fix."

"Hey, thanks; you're not wrong about that. See you, Isabel. Take it easy, Ms. Willner."

She picked up the counter cloth as she completed our ritual. "You too, Ms. Fielding."

Back home, I fled immediately upstairs to my office. Odd, I thought as the door knocked over an unseen obstacle, the room should be clean. I thought I'd cleaned it earlier this summer. Once I fought my way in, I realized that I had, and I could see that the rug was recently vacuumed. But between the notes and crates of artifacts dumped after the fieldwork, and the piles of books pulled for lecture writing, on top of the rush at the beginning of a new academic year, you were bound to lose a little surface area.

I saw a note stuck to my computer, reminding me that I'd promised to bring some books on introductory archaeology to Raylene Reynolds. She and her husband Erik ran the Lawton Yacht Club and Tiki Bar, one of my favorite haunts. Raylene homeschooled her kids. I had piled the books up and left them by the door, so I'd remember to get them to her.

After I got the fans started up and the place began to cool down, I pulled out my collection of near-completed syllabi. Four courses this semester, one of them brand new. Yuck. While it was indeed better to burn out than rust out, I could have done with a little more rest and oxidation.

I worked out the updates for the first three classes, and then tackled the new one. Inspiration hit me, and I thought of a topic for a lecture that would round things out nicely and get me the basis for a paper that I promised to present later in the fall. I got a tingly feeling at this bit of deluxe recycling. No, not recycling. Multiple use and good planning. Yay, me.

The lights went out. The fan blades became visible as they slowed to a halt. The CD player died.

"Seven variations on six filthy words!" Deep breath; no problem, I'd prepared for this. I turned off the lights and the fans and the radio. My computer was running on its battery, and I'd squirreled away some bottles of water to keep me going a little longer.

I kept at it for another two hours and made some good progress, but it was getting hot up there. Moving downstairs was not an option—I'd be way too distracted by the work that I hoped was going on—but outside . . . I was never good at working outside, and besides my battery was running low now. I backed up my work and then the phone rang.

"Hello?"

"Em, it's Meg. Are you going to be on campus any time soon?"

"Um, not sure. Anything wrong? You sound anxious."

"I am, I guess. I wanted your opinion on something."

"Can't do it over the phone?"

"Not really. It's not . . . about anything . . . you know. It's the wedding."

"Okay. But I'm not sure what I can do about that." I glanced over at my clock, a battered and battery-run near antique that had also seen use in the basement and barn. "Actually, I could use someplace with power; we're out here. I'll see you in my office in an hour?"

"That would be great!" The relief in Meg's voice made me wonder whether my student had been telling me the whole truth. "See you then."

I gathered up my stuff, told Artie that I'd be about three hours, and called the alarm company to let them know that our power would be out for the day and they shouldn't call in.

The trip took less time than usual, in part because the traffic was long gone, and partly because I was indulging in my latest bad habit of driving too fast. My first new-new car, a sound and eager engine that didn't shudder over sixty-five, and suddenly, I had discovered my inner speed-demon. Okay, maybe it wasn't so much as a walk on the wild side as edging one toe over the line, but it was a small escape.

I got there early enough to dodge into the library and find one of the books I needed to check for my class. Ha! Another week and it would have been on reserve or out. As much as I love teaching, I get so much more work done when there aren't any students around. Now was a great time to be on campus, as everyone there was trying to prepare for the mob scene that was freshman orientation.

A woman hurried from the library to the Fine Arts building; something about her long black hair was familiar, but I couldn't place it. I craned to get another look at her, but a pack of male students heading down Maple Walk erupted with bawdy laughter, and I scurried up the stairs to the department to avoid them.

I was on my way to my office when I heard a raised voice down the hall by the main office. Veering down the other corridor, I was confronted by the unlikely spectacle of our department administrator, Chuck, exchanging words with my colleague from the Art History Department, Dora Sarkes-Robinson. It was her voice I'd heard. The contrast between the two couldn't have been more marked: Chuck was a white, five foot hippy in granny glasses, and Dora was black and she towered over him, an imposing figure of a queen crowned with a lattice of intricately woven braids. Chuck was wearing a hemp shirt and a pair of army surplus pants. His hair was in dreads, possibly last combed shortly after his birth, which had to have been just after the Bicentennial. Dora was dressed in something impeccable and Italian; Cerruti, I was willing to bet, only because she told me so repeatedly, and it was something the gods themselves would have envied.

"Huh, so your paper's on Raphael Santi, then?" Chuck, whose pronunciation usually reminded me more of West Coast surfers than his actual Maine upbringing, spoke the Italian carefully.

"Yes." Dora seemed amused, which in itself was reason for curiosity. And reason for caution. She highjacked other people's lives when it suited her, and generally carried on her own affairs with the noble disregard of a Medici pope. I had reason to know this for a fact: Dora's insinuation of herself into my affairs several years ago had involved me in a criminal investigation and led me in the right direction to identifying a killer. Two killers, to be exact.

"And you think that it was him, and not that other guy—"

"Perugino, an influence in his early years," she corrected, a slight trace of irritation barely concealed. Raphael was Dora's specialty, kind of the way architecture was Frank Lloyd Wright's. And she was used to getting her own way.

"—who was responsible for the painting? Neat!" Chuck's enthusiasm was as genuine as it was all encompassing. I think that part of the reason he was a sixth-year senior was that the classes at Caldwell College provided Chuck with an endless kaleidoscope of neat experiences. For my part, I thought Caldwell was probably the safest place for him: The world wasn't ready for Chuck, and he wasn't ready for it. Plus, on a more selfish note, despite his occasional trips to the outer rings of Saturn, he kept things going remarkably smoothly at the Anthropology Department.

"Yes." Again, it was more of a cat watching a particularly playful mouse that characterized Dora's response. "And now, may I have the slides?"

If Dora was at this stage, they'd been going at it for some time. Her patience—never Olympian—was wearing out, but interestingly, Chuck was immune to the signals that would have had the rest of us scurrying.

"Oh. No, sorry. I can't let anyone who isn't in the department take slides. Sorry."

I watched as Dora drew herself up ever so slightly—this wouldn't call for all her formidable force of personality—to respond. "Ah, I understand completely. But I need those slides. Surely you can make an exception."

"Nope." He shrugged and smiled. "Sorry. Rules."

"Of course, naturally. But I'm sure the rules are more to keep the undergraduates from running amuck"—Dora wrinkled her nose—"and getting their jammy fingerprints all over the slides. I'm certain that it doesn't apply to the faculty."

"Oh, especially to the faculty," Chuck said, nodding emphatically. "You wouldn't believe what some of them will do, given the chance. It's like they didn't learn how to share in kindergarten or something. They'll hide things they think belong only to them, they'll lie, they'll sneak. Just like the sandbox."

I watched the amusement leaching out of Dora like water out of a rusted-through bucket, and decided that maybe I could help. "Hey, Chuck. How's it going? And, hello, Dora—how's your summer been? Productive so far?"

"Emma!" Dora was pleased to see me, though probably more to do with the slides than anything else. "Perhaps you could help me. This—Chuck, is it?—won't allow me to take a couple of slides from your slide collection. Now, it's only a nice detail, but the ruins in the landscape are exactly the sort of thing I need to make my point about the influence of the Urbino countryside where Raphael grew up. A small thing, but just the touch I need to—"

I nodded soberly. "Chuck's right. It's not department policy to lend the slides."

Chuck beamed at me. I beamed back. Then I saw Dora pulling herself together for a really good blast, and decided I would back off. I was too close to ground zero.

"But what if I checked them out, Chuck, took responsibility for them?" I said in a hurry.

"Well, I can't really . . . but then . . . I have no way of knowing what you do with a slide once you check it out, do I, Professor Fielding?" Chuck gave me a big, theatrical wink. "And since you're so good about turning your slides in when you're done with them . . . I suppose it will be okay."

He slid the key across his desk to me. I resisted sticking my tongue out at Dora, and she successfully held her own tongue, now that she was getting what she wanted. I tilted my head toward the slide library and she followed me.

"I suppose he took pleasure in that," she said to me, when we were just out of earshot.

"Of course he did. Chuck likes being able to solve problems, especially when he can do it by the book." I let us into the library, which was warm and stale and smelled of sunlight and undisturbed dust.

"No, I mean . . ." She frowned, even as she reached for the index I handed her.

"I know what you mean."

"Or perhaps he was just being mulishly dense? Chuck—that's not a name. It's a cut of beef."

I figured it mattered not a whit to her that his name was actually Charles Carlton Huxley III. "Chuck's not dense, he just has a way of looking at things that isn't always clear to the rest of us. He would have let you have the slides if you were affiliated with the department, but otherwise it wouldn't have been fair to the rest of us, not with the start of semester around the corner."

"He knew you were going to lend the slides to me. That doesn't seem commensurate with his 'fairness.'"

"You have to earn that brand of fairness with Chuck first."

We found the slides and I extracted a promise from her to return them as soon as she had copies made. "Of course. I'll catch our slide tech before he leaves tonight."

And make him work late, I finished. But that was Dora's domain and her people knew what to expect of her, and it was none of my business. We made our goodbyes, Dora promising to email me to meet her for coffee, then she swept off.

Ten minutes later, in my office, I was trying to make sense of two conflicting entries in a field log. Meg was there too, having a fit.

"I look like a human sacrifice waiting for the volcano," the short, spiky-haired platinum blonde announced.

"I've already told you. You look gorgeous, the dress is beautiful," I said, not looking up from the smudged papers I was trying to decipher.

"Don't you think it looks a little too *ritualistic*?" she asked, standing on her toes, trying to see her backside in the tiny mirror hanging from the back of my office door.

I sighed. At first I was pleased to have the distraction of Meg showing off her wedding gown—the field notes seemed more than usually screwed up—but when after ten minutes she'd neither budged from my office nor stopped agonizing about the upcoming event, I decided she wasn't listening to me anyway and went back to work. The problem with graduate students is that they overanalyze everything.

"Do you think the white is too . . . virginal?" she asked.

"Oh, for God's sake, Meg!" I said, tossing my pen aside. "You're supposed to look virginal! You're supposed to look ritualistic! Unless you don't want to—no one says you have to wear white these days!"

Meg gave me the wide Bambi eyes and I knew I'd gone over a line moved a little closer by her wedding nerves.

I sighed and tried again. "Look, that dress is fabulous on you: It's short enough to be hip, the flapper cut and the lace are extremely elegant, and the fact that it was your great-grandmother's is extremely good family karma. It doesn't make your butt look big, it hints at cleavage, and Neal will be blown away. You can't lose."

"My butt looks big?" Meg asked apprehensively.

"I think you'd better change now," I said, with all the patience I could muster through clenched teeth.

"I'm sorry, Emma. It's not the dress," she said, taking the overdress off.

No shit, I thought.

Whoever restored the dress did a great job, but Meg was pulling the underslip off at the same time, and I rushed over to help her before she ripped it.

Meg was most uncharacteristically on the edge of tears. "It's just we started out so perfectly. Neal and I both knew what we wanted. Then we had to make a compromise here, another there, and now it's just turned into something neither of us recognize. It's a total zoo. I hate it. I don't know what to do."

"Hold still." I carefully worked the layers loose. I thought about what kind of trouble unsolicited advisors get themselves into. She didn't exactly ask, but Meg was usually so decisive, so sure of herself, that I decided I ought to give her the best advice I could.

"Look," I said, after I had the dress safely removed. I hoped that the Sponge Bob underpants and jog bra were not going to be a part of the regalia on the big day. "As I see it, you've got three choices. You could tell everyone to back off and do precisely what you want. You stand a tolerable chance of bruising a few feelings, but you remain true to what you and Neal imagined."

Meg nodded grimly. Unless she was made of even sterner stuff than I knew she had, that wasn't a possibility.

"You could keep your mouth shut, and let your relatives and his 'help' when they offer. Things might not be the way you planned, but everyone else *may* be tolerably happy. Emphasis on the word *may*. You're never going to get consensus from a gang of relatives."

She carefully folded the dress back into its box with a small frown of concentration.

"Or you could run away and avoid all the hassle now, and pay for it later. In all of these three scenarios, you get married and no one dies; in at least two, you get presents. Pick one, stick with it, and accept the consequences."

"It's only one day," the young woman said, pulling up her jeans. She smiled with relief. "You're right, Emma."

Meg is probably the best student I ever had, but even she couldn't have guessed that I was only about two-thirds right.

When I got back from campus, Artie was gone but had left a pile of tools in front of the basement door, perhaps suggesting he would be back again sometime soon. The light on the answering machine was strobing, fit to beat the band. At first I thought it was only because the electricity had been off—the counter was flashing in that odd hieroglyph that indicates a failure of some sort—but then realized the lights in the kitchen were on. There might actually be messages for me. I listened to them all, frowned, and then took them one by one. Something strange was going on.

The first call I made was to Brian's mother Betty. "Emma, I can't tell you how beautiful the leis are!" she said, after she recognized my voice.

When I'd listened to her message, it had taken me a minute to figure out that she was not talking about epic poetry, but Hawaiian flower chains. "Um, that's great. What leis?"

"Silly! The one you sent me and Stan, thanking us for your visit! Completely unnecessary—you're our family, you're always welcome—and after such a lovely dinner out! That was more than enough thanks."

I thought the dinner was the thank-you, too: I'd never sent flowers.

Betty was still talking, with all the bubbling enthusiasm that came with her love of plants. "—really too much, but thank you, they're just stunning. I'm going to take pictures of them so I can figure out whether I can grow the same plants. Maybe I'll take up lei-making myself."

She sounded so excited that I was mentally kicking myself for not having thought of doing that in the first place. Considering what I'd received in the hotel, alarm bells began ringing in my head.

"Betty, I didn't send you any flowers. I don't think Brian did either, though I'm going to check with him."

"But . . . Emma. They have your name on them. Even on the card, it says 'Thank you for a wonderful visit and hope to see you again soon, Emma.'"

I shook my head. "I didn't send the flowers. I'm a little worried about this. I—I have been having some problems with . . . identity theft lately. Someone may be using my credit cards since we were on vacation. Would you do me a favor? Get me the name and number of the florist or maker who sent them? I should check this out."

"Oh, no, Emma! I read about that kind of thing in the news all the time. I'll get the label right away. Hang on."

As my mother-in-law put the phone down, I prayed she'd be so distracted by the thought of identity theft, that she wouldn't ask why any identity thief would use my name to send her flowers. My stomach began churning acid as I waited for her to get back.

She gave me the information. "Thanks, Betty. I'll call them right away, make sure everything's okay. Maybe . . . maybe it would be a good idea if you didn't handle the flowers"—I couldn't bring myself to say, In case there is something dangerous in with them, but then my mother-in-law helped me out.

"Okay, you're right. They might be meant for someone else."

She sounded so sad that I could have kicked myself for not sending them. Damn. "Okay, you know, it might just be . . . I don't know what it might be. I'll call you right back."

"Please do."

"And, I'll call Brian, too. Maybe he sent them, and they messed up the card."

"I bet that's what it was," she said, and I could hear the relief in her voice.

We said goodbye and hung up. I called Brian, who had no idea what I was talking about, then I called the florist.

"I can't tell you the name of the person who sent them," the woman on the line said. "That's a matter between the recipient and the sender."

"What if I told you that I was afraid it was a matter of identity theft?" I said.

"I doubt that very much," the woman replied. "The customer paid with cash."

I racked my brains. "Okay, I understand that you can't tell me who sent the flowers. Can you . . . can you at least tell me whether you made up the leis yourself? Maybe not you, personally, but in house?"

"We would never send anything out that we hadn't prepared ourselves."

"Straight from you to the address in San Diego?"

"Absolutely, yes."

Okay, that at least ruled out the idea, crazed as it might be, that Tony or whoever it was had tampered with the flowers. A distant memory of Nancy Drew and a funeral lei came back to me, and I couldn't shake the feeling that Betty might be in danger.

"Thanks for your help." I hung up then dialed Brian's mom again and told her that there had been some confusion at the hotel where we'd been staying; they sent a thank-you gift to us, not to our address, but to our 'in case of emergency' address. "It's some kind of premium, you know. You get a tour package and 'thank-you gift.' It wasn't 'from Emma,' the card was saying but thank you 'to Emma.' "

It was a lame excuse, but the best I could do with the information I had at hand. "I'm just glad that they went to you, instead of getting lost altogether. You enjoy them, and make a lei for me next time I come."

"Oh, dear. Well, if you're sure . . . ?"

"Absolutely sure. You'll get more out of them, than I would. What am I going to do, wear it to class? I don't think the orchids and other stuff would go well with khakis in Maine in the fall."

Then Betty laughed and I knew she'd be fine.

I, on the other hand, was having a fit. If it hadn't been for the lilies of the valley at the hotel, I would have been able to convince myself of some hospitality error as well. But *Convallaria* would always be associated, for me, with the death of my friend Pauline and the death of her killer by the poisonous plants that grew in her yard, and another coincidence with flowers just didn't work for me.

And the note. I surely didn't relish seeing Tony soon. Even if it wasn't him, it still struck me as threatening.

I pressed the button and listened to the next message again. "Emma, this is Beebee Fielding," a crisp voice announced.

As if I knew thousands of Beebees. I sighed. My father's second wife. Maybe she was just making sure that I knew that they were still married, maybe she just never shook off her business background. I tried to give her the benefit of the doubt.

"I'm not really sure how to say this. While I think it's very kind of you to remember your father's tastes, and to think of him, occasionally—"

Okay, that was when I decided that there would be no more benefit of the doubt. Bitch.

"—I really must insist that you don't send him any more 'presents.'"

There it was again—presents? And I could practically hear her making quotation marks with her fingers.

"You know as well as I what the doctor says, and you know, equally well, that he, like most men, is incapable of curbing his appetites—"

Dear Beebee. I have no clue what you're talking about and I refuse to be lectured by someone five years older than me. You could be one hundred years older, and I still wouldn't take it.

"—and so, please. No more steaks. I will not be placed in the situation of being the bad guy, trying to keep him healthy. I must insist and I hope you will understand. Bye for now."

Steaks? I could barely make my fingers work the phone to call Beebee back.

She answered at once. "Beebee Fielding."

"Beebee, it's Emma. I got your message, but the thing is, I never sent Dad any steaks. I wouldn't, you know that." Quite apart from respecting her wishes, at least when it came to Dad's health, I'm not the steak-sending sort. She knew that as well.

"Well, the package had one of those preprinted labels, you know, the kind with the printed note from the sender. It said, 'Dad, have a blast. E. Fielding.' What am I supposed to think?"

"Beebee, this is important. Did Dad eat any of them?"

A delicate, frustrated sigh. "I told you in my message. The delivery truck no sooner left the driveway than he had the grill fired up and all six of them on the fire. I caught him, but he pleaded, and so we had our neighbors over."

"Is he . . . was everyone all right, after?" I couldn't believe how stupid I felt, or how shaky my voice sounded even to myself.

"Yes, of course. They were very good steaks," she said grudgingly. "He had a little bellyache, after, but that was simply because he'd eaten too much, too fast. And he can never stop with just one treat, he had to have blue cheese dressing on his salad, and potato salad from the deli, and too much whiskey after his beer—"

I breathed a sigh of relief. "That's good. Not the stomachache, but that there was nothing worse."

"Emma, what is all this about?"

"I think someone is playing practical jokes on me. I'm afraid that they might turn nasty."

There was silence from the other end. "So why would they send very expensive presents to us?"

To show me just how closely I'm being watched, I thought. To show that whoever it was knew me, knows my family. "I don't know. Maybe it's just to embarrass me, when I have to confess that I'm not that thoughtful. When was all this?"

"The day before yesterday. I waited to call because I wanted to calm myself. I was very upset that you might have . . . even though he loved the idea that you . . ."

While Beebee tried not to offend me, while trying to correct me, while telling me how much Dad had enjoyed the treat that I hadn't sent, I recalled what I knew about food poisoning. If the meat had been tampered with, it would have shown by now, I figured. "And it came straight from the source? Not a private home?"

"No, it looked as though it had been sent straight from the company in Omaha. What am I going to tell your father?"

"I . . . don't know. You can tell him the truth, I guess. Just do me a favor?"

There was a guarded pause before she answered. "Yes?"

"Give me the name of the company that sent it? And if you get any other packages that look like they're from me, give me a call, would you? Like I said, I'm just worried that this joker might turn nasty."

Beebee met my father through their mutual dealings in real estate, in the upper-end market in Connecticut. She knew something about competition and nasty tricks. "Of course. Thanks for calling."

"Yeah, you, too." I hung up, then glared at the answering machine. There was one message left, and I almost didn't dare to listen to it again.

"Emma, it's your mother."

Oh, hell.

"You know I hate this machine."

So I've heard. Repeatedly. Never stops you, though.

"In any case, thank you so, so much for the yummy, yummy chocolates. You shouldn't have. I mean, you know I'm watching my figure—"

A refrain as oft-spoke as it was false.

"—but it was too, too thoughtful of you. You know I love these little surprises, though it would have been even a nicer treat if you'd brought them yourself."

She giveth with one hand, and with the other, taketh away.

"I'm saving a few to share together. I know you're awfully busy with . . . whatever you're doing this summer. I haven't heard from you since the postcard you sent from Hawaii; lucky Mrs. Chang, she gets to see you."

Lucky Mrs. Chang.

"Well, give me a call. Or you could visit. You know I live on your visits. Bye."

Live for my calls, my pale pink butt. Ma was never in the country long enough to sit around and pine for me. If I called, I was being needy; if I didn't call, I was being thoughtless. And I recalled that the whole "I live on your visits" thing started just after she'd read Dorothy Parker in one of her many literature courses.

I had to call now, though. Had to find out about the chocolates.

But, as usual, Ma had called and gone, and who knew when she'd get back? She could be in Peru by now, which under other circumstances wouldn't be such a bad thing, but this whole things-I-hadn't-sent people thing was really creeping me out. I left a message: While she might hate my answering machine, she found her own invaluable.

"Hi, Ma, it's me. Look, I didn't send you any chocolates, and it's very important that you call me and tell me where they came from, what kind they are, whether you ate any. I'm sure it's fine, but just in case . . . well, I'm thinking that someone is playing practical jokes on me and I wouldn't want you to get hurt. You know, maybe they fixed them with Exlax or something. If you haven't eaten any, well, don't. And call me if you get anything else that says it's from me. Call me right away anyway, okay? Talk to you soon." I put the phone down, only to realize that my hands were shaking. The rest of me was shaking, too.

Okay, if this is Tony, he wants me to see him, he wants me to know that he's got an eye on the people in my life. That he's got an eye on me. Everything so far, well, it's been pretty benign. Flowers, chocolates, steaks. Sounds like courtship presents. Maybe that's how his mind works. He'd been flirtatious with me, but I'd always just assumed that it was a ruse, a way of feeling me out, so to speak. Find out what kind of person I am. So maybe, in his weird take on things, this is a kind of gesture. Gifts to me, to my family . . . well, it could be worse. Hell, who am I kidding? It will get worse. But if he's spiraling in, I've got the time now to start thinking about this, follow the leads, track him down before this gets really bad.

I was home for the next call, the next morning. It was from my sister, Bucky.

Someone had tried to burn down the Pollock Farms veterinary clinic.

Chapter 5

WASN'T THERE," SHE SAID. "I JUST GOT THE CALL from the old man. Excuse me, our senior partner."

"Was anyone hurt?"

"One of the older dogs died, probably from smoke. But I don't think the racket did them any good."

I took a deep breath. "I mean, none of your colleagues were there?"

"No, a car passed by and the driver saw the smoke. Thank God for cell phones."

I waited for her to continue, and when she didn't, I started to get scared. "I just need an hour to get my stuff together," I said. "I'll be down by noon."

Some of the sharpness returned to her voice. "No, no. Don't bother. I just wanted to tell you."

I hated when she got like this. "Wanted to tell me. Bucky, someone tried to torch your office. I know that place means more to you than—"

"Yeah, well, what are you going to do? I'm not hurt, we were lucky that no more of the animals were hurt badly, and the fire was reported before it got too far. What can you do?"

I didn't say: I can comfort you, I can help you get through this. That would have had exactly the wrong effect.

I didn't say it, but she picked up on that anyhow. "Look, don't bother. Joel's down here being a big enough girl for all three of us. I just wanted to tell you, because I know you like to hear about what's going on with me. That's all."

The fact that Bucky'd called me was proof enough that she was rattled. I was glad that her sensible boyfriend Joel had moved in with her last year, and that was the only reason that I let her get away with her lame excuse. Or calling him "a big girl," just because Joel was capable of dealing with emotions, and tried to address hers.

"Yeah, you're right. I'm glad you told me. And . . . I hope . . . you'll tell me if anything else happens."

"What the hell is that supposed to mean?"

I told her what had been going on with the phone calls, and my suspicions about Tony Markham. "I think they might be related."

"I think you might be *high*," my sister said. "Emma, for fuck's sake—a little evidence, please? Above and beyond the circumstantial?"

"What more do you want? *You* don't think that this suggests that Tony might be back?"

"Sure it suggests it. Who wouldn't think that?" Sarcasm is my sister's oeuvre. "But let's pull up a moment. The guy is supposed to be dead."

"I saw him," I said.

"You saw a guy at the airport, when you were half asleep and jetlagged. Okay, let's go with that, then. Maybe he isn't dead, but we can't prove he isn't dead, not conclusively. We can only say that odds are, he is. Let's look at where there is better evidence—"

"You sound like Brian," I muttered. I tried to relax my clenched fist, wiped my palms on my shorts.

"Thanks. Okay, if you're curious, I think it's a guy we just reported for animal cruelty, Fred Gamble. You should have seen what he was doing with that puppy farm. And we shut him down. Now, anyone who is willing to do that has got to have a few screws loose, and with Fred's temper and talent for expressing himself forcefully, he immediately shoots up the list of my favorite possible suspects."

"Fine. But that would also work for me. Tony has a talent for finding someone with an axe to grind and pointing them toward the nearest tree."

"That doesn't actually scan. Wouldn't it make more sense if you said, 'pointing him toward the nearest whetstone,' or whatever?"

"Bucky! Will you stay on the topic!"

"I am, you're the one haring after long shots and referring to a dead guy in the present tense. Fine, let's say all of these hinky coincidences aren't coincidences, and I'll step out farther onto that shaky limb and say that the fire is related, too. Your Tony, from what you've told me, is scary smart. This looks like someone busted a window and chucked in a Molotov cocktail. Why wouldn't this evil genius of yours have gone straight for the oxygen or nitrous canisters we have here? Would have done the job a whole lot more efficiently."

"Tony doesn't work with brain trusts. He finds angry idiots and manipulates them. If he wasn't actually there, on the scene, then it could have happened any way at all."

"Sounds like a stretch to me. What about fallout from the plagiarism thing from last year? Isn't that a possibility?"

I sighed. "Bucky, I really don't think that has anything to do with it."

"Okay, if you want to get willy-nilly with the facts, the probabilities, and the possibilities, we can move closer to home. Duncan Thayer."

Bucky hated my ex-boyfriend. Maybe even more than I did.

"Bucky, I think that Duncan's got better things to do—"

"He may well have, but remember, he's the one who brought this up at the conference in January, right? And didn't you tell me that he'd asked you for a reference? That you did not give? For a job that he subsequently did not get?"

"Just because he didn't get the job is no reason to—"

"Since when does reason come into it, if Duncan thinks he's been screwed over?"

I said nothing.

"And didn't this whole thing start with him? He asks, you say no, he tells you hello from Billy whatshisnose."

"Griggs." While Tony had tried to kill me and two of my students, he actually murdered Billy Griggs in front of me. And tried to pass it off as a favor to me. A token, if you will.

"He thinks about it, has someone send a postcard from Caldwell—how hard is that? Presumably he knows people in the college, right? He doesn't even have to be there himself."

"I don't know, Bucks . . ."

"He doesn't get the job. He's pissed. Rather than blaming himself, or the search committee, he blames you. He knows Ma and Dad, hell, he knows their tastes well enough. Any suck-up in his class would. And he knows what drives you up a wall. He knows what buttons to push."

"I think this is dealing with ancient history, Bucky."

"It's not ancient history, you moron. This has all happened within less than a year. Pull your head out of your ass and wake up and smell the coffee."

"Yeah, well, thanks for that charming image. I'm glad you're not hurt. Thanks for calling—"

"Don't pull that frosty professorial bullshit with me, Em. If you're pissed off at me, just say so."

"Well, I am. It's like you don't even care that I'm scared. That I'm even scared and concerned about you—"

"I do care, Emma, but it was Fred Gamble. And I can take care of myself—"

I ignored her, a sister's prerogative. "—on top of that, you're not even here, you don't know what's going on, and you already assume that you know better than I do."

"At least I'm not happier making up a fairy tale because I'm too egotistical to think some small stuff might be a small problem and not some frigging Greek tragedy. You're taking something that happened to me, and making it about you. You ain't the center of the universe. Get help, Em."

I hung up then. "Damn it!" I said to the wall.

"What's wrong?"

Brian was leaning in the kitchen doorway, dressed for work. I told him what happened and how Bucky had left things. "She'll be okay," I concluded, more to reassure myself, I suppose. "She said there wasn't even all that much real damage, but there'll be a hell of a mess to clean up."

Brian didn't say anything. I looked over at him. "Yes?"

"And she's right. This may have nothing to do with you. You may be looking for a connection where there isn't any."

I hated how carefully he kept his face neutral, kept his voice so reasonable, almost to the point of condescension. "I hate how everyone thinks I'm going off the deep end. It's not like I'm making up any of this stuff. It's actually happening. And yet, somehow, you and Bucky both seem to be forgetting that I am one of the most eminently reasonable people in your acquaintance."

"If we accept that you're an overwhelmingly reasonable person," he said, in that hateful, measured, cautious voice, "maybe you can remember that we're not stupid people either."

"I never said you were stupid."

"Great. So look at it from our perspective. You've been suffering a lot lately. Last semester took a toll on you and, frankly, things have been very stressful for you for a long time. You're starting to strain at relationships where there is no strain, almost like you want there to be something wrong. What would this look like to you, if you were in my shoes?"

"I'd think something was up. I'd be trying to find out what is going on."

"There's something going on, yes, but I just don't believe it's Tony. There's no proof of that. I want to find out what's happening, but I won't go looking for the bogeyman when there's a better answer."

One of our two cats, Minnie, sauntered through the other doorway from the dining room, and she perked up when she saw me, her tail went up as she hastily padded over. I scooped her up, and kissed her velvety head. "At least the cat still loves me," I muttered into her fur.

"I still love you," Brian said, but he left the room.

I followed him out, still hugging Minnie, who was batting at my ear. "Do you ever stop to wonder whether your adamant determination that this isn't Tony isn't pure denial? That you say it can't be, that it isn't, because you don't want it to be?"

He stopped. "Sure. Do you ever consider why it is that you seem to *need* it to be Tony?"

"Need it to be? Don't make me laugh."

"I ain't laughing, Em. You know, it's kind of creepy, like some weird kind of infatuation. Obsession, even. Occam's razor—"

"Don't give me that. You can't give me philosophy and science without applying them to your own arguments. Of all the people who might have a grudge against me, Tony has the most reason. And if it isn't him, then someone is going to a lot of trouble to make it look like it's him, and has a lot of knowledge about him and me. A copycat? That seems more unlikely than it being Tony himself."

Brian's jaw tightened. "The fingerprints weren't his. The handwriting wasn't his."

"But it was close. I'm not claiming to understand it all, but he's in this. You know he is."

Brian wouldn't look at me, kept staring at the boxes in the dining room. "He's dead, Em," he repeated woodenly.

"Again, when we apply logic, we don't have good proof of that. We never found a body. There was another way for him to have escaped. He had funds. He's got the wits to survive and pull something like this off. None of this stuff is the work of a pissed-off freshman, and everyone else who might have a stronger reason is either in jail or dead."

Brian shrugged. "Look, I'm going to call the bank and credit card companies, make sure that someone isn't ripping us off that way. Then I'm heading to work, okay?" He kissed me, left, and I was forced to confront my own thoughts in the solitude of my office.

Whatever I did, Tony, or someone, seemed to take it into consideration, even as I flailed about ineffectually.

I'd been retreating too long; I needed to press an attack. And while it was all very good to say that, I had absolutely no idea of what to do about it. Brian might be keeping his eyes open for identity theft, but he was purely in denial about Tony. It was up to me.

I might be able to fight, but I couldn't find an enemy to attack. And my fighting skills were theoretical, at best.

I had brains, but Tony was at least my match. Probably a lot smarter, and he had an agenda, which now looked like it had been planned over the past four years.

Hell's bells, chica. You're starting to make me scared. You're acting like you're weak, that you're not up to the task. What would you say if someone—not you—called you weak, ineffectual?

I'd tell them to get stuffed.

Right. So, what else did I have?

A mortgage. The love of a good man, even if he wasn't on the same page as me. A more than passing familiarity with the local constabulary. A burgeoning interest in criminalistics.

Not bad . . . keep going.

A kickass collection of reference material. Degrees with honors from a couple of prestigious universities. Tenure.

There you go. That's a lot, right there.

Oh, yeah, maybe for when they ask me to submit to *Who's Who*. But how am I supposed to make archaeology work for me—?

I hadn't even finished that thought when the answer came to me so suddenly that I had to sit down.

It's just what I'm always telling people: I reconstruct things that happened in the past. If I can't figure out where Tony is now, I can start from the last time I definitely saw him.

Penitence Point.

I had been staring at my blank computer screen when the thought first hit, and now it was like watching a movie of the events that dark afternoon so long ago. I watched, up to my waist in freezing water, body broken and bruised, as Tony fled into a storm with a bag, probably bags, of gold. Later, the wreck of that motor boat had been discovered and Tony presumed lost, but there was also a missing sailboat from a nearby marina. The authorities, rightly having no other evidence to go on, couldn't assume that there was a connection, but I had always believed I knew better. Tony had survived the storm and had headed for parts unknown.

This was nothing new, my balloon-bursting internal editor reminded me. You still don't have anything to work with.

I do. I never thought to try and follow him from that point, so to speak. I had been too easily reassured that he was gone for good and life had taken over from there.

I look for clues to events that happened centuries ago. Now I'm going to see how good I am at tracing a four-year-old trail.

I dumped the cat unceremoniously onto the floor. Right, Brian says he wants evidence, wants to get some solid evidence? Me too. Time to cross some names off the list.

I got in the car and headed for campus. Every once and a while, when my concentration slipped and I remembered what I was actually doing, the knot in my stomach tightened unbearably. It was no surprise that I'd found it difficult to eat over the summer, and I couldn't plead the heat as an excuse, even. I'd made a bit of progress while on vacation, when everything seemed unreal and I could pretend that I wasn't coming home to real life and anxiety. If one more person told me how great I looked, that I'd lost so much weight, I'd kill them. Weight loss sometimes seems to be the only hallmark of good looks in this society. It's not even near the best one, not when combined with bags under eyes and short temper. I didn't like feeling like this, and didn't like knowing that my disturbed state of mind was starting to affect me physically.

I found a parking space readily enough, and headed down the main path on the quad toward a group of buildings I usually had no business with. Actually took pains to avoid, truth be told, for what they represented to me, not just with that business last semester, but in general.

A knot of young men stood outside the frat house, and seeing me, a couple of them gazed frankly, no trace of embarrassment or self-consciousness on their faces. I could have chalked it up to basic male chemistry—a tolerably fit, unmistakably well-endowed, nearly youngish woman in shorts and a T-shirt might reasonably expect a few glances—but they didn't turn away when I looked at them.

That is, they didn't turn away until they recognized me. Then a few actually turned and fled inside the house.

They didn't run, not really, but it was a definite retreat. One didn't move fast enough. I called him. "Ryan! Hang on a second!"

He was either too dumb or too honest to pretend he hadn't heard me. He did pretend, however, that he hadn't noticed his friends taking off like a pack of scared wildebeests. I could give him that; it wasn't a matter covered in most etiquette books. "Oh. Hi, uh, Professor Fielding. Are you having a good summer?"

"No." I looked around the porch, but it was completely deserted. "Where is he?"

"Uh . . . who?" He tried to look baffled, but gave it up after a moment. He then tried a look of delayed recognition. "Oh. You mean . . . Tyler?"

"Yes, Tyler. Where is he?"

"Uh . . . Belgium?"

I crossed my arms over my chest and sucked my teeth. He had exactly ten seconds before I . . .

He must have seen something in my face, because there was genuine panic in his now. "No, I'm serious! I think he's in Brussels until the end of the week, and then he'll be back. He's not due back at the house for a couple of days, anyway, and if it's not Brussels, it's somewhere else in Europe. He's been away for almost two months."

"Excuse me. He's in Europe? He gets caught cheating on a paper—by me—handing in a paper from one of those Internet term paper mills, gets subjected to a college disciplinary hearing, is reprimanded, flunks my class, and you want me to believe that his parents sent him to *Europe*? For two months? Try again."

"I'm serious. He's been away the whole summer. But they didn't let him go by himself. They made him go with them."

"Forgive me if I don't see the punishment there."

"But he didn't flunk your class," Ryan blurted.

I turned on him. "The whole sordid episode has been burned into my memory for all time. I believe I recall quite clearly the moment I hit the enter key and submitted my grades." I recalled quite clearly thinking the entire ghastly mess—the hearing, the wrangling, the pleading—was behind me.

"Oh, sure, you might have. But what he told me was, the dean told him he could just not get credit for the class. He could take another one and it would just be . . . gone." He shrugged.

Oh, dear God. The dean. "He . . . I never signed a drop form. I wouldn't . . ." But I knew that Dean Belcher would. Especially if . . .

"Ryan, remind me. Tyler's family. They're the aluminum Tuckers, aren't they?"

It made them sound as if they were cut out of shiny foil, but Ryan knew what I meant. At least the little wiener had the grace to shrug again as he nodded.

That explained a lot. Dean Belcher was a sucker for a sob story, especially if it was backed up with a significant family fortune and the possibility of incoming funds. "I cheated because I was scared that I wouldn't pass" sounded so much more logical when accompanied by the potential, perhaps the promise, of big donations.

"Okay, thanks."

Ryan looked relieved and turned to climb the porch.

I waited until he was almost at the top step. "One more thing, Ryan."

Give the kid credit. He didn't bolt for the door. "Yeah?"

"He's been with his folks? The whole time? You see, there's been some . . . oh, let's just use the coy euphemism 'unpleasantness' . . . this summer. You don't think that he . . . ?"

I sounded like an idiot.

Ryan shifted his weight, back and forth, as he tried to decide what to say. "Professor Fielding, I won't lie to you. He was pretty pissed off at you, during the whole . . . thing, but—"

Pissed off at me, I thought. Because he got caught cheating.

"—but after his parents . . . and the dean . . . after the dust settled?" Ryan shook his head. "I'm sure he doesn't even re-member you exist."

I nodded, a bit numb. "Sure, fair enough," I said, mar-veling at how stupid the words were even as they left my mouth. I turned back to the main path.

Ryan hesitated, before he opened the door. "I really en-joyed your class. I mean, I didn't do really well, but it wasn't because I didn't like it."

I nodded. I couldn't bring myself to say thanks, not for the information, and not for the pity. Because now I was getting pity from undergraduate fraternity porch ticks.

Great.

I walked back down Maple Walk. My stomach was still in turmoil, but for a completely different reason.

Long before I reached my building, I had convinced myself that Tyler was no longer on my list of suspects. He couldn't have done it, not while still in Europe, not with whatever lax parental observation—exerted in response to having had to deal with the dean—was present.

Other suspects wouldn't be ruled out so easily. Not by me, anyway.

Okay, say it is Tony. How on earth do I go about finding where he might have gone and what he might be up to now, without getting the police involved and without getting

Brian more convinced than he is already that I'm a mental case? I just don't have the skills to deal with—what? Stolen gold, double identities, that sort of thing. And everything I do know is four years old, to say the least . . .

Shit, Em. Everything you spend your days learning about is three or four hundred years old, depending on how you look at it. You want to talk about partial evidence, the impositions of time and space on your work, and you're worried about four years, in the age of the Internet? Where simply everything is documented?

Most everything. Most everything legal—you can't imagine that Tony has been doing everything on the up-and-up, can you? But still . . . this might not be impossible.

Of course not. In fact, more than half of the problem is asking the right questions. Start there—

Work from the known to the unknown. Begin at the beginning.

—and move to what you know now. Give it a shot, at any rate. Give yourself some peace of mind, maybe, finding out one way or the other. Maybe you'll find out he's dead.

And that would mean I have no idea who's behind these events? That's comforting how? I've crossed one name off a list of four and a half billion, that's all.

Pish and tosh. You're not that important, my girl. How many people have you ever taught, all together—thousands? How many of them might want to mess with you? A dramatically smaller number, never mind that little turdbag Tyler, who apparently we can temporarily shelve as a suspect. I ditched my parents all the time when I was growing up, and all the little rat needs is a credit card and a cell phone or an Internet café . . .

He's off the list for the moment.

I arrived at my office and flung myself on the couch there.

Okay, so subtract Tyler, add in colleagues, competitors, neighbors, people you accidentally cut off in the supermarket parking lot, most of whom can be written off the list immediately, and you're dealing with a hundred, maybe. Instantly, your list is magically, logically, smaller.

Okay, so you've talked me into it. Where do I start?

You start with gold.

Don't know a thing about it. Don't know where you'd turn gold into cash, don't know who might pay attention to those things . . .

But you do know folks who know about stolen antiquities. Time to get online and start asking some pertinent questions.

That got me out of my funk and off my couch. I pulled out a couple of books from the shelf, on the antiquities trade, and my ASAA directory. I flicked through the articles, and realized that they were all dated and most of them dealt with areas other than the ones I suspected—the Caribbean, Mexico—but they had some anecdotal evidence that suggested I was on the right track. The rates of antiquities theft these days were quite staggering, partly because of collectors, who were a constant plague, and partly because of countries that sold the antiquities to raise money, though this was usually for arms and not the populace at large. I learned a bit about how sites were looted, and how the collectors, looters, thieves, call them what you will, were almost as skilled as my archaeological counterparts. I learned that the trade in illegal antiquities was third behind drugs and weapons dealing.

I also learned that archaeologists were killed by site looters.

But it didn't tell me where the artifacts went. How one turned them into cash, and more, did it without being caught. I was just too law-abiding for my own good.

I figured I had two options then. I could go the usual route, check colleagues I knew might know. Then I could branch out a bit, check out some folks who might have the information and be amenable to sharing it, if I put the question just the right way.

My first call was to Rob Wilson. Rob's been a friend since the bad old days, even though we hardly ever get the chance to hang out anymore. As much as I missed that, I knew that if I had a question that he could answer, he wouldn't rest until he got what I needed. Actually, it was kind of unfair to ask him anything, as he was as bad as me about obsessing over tracking down a fact.

On the other hand, I was more than willing to exploit that and his guiltiness for never hanging out with the old crowd at the conferences.

Getting to be quite the coldhearted creature, aren't we, Em?

Sod off.

I lucked out, he was there, for once, and more than that, answering his phone.

"Hi, Emma! How're you?"

Damn caller ID. Always took me by surprise. "I'm doing okay, Rob, you?"

"Can't complain. What can I do for you?"

Was there just a touch of impatience there? I didn't care. "Got to ask you some questions about the antiquities trade, if you've got a minute."

"Just about five, but I'll see what I can do for you. Shoot."

I outlined the problem, without giving him the reasons I was so interested in it. "I'm hopelessly out of date when it comes to the latest bulletins, and such. Where are the best places to sell gold, or rather, golden antiquities, these days?"

There was a heavy silence on the other end. "What the hell are you getting into, Em?"

"Um, let me rephrase that—"

"What did you find this time, Emma? Exactly what kind of trouble are you in?"

"I'm not . . . I didn't find anything, it's not me." None of it was me, I thought angrily. "Look, I don't know if you heard, if you remember what happened a couple of years ago—"

"Is this the stuff that Duncan Thayer was going on about, back at the ASAAs?"

There's that name again. "What? No. Well, yes, but probably not the way he was . . . why? What did he tell you?"

There was a long pause. Rob was going to be diplomatic. It was one of the things that I loved about him, ordinarily. Now, it just seemed like he was covering for my evil ex, the oft-wished-I-could-eradicate-him-from-the-record-of-my-life, Dunk the Skunk.

"You know everyone was pretty well jarred by what happened at the end of the conference this year, up in New Hampshire?"

How could I not know? I'd exposed a killer, one of my colleagues and someone I'd accounted a friend, and nearly got myself killed in the process. "Half of the folks blamed me for causing trouble, half thought I was a liar, and half of them just thought I was mental."

"Um, okay. Jarred. But Duncan falls into that third half. He claimed that he passed along a hello from someone and you assaulted him."

"Assault is a strong word," I said carefully, knowing it wasn't too strong: I'd gone ballistic, true, but with good reason. Didn't make it less of an assault, I guess. "He gave me greetings from a murdered man, and the person using that man's name was probably the murderer. The same guy who tried to kill me."

"This is to do with that thing out at the site that time? Three, four years back?"

Rob was an old enough friend that he knew about the murders at Fort Providence on Penitence Point. "Yeah. You know, at the conference in January, Duncan made a point of telling me that a guy approached him. I don't think Duncan was lying, now. I think the guy is back. Looking for me."

"Give me some context, Em."

So I told him about Tony and the gold he'd stolen and why I thought he was back. "I was trying to figure out if I could trace him by the British gold he took from the river. I never saw it, but I figure if I could track the dealers, find out which illegal antiquities markets would be the most like to give him a good profit and yet not send up any signals to the authorities—"

"Emma, believe that I say this from a place of love: You think way too much. Always have, always will. You're over-complicating this to extremes."

"Yeah? So tell me how you'd approach it." Okay, I was feeling prickly.

"Shit, if it were me? Either the gold is in bars, in which case you melt it down and sell it to your local refinery, or it's in coins, and you don't melt it because of the numismatic value. Also more portable that way. Go to your local coin dealer and say you found Grandpa's collection in the attic and you'd like to cash it in. They're not going to ask."

"They don't have to report it to the authorities, or something? The IRS wouldn't—?"

"Look, kiddo, you could find an auction house—you said it was British gold, right? Find a large British auction house, if you want, and get the best price. But that's too high profile, even. You could go and sell it online. Or you could just go down to the corner—"

"Yeah, yeah, the corner coin store. Rob, seriously? Is it that easy?"

"It's that easy."

I shivered. That not only meant that it would be nigh on impossible to track Tony, if it was bars, as I bet the dealers wouldn't be likely to tell me who'd been selling them what. It also meant that he had a very large amount of very dispos-able income.

"Look, I can tell you the other stuff if you want, Em, but really? You don't need it."

I didn't need it: I was already hosed. "Okay, gotcha. Thanks for your help, Rob."

He laughed, and in other times it was a noise that would have brought a smile to my face, too. "You make a shitty criminal, Em. But if you ever stopped thinking so damn much, that would be different."

"Yeah, yeah, rub it in, why don't you?"

Maybe he could hear the frustration in my voice; it had nothing to do with my lack of criminal genius. "I'll email you, if I think of anything that will help you, okay?"

"Thanks, Rob, I mean it. Catch you later." I hung up and rubbed my head. I guess if it ached, it was from running head-long into so many dead ends.

Chapter 6

WITH ARCHAEOLOGY, YOU'D THINK THINGS WOULD be straight forward, but they never are. Read the books, dig the site, wash the stuff, write up the report, reap fortune and glory. And while that is essentially correct, it leaves out the details of schedules, paperwork, personnel, budgets, meetings, PMS, home life, and homicidal maniacs. So it was a relief to be able to actually get out into the field the next two days to do some testing out at Penitence Point.

There wasn't a lot to be done, and so it worked out to be just Meg and me, again, out at the Point. Neal had gotten his doctorate in the spring and was trying to set up his own company, and so didn't have the time, even if he could have used the money; Dian was gone, out of the picture, having been offered a job as an office manager that was going to keep her a lot more secure than any job in archaeology would. It was a little sad, too, to think this might be one of the last summers that Meg and I would work in the field together, as she was working full-time on her dissertation and would be gone, probably, in a year or two.

There were lots of emotions that I was trying to clear out of my head so I could concentrate on the work. A nice collection of one-by-ones, all along the western boundary of the site, near the line of silver birches that led down to the edge of the bluff and the river. Meg looked a lot happier than she did in my office; now she was more surely in her element.

"Did I remember to mention in my email yesterday?" Meg said. "I asked Katie Bell if she wanted to join us, just for the experience. She was back for a visit, before she goes off into the wide world of graduate school next year. Told her we'd be dropping some phone booths and maybe some TPs, and did she want to come along?"

"Let me guess," I said. "She had no idea that you were talking about."

"Right. I mean, she knew TP was 'test pit.' But it wasn't just that she didn't know that I meant square-meter units, she didn't know what an actual phone booth was."

"Surely she must have seen them in movies," I said. "How old is she? Twenty-one, twenty-two?"

Meg nodded. "She finally did remember having seen them in movies, but that was her only reference point. I bet she doesn't know what a vinyl album is, either, or that you can make tea without a microwave, or that floppy disks used to be floppy."

"She's a smart kid, but a very new soul," I agreed. "Ah, well, now she has a bit of dated jargon, which she will probably think of as 'lore.'"

The fact that it was just the two of us had struck me from the moment our plans were set. Meg and I had been alone on the Point before, and bad things had happened. Good things too, but the stuff that was on my mind was directly rooted in our first experience there, and a particular night that had involved gunplay, a death, and Neal being wounded—by Tony Markham.

If Meg was bothered, then she didn't show it; as far as I knew, she still thought the mention of Billy at the conference had been a parting jab from Duncan. For my part, after the flowers, mysterious deliveries, and fire, every noise that might have been a footstep, or might have been nothing at all, caught my attention. Finally, it was only the physical labor itself and the concentration that digging a neat square hole in the ground required that diverted me. The fact that Tony had used fire to destroy the house that had once stood on this site, and conceal the murder of my friend, just gave me an even worse case of the jumps.

I finished the balk drawings that were left over from yesterday and Meg had just finished sifting and sorting the artifacts into carefully marked bags. As I gazed across the site, I realized something wasn't right.

Even as I felt myself frown, Meg asked: "Emma, how many meter squares did we do yesterday?"

"I thought you and I each did one—it's pretty shallow around here—and we did two more today. Four"

"That's what I thought. I remember because I emailed you to bring more string for today."

We both counted again, and finally Meg asked, "So why is there an extra test pit?"

I shook my head, unable to figure it out. I flipped through the notes, and checked. Sure enough, our memories matched the notes. There was a unit that wasn't here yesterday.

"Do you think it's looters?" Meg asked.

"I don't know. Was someone camping here? It looks awfully regular, though."

"It is."

We walked over to the hole that we didn't remember digging. It was in fact, just as square and regular as the rest of our units, but smaller, and to my all-too-practiced eye this one looked to be exactly fifty centimeters square, each side roughly the width of two shovel blades. Every profession has their own informal metrics.

The walls were straight and clean; I would have praised the student who showed me such work. The location of the unit also puzzled me; it was exactly where I would have placed another unit, had we the time to spend on moving out from the core of the area I was most interested in.

"We didn't dig this," Meg said.

"No."

"But it looks . . . real."

"Like we did it," I agreed. "But we didn't."

"No."

A cloud passed from over the sun. Something was at the bottom of the unit.

"Hang on a second," Meg said, and she knelt down to get a better look.

"Meg, wait," I said. "This is bothering me."

She smirked. "What, are you afraid that there's a land mine or something down at the bottom?"

"You can laugh if you want, but . . . yes. Something like that."

She shook her head, serious now. "I won't touch anything, I'm just going to get a better look."

She leaned over, and as she set one hand down on the opposite side, she suddenly jerked up. "Shit!"

I stepped toward her. "What is it?"

"Ah, nothing. You got my nerves going, that's all. I put my hand down on a rock and it bit me." She looked at her hand, saw nothing, and leaned over again.

And jerked back much more quickly. "Ouch—goddamn it!"

She held up her hand and this time blood was running down the palm of her hand. "There must be a piece of glass or something over there. Hold on."

"Meg, don't," I said. "Get out of there, please. Now."

She looked at me suddenly; it must have been the urgency in my voice. "Okay."

I did not move for a moment, just studied the ground before us. The grass around two edges of the pit was untrampled and most of the ejecta—the soil dug from the hole—was piled tidily not too far away in the familiar inverted cone. No doubt about it, someone had taken a good deal of care in excavating this unit. Call it, rather, the very square hole someone else had dug on our site. A spark of indignation began to burn: it wasn't a unit unless *I* said it was.

The ejecta. The edge of the pit. Finally, I figured out what was wrong.

The hole had been dug to look like an archaeological test pit, but that's as far as it went. The cone of excavated soil should have been sifted, if we'd been doing the work, with all of the rocks dumped on the top of the sifted dirt. So what I should have seen as the result of proper archaeological work would have been a cone with nicely sorted, fine soil on top, with the rocks and roots having rolled to the bottom of the pile. Different color soils would have been visible, separated out.

This was just a pile of dirt, uniform color, no sorting whatsoever. That told me to reexamine the edge of the unit again. If it had been genuine archaeology, there would have been more trampling of the yellowed grass, where the excavator had squatted or kneeled or rested her hands or, heaven forbid, sat at the edge of the unit. I saw no knee prints, hand prints, or butt prints on the grass on two sides of the pit. So, it only *looked* like professional work.

It was in staring at the untrodden grass, remembering how Meg had leaned on the edge, when I found what I was looking for. A glint in the grass, as the sun came out from behind clouds again, and I saw the pattern. Making sure that I had seen all of it, I gingerly got to my knees and carefully moved the taller grass stalks aside so Meg could see, too.

Someone had stuck nails into the ground, points up, in an irregular pattern, around most of the square. Anyone kneeling or leaning within six inches of those edges would put her full weight on them; Meg's quick reflexes—and a dash of luck in kneeling on the side where it was too trampled to hide the nails—had saved her from worse injury. And if Meg's "joke" turned out to be no joke—if there *was* a land mine at the bottom—the nails would make excellent shrapnel.

I stood up, brushing the dirt and grass off my hands. "My guess is that whoever it was cut the heads off, then stuck them in: points on both ends."

"Whoever it was also knew that we'd be on the ground, checking this out in no time," Meg agreed. "Knew that we'd crawl all over the place near a unit. Knew we're not afraid of getting dirty."

"Still want to see what that is down the bottom of the pit?"

"I'm not that curious," she replied. "But how—"

"Let's call the cops."

"Why, Em? I'm not hurt that bad." She held up her hand, to show me that the flow of blood had slowed. "It could still just be someone else's idea of a sick joke, it might not have anything to do with Tony." She knew my fears, even if she didn't think they were anything more than a parting blow from an angry ex-boyfriend.

"I'm not much for coincidences right now," I said. "I think someone is watching us closely, someone who knows how we work and move. I don't want anyone else to get hurt, if possible." I was thinking of Bucky's clinic.

"And you think, whoever it is, might be thinking about other people associated with the site, in this area," Meg said.

"Yes. Let's see if Sheriff Stannard is in today."

About forty minutes later, Dave Stannard was standing beside us, looking down at the nails with an unreadable expression. He shifted his gaze to the water for a moment, then looked back at the ground.

"Deliberate. Nasty." Dave paused, then glanced at me. "For you."

I nodded, my stomach roiling. "I'm wondering how they knew we'd be out here. It's not a state secret or anything, but . . . it's not like there's any cover for someone to hide out and watch."

"Hmmm. Might want to check with the Anthropology Department." He turned to Meg. "How's that hand of yours?"

She held it up for him to see. "It's fine. I cleaned it out real good, bandaged it up. It's no big deal. I've got my shots, and it's already stopped—"

"Do me a favor?" I was surprised: Dave Stannard rarely interrupted people. "Keep an eye on it. Just in case."

"Just in case . . . there was something on the nails?" I said.

He shrugged. "You never know. You might just stop by the hospital on the way out, make sure." The sheriff kneeled down, pulled some latex gloves out of his pocket, and put them on. He took a few of the nails and put them into a plastic bag. "You never know."

I couldn't respond. As bad as I'd thought the situation, he was able to imagine it so much worse. I wasn't used to thinking like this.

"We took some photos of the site," Meg said. "If you like, we could send you some."

"Thanks—do that. Em, any ideas about what that is down at the bottom of the pit? Did either of you touch it?"

"No," Meg and I answered simultaneously. I added, "It was deeper than ours, maybe arm's reach. I didn't dare touch it."

He nodded. "I'm willing to. I think that after the nails, it would be silly to put the real danger down the bottom of the hole. I mean, who'd be stupid enough to warn you away from it with the nails?"

"I don't know what this is about," I said. "I only know that I don't want anyone getting hurt."

He shrugged. "It isn't your call." But he had us stand back and he probed the bottom of the pit with a long stick before he knelt on the safe side of the hole. He reached in. I tensed.

Dave pulled out a crumpled and dirty brown paper lunch bag. Maybe it was the bag that once held the nails, I thought; it looks like the sort you could get from the hardware store. He slowly uncurled the top of it, crumpled and dirty and damp from having spent the night in the bottom of the pit, and looked inside.

"I think we've got trouble here," he said.

"What is it?"

"Bones." He shrugged. "I'm not an expert, but they look human to me."

"Human bones?" Meg looked more curious than scared or ill, which is more than I could say for myself. "What sort?"

"Little ones." Stannard smiled, a little sick, pale under his summer work tan, and shrugged. "I said I wasn't an expert."

"Can we—?" I asked.

"Just don't touch them." He shook a few of them onto a large plastic artifact bag that Meg whipped out of her backpack and spread out on the ground.

"Shit," she said. Something like awe was in her voice. "They do look human to me. Emma?"

She knew that osteology wasn't technically part of my specialty—colonial archaeology—but that I had been reading a lot on human remains lately, with an eye to expanding my professional horizons.

I leaned over the bones. "Sometimes, if they're in rough shape, the bones can be misidentified as some other carnivore—bear, maybe even a wildcat." Sure enough, they were about the right size, certainly the right shape for human, but there was something distinctly odd about them, considering what I was expecting to see and where I was seeing them. "Yes, human—but holy cow! They've been prepared!"

"Prepared?" Stannard looked queasy.

"You know, someone cleaned them up, boiled or bleached them clean. Like they were being used for a study collection. It was strange; at first, I was just assuming the bones were something found here by whoever dug this hole. But there are no stains and they're not weathered—they've not been in the ground at all, as far as I can see—and there's no sign that they . . ." I stopped myself, trying to find the best way to phrase my grisly thought.

"No sign, what?" Meg asked.

"No sign that they . . . recently came off someone alive. There's no tissue, no, uh, bloodstains. The thing that tripped me up was that they look exactly like the ones we have back in the faunal lab, the skeletons and bones that are known examples, to be used to compare with what you find in the field. I'm so used to seeing them there, that it didn't register with me for a moment."

"Yeah, you're right. Damn." Meg sounded like she was disappointed that she hadn't caught that. At least, I hoped she wasn't disappointed that the bones were not . . . recently acquired.

"Jeez, you know—hey, check this out!"

I was using a pen to roll the little bones around—they were short, roughly cylindrical with knobby protuberances on either end—when I saw the markings. Clear, but cryptic, black markings along the short shafts of some of the larger ones. Letters and numbers . . .

"I'll be damned," Meg whispered. "Are those . . . ?"

"Yeah," I said. I was actually more creeped out now than I had been when I still worried that the bones were fresh. "I think they are. Look here." I pointed out a particularly good example.

"Will you tell me what's going on?" Dave said. "What are those marks? Some kind of occult thing? Or is it just 'cult'?"

"Kinda," Meg said; I frowned, she wasn't wrong, but it wasn't the time for humor. Everyone needs an outlet for anxiety, I guess.

"Only if you consider accession marks on a study collection an occult practice. Imagine a room full of people dedicatedly washing each bone fragment as if it was precious, then marking each one just so, with the attention that is usually reserved for relics. These were part of a faunal collection, once, or an archaeological assemblage. The thing is," I said, squinting at the numbers, "I'd be willing to bet that they came from Caldwell College."

"Not one of your sites?" Meg asked quickly.

"No, I don't think so," I replied. "Caldwell's collections, but not one of mine—we don't have any human stuff from my sites. There's a lot of stuff that was recently recatalogued, collections curated by my predecessors." I finally looked up at Dave's worried face. "They're human. Finger phalanges, I think—you can see they're a little flattened on one side. Toe bones are rounder, if I recall correctly. But these marks, the writing, indicate where these were found, and on what site. We do exactly the same thing."

"So that means . . . what?" asked Meg.

"It could be a couple of things," Stannard said. He was looking at the water again, rubbing his hand back and forth over his head, rumpling up his brown hair. Completely unconscious about it, as usual. "It could be someone from Caldwell. Obviously, whoever it was knew you'd both be here, knew enough to make it look like one of your units, had access to the collections."

"I don't think so," I said. "Most of the department is scattered to the four corners of the world. Most of them will be coming back in a couple of weeks. I'm thinking of faculty, not students, though I've got an idea where most of them are. The archaeologists, at least."

Meg and Dave looked at me skeptically. "Okay, well the graduate students. Keeping track of undergraduates is like keeping track of fruit flies. There seem to be millions of them, and they're always in constant motion."

"Doesn't mean they couldn't have come back early," Meg said.

"I know, but there's none of them that would do a thing like this," I said, a little impatient. We had to narrow it down somehow. "We can ask Chuck, our administrator, if he's seen anyone—crap!" I slapped my forehead. "The keys!"

"Right!" Meg said.

Stannard furrowed his brow, confused.

"There are only a few keys to the storage areas," I explained, "and it gets recorded when they're given out. I have one, Neal—that's Meg's fiancé—had one, but he turned it in—"

"I remember him. Nice kid. Congratulations, you," he said to Meg. She nodded impatiently, wanting to stay on track.

"I don't know who else would have a key right now," I finished, frustrated. "Since I'm the only archaeologist, I can't think that the linguists or social anthropologists need to get at the curation facilities. So it's got to be Professor LeBrot's stuff—he's our physical anthropologist. We can double-check, and ask Chuck too."

"There's another possibility," Dave said, looking troubled now.

I nodded.

"It could be that someone broke into the storage. Someone pulling a stunt to play with your head, as well as cause you some kind of injury."

"Maybe they didn't need to break in," I said.

Meg looked up.

"Maybe Tony's still got a key," I said to Dave, then explained my current theories. His frown deepened as my story worked its way up to the present.

"Even if the locks have been changed since that time, I'm sure he remembers enough of how to get in some other way. Nick another key, break in during the night, follow someone in, something like that."

"You should make sure you speak with the administrator, and the people in your department," Stannard said after a pause. "This is serious. Even if it isn't Tony Markham, someone deliberately tried to hurt you two—"

"And if it is Tony," I said, a little impatient, "you need to be careful too, Dave. I think . . . he's reaching out to people I know. Some of them were related to his case, some are people who are close to me, family, friends. I think that with your involvement with the case, you should be extra alert. And your family, too."

"You know, Emma, we've discussed this before," he

started slowly. "Last time we had this conversation, after the conference in January, I was pretty sure Tony Markham was dead. I still am, truth be told."

I shook my head. "I still say, there's no proof that he's dead. No body, nothing. And even if it isn't Tony, it's someone who knows enough of the details of my history, and therefore our association with this site and Pauline's murder. Information that isn't readily available—"

"Most everything is readily available, these days," Dave said. "Do enough digging into public records, the Internet, you can find a lot of stuff. I don't need to tell you that."

I waved one hand. "Okay, say it is someone else, just for the sake of argument. It could well be someone from around here who might have been on the scene four years ago. And if that's the case, there's still a good chance that you and your family may . . . be at risk."

Maybe my argument was convincing enough, maybe it was the strain in my voice, or the look in my eyes that said, yes, I am going to keep arguing until you at least pretend to agree with me, but the sheriff finally nodded.

"Okay. I'll talk to my people, have them do some nosing around. I'll talk to my wife, tell her keep an eye out. You write me up an account of what happened today—you too, Meg—and then, Emma, you write me another summary of what's been going on. At least that way, if I find something on this end, I'll be able to see where it fits in."

I nodded so eagerly I'm sure I looked like one of those little dogs that people have in the rear windows of their cars. I didn't care. Even if Dave didn't entirely believe me, he'd do what he said, and that's all I cared about. It was one of the many things I liked about him. More than that, he was taking my fears at least a little seriously.

Though it would have been nice to think he did believe me. I liked and respected Dave and didn't want him to think I was a basket case.

"Good," he said, relieved. "We'll stay in touch then. So, how's your husband?"

I told him, asked after his wife and his two daughters, the oldest of whom was now nearing junior high school age. He turned to Meg.

"So, when's the big day?"

"Weekend after Labor Day," she said. Meg had on her game face, the one she reserved for public speaking and other tasks that made her uncomfortable. "That way, everyone will be home from the field, everyone will be back at school."

"Wow, just a couple of weeks. Less. Got everything all set?"

A thought hit me then, and I think it occurred to Dave, too. Meg was too preoccupied to pick up on it, though. "I've got a bunch of stuff left, but all little things. You're right, it's not long." She looked panicked, then got control of herself, straightened her shoulders, gritted her teeth. "But I can do it."

"Of course you can," Dave said. I thought there was just a trace too much forced heartiness in his voice. "Well, I must get back to the office. You all take it easy."

We all shook hands, and Meg and I finished loading up the truck.

"Wild day, huh?" Meg said, as we found the highway that would lead us back to campus.

"Yeah." I wanted to chat with her, wanted to pretend that everything was fine, but I couldn't.

All I could think about was the wedding. And how close it was. And how perfect a target it would be if someone truly wanted to do us harm.

Chapter 7

I WAS PROBABLY TOO DEEP IN THOUGHT ON MY WAY home later that evening, or else I might have noticed the dark-colored sedan behind me a bit sooner. It was just as I was pulling out of Lawton's center and finding my way down the road that would lead me to my road and the Funny Farm.

It was dark outside—Meg and I'd been delayed by the surprise at the bottom of the pit and Dave's questions—and I was running late. The streets outside Lawton center are very quiet, apart from rush hour, when some folks cut across country rather than follow the more congested arteries through town. After six or seven o'clock, the only cars I generally see are those of my few and distant neighbors and their visitors.

It will turn at the next intersection, I thought. They're just late coming home from work. It's really unlikely they'll follow me down Harrison Farm Road, down there it's just us and . . .

The car did follow me down Harrison Farm Road. I glanced back at the driver, but could hardly see anything behind the tinted windshield. Just a flashing blue light swirling on the dashboard.

I frowned, and began to pull over, simply out of habit, but then something checked me. I continued to move, albeit a bit more slowly, along the side of the road, waiting for him to pass me, if he wanted to. No such luck: He kept on my tail. And yet, something kept me from pulling over and stopping completely.

I didn't have time to figure out what it was that was bothering me. Suddenly, I found myself jolted violently forward. The other car had bashed into the back of mine.

Omigod, was he trying to kill us both? And yet, he kept right on my tail, dangerously close . . . why didn't he back off?

That's it, I thought. Cops will give you a moment, use the loudspeaker, something, to get you to the side of the road. Without another thought, I shifted into high gear and floored it.

The road was largely unlit—it was too far off the beaten path to warrant many streetlamps—and I knew the area as well as anyone local. I knew what I was going to do. I just needed to keep my head and I needed to keep at least a foot ahead of the other car. If he hit me, and I rolled off the road into the fields that surrounded my house, I would be in big trouble. I couldn't take my eyes off the road long enough to get any of the plate. Besides, he was too close behind me now.

I tore down the road, past my own house, not even pausing. If this guy wasn't a cop, then no way was I going to lead him home. I passed the neighbor's house. He was out by his mailbox and I saw the startled look on his face as he recognized me and realized that I was being pursued at high speed by what looked like an unmarked police car. I hoped that I'd have the chance to explain it all to him later.

The intersection with the other tertiary road came up sooner than I expected—I wasn't used to traveling this fast on this road. I hit the left directional, and then yanked the steering wheel hard to the right. I didn't think for a second that he would buy it, but trusting the idea that most people signal as a reflex, I saw that he had to swerve hard around to keep on my tail. Good.

The steering wheel slipped in my hand, and I was going so fast that the Jetta almost jerked out of control. My hands were sweating as I clenched the wheel. I wiped them off, one at a time, on the leg of my jeans, and strained my eyes looking for the shortcut I knew was coming up fast. It was so hard, in the dark, when everything was so overgrown, and if I stopped to think, I'd be too petrified to continue.

Don't think, act, Emma.

There . . . I left it for the last possible second, and then turned hard, right. This was a dirt road, an access road for a farmhouse that was no longer in existence, even less traveled than the one I'd just left. Even darker, if that was possible: there were no lights at all, here, just the beams of our headlights. I would have to be very careful, hoping that anyone who might come from the other direction would have their headlights on; it was just too narrow for two cars to pass each other without slowing down. And at these speeds . . . I pushed away the memory of the two kids who had been killed while drag racing two summers ago.

I was in luck, for the first time in days. There was just one more leg to travel, and then we might find out what was—

I felt another hard smack against the back of the car, but it wasn't as bad as before; he was having a hard time keeping up with me. Correcting my steering, I realized that his car wasn't handling as well as mine on the badly repaired road. All I had to do was keep it together for just a few more minutes . . .

The ambient glow of the lights from my destination made me almost swoon with relief. With any luck, my pursuer wouldn't have any idea of where I was actually heading. I turned right again, and hit lighted pavement with a jostling bounce. My jaw clacked shut, jarring me, reminding me that

I was now breathing through my mouth, as though I was fighting. There were more cars here, and they weren't pulling over—the guy behind me had no siren. I had to swerve around them, using the suicide lane and breakdown lane to pass. I hated driving so recklessly, but I didn't want to find out what the other driver was after, either.

There, an open space, a straight shot, and still the sedan behind me didn't slow down: He didn't know what I was up to. I turned right, signaling, hoping that he would follow me.

I pulled into the Lawton Police Station, grating undercarriage on asphalt, and the sedan followed. For a moment I believed that I'd been evading a genuine police officer, but then the dark sedan wheeled out of the parking lot with a screech. He made a U-turn, causing several other cars to brake suddenly, and took off in the opposite direction we had been traveling.

I had just enough sense left in me to put my car in park, and then I sat there, shaking like I had a fever, my head on the steering wheel. There was a sharp rap at the window.

Cursing loudly, I jumped, my left hand smacking out against the glass. I saw that there was a uniformed officer outside the car. I lowered the window.

"Evening. You mind telling me what that was all about?"

It wasn't a request. Dry mouthed, I told him what had happened. At another nonrequest, I handed over my license and registration.

After assuring himself that I wasn't the real trouble maker, he asked the question that I had been asking myself since I pulled over. "How did you know it wasn't a real officer following you?"

"I think it was the car," I said slowly, just working it out for myself. "I thought at first that it looked like an unmarked police car, but there was something about it that wasn't right."

"How not right?"

"It was the way the grill and lights looked," I said, finally able to identify the problem. "It looked like more like a Japanese-style sedan, rather than an American one. All of the police cars around here are American-made, I'm pretty sure. And the light on his dash, it whirled. Don't you guys use strobes?"

He cocked his head. "You notice all this when someone is trying to run you off the road?"

"Trust me, the screeming meemies have just caught up with me." I took a deep breath, swallowed, tried again. "There was also the bashing into the back of me. I'm assuming you give people a fighting chance to pull over before you start trying to ram them off the road."

"You're funny." He nodded, frowning. "Okay. You did the right thing. Did you get any other details?"

"I couldn't see anything else," I said, apologetically. "Dark, late-model sedan."

He nodded, then walked around to the back of my car, where he could see the evidence that I'd been hit. "Well, it sounds like you had your hands full. How about you come in, fill in a report, and then we'll get you out of here, okay?"

I went in, and that's when the tears started. Officer Franco found me a tissue and waited patiently while I finished, but even then, I couldn't stop shaking. My knees were like sponges: I'd had the benefits of an adrenaline rush, and now I was deep in the aftermath of the adrenaline dumps. Still, a tiny corner of my mind was active enough to be grateful. I didn't have time to think, I'd acted on souped-up nerves, muscle memory, and a fast inspiration. I got out of it alive.

I told him the story, as best I could, hesitating when I got to the part where I admitted that I was afraid that it might be Tony, or someone in his hire. I told Officer Franco this, and he stopped chewing his gum.

"Put it in the report and I'll give this Sheriff—Stannard, did you say?—a call. It sounds unlikely—it could just be some random nut case—but if we get any other complaints, we'll want to know everything. That light on the dash is worrying. Could be a ruse to get young ladies such as yourself into . . . a bad situation."

I nodded, and picked up a pen, willing my still-trembling fingers to be steady. Young ladies such as myself were already in a bad situation.

Chapter 8

IT WAS WITH A STRANGE MIXTURE OF APPREHEN-
sion, vindication, and nerves that I told Brian about the
chase when he got home. Apprehension, as if I was the
one responsible for the chase and would be rebuked. Vindication, because trouble just kept coming, and sometimes, it
still means something to be right, even when it's your neck
on the block. Nerves, because I had to relive the chase yet
again with the second telling of it. There's only so many
ways that you can keep something at arm's length before
you have to face the reality of it. Then I realized I had to
backtrack and tell Brian about what had happened at the
site.

Brian let go of my hand, ran his hand through his hair.
The blood rushed back into my fingers.

"Okay, whatever this is, is getting way out of control," he
said. "And this was aimed directly at you. The site, now this
asshole in the car. There's no doubting that."

I kept my mouth shut and did a fair job of not looking like
I'd finally made my point.

He squeezed me in a bear hug. "You've done all the right things, going to the cops, keeping your head. I'm so proud of you."

"And I was right." Then I blurted, "It is Tony."

Brian looked at me quizzically. "You're right, someone is gunning for you. I hate that it's true, but yes, that's what seems to be happening. As for that other thing, I don't know. Even if it isn't Tony, we need to be careful. I'm glad you went to the cops, glad that Stannard knows now, too. I say that we keep our eyes and ears open, do a little research into the laws about stalking or harassment laws or whatever they're called in Massachusetts. Maine, too. Start a file, keep track of all this stuff, be extra careful about the house, your office—"

"And your office," I persisted.

"Okay, sure, whatever." He said it so quickly, I got the impression that he was doing that male denial thing, where an unpleasant situation is dismissed out of hand.

"I'm serious, Brian." I put my hand on his shoulder. "This is getting . . . closer to home. Literally and figuratively, okay? And if it's getting closer to me, then . . . you need to worry, too. About you."

I watched him frown, but held his gaze until he nodded. "Okay. I'll do my best." He chewed the inside of his cheek a minute. "What if you take a leave of absence from school, this semester?"

"Brian! I can't do that! It's too late . . . it's too much." Talk about going from one extreme to another.

"Okay, okay, maybe that was a little much. What if . . . I work at home? And you work at home?"

"I can hardly teach classes from home," I said, frowning. "And you've got a project deadline coming up, you know that. It's all you can do to keep off a death-march schedule as it is."

"I just hate the idea of someone knowing your schedule. I mean, it's on the department website and everything, right? I could drive you to work."

"Brian, you can't drive me to work—it's exactly the opposite direction of where you need to be going. And like I said, our schedules won't allow it."

"Hey, I'm on your side, remember? I'm trying to make sure you're, uh, we're both safe."

"Yeah, but you can't do that by locking me in the house. And I'm not going to let anyone curtail my life like that. I just can't. Plus, I don't want to be a sitting duck, which I will be if I confine myself to the house."

Brian was annoyed, I could tell, but he didn't make any other outrageous suggestions. I was glad, because not only did I not like the idea of being kept under lock and key, I hated the idea that I was responsible for making him uneasy. I also hated the notion that he might be in danger. His earlier denial of the situation was almost preferable to this new attitude, however.

"Okay," he said finally. "But we're both going to be extra cautious, right? There's a weirdo out there."

"You got it." I could live with that: I hugged him then, a long time, grateful that I no longer felt so alone in this. Unanchored, it was all too easy to imagine that I might be making things up, seeing connections where there were none, but neither one of us could doubt it now. A gap between us had been bridged or the existing bridge made stronger, but it was terrible to think that I had to convince him of his own danger.

When I let Brian go, there was a thoughtful look on his face. I kissed him again, and went up to my office.

The next day, I got home late from errands, checked my email, and began putting together a batch of chili. I'm not a great cook, but I can do it when absolutely necessary. I even try to avoid using frozen foods, and so by most standards, I was pulling out all the stops. It made a change from working on lectures and fretting, at any rate. I set the table, cracked a beer for myself, and heard a car door slam in the driveway. And then another.

Frowning, I looked out the back door window, and saw my sister's boyfriend, Joel, getting out of his Beemer, which was parked behind Brian's pickup truck. There was no sign of Bucky. Strange enough that Joel should stop by unannounced and without my sister; it was odder still to see Brian and Joel do the handclasp–back slap greeting that's become de rigueur among males of a certain generation.

Brian and Joel don't get on all that well. I loved them both, but they'd never quite managed to become friends.

As I watched them talking in the drive, I was struck then by the similarity between the men. The physical likeness was limited to similar height and brown hair—Joel's was blonder, cropped close to his head, his almost stylish small beard was a bit too self-conscious, and he had a slight paunch developing. Brian was looking a little more cut these days from the exercise at Krav, and he needed a haircut to disguise his cowlicks. I couldn't help but notice that they were both wearing polo shirts, baggy shorts, and sports sandals. Both were geeks by trade, by nature and inclination. Both loved music and were devoted to good food. Both were problem solvers, both tended to be alpha, leader-types . . .

Maybe that was it: They were far too similar to find it easy to be friends. And then there was this protective thing Brian had going with Bucky: not having any siblings of his own, he'd adopted my sister as his own, and in some ways, the two were close friends, as close as my perennially guarded sister allowed. Brian'd been happy to hear about Joel being in Bucky's life, but had never warmed to him personally.

And yet, here they were, looking for all the world like . . . friends.

I opened the door. "Hey, guys! Joel, this is a nice surprise."

Brian started guiltily.

Joel waved. "Hey, Em. Yeah, well, when Brian called me last night, I figured I should come as quick as I could."

Now I was really confused. "That was nice of you. What did Brian tell you?"

Brian was now shifting from one foot to another. "Uh, well, I told Joel the whole situation. That we've been worried that someone's been watching the house or stealing our identity, and somehow they knew you'd be at the site. So figured, maybe they might have left bugs or spyware on the computers, or something. I thought maybe he could help me . . . us find out."

Joel nodded. "Yeah, and after Carrie told me what happened—"

To me, my younger sister Charlotte was Bucky; I often forgot that the rest of the world not only saw her as a functioning adult, but called her Carrie. I was still surprised that my somewhat asocial sister was living with a guy; I had no idea what she told him, and every time I tried to guess, I got it wrong.

"And what with the fire at the vet clinic and everything? Well, I figured I could sneak out of work early, give you guys a hand. Like I was telling Brian, I'm not sure what I can do, but I'll have a look, you know? I mean, we computer guys talk a good game and occasionally threaten to hack someone's credit report, but—really? I'm just a software engineer. I've got a few tricks, but I don't like hackers or what they do, so I'm not all that sure I can do anything much for you."

"Still, it's nice of him to come all the way up from Connecticut to help us," Brian said. He glanced at me nervously, hoping that I'd be polite enough to refrain from arguing in front of Joel.

"Sure. You want some chili, Joel?" I said, standing back so they both could come in.

Joel entered the kitchen, sniffed and said, "Hey, are you sure that's not spaghetti sauce?"

I got the hot sauce out of the cupboard for him. Joel likes his food with a kick. He put hot sauce on pancakes, once. "You're very funny. Never insult the one who is feeding you, boy."

Brian jumped in, eager to keep things going smoothly. "Joel, do you want to eat first, have a beer first, or start snooping?"

Joel shook his head. "I'm starved. You got any wine?"

"Uh . . ." I said. "We got some white in the fridge. Sauvignon blanc, I think."

Joel made a face. "With chili? I'll stick with the beer, thanks." He glanced at Brian, who shrugged, as if to say "Hey, I've tried to teach her."

We sat down and ate quickly.

"Do you have any bread?" Joel was sweating profusely now, the beads glistening on his pale skin more to do with the extras he'd dumped onto his chili than anything I had put into it. Red pepper flakes, Tabasco, and something scary-looking he poured from a bottle he kept in his briefcase.

"Yeah, but I made the rice to go with it . . ." I gestured to the bowl, but he'd already eaten it.

"Just to mop up."

I got him the bread, and another beer for myself and Brian, who was more than usually chatty. Again, trying to prevent me from saying anything in front of Joel.

And then we got to work.

We all went from room to room—there was no way that I was going to be left out—and in each instance, Joel looked in the most likely places for a camera or bug. He told us why he was looking where, and we were able to give him the recent history of most of the rooms, having been intimately acquainted with the woodwork as its installers. After I told him about what had been in the room before the new molding, he looked approvingly at me.

"You really pay attention to details."

"Brian did most of the finish work," I said.

"Yeah, but it's good, you know when things happened and how. You know what cracks are old and new." He struggled to find the words for what he meant. "You pay attention to your surroundings. Most people don't."

"I'm sure it's the archaeology," I said. "Or maybe the up-tightness. Maybe paranoia, these days." I looked over at Brian.

My husband frowned and shook his head, wondering if I was going to start something.

Joel waved the comment aside. "You know, a lot of scientific types are a bit paranoid. It's a part of being tuned into trends and paying attention to detail. It's not always a bad thing."

"No," Brian and I both said quickly.

"Okay, that looks good, far as I can see," he said when we finished the last room. We'd spent a long time looking at the new plumbing and electrical box. "Let's see your office, Emma, then we'll figure out where to put the cameras outside."

"Cameras?" I asked.

"We can put some cameras up, keep an eye on the outside," Joel said. "It was a good idea that Brian had."

"Cameras?" I repeated at Brian, who pretended to be paying rapt attention to Joel.

"Sure," Joel said. "I've got a couple that will do the trick—Freddie the Freak will have to watch other people's porn for a while—"

"Dude, we don't want to know your friends' habits," Brian said.

Joel laughed. "Seriously not my friend. Co-worker. And it'll be good for Freddie to watch professional pornographers for a while. And these cameras are out of date for what he's into anyway. As for your present problem . . . you know, most hacks are worked inside the company, not outside. So if the facility is secure . . . then that helps. You keep the place locked up, right? And you use your alarm system?"

Brian and I both nodded.

"Good. No one with keys you don't trust? The guy doing the work on the house?"

"I haven't given him a key," I said, but suddenly, I wondered about Artie and his unreliable nature.

"Good to hear."

"You said you weren't an expert?" I asked.

"I'm not, I'm just a guy. But I know enough to be paranoid and I know plenty of security freaks and I know my way around a Radio Shack. I can fake it good enough for your purposes. So, lead me to your office."

I hurried up ahead, and quickly cleared a path to my desk. This resulted in a new pile off to the side. The CD I'd left playing while checking my email before I'd started dinner was still cycling.

Joel cocked his head thoughtfully. "Beethoven?"

"Yep. You need me to turn it off?"

"No, turn it up."

I obliged, he sat down, cracked his knuckles and got to work. After a glance at the router, he looked at the monitor and frowned. He tapped the keys, bringing up screens I'd never seen before and didn't know existed.

Finally he looked up, wary disbelief on his face. "You don't have your encryption enabled?"

"Oh, the router has a firewall," Brian said. "Don't worry about it. Kam helped me with it when we set up the network."

Joel went even paler than usual. "Brian, how long have you had this wireless network?"

The panic in his voice scared me.

"Not long, just about a month," Brian said slowly. "We put it in just before we went to Hawaii."

Joel shook his head. "With the wireless access wide open, anyone can see all your machines from behind the firewall. Damn it, you could have all sorts of crap on there."

I exchanged a look with Brian: this was all news to both of us.

"Dude, you need to encrypt your wireless network, and install a firewall *and* some spy-detecting software on each machine."

Brian looked at me, one eyebrow raised so high it was lost under his hair. He needed that haircut soon. Maybe I was trying to ignore the note of anxiousness in Joel's voice.

"Why?" Brian said. "You really don't need encryption if you're as far out in the country as we—"

"No, man, that's not true. Anyone could get on your network from outside the house. And the firewall in the router is wimpy-assed; you should have them on each of your machines as well." Joel explained in detail what was wrong as he worked. "I didn't find anything too suspicious, but I think you'll be a lot safer from viruses and stuff, at the very least."

Brian fancies himself the technologically literate one in the family, and he was particularly proud of having installed the new network. Although Joel had done a good job of explaining without pointing fingers, I could tell my husband was far from happy. But I had to hand it to him, he didn't make excuses to Joel and he didn't try to argue the point with someone who actually worked in the field. Taking even a gentle rebuke from Joel was hard, but Brian did it.

"Hang on a second." Joel pulled out his laptop notebook and spent a little time with it. "I've got some software on here that helps find open access points. You know about wardriving, right?"

Brian said, "I've heard of it."

"No clue," I said.

Joel blew out his cheeks in frustration, then turned his machine so we could see the screen. I didn't see anything I recognized; it was all just random numbers and letters, to me.

"Look, right there? That's you. That's your wireless router shouting, "look at me, I'm a wireless access point at the Funny Farm!"

"That sounds bad," Brian said.

My stomach felt like it was ready to be rid of the chili, and I concentrated on taking deep breaths.

"It *is* bad. It means people could have been using your machine to look at your files, your email, use your computer to transmit files . . ."

"Can we fix it?" I could feel sweat running down my back, something that had nothing to do with the heat in my office.

"Yep, I'll set the encryption on the wireless network right now, but then we'd better do some shopping."

I said nothing, just followed him out of the house and into his Beemer. It was parking us in, and besides, Brian's truck was too tight a fit for all of us. My car was was full of field gear, and a pile of books I'd meant to lend to Raylene Reynolds for her kids. To me, the BMW didn't match Joel's personality—unless you chalked it up to gadgetry and you thought of the ways in which geeks compete.

Twenty minutes later, we were at the nearest computer megastore, and ten minutes after that, Brian was paying out a shocking amount of money for things I'd never heard of or believed I needed. He seemed to vaguely get what Joel was talking about while he threw things into our cart, but I still had no idea.

Joel saw me flinch when I saw the total. "Trust me. It's all necessary."

"You told us you weren't an expert on security!"

He shook his head. "This is just basic stuff. I know you guys love Kam and all, but next time you're doing something like this? Give me a call. I don't mind, I don't want anyone getting exposed to the creeps out there."

Brian didn't say anything, but he colored, and nodded. I could tell that he felt guilty, or at least remiss, as the network had been his idea. "Sure. Definitely."

When we got back to the Funny Farm, Joel installed the new software and hardware, and then we started installing the cameras he brought outside. We reassured him that the barn had been padlocked, and the access to the connected buildings was kept locked as well. We finally put up a birdhouse Brian and I had bought, but now it camouflaged a camera.

"There you go," Joel said with satisfaction. "Beautiful job, if I say so myself. Just keep an eye on the cameras, try to make sure they don't get wet. I'll monitor the images, and I'll send you an email with the directions so you can, too. I'll let you know when the batteries go or anything."

"Okay," I said, a little overwhelmed by the past few hours. I gave Joel a hug. "Thanks again, Joel. Any chance I should call Bucky, try to patch things up with her?"

He tchhed, and shook his head. "Do you remember what happened when your parents tried to make you both take tennis lessons?"

When we were kids, I had plodded on until the instructor finally said I had no talent and no desire. Bucky had picked up the racket, and threw it at the teacher. He only avoided injury by dint of a lifetime of lightning movement on the courts. "Right. It doesn't pay to push her. Say hey to her for me, though, would you? And tell her to call me."

"You got it."

"Thanks again, man," Brian said, and did the hand-slap thing again.

"Thanks for the chili, Em. Good effort." Joel got into his car, waved, and pulled out of the drive with a spray of gravel.

Brian and I were left alone outside the house.

"Hi," I said.

"Hi," Brian said, looking nervous.

"Cameras . . . seem extreme to me," I said carefully.

Brian jumped right into it. "Well, it's really like you said. There's so little we can do about what's happening, I figured it was better to try and do something, rather than just sit locked up in the house. And plus . . . you're always after me to get along with Joel."

"Yeah, I'm glad about that, but can we stick to the topic at hand?" I said.

Brian shrugged. "You know, Joel's going to talk to Bucky, see if she can get the partners to do something like this at the clinic. Get something professional, though, not a kludge-job like this. I bet that would make her feel better. About the animals. It's no big deal, and if it makes her happy . . ."

"Yeah, but you . . ." I headed toward the back door. Brian followed me as I started clearing the dishes off the table, loading them into the dishwasher. I couldn't help a purely communicative bit of banging and slamming as I dumped the leftover chili into a plastic bowl.

Brian stood in the doorway. "Don't take it out on the kitchen. We'll have to pay the contractors extra to fix it all over again."

It was supposed to be a joke, but I just didn't feel like it. "We have an alarm system. That isn't enough?"

"I just want to know whether someone has been hanging around. The alarm will only tell us if someone got in, while it is armed."

"You don't think it's a little much?" I asked. "A little paranoid?"

"I don't think it's paranoid. I mean, now we know why things have been happening when they were happening. That someone could watch your email and know when you were going to be at the site, in Hawaii, or whatever."

"But, Brian . . ." I tried to sort out my jumble of thoughts. "You could have told me. That you called Joel. We . . . could have talked about it, first."

"I thought we were both going to try to be careful. This was my compromise. I thought you'd be happy about that." Now all the defensiveness that Brian had kept from expressing around Joel came rushing out. "I thought you'd like that I was taking your concerns seriously."

"Yeah, but . . . this feels like you went behind my back." It wasn't a very strong argument, but somehow I'd just wanted to keep Brian from getting *too* involved. Like acting on the threat would make the threat more real, would direct it toward him.

"I thought it was a good idea. I went for it." Brian bit off each syllable, almost glad to have a real opponent, no matter how minor the issue. "Emma, I had to do something. This is real, there is a threat to you."

I reached out to him. "And I'm glad that you believe me, now, that Tony's behind this."

Brian pulled back. "Whoa, I didn't say that. I believe someone is acting against you; I still don't think that Tony Markham is necessarily the best suspect."

We glared at each other.

Brian tried again. "Look, like I said, I had to do something. You've stopped trying to look forward. You don't even care about what the Red Sox are doing, and they're having a pretty good year. You used to talk about doing forensics or criminalistics or whatever—you know how that guy who was investigating the crime scene at the Chandler house was trying to get you into it?"

"Stuart Feldman. With the State Police lab."

"Yeah, well, you don't talk about that anymore, not since you got back from the conference in January."

I got a bottle of water and threw the cap angrily toward the trash: I missed. "How could I? When I was afraid that it was my . . . involvement in these things that was bringing this on us?"

"Bringing what on us? Coincidences! At the conference, all someone had to say was 'Tony Markham,' no, not even; they said 'Billy Griggs,' and you flipped out. Yes, something is going on and we're trying to take care of that. But you, something happens and you go to Def Con one: Against all logic, it *has* to be Tony."

I couldn't stand that he was saying that, and I couldn't dispute it either, not sensibly, not without sounding like a broken record. He made it sound so crazy, and I knew what I saw. "Whatever. I still think cameras are too much. What's next? Dogs? Barbed wire? An armed guard?"

"You're picking a fight, Emma. You're overreacting, and it's not fair to me. I'm trying to do the right thing."

Again, Brian made me sound like a lunatic, just by being so damned . . . reasonable about it. "Yes, I'm mad you went behind my back. Yes, I'm glad you're trying to come up with a solution that will work for us. I just don't want . . . any of this. I didn't do anything wrong, and yet . . . I don't want this to be happening to us."

"I know. I'm sorry, and next time I have a brainwave, I'll talk to you first. It's done now. It won't hurt you any, and maybe it will help. And besides, Joel cleared a whole pile of spyware and crap from the hard drive."

We were trying to make up, but I still felt like Brian was overcompensating for not being able to make the threat go away. Maybe even for trying to take care of me, I thought, as ungrateful as that sounded. I just wanted it all to go away. The fact that I *did* feel like it was my fault was no help.

I nodded, and finished clearing up. Brian took the vegetable garbage out to the compost heap and returned a moment later with the newspaper, a look of shock on his face.

"What is it?" I asked immediately.

"The front page. They found the car that chased you, not too far away from the police station."

"Huh?"

"Someone torched the hell out of it. By the time the firemen got there, it was nothing but a smoking shell."

Monday, I stopped by CaféNation as a treat for breakfast. As I waited for the miracle of coffee to overtake me, a shiny red object on the register caught my eye. A closer look revealed that it was a key chain, a metallic red carabiner with a couple of keys and a charm, a shamrock that looked like real gold with a tiny diamond in the center. I picked it up, flicked the carabiner; there was a Volkswagen key and a couple of house keys, I noticed. I had to resist the urge to clip it on my own belt as I watched the play of light on the shiny red surface. A ready-made Emma toy.

"Shoot, Tina, someone lost their keys?"

"Yep." She bustled with my coffee. "I found them right after the lunch rush, couple of days ago. Can't imagine that anyone isn't missing them, you know?"

"Yeah, for sure. Lost house keys, you can work around, maybe. Lost car key, not so easy. Nice car, too." I shrugged. "Maybe it was their Tuesday car, and they won't miss it until next week."

"If that's the case, we could just walk down the street with the key and keep pressing the alarm button until we get a hit." She glanced over the espresso machine and smiled. "Go for a little joy ride. Got time for a run to the border today?"

When I opened my eyes again after that first sip, I pretended to consider, "Which one?"

"I was thinking Canada. Go up, get us some beers, Cohibas, a few Mounties. Have ourselves a party. What do you say?"

"Shoot, I can't. I have lectures to write." And a husband to placate, and a contractor to chase, and a house to patch up, and a villain to find . . .

"Aw, you're no fun."

"Not me."

Back at home, the phone was ringing as I juggled my bag, the keys, my coffee, and the alarm code. I caught it on the last ring before the machine picked up.

"Hello-ow!" I tried to take a sip, but the cup had twisted around and coffee splashed out, burning my hand.

"Emma, what the *hell* are you getting into now?"

I set the cup down and brushed off the coffee. "Huh? Marty?" It sounded like my best friend, but she seldom used any kind of bad language since the baby came and her voice was high with hysterics. "What's wrong?"

"It's Sophia! How could you get her involved—?"

"Wait! What's wrong with Sophia? Is she sick?" My stomach plummeted at the thought of anything at all happening to my goddaughter. Marty's usual dramatics were never about anything serious . . .

"—you don't even think of what you're doing, of how it will affect anyone else! And now Sophia—!"

"Marty! You have to calm down! Tell me what's wrong with Sophia! Is she hurt?"

"Not hurt, but . . ." I heard my friend take a long, shuddering breath. "Her picture! It came to us . . . from a prison! The one we gave you! From a . . . oh, my God!"

"What picture?"

"The one I sent you last week! The one of her at her little friend's first birthday party!"

It took me a minute to remember the occasion, but one thing I knew for a fact . . . "Marty, you never sent me a picture. I don't know what you're talking about."

"Emma." I could hear her summoning up patience. "Last week. I sent you a card, with the pictures of Sophia, the ones I took of her with the baby rabbit that the next-door neighbors have. I finally got them printed and so I sent one to you."

"I never got it."

"But you must have . . . the one I got in the mail, it's the one I sent you. I know because I had Sophia draw on the back and I wrote your name and dated it myself. It's the same one, I'm telling you!"

Marty's voice was hoarse; she'd been crying a long time.

I went cold, my mind racing. "Marty, listen to me. I never got the picture you sent to me. It never came to the house. Now . . . where are you telling me it came from? How did it get back to you?"

"That's why I'm so . . . Emma, it came from a *prison*. From a *prisoner*. And the . . . implication was that he was getting out and going to come for . . ." She couldn't even finish; I heard hard breathing and muffled sobs on the other end of the line.

"What!"

It took her a full minute to regain her composure. "All it said on the letter—just a piece of paper, really—was a name and the words "expected release date: September 10, 2004." Emma, that's in two weeks!"

I bit the inside of my cheek. "How do you know it came from the prison?"

"What? There were marks on the envelope. Official ones."

"What prison was it?"

"Emma, what does that matter? Some bastard is threatening my daughter, and somehow, he's got the picture I sent to you!"

"I'm trying to help figure this out. Did you call the cops?"

"Yes. Kam's talking with them now."

"Okay, that's good. Now, look Marty, this is important, this can help. Someone's been pulling . . . no, I can't call it pranks. The other things, they'd been threatening, but so far, harmless. This might be more of it." I tried to ignore the site and being followed the night before; they were aimed at me. "Now, which prison is it?"

She hesitated before answering. "Pine Island. I can't believe that you are asking—"

"But don't you see? This is good: Pine Island only houses minimum security prisoners. Not the sort of person who . . . might be a threat to Sophia. And I'm not sure they're actually allowed to mail anyone anything besides the letter, you know? I think there's a good chance it's a hoax—"

"There is no one who's going to be a threat to Sophia," my friend said, her voice steadier, surer now. "Emma, you tell whatever freaks you've been hanging around with, or following, or pissing off, or whatever that they don't get near her. I see anything, anything at all and I . . . I have a gun. I'll sure as hell use it. You tell them, Emma."

I'd never heard of Marty having a gun before. The sound of her voice drove whatever warmth there might have been from my body. "Marty! It's not me, I . . . I'm trying to help, listen to me!"

"Do you hear what I'm telling you? I'm telling you that someone is threatening my baby, and you . . . you ask me questions. Jesus, Emma, do you need to sound so goddamned calm? Do you even care?"

Marty'd never cared about my investigations before, but I'd always turned them into anecdotes for telling over margaritas. And . . . this was Sophia. It wasn't that I was calm; I was just trying to cope. "Yes, of course I do. And I think . . . I think it's Tony Mar—"

"Yeah, so you've said. And so Brian told Kam, who's told me that he's worried about you. And why in the name of God are you making this about you rather than my baby's safety?"

But Brian believed me now, I thought irrationally. "I'm not, I swear to you! Marty, I'm trying to help—"

"I don't care who it is, Emma. I don't care what it might be. You brought this on me, on us, you fix it—"

"I'm trying—" I found myself close to tears now.

"It's one thing if you're going to get into stuff that has nothing to do with you, that's your business. But you've got no right to get Sophia anywhere near any of this. You keep the hell away from us."

And then she hung up.

Chapter 9

AFTER MARTY HUNG UP—SLAMMED DOWN—I
stood there for a while, trying to take it all in, trying, in
some small, selfish way, to minimize the danger, to be able to
dismiss Marty's anger much as Brian had tried to maintain
that I was imagining Tony was behind all these events. But
all I could do was remember that day at the hospital. . . .

The first time I met Sophia Asefi-Shah, I thought she was
the least convincing person I'd ever seen. Marty looked like
hell and I could fully believe that Sophia'd just come out of
my best friend because she looked like something that had
just been removed from a human body. I held the baby and
tried to hide my reaction and realized there wasn't really
much to recommend her; in addition to scarlet lumpiness,
her head was huge in comparison to the rest of her body, she
had all sorts of spots on her face where she wasn't covered
in thick, downy black hair, and her eyes were screwed shut.
Yet, she was tiny and infinitely vulnerable; she weighed so
little in my arms that I worried lest I forget she was there and
she simply float off. I had to hold her tightly, but not so tight
that I would crush her. Then one eye opened, brownish and

opaque, her froggy little lips yawned wide, and her eensy little hand flexed open and then closed, grasping for something she didn't know she wanted, something that might not even be within her reach.

Suddenly, I wanted to take piano lessons.

I wanted to brush up on my French, really learn which constellations were where, improve my writing skills, and take first-aid classes. I wanted my green belt in Krav Maga, and vowed silently to redouble my efforts toward that goal, because I understood with perfect clarity the ancient instinct that Sophia was now a part of my herd and I would die to protect her. Everything I knew, I wanted to teach to little Sophia. I was already planning how I would introduce her to Shakespeare, starting off with the sonnets to get her used to the language and the images, and then introduce the plays and their characters. I would teach her how to pee in the woods without getting her feet wet, how to use my power tools safely, how to look at a recycling bin and identify the ethnic background and economic aspirations of my neighbors, the best way to tie your sneakers, so that you didn't get shin splints when you went for a run. I wanted to teach her everything I knew. I wanted her to be ten times better at it than I was.

It was over in a heartbeat. But the memory of it was imprinted on me forever.

"Funny looking, isn't she?" Marty had yawned. "The doctors say she'll improve over time, but I'm not counting my chickens just yet."

"Don't be ridiculous." Kam took Sophia away from me with an ease that suggested he'd been wrangling babies all his life. "My Sophia is the most beautiful girl in the world, the nonpareil of babies." He pressed his face close to hers. "Yes, she is. She's magnificent."

Kam now had another woman in his life to worship.

"And I?" Marty hauled herself up in bed, wincing, and I handed her a glass of water. She looked like hell, which scared me, but if she was fishing for compliments, she couldn't be too far off her usual form.

"You, my dear, are the only person in the world who could have produced such a miraculous baby. It is clear that she got all of her looks from you, and the best thing she could do with her life would be to imitate you in every respect. She is the most beautiful girl in the world, but you my dear"—he kissed his wife on the forehead—"are a goddess."

Marty's hair was slicked back with sweat, her eyes were puffy from crying and dark-lined from lack of sleep, and her skin was slack and sallow. Still, she smiled; and if Kam had been telling me that—he believed it with every fiber of his being—I would have believed him too.

Putting down the phone, I thought about what Marty had told me and, suddenly, I felt my stomach heave. I made it to the bathroom, felt the tiles dig into my knees as I stumbled across the floor to the toilet, just in time. I wiped my mouth, flushed, and then washed my face. That's m'girl, Emma. Keep your cool when your friend needs you to melt down, and lose it after.

I didn't look in the mirror, I didn't want to see what would be looking back at me. I felt the shakes come on, and clutched the sink until it had passed.

God, what was I doing? It was one thing to get myself into this, it was another to drag everyone else into it.

But I wasn't dragging anyone, I protested; they were being targeted by a crazy man. It wasn't my fault. I tried to stop him, had at least got the police pointed at him, exposed him at least. If he couldn't stay decently escaped, then that wasn't my fault.

Sophia wouldn't be endangered, at least not in Marty's mind, if it weren't for you . . .

Yeah, well. How the hell was I supposed to predict this would happen? And if I had, wouldn't I have taken steps to avoid it?

Marty wants me out of her life. Away from her and Kam and Sophia, and oh, God . . .

How the hell did someone in the Pine Island lockup get Sophia's picture? A picture that was mailed to me? I mulled over that a while and realized that I'd been at home when Marty claimed that she'd sent the picture. When I hadn't been home, the alarm had been on. Something gnawed at me, and I realized that I'd left Artie alone one day when I'd gone to CaféNation. I'd ask him if he'd noticed anything. The mail usually came late morning; maybe he could shed some light on this. He might have seen someone at the box at the end of the driveway, especially if he was on a cruller break.

The phone rang again; it was Kam.

"Emma, I've just finished with the police. It's just as you said, it appears to be a hoax." I'd never heard him sound so serious and he was a serious guy.

I exhaled in relief. "Thank God for that. Did they say—"

He continued on, as if he hadn't heard me. "It doesn't much change things for us. It still remains: Someone has threatened my daughter. And you seem to be connected."

I almost protested, but caught myself: He had a point. "At least tell me, what did the cops say?"

"They said it was a fake but it had all the right marks. Very convincing." He paused, then said, "They wanted to know where the picture came from. It had your name on the back, of course. And I assured them, it couldn't be you."

"Thanks for that." I tried not to sound as bitter as I felt. "I never even saw the picture. Marty says she sent it to me? Then someone must have intercepted it, taken it from the mailbox—"

Kam had no time for my speculation. "Emma, the police believed me. But . . . they took less convincing than Marty will. She's not sure what's going on, but I strongly urge you to . . . give her some space. Until we know what is going on, for certain."

I had to protest now. "She knows it isn't me! How could she ever—?"

"She doesn't think it's you, not truly, but there's some connection and, Emma . . . this is our daughter. I think you'll agree that whatever your friendship with Marty may be, Sophia and her well-being will always come first. And Mariam's . . . more than scared. Please, just don't call, don't come by until we get this sorted out. Please? For me? I know you'll understand. It's *Sophia*."

"I understand," was all I could bring myself to say. "I won't call." Then I blurted angrily, "Does Brian get to talk to you at work?"

"Don't be like that!" Kam pleaded.

"Be like what? I'm not the one who's talking crazy about guns. I'm not the one who threatened Sophia—we've even found out it's a hoax! And if I talk to you, I might be able to help."

"Marty doesn't agree. I'm sorry, Em."

He hung up.

I don't believe this, I thought. I'm getting out of here.

I called Brian and told him about Sophia; irrationally, I didn't want to, but I knew that Kam might say something next time he was at work. Brian said nothing for a moment, then asked all the same questions I had. It was so frustrating; he couldn't make any more sense of it than I. Finally, he just asked me to be careful, and we said goodbye.

I checked my email upstairs to confirm the time that I was supposed to have coffee with Dora. Now, because it was Dora, it wouldn't be a watery cup of something brown from a cart on the quad. Dora had her own espresso maker in her office; as far as I knew, only her TAs were allowed to touch it, and only after extensive training and a probationary period. I could use a dose of Dora's bravura, too. I needed something.

The drive up to campus gave me a chance to think about things. Traffic was still pretty light, but in just a week, the roads would be clogged with cars full of parents, students, hopes and expectations and dread.

I realized that even before I saw Dora, I needed to see my painter, Dominic Harding. Known primarily as a portraitist in the eighteenth century, there was a tiny landscape of his I'd fallen in love with. Fortunately, Dora and Dominic's landscape were both in the Caldwell College Fine Arts building.

The stairs to the building were uneven and worn, the stone buffed by generations of feet and thousands of first-year art students' bottoms as they sat pondering art, philosophy, and the hot guy in the black jeans. The doors opened, the smell of floor polish and old canvas hit me, and a calm stole over me.

I was in no particular hurry, I had time before our meeting. Strolling past the temporary installation of student work in the central hall, none of which I understood, a scuffling and a crackling of radio static caught my ear. Campus police, Caldwell County police, and EMTs with a stretcher invaded the gallery from behind me, and moved past me in a phalanx. It wasn't that I was following them, it was just that they were heading in the same direction I was, toward the American room.

Brightly lit with indirect sunlight, the high ceilings of the room had always been more of a church to me than any holy structure. I came here for repose, meditation, recreation, to visit art that was not a professional specialty, but a comfort as familiar to me as my face in the mirror.

That sanctuary had been violated. I picked up my pace, curious, a knot of dread tightening in my stomach. It couldn't possibly have anything to do with me, I told myself, but I was going to find out for sure.

The first thing I noticed was that the Harding landscape I had wanted to visit was not in its usual place. That wasn't cause for alarm as the pink notice signaling the removal of a piece of art was taped conscientiously in its place. It was the rest of the scene that was wrong.

The EMTs were busy in two areas. One was tending to a young woman with dark hair, her slight build made smaller by a white lab coat. She was hyperventilating and her brown eyes were wide: the police were gathered around her. Another group, the one with the stretcher, was in the room just beyond.

I had just decided that I would come back later—surely it was a nasty coincidence, none of my business—when Dora stormed into the room. She ignored me, saw the empty space, frowned, and addressed herself to the woman in the lab coat.

"Ms. Reibach, what is going on here? What's happened?" Dora's words were, as usual, a command, but there was something in the way that she said it that seemed to reassure Ms. Reibach, who was able to catch her breath.

"Professor, I . . . there was this man. He . . . started talking to me. Asking me strange questions. But . . . then he . . . he just took the little Harding landscape and put it into a backpack." She took another shuddering breath, trying to collect herself. "I tried to stop him. He shoved me, and I fell."

"I don't think there's a fracture," one of the EMTs said. "But you might want to come along with us, get an X ray. Could be a concussion."

The young woman wasn't registering any of this. "I think I was out of it . . . maybe. Just for a couple of seconds," she said, measuring each word carefully, as if that would help her make sense of what had happened. "When I came around, I called security. And that's when I found . . ." She began to gasp again, waving toward the other room. "Jim wasn't moving!"

Not Jim, I thought, I've heard wrong. It can't be, this wasn't happening. He was the nicest guy, loved his job, always said hello to me, always happy to help people—

"Lois? Lois, it's okay. My buddy Cliff is in there, and he's going to do his best job on your friend in there—Jim's his name?"

She nodded. "Jim. He's going to be okay?" she asked, hanging onto the sleeve of the EMT.

He avoided her eyes as he worked. "My buddy Cliff is the best there is, even better than me. You can bet he's going to do everything he can, give Jim the best care until we get him to the hospital."

The EMT's face didn't match the hopefulness of his words, which sounded rote and forced to me. But the distraction seemed to work: Lois was calmer now.

The campus police arrived. One officer took her name, then Dora's, and turned to me.

"Did you see anything?"

"No, I just—" Out of the corner of my eye, I saw Dora reaching for something on the wall.

"I'll going to ask you to leave, then. We need room here."

I was nodding, grateful to be dismissed, when Dora sank down on one knee, the pink slip tearing from the wall as she slumped. At first I thought she was genuflecting for some strange reason. Then she moaned.

"Professor!" Lois's voice was strained, shocked. She struggled to get up.

"Dora!" I rushed to her side. "Somebody help—!"

She came to almost as soon as the EMTs reached her side. Her eyes were blank, her face slack, and that scared me to death.

"What was it, Dora?" I grabbed at her, but she was too heavy to support on my own, and we both sank down. "Are you all right?"

"Oh my God." She seemed to realize where she was, but not how she got there. Then she held up the hand with the pink memo, and her eyes rolled back in her head again. They fluttered and then she seemed to pull herself together. She staggered to her feet, managing to dislodge the men who were trying to keep her sitting.

"I can't, I have to leave, I have to go now!" she said, and there was something in her eyes that made me step back. "Leave me alone!" she said, shaking off the hand of one of the cops.

They moved her away to a bench, and it took three of them to keep her from storming out. She was making no sense, waving the paper, and finally, one of the cops had to take it from her. It took some doing, almost as if the paper itself was precious to Dora. She said something to him, and he reassured her.

I couldn't understand what was happening. Dora knew the painting was stolen, her assistant Lois had told her that. And I knew she hated that painting, rode me every chance she could about my affection for it, derided it as "a game but failed tribute to bourgeois land-grabbing colonials and their so-called social status."

So why did she faint? I didn't think it was the sight of the medic working on Jim—my breath caught when I saw Cliff look at his partner and shake his head. And it wasn't concern about her assistant, Lois, either. It was the accession slip.

"I have to get home," she kept repeating, then she looked up, pleading. "Emma, help me."

Taken aback by this change in Dora, I was eager to help, make this better. "What can I do?"

"Go to my office, tell them to cancel classes. Then if you—"

"Hang on a second," one of the cops said, turning to me. "What's your name?"

"Emma Fielding. I teach over in Anthropology."

He held up the accession slip. "E. Fielding" was down in the corner, where the person removing the piece was supposed to sign. "This you?"

I stared at it. "What? No, it's not me. I mean, it's my name, but I never signed this. I don't have the authority—"

Dora gasped again, her eyes fluttering.

"But it's your favorite painting, isn't it?" Lois said, all of a sudden. "That's what the man said. When I came in, he asked me if I was Emma, and whether this wasn't my favorite painting. I couldn't understand what he meant."

Suddenly the cops weren't telling me they needed me to clear out anymore. They wanted to know what I knew about the missing painting.

"I don't know anything about it," I protested. "I mean, I was coming over here to have coffee with Dora. I came early to look at the picture. It is one of my favorites, I come here a lot to look at it." I shrugged helplessly.

"Do you have any idea who might have—?"

I told them about what had been happening to me. That Tony might have access to the college facilities still, that they should check. But it might be unrelated, I said, anyone could sign any name to anything—

"What else was on that slip?" I asked. It wasn't just the picture that had Dora this angry and afraid.

"Just an address. It's not yours, so don't worry about it."

"Don't worry about it?" Dora was there suddenly, towering over me, it seemed. "How could you bring this down on me, Emma? And who is this Tony Markham?"

I reminded her of what had happened to me just after I'd started at Caldwell. She recalled the story quickly enough.

"Are you telling me that he's back? That he's making threats against—?"

I nodded. "I think so. I think we'd better call—"

She held up a hand. "Quiet! I need to think."

"Dora, I—"

"You be quiet while I decide what to do about this." She looked at me, her face set in an expression I'd never seen before. "You brought this. You keep away from me."

Dora had been rude to me before, hell, Dora was rude to everyone; it was her stock in trade. I'd come to expect it as a part of her personality and had learned to ignore it, even enjoy the spectacle that she created. I actually realized a while ago that I envied her ability to disregard how other people felt, how that kept her focused on her work, on what was important to her. She was her own person, and she let nothing and no one interfere with that. I would have given anything to develop that talent.

But this was different, this was downright hostile. Whatever it was that was on the note, it had affected her deeply, on a personal level.

And I had brought it to her.

My hands were freezing, the world spinning. Don't be an idiot, Emma; you're not responsible for this.

Well, Tony's not back here for Alumni Week. He's not stealing pictures because he needs something that will go with his couch or he's into Harding's brushstrokes.

No, Emma. Tony's here for you, and he's not the kind of guy to be interested in gestures for long. There's something else, he's got a plan, this is all getting worse and worse, and everywhere I turn, there he is.

I shivered, feeling suddenly exposed, panicky. I'd better get a plan, too. Because I didn't think that anything that Tony might have in mind was going to end up well for me, or anyone around me.

As if from a distance, I saw Dora sweep past me, police in tow. One stayed behind to take my statement.

I clutched at Ms. Reibach's sleeve. She was left behind; Dora didn't even want her nearby. "What else did it say on that slip?" If I could find any sense in this, maybe I could stop feeling so damned afraid.

She glared at me. "Why should I tell you? She said that she wanted you to stay away from her."

As much as I admired her for protecting Dora, I had to find out what was on the slip. "Please! If I can help fix whatever is going on here, I need to know."

Lois stared, still deciding. Then she nodded, finally. "Only because you might help Dora." She took a deep breath. "It was an address, over by the coast, in Haver's Falls. It's one-o-three Burnt Oak Way."

I nodded, grateful. "Thank you! Please, if there's anything else I can do. Please tell me."

"I'll see," she said, as she was escorted from the museum to an ambulance.

I told the administrator to cancel Dora's classes, and was hurrying back to my office when a familiar gesture caught my eye, a flip and a flash of wavy raven hair. I shook it off, dismissed it as a student I'd seen before, when the memory sorted itself out in my head and I understood it was an archaeological colleague, Noreen McAllister.

Noreen and I hate each other to the point of public outburst.

I quite reasonably dislike Noreen because she whines a lot, blames her problems on everyone but herself, and has fashion sense that is best imagined as "fishing lure chic," all bright colors and dangling, brash metallic accessories. She also seemed to be putting the moves on my unlamentedly-ex-boyfriend-from-another-lifetime, Duncan Thayer, which wouldn't bother me a whit except that he was married and the thought of two of them scheming together—her vindictiveness and his smoothie-boy sliminess—gave me the heebie-jeebies.

I don't know why she has such a hair across her ass when it comes to me, but she has more than once flung my family connections in archaeology in my face. I chalk it up to jealousy.

To see her here, on my campus, was more than strange. I'm not surprised that she didn't call me—there was no point in even trying to be cordial to each other—but I had no idea why she might be here.

I realized that she'd been the person I'd seen but not recognized right before Meg showed me her wedding dress. It seemed awfully odd that she was here, now, at this very moment. I was going to find out now why that should be.

"Noreen! Noreen!" I called after her retreating back. I saw her hesitate, as if she recognized my voice, move another step forward as if she was going to keep going, and then stopped.

She turned. "Emma."

I had no idea of what I should say to her. "What are you doing here?" I blurted.

She shrugged, looked off to one side. "I'm visiting a friend."

Liar. "Which friend is that?"

She stared back at me in disbelief. "That's none of your damned business."

"I'm surprised to see you here. Now. What about work?"

"Who are you, my mother? Damn."

The way she said that lit something in me. "I need to know what you're doing here." I stepped forward.

"What are you doing, you freak!" She stumbled as she backed away a few paces.

I never figured Noreen for a good actor, she's way too conscious of how she's coming across to people. And she never bothered trying to convince me that she was my best friend or anything. She was scared now, though, that was for sure.

Thing was, the direction she was going, she could only have been coming from the Art History department. Which is connected to the museum.

"What do you know about the Dominic Harding painting," I said.

"What? Nothing!" She shook her head violently, hair and dangling earrings flying. "Will you get away from me!"

We were starting to draw attention from passersby. Was it possible that she was just afraid of me? Or was it something else?

"Fine. I'm leaving," I said. But I wasn't done, not when there are this many coincidences.

"Freak!" she screamed again.

I waved my hand, dismissing her, then hustled up to my office. Two quick chores, and then I was out of here.

First, using an abandoned office on the first floor, near the dean's office to avoid caller ID, I called the Art History Department and asked for Noreen McAllister, who was visiting. The receptionist said that Noreen was out; I asked who I could leave a message with. Professor Jones would get back to me, I was told. I didn't know the name, but promised myself to investigate as soon as I could. I hung up when the receptionist asked who was calling.

It couldn't just be a coincidence? I asked myself as I climbed to my office. Not when there is so much else going on. Or was it that I was, as Brian suggested, seeing connections where there were none?

In my office, it just took a few minutes on the Internet to find directions from the Caldwell campus to the address on the pink slip. I knew it wasn't Dora's address, as she lived very close to campus in an awe-inspiring stone Victorian that reminded me of a castle. It had once been the president's house, before a larger house was built closer to campus. I asked her, after I'd stopped gaping, why she hadn't actually found an Italianate style, with tall rectangular windows and a tiled roof to better reflect her tastes. She'd given me a withering look, and told me that there weren't any, but she was looking in to having a folly brought in, just as soon as she found one. I asked her why she didn't build a folly, as they were all imitations anyway, and was promptly dismissed as a cretin. Older was better, authentic was better, even if it was only something built in tribute to the Renaissance.

I locked up my office. To hell with work. I knew that the town was by the water, and I didn't mind cutting out of school early. I noticed a dark car behind me in the road leading from the college to the main highway, and started before I remembered that the car that had chased me was probably still a burnt out wreck in Lawton. He turned left when I went right. I was content to assume that I knew the car from the line always heading to the highway.

I cranked up my Corelli CD and turned east. I passed through the downtown of Haver's Falls and on another mile, before I found Burnt Oak Way. The houses had been few and far between as I left town, but they were all large, old, and well-maintained. Even as I was cataloguing architectural styles and elements—here a quoin, there a dentil—I showed I was still, at least in part, my father's daughter and assigned a healthy price tag to each and every one of them. Add in the maintenance and the landscaping, and I knew that I was in old money country.

I found the correct turn the third time I doubled back, working off my web directions and odometer. The road was essentially private, marked by only a mailbox shaped like a barn. When I found what I was looking for, however, I saw that the street and number were clearly marked on the mail-box, and that there was actually a street sign, obscured by pine boughs. The name on the mailbox was Sarkes-Robinson.

I pulled down the road, which showed signs of being recently paved. Down one more turn, and suddenly the vista opened up, and what both Brian and my father would have referred to as "a fine pile of bricks" sat in front of me. The house was made of brick, but the cube shape, fanlights over the window, and columns told me it was Federal style as well.

There were two vehicles in the circular drive, and another in a space off to the side. In front was a delivery truck with a logo for hospital supplies and oxygen, and there was Dora's car, a Mercedes. I had also asked her why her love of things Italian didn't extend to her wheels, and she promptly replied that there was a place for everything and she preferred Italian in the bedroom and German in the garage to the opposite. Another car parked off to the side was a black Mercedes sedan about twenty years old.

I slowed to a stop, considering. Dora's pied-à-terre? I thought she was well off, but this place was more than I figured for her, and not her style either. The name on the mailbox was the same as hers, so between that and the delivery truck, I was betting on relatives.

The front door opened, the delivery men came out wheeling empty handcarts. They prepared to pull out, and I had to either back up or follow the drive around and clear the way for them.

Dora came out after them, and shut the door behind her. She noticed my car immediately, and then, upon recognizing me, folded her arms over her chest. She spoke to the driver, and then the truck moved forward. I had no choice but to pull up and let them out.

She stood between me and the house, to remove any thought that I would be invited in for tea and cookies. I could tell that she was none too pleased to see me. I wasn't sure what to do, but I felt it would be too strange to just pull away.

I cut the engine and got out, not shutting the car door, just leaning over the roof so I could see her and she could see that I wasn't going to get comfortable.

"I'm sorry," came out of my mouth before I knew what I was going to say.

She nodded. "My parents' house. Both quite elderly, both quite ill."

"I'm sorry," came again, whether for the family's troubles or revealing them to outsiders, I couldn't have said.

"The security people are due any moment. I doubt there's anything more they can add that isn't here already, but I'm not taking any chances." Her face was empty of her usual passion, and there was no sign of the flamboyance that characterized her behavior for me. No hauteur, no *froideur,* no disdain. Nothing, but grim determination and fear. It scared me, seeing her so . . . it wasn't that she was reduced. Exposed.

"Dora, I don't know what's going on, not exactly. But I swear to you, I'm doing everything I can to find out and make it stop."

She shrugged, as unconvinced as I that there was anything I could do. "Please leave. Don't come near me—or this house—until you fix this."

I nodded, got in my car, and went back, out of reflex, back to Caldwell. At least in my office, I didn't feel so damned lost.

Chapter 10

I SAT IN MY OFFICE, WONDERING ABOUT DORA AND the painting. I thought about poor Jim, who I was now convinced was dead. And it was all so specific. Why, if Tony had survived the storm, had gotten clean away with a bunch of gold, the whole world at his disposal, would he ever have come back? If he was as bored as he'd said he was, why wouldn't he have just created a new life for himself, from scratch? He could have done anything in the world he wanted to, so why come back?

He needed an audience. A particular audience. Me. I shivered, feeling numb. That's why things were spiraling in, closer and closer, with more and more violence each time something happened. And if this kept up—

The phone rang, scaring the bejeezus out of me. "Hello?"

"It wasn't you, was it?" said a male voice after a pause so profound that I almost hung up.

"I beg your pardon!" I hate obscene phone callers, and this guy's voice was classic. Not actually breathy but a little too much oomph behind the words for polite society. Good, careful pronunciation, though. Weird.

"You never would have sent me that letter, would you, Auntie?"

"Who is this?" But I was starting to recognize the low, depressed voice and erratic telephone manner already. A darkened room, a library at the western part of the state, a raincoat like a security blanket, scholars dying under mysterious and violent circumstances . . . and there he was, in the midst of it all, as ridiculous a suspect as he was a compelling one.

"It's Michael Glasscock." He said it as if he was the only one in the world with my phone number and I was a dope for not recognizing that fact. I was his dull old "Auntie." "And you never sent me the letter, did you?"

"What letter are you talking about?" My heart was still pounding. There was really no point in asking how he was. For Michael, it was either agony or ecstasy and he could rationalize his way from one to the other in a microsecond, the benefits of a staggering ego, a brilliant mind, a mercurial wit, and too much philosophy, or not enough.

"The really filthy letter, detailing your undying lust for me and what you were willing to do to prove it."

Michael's sense of humor, such as it was, did not run to practical jokes. And yet, I still hoped. "Michael, this isn't funny."

"You're telling me. It was so good that I almost believed it. Nearly thirty seconds of unalloyed shock and excitement. How often do humans get that, really, these days? We're a jaded lot, we modern humans." I heard a massive sigh, the sound of a man who'd come to grips with the fact that he'd been robbed. "But of course, it wasn't you. Couldn't have been."

"Why not?" I couldn't tell why I was so annoyed by this.

"Well, the handwriting was pretty similar to yours, in some ways—the downward stabs, characteristic of someone who digs, a gardener, perhaps—but it was the crowded left margin of someone clinging to the past that suggested an archaeologist to me. But the rhythm was off, the spacing was strange—with those too-wide spaces between the words? Shit, it was nearly as antisocial as my own. And the variation from the baseline showed me that it was someone with no interest in conforming. Dangerous, even. And that my dear, is not you."

"Thanks a lot. Now you're telling me that someone sent you a letter, and signed my name?"

"That's about it, Auntie. Except for the picture. That almost killed me."

"Picture?"

"I'm going to leave orders that it be buried with me. Or cremated, I haven't decided which I favor, yet. The jury's still out on the afterlife."

Michael might have been a philosopher, but it never seemed to do anything for him, except provide rationalizations. "What kind of picture?"

"As a man, I'm a connoisseur of pornography. As, well, *me*, I take my hobbies seriously. This . . . whew. Like I said, if I had really believed you'd sent it to me, I would have dropped everything, run out, and bought new underwear, just on the possibility."

I took a deep breath. "Michael, please! Start over. Someone sent you a dirty picture?"

"Yes. One of you."

I gasped. "It couldn't be—"

"No, of course not. But it was a good enough fake to keep my interest. Someone put your head on an astoundingly inventive, and might I add very flexible, body. God bless the Internet. Not that you aren't flexible—I'm sure you are—and frankly, since I got the picture, I've been speculating about that. But there was a certain quality about the upper body that, while similar to yours, was just a trifle too . . . enthusiastic. Enhanced, but an outstanding job, in my considered opinion."

"Damn it, knock it off, Michael!"

"I'm just building the proof, don't take it out on me." Another pause, and I could almost hear the effort it took to wrench the conversation back around to me. "So it seems like you've got some problems. Someone's got it out for you, and they're not playing nice, are they? Am I the first?"

"The first to get smut," I said.

"Why me?"

"I couldn't tell you." I told him about the "gifts" sent to my family, the fire at the animal hospital, the picture of Sophia. The site, the chase. The art museum guard, the painting, and Dora's parents.

"It's not like you're a member of my family. Or a particularly close friend." As soon as I said it, I felt uncomfortable, but it was the truth.

It didn't seem to even register with Michael. "Hardly. I would have said that the odd email now and then didn't actually constitute a relationship. But people are getting married on the strength of just that these days, and the odder the email, the better, in some cases. Perhaps, if you've got a stalker, which it seems to me you do, he's trying to indicate how well he knows you, knows your movements. How long's it been since we were at Shrewsbury? Year and a half?"

"Something like that." I shuddered, thinking that if he was right, Tony'd been very, very busy.

"Huh. That's scary, isn't it? Someone who's willing to go to that kind of trouble, spend that kind of time?"

"Yeah." Suddenly, I felt my eyes welling up. As much of a weirdo as Michael could be, he was taking my fears seriously, and I found myself promoting him to friend status on the spot. "It is scary."

"Hmm. Kind of obsessive, if you ask me." Asking Michael about obsession was kind of like asking the Pope about Rome. "Once I started really studying the letter—"

"Oh, enough already!"

"Emma, please." His disdain was so palpable I could almost hear Michael drawing himself up out of his perennial slouch over the phone lines. "I meant, once I realized it wasn't you, I started to analyze it. I've picked up a thing or two about graphology, studying personal documents as I do, and a little bit about forensic attribution along the way. And it's my informed opinion that whoever's responsible for this is a nut case."

"That's a big help. Huge."

"Also highly intelligent, perceptive, inventive. An egoist of galactic proportions, he's as desirous of an audience as he feels impossibly superior to any one else in the world."

"You got all that from the handwriting?" Frankly, the description sounded like Michael himself.

"Not all. Handwriting is not a good indication of gender, but, well, men and women write porn differently. In my considered opinion, this felt like a guy trying to sound like a woman to me. Do you have any idea of who might be doing this?"

The flesh at the back of my neck crawled. "I've got an idea."

"Presumably you've been to the authorities?"

"Yes, but it's only recently that there's been a crime—or any evidence—worth troubling about. No one's seen this guy, and they're also mostly convinced that Tony is dead."

"Well, that's what I call dedicated. Good work, from beyond the grave. Do they have Kinko's in Tartarus?" A pause. "Can you get me a sample of Tony's handwriting?"

"Uh, yeah. You think you could compare them, find out for certain?"

"No. But I have a friend who could. Specializes in attribution. I'm just more of a talented amateur. Developed while I was stalking women as an undergraduate—oh, and doesn't that word have such a rotten, narrow, loaded connotation these days? Send me a more recent sample of your handwriting, too. For comparison."

"I will. And you have to send the letter and the photo to me."

"I can't!" he said petulantly. "I'm going to have it buried with me, I told you!"

I counted to ten, then to twenty. "Make a copy, if you must, but get me that letter. The original."

"Okay, but after I show it to my friend. She works better with the original."

"Fine. I want the cops to be able to check for fingerprints. I want them to have every opportunity to nail this guy."

"Interesting choice of words, given the situation. Emma, this letter troubles me. This guy seems to know exactly what buttons to push, on you and those around you. A person with a less subtle grasp of the situation would be impressed. I'm just scared."

Michael's frank admission surprised me. "Me too. I don't think Tony would do anything to you, but be careful, would you?"

"Oh, sure. He'll have to cut through the swathes of adoring women."

"Sasha's out of the picture, then?" Too bad, I thought. I liked Sasha, and if anyone had a chance of taming Michael, calming him down, it was she.

"Oh, not a chance. We've moved in together. But the woman—she's a devil, Emma. She'll do everything but marry me. She drives me to distraction, as elusive as she is."

You can be elusive and still live in the same house? It struck me that Sasha was doing things exactly right; Michael's obsessions usually ended with a trip to the altar, at last count, four. If Sasha could keep him entranced, while still enjoying domestic bliss, then she was even cannier than I gave her credit for. Not marrying him, for example, apparently keeping herself unattainable, by his lights. "And these other layers of women?"

"Oh, nobody. Just the usual armies of enthralled. Send me the sample text when you get it."

"Right. And then make sure I get the originals."

"It might take a while," he said. "The tattoo artist works better from originals, too." He hung up.

I remembered that I'd wanted to speak to Artie, find out if he'd ever left the house when I wasn't there. I tried his number, got nothing. Called his boss, got a gum-chewing secretary, and was told that Artie wasn't due at my house that day.

"I know that," I said.

"So why do you want to talk to him?" The gum stopped for a moment.

"I need to find out something from him. Can you have him call me?"

"Is there some complaint?"

Not yet, I thought. "I'd just like to speak to him."

"I'll leave a message . . ." she said doubtfully, working the gum back up to normal speed.

"Thanks." It all led me to imagine that I'd hear from Artie when next I saw him, whenever that might be.

I waited until the department was even emptier than when I came in, and then went down to the map room. There had never been anyone to claim Tony's papers and files and books and things; after his disappearance, the college boxed up the materials in his office, and were presumably charging rent against Tony's estate or the day he should reappear. Didn't make things easier for me; a few friends in the department, while shocked to hear of what had gone on, had always seemed a little more distant to me since then. Tony wasn't there, and since I was, it was almost as if I was to blame for disrupting things so much. The three new professors that had to be found, the gaps in the table at faculty meetings were obvious reminders that I had rocked the boat.

I couldn't really blame my colleagues; it was a lot of upheaval. We were lucky to get the slots filled, not lose the lines or the funding. That was the quick work and diplomatic ways of our new chair, Jenny Alvarez.

The rest of the files were in Professor LaBrot's office; I could get at the map room, though, and assumed that some of them would be annotated.

I was in luck. A terse, irritated and threatening note from Tony about the return of maps to the correct places was stuck near the top of the pile in the map room. Long enough, complex enough, to possibly be of some use.

I cast about for a piece of paper to leave a note and realized how foolish I was being. Yes, I was taking something from the files and not leaving the appropriate paper trail. No, it didn't really matter.

Still felt funny, though. I didn't like skulking and sneaking and taking things that didn't technically belong to anyone. Stealing wasn't my style.

I made two copies of it, replaced one in the files, and then packaged up the original to send to Michael in the next day's overnight bag. I put the other in the file I'd been keeping, just to keep track of what I'd done and why, in response to what. It was getting rather thick, I thought glumly.

The next day, I stopped by the office to check my mail. A strange young woman was sitting in Chuck's seat, filing folders. Not just strange because she was unfamiliar to me. A long, burnt-orange dress in velvet with a long row of jet buttons from the high neckline to the skirt swept the floor—it looked like something from a vintage store. As she rolled the chair back to the desk, little black boots with matching buttons skittered beneath her. Short black hair was a surprise—I would have expected Beardsley's flowing locks to go with the dress—but her beautifully shaped face could have taken any haircut easily. The kohl around the eyes and dark lips told it all, and I was putting my money on first-year fine arts major.

She must be roasting in that dress, I thought. Even with the air-conditioning.

I waved as I stuck my head into the mailbox area. Nothing yet. "Hi. I'm Emma Fielding. Chuck's out today?"

The look she gave me was fixed and poisonous. "I know who you are."

Not "I've seen your name," not "Oh, hi! I'm Trixie!" "I know who you are." I shivered in spite of myself. "Oh? How is that?"

"You were in the museum yesterday. When the guard was killed and Professor Sarkes-Robinson collapsed. I heard that you were responsible."

"She collapsed because a painting was stolen. Apparently there was a threat made against her as well." Why on earth am I explaining myself to this child?

"I see." But clearly she didn't. She sniffed and turned to her computer.

"Any messages—?"

She looked up at me. "Justine."

Of course it was. I was also willing to bet it wasn't the name on her birth certificate either. "Justine. Any phone messages?"

"I put any messages in your mailbox."

"Okay. I'll be in the lab."

Justine didn't bother to reply. I didn't bother trying to make her.

I let myself into the lab, wondering how the bones at the site had been removed from the storage. There were three students in there; two of my undergraduate majors were wielding toothbrushes, carefully washing artifacts, and yammering to beat the band. It was impossible to walk past them without picking through the goodies to see if there was anything new that I hadn't seen in the field. It's amazing what can get collected unknowingly, and then, when the dirt washes off, you find you've got a little jewel, artifactually speaking. Archaeologists get excited about odd things.

They glanced up when I came in, of course, but they didn't quiet down a bit. I must be losing my terribleness for them, I thought. Have to fix that.

But their work was fine—the dirt was coming off the artifacts, everything was being kept with its original artifact bag so that we wouldn't lose the important associative information, and there were no unpleasant surprises like modern nails mixed in with nice eighteenth-century pottery, which would mean that our context was not sealed.

I'd let them live.

"We have a question," John said.

"Shoot."

"What's that that Nick's got?" John pointed to his friend, who had a brownish lump hanging off his tongue, a grin on his ugly face.

"It's not his best look, whatever it is." I reached over and pulled it off; Nick made a yuck face. I glanced at the artifact. "Well, if it's sticking that good, it's probably earthenware, right?"

"Yeah, we know, but it's really thin. Delicate. It looks like it could be a teacup or something, but it seemed too nice for earthenware."

"Refined earthenware," I said. "Go check Noël Hume, for a start; there was an attempt to reproduce some of the Asian dry-bodied red stoneware. It works for the period."

"Cool," Nick said. "John said it came from the privy."

John was fibbing; we hadn't excavated a privy at the Chandler house. "So how'd it taste?"

He shrugged. "Oh, fine. No worse than that piece of sewer pipe I tested yesterday."

Twenty years old, and you still can't break them of an oral fixation, I thought. "Fine, good. Don't actually eat anything, will you?"

"Not intentionally. Say, Professor Fielding . . . we need some more storage boxes."

I eyed them suspiciously. "Are you sure?"

"Oh, yes. We need them for the stuff we finished processing."

I glanced down the long table covered with cleaned and labeled artifacts; they'd made good progress, for all their fooling. "Okay, you can make two each."

"Three," John said quickly; he caught my eye and backed down.

I glared at them both. "You can make two each. No more. And I'll count."

They exchanged sheepish grins. "Okay. Thanks."

I walked to the back of the lab where a young woman was reading an osteology text. While she read, she took notes, and with her other hand, rolled a tennis ball down the table. She caught it when it hit the wall and gently rolled back. That was one way to keep from chewing fingernails, I thought. Her lowered head was bobbing, as if to music I couldn't hear. A thin white wire snaking through her thick dark hair told the story; she had earbuds in, listening to her iPod. Made sense, given the racket my two reprobate students were making.

I waved my hand, trying to get her attention. No luck. "Ms. Shepherd? Phoebe?"

She looked up, and pulled her earbuds out as soon as she saw me. She had a foxy, pointed face, and eyes that were so deep, and bewitching that I'd actually caught Brian staring into them when he met Phoebe at the last departmental party. "Sorry, Professor Fielding. I was just trying to—" She waved her hand at the guys.

"I understand. I don't know how you manage to get any work done. You can tell them to keep it down, you know."

"Oh, they're okay. But . . . you know that they were putting things in their mouths? Won't they get a disease or something?"

"Probably," I said. "But not from that. It's okay, it's a porosity test. Generally speaking, if it sticks to your tongue, it's probably earthenware, low fired, porous. If it doesn't, it's probably stoneware or porcelain, which are higher fired, harder, less porous."

"Right, I hoped that was the case, but with them, you never know." Phoebe was relieved. "And . . . I don't want to say anything, but . . . they're making boxes again."

"It's okay. I gave them permission."

Phoebe's concern was well-founded. The acid-free artifact storage boxes came flat, ready to be folded into shape.

They were an elegant design and, well, really fun to make. Nick and John had discovered this one day, and decided to get a head start on the busy field season with a "box-off." They'd constructed twenty of the boxes before anyone caught them. Twenty boxes for which there was yet no storage space in our increasingly small lab space, most of which had to be unmade later.

I handed her the bag of bones from the site. "I have a puzzle for you."

She stuck the tennis ball between two books and her eyes lit up. "Cool. Lay it on me."

"Any idea where these might have come from? And how they might have gotten out to the Point?" I told her the story, and her look of disbelief grew as I finished.

"Wow. Human hand phalanges. Strange." She shook the bones out of the bag and picked up one of them, searching for the number. "These are from an older collection. Not one of Professor LaBrot's."

Professor LaBrot had replaced Tony when he'd vanished. A physical anthropologist, he taught the prehistoric archaeology classes, including the Maya, and science, while I covered the historic ones and theory. Phoebe was his TA.

"Let's have a look." She pushed back from the desk. I noticed she wore a black T-shirt with a crude cartoon picture, half dragon, half man on it, labeled TROGDOR. I'd have to ask Brian what that was about. Phoebe was rubbing her hands and muttering something in a singsong voice as she turned to the cabinets where the faunal collections were kept.

"I didn't catch that," I said.

Phoebe turned and giggled. "Oh, just silliness. I said, 'bring out your dead.' You know from Monty Python?"

I nodded; I might not know who Trodgor was, but I wasn't so irredeemably unhip that I didn't know *Monty Python and the Holy Grail.*

"Over here. The human remains are kept locked up." She unlocked the first cabinet, pulled out a box, and examined the contents list on the lid. She dug through the bags, frowned, then pawed through them again. "Okay, well here's where they should be. And there's no note to say why they're not. Damn."

"Who has the keys to this room? And the cabinet?"

"You and Professor LaBrot. There's probably a set in the main office, and I suppose someone in the physical plant does, for emergencies. But for students, well, there's me and a couple of other graduate students. Chuck does—oh, hey, you heard about him, right?"

"What about him?" I saw her serious face and felt my stomach fill with ice.

"He got mugged. Beat up pretty bad. Right here on campus."

"What!" I sagged against the cabinet. "Are you kidding me?"

"No way. He's been out of work almost a week."

"Oh my God. I thought he just . . . was on vacation or something."

"Hey, I'm sorry, I thought you knew. What with Wednesday Addams out there, and all."

I felt light-headed. "Did they catch the guy?"

"No, but campus police are in a tizzy about it."

"Yeah, I'll bet. That sort of thing—"

"Doesn't happen." Phoebe nodded sadly. "Not here, no."

I shook myself. "Anything else that you might have noticed missing? Odd, off, anything like that?"

"I haven't noticed anything, but now I'll keep my eyes open," she offered. "I'm sorry I had to tell you about Chuck. The whole thing sucks."

I nodded. "Yeah. Thanks for your help."

"Thanks for bringing my bones back."

"Sure." I wandered over to the window, hoping to find solace about Chuck, or maybe inspiration, an elegant solution that would neatly tie up all my problems. Whatever else the bones meant—and it seemed as though they were just the nearest thing to hand—whoever put them on the site wanted to let me know he had access to my world. Knew how I felt about the museum, and what the thought of the violence there would do to me. The assault on Chuck—and I was convinced that was also connected—sealed that as fact for me. I rested my head against the pane of glass . . .

. . . and saw Tony Markham looking up at me.

Chapter 11

HEY! HEY!" I SHOUTED, LOOKING FOR A WAY TO open the windows . . . didn't they open? Ventilation was all through hoods and air-conditioning, the better to keep the artifacts in a stable environment. I banged on the window, trying to get the attention of someone, anyone, who could stop him.

"Uh, you okay, Professor Fielding?" All three students were watching me, shocked.

"—right back," I muttered, and tore out of the lab.

There were already people waiting for the perennially slow elevator. I opted for the stairs, taking them two and three at a time. I hit the front doors at a run, knocking into a student as I crashed through.

Tony was already gone by the time I got to where he had been.

I looked around wildly, but there was no sign of him. Where could he have gone? There were too many buildings that someone—Oh God, with *keys*—could get into.

Think.

Can't find him by running around, so find him by walking.

I went to the maintenance office. They knew me well enough there, having had my share of climate-control emergencies in the lab and more than my share of encounters with them on the weekends, when it seemed that we were the only people on campus. I was also known for keeping the coffee maker running while I was in the lab, and didn't care if they had a cup or two, so I actually knew most of the guys by name, and knew a bunch more by sight. Once or twice, they'd given me a break, letting me park in spots that were usually off limits so I could move equipment or finds. More than once they'd held the door for me, using their own security passcards to let me out, joking that they hoped I wasn't stealing any valuable artifacts. It wasn't that I was stealing them—I always brought them straight back—but sometimes it was easier to work on the goodies at home. And they weren't all that valuable, anyway, unless you count the information that they represented. And I always brought them back.

"Hey, there . . . missy." Everyone was "missy" or "mister" to Duffy, who was bad with names but good with furnaces. "What can I do for you? You been running or something, or are you just glad to see me?"

I smiled as best I could, but it was weak. "Oh, I've been running, Duffy. Trying to catch up with someone from maintenance. I hope you can help me."

"Sure, I bet I can. What do you need?"

"I'm trying to find someone. Might be a new guy, the last year or so, maybe. He's about this tall, darkish hair, maybe in his late fifties or sixties."

"That could be most of us, you know."

"I know, and here's the problem. I can't remember his name. There were two guys I met at the same time. My building. One of them might have been a vendor or outside contract, or something. Ring any bells?"

"Not really. You got a name?"

"Tony Markham? Billy Griggs?" It was worth a shot.

"I can tell you right now, we got no one named Markham. Griggs, neither."

"Is there any way I could look . . . are there photos in the personnel files?" I said, a little too quickly.

Duffy's eyes narrowed and he pulled back; and I knew that I'd gone too far. "That's not something I could . . . say, there's no trouble is there? Because I'll tell you missy, I can't go giving out information like that. We got rules."

"I know, I just . . . he was asking me about something . . . to do with the local history, and I thought I saw him coming in here, and I figured I'd tell him what I remembered, but he wasn't here, so . . ."

Duffy still wasn't happy. "Oh, I couldn't go showing you that sort of thing. You're sure there's not some problem? I'd have to do it official, but we can sort out problems, you know. Thefts, breakage, it happens, and we take care of it. But we do it official."

"No, I promise, nothing like that. I just thought I'd, you know, tell him. But it's not that big a deal."

He nodded, still disturbed by my incursions beyond regular bounds, but then the door opened behind me and a smile crossed his face. "Well, hang on now. What about this young fella, Ernie, behind you?"

I turned to see what he was talking about. The "young fella" was right behind me—I gasped. There was a superficial resemblance to Tony—same height, weight, general build, coloring, and age—but not more than that. Just enough to make the mistake from several floors up.

"Can I help you?" The guy's name tag said 'Fishbeck.' " He looked between me and Duffy, wiping his hands on a dirty rag.

I looked at him and shook my head. "No, sorry. Sorry to be such a pain."

"And here you were, trying to do something nice." Duffy clucked. "Well, you let me know if you find the guy, okay?"

"Something wrong?" Ernie asked.

"Nah. Missy . . . Fielding here was trying to find a guy who'd asked her a question, that's all."

"Oh." He shrugged. "Not me. Sorry."

"Thanks anyway."

I left the maintenance office shaken. I couldn't have been wrong, in the airport, could I?

Ernie looked like Tony, who looked like any number of men. And if he was in any kind of disguise . . .

But everything else? Surely it all couldn't be coincidence?

Why was I seeing Tony everywhere? Maybe it was exactly as Brian had said, like seeing Oscar after he died and I was in a state of distress. We live on a small planet with a very shallow gene pool. There was bound to be a lot of overlapping resemblance in a given population.

I know what I saw. I know what's been happening to me. I can't be imagining all of this, I just know I can't.

And yet here I am, with a double handful of nothing to prove it.

I'm starting to be scared for reasons that have nothing to do with Tony. What does it look like when you're going out of your mind?

Maybe being a little depressed isn't going out of your mind. And there's something else at the root of this.

It doesn't explain seeing things that aren't there. It doesn't explain conjuring nightmares in midday.

I went back up to the office and the mysterious Justine. "Can you tell me if there are any keys missing? From the office collection?"

She glanced up at me, smirked, and put down her nail file. "How would I know?"

"You wouldn't. But you and I will look at the cupboard together. I'll see if there's anything missing."

Justine got out her key; I held out my hand, which she studiously ignored, then she went to the cupboard where the departmental keys were kept. Everyone of them was accounted for, or had been appropriately signed out. No luck there.

"Done?" Justine stood waiting for me, not quite tapping her foot.

"Not by a long shot. But I'm through here." She locked up, and without a word returned to her desk.

Okay, I thought as I returned to my office. But Tony doesn't need a key, if he's got a job with the physical plant . . . he might be using another name.

After I finished with my email, I stopped by campus police and asked if I could talk to the officer who'd handled Chuck's mugging. I gave him my staff ID and tried to seem as little like a thrill seeker as possible.

He looked at the plastic card, grunted, and shoved it back to me. "Why are you so interested?"

"Because there've been several other incidents connected to the archaeology department," I said. "And that theft at the museum might well be connected. I might be able to identify the guy."

The campus police officer looked up sharply. "We'd love to get this guy. Jim was a friend of all of ours. There's been way too much trouble around here lately."

I nodded. When I'd seen the confirmation of Jim's death in the campus paper, I'd felt the world tilt away, couldn't feel my feet beneath me. One more thing to nail Tony for.

The officer's face was taut, the muscles of his jaw flexed. "He was declared DOA when he got to the hospital." The officer watched me a moment, then seemed to decide. He made a quick phone call, speaking in phrases so clipped that I could barely tell that the officer was available. He hung up. "Come with me."

I followed him down another hallway to a back office, and he told my story to another uniformed guard. "We're working with the Caldwell Police on this," the second guy said. "Nasty thing, but if you think you can help, I'll send you to them. Take a seat."

They sat me down and set a file in front of me. I wasn't sure what to expect, but nothing they might have told me would have prepared me for what I saw.

The file held a series of indistinct photographic images, obviously taken over time by some security camera. Then, as I understood what each successive image meant, saw what was happening, I wished that it was video, so it would be over that much faster. Even the illusion of speed would have been better than this.

And the pauses between the pictures only left that much more to my imagination.

Chuck was immediately recognizable, even in a bad image. Not just his dreads, not just his recycled basmati rice bag book tote, there was something upward in his gait that wouldn't be confined, even by a still, two-dimensional picture. There was a little flash, and I knew he'd turned his head, toward a light that he couldn't see. He was turning because someone had called him and a streetlight reflected off his glasses. That someone came out from an alley between two buildings. A man, large and powerfully built, face and hair covered with the hood of his sweatshirt, for which it was far too warm this time of year. Loose fitting pants, sweats, maybe. Running shoes.

In one frame, Chuck looked down at his watch: He'd been asked the time. In the next, the man was swinging, his legs a blur as he dove into Chuck.

Do something, Chuck, I whispered to myself, don't let him hurt you! Scream, run, kick him . . . do anything.

But it was already done. Already too late.

Three more shots, like a slide show. One: Chuck was down, the man on top of him, arms raised and blurred with motion. Two: Chuck's hands were over his face, but it did him little good, and the attack continued, a brutal pantomime. Three: Chuck's hands were limp, on the ground beside him and there were dark patches on his face and shirt. I realized it was blood.

I tried not to, but I found myself doing the math: one picture every thirty seconds. Two minutes of a beating is a very long time. Most people would be exhausted, fighting back after thirty seconds, even if nearly none of the punches landed.

Chuck didn't fight back. He never had the chance, even if he wanted to.

It wasn't over.

The next picture there was another blur, another flash, and I saw—or at least imagined that I now saw—a knife. The man pulled something from Chuck's trouser pockets.

Leave now, I thought. You've got whatever it is you wanted, not that Chuck had anything much to begin with. If you'd asked him, he would have given it to you. All you had to do was ask: Chuck would have done it and been happy about it. There was no need for any of this, not ever, but especially not Chuck. . . .

It wasn't over yet. And it had nothing to do with Chuck, I knew it in my bones.

In the next picture the man was back, leaning over Chuck's torso. The knife was clearer now, and in the next shot, I could see what was going to happen . . .

He was leaning on Chuck's arm. Going to slice into it.

I heard noises, off in the distance. A split second passed before I realized that I'd shoved my chair back, and was moaning.

"There's more," the officer said quietly.

The spell was broken, though, and I came back to the small office where I'd been sitting all along. Now I felt more like the distant observer I was rather than being there, helpless, while it happened. I forced myself to finish looking at the pictures.

The attacker suddenly was up—there was no interval between whatever had moved him and his standing upright. Then he was a blur as he ran away, and a young woman entered the frame. The next few images were of her kneeling by Chuck, looking around for help, then reaching, God bless her, into her bag for a cell phone.

"That's about it," the officer said. He leaned over and closed the file. "She called an ambulance, stayed with Charles—"

"It's Chuck," I said, a little louder than I meant. Somehow, that was very important.

He nodded. "She stayed with him, Chuck, until it arrived. Even went to the hospital with him."

I pushed back from the table, feeling the pain in my shoulders slowly subside. My fingers ached from gripping the arms of my chair, and when I looked, I saw I was bleeding from where a fingernail dug into the soft flesh of my palm. I'd been wrong when I imagined the worst was over. I still had to go see Chuck.

"Can you tell us about that man? Do you recognize him?" He slid an enlarged print of the man across the table to me. It was only good as a reminder of how large the attacker was; his face was a blur.

I stared at the picture, but it only seemed to become more abstract and pixilated the longer I looked at it. Tears filled my eyes, and it blurred away altogether. I brushed at my face impatiently, and shook my head.

The officer handed a box of tissues to me, and I blew my nose. I tried to memorize the attacker's build, his sweatshirt, something. Because if I ever found this guy . . .

"Can I have a copy of this?" I asked on impulse. "Maybe someone at the department will recognize him."

"I suppose we could do that," he said slowly. "But you have to tell me, why do you think this is connected with you?"

"I believe Chuck was attacked because of me, or if not specifically to scare me, possibly to get his keys to the lab." I told him about what had happened at the site, about the bones in the bottom of the pit from the Caldwell collections. I told him about the other incidents. Finally, I told him my suspicions about Tony Markham.

The man was silent for a moment. "That's quite a story you've put together, there."

"I'm not putting anything together," I said. I swallowed and tried to relax my jaw muscles. "I'm telling you what's happened to me, and what I think is going on. You can contact the police officers in Lawton or Sheriff Stannard, if you like."

"Uh-huh. I wasn't implying anything. It's just . . . quite a story."

I couldn't be bothered to rise to the bait. "What can I do? Is there anything else I can do to help?" Not that I'd been all that helpful to begin with. "Is Chuck all right?"

"He was released from the hospital, he's doing fine. Cuts and bruises, no broken bones, nothing major." The officer stopped suddenly and looked at me. "Were you and Mr. Huxley involved?"

"Involved with what?"

"Each other."

"What? No! Are you kidding me?"

"Why is that such a strange question? There must be some reason that he was targeted, if that's what's going on here. What exactly is your relationship with him?"

"Chuck . . . well, I'm fond of him. We're not really friends, we don't hang out or anything, but he's been over the house when I've had departmental parties. I like him . . . and I feel protective of him. I think Tony knows that."

"Why protective?"

"Chuck's . . . not naïve, that's not it, not entirely. He just tends to believe the best of people, even when they've given him no reason to expect it. He thinks people want to be good."

He scowled. "That's not very bright, these days. My friend Jim lying in the morgue will tell you that."

I found myself getting angry, even though I knew he was right. "Maybe not, but it doesn't deserve punishment like this."

As he apologized, there was only one thought that kept going through my head, and it was exactly as Tony had planned, I was sure.

Scars last so much longer than bruises. If it hadn't been for Chuck's rescuer, he'd have been marred for life, with marks both he and I could see.

I walked out in a daze. There was little comfort in the young woman's rescue of Chuck, and while I was grateful, all I could remember was Chuck's limp form and the dark blood stain on the pale fabric of his recycled book bag.

* * *

As always, there was plenty of work for me to flee into. I presently was tracking down more leads on the Chandler family, who were leaders of the community of Stone Harbor, the next town over from where I lived. Although there were a number of interesting primary documents that mentioned the English-born Matthew Chandler and his work as a judge in the early eighteenth century, I was actually more interested in his wife, Margaret, whose diary I'd had the chance to study.

The accounts that didn't fall in line to praise her were the interesting ones. I'd only recently come across one, by painstakingly going through every period diary and collection of letters that I could lay my hands on that had anything to do with anyone in coastal Massachusetts. While locating the diaries was time consuming, reading them wasn't as arduous as it sounds. Usually they weren't too hard to read, if they were in good condition, and the handwriting wasn't too awful. Awful, you could get used to, especially reading the scribbled exam papers of panicked and hyperventilating freshmen. And sometimes, rarely, there was even a transcription, though you were usually better off rereading the original for yourself, to avoid errors the transcriber made, intentionally or not. The problem, as far as I was concerned, was that oftentimes these diaries were one-line accounts of weather, ships arriving and departing, or amounts of grain harvested. That was fine, and the right kind of scholar could do a lot with them.

What I had was a fragment of a note that mentioned Margaret. It described her as an "iron-hearted wretch," which was remarkable to me, given her reputation.

This was the best part of my work and I couldn't stomach it. I couldn't concentrate, but worse, I found myself not wanting to. I'd been tired before, overworked and pressed for time, but had never been able to put something as juicy as this aside with so little regret. I couldn't bring myself to care.

I thought about eating the sandwich I'd brought with me, but these days, the thought of food just made me queasy. I knew what I was avoiding, so I decided to confront it head on. I went to Chuck's apartment.

Chuck rented the top floor of a three-decker not too far from campus, in the center of Caldwell. As I had come to expect, the Christmas lights were still up, though the bulbs were still red, white, and blue, for Independence Day. Chuck believed that if lights on a house were pretty at one time of year, they were pretty all year round: What his landlord must have thought, I didn't know. The windows were uneven, giving the house a rather cockeyed look.

I climbed to the third floor. The front door was propped open. I knocked on the door to his apartment, and after a moment, heard shuffling, the chain being drawn across, and then the door was cracked open.

Chuck peeped out, a black eye turning to green and yellow behind thick glasses that replaced his usual granny glasses. Something as fragile as they were wouldn't have survived that brutal attack. Chuck had a cut on his mouth, and his grin at seeing me rapidly turned to a grimace of pain as it pulled at the scar. Then something clouded in his eyes, and he looked wary.

"Hi, Professor Fielding," he said. "Uh . . ."

The fact that he hesitated worried me. Whatever physical damage he'd escaped, there was a blight on his trusting nature now. Understandable. To me, heartbreaking.

"Would you like to come in?"

"Yes, please. Just for a minute. I wanted to see how you were doing."

"Oh, I'm okay." He looked dull, the light had gone out of his eyes. "A little shook up still. I still can't believe . . . it doesn't seem like it happened to me, somehow." Then his face became fixed; Chuck had thought of something and was trying to conceal it. It was a look I'd never seen before.

"I brought you a carrot bran muffin," I said, handing him the bag from Joey's Sandwich Shop. They were his favorite.

"Oh, thanks. That was really . . . maybe I'll eat it later. I'm not much hungry, lately."

"I see." You and me both.

He led me into the living area, and offered me a choice between a beat-up love seat and a beanbag chair. As there was an afghan on the love seat—for comfort, certainly not for warmth—I took the beanbag. Sank in, my knees up to my chin. Chuck settled under the afghan.

I cleared my throat. Chuck looked away. Then we spoke at the same time:

"Chuck, look, I have to tell you—"

"Uh, Professor? There's something—"

"You go first," I said.

"Um. This is hard. I think . . . it's hard for me to remember everything—it happened real fast. But I think, I think the . . . the guy who beat me up? I think he mentioned your name. I thought you should know, if it isn't, you know. My concussion talking or something."

"Oh, Chuck—!" A lump rose in my throat.

"He said your name. He said, 'Ask Emma.' Or at least, that's what I thought he said. But I could have heard wrong." He laughed, but it wasn't convincing. "I was kinda busy at the time."

The words froze me: At the conference earlier this year, a hotel room had been trashed—and students threatened— because I was believed to be looking into a murder. The same words, "ask Emma," had been written on the walls. Duncan Thayer knew that; everyone at the conference knew it. I felt myself go clammy.

Chuck had gone pale, and that brought me back to the sunny, warm little room. "Are you okay?" I asked. "You look a little peaky."

"I feel okay, not even headachy anymore. A little Tiger Balm, a little ice, a little Motrin . . ." He shrugged. "But I've been afraid. It comes in flashes, you know?"

I hated that I had brought this on him. "It's understandable," I said. "You've been traumatized."

"Yeah, but it's not just that. I . . ." He played with the fringe of the afghan. "I was afraid to tell you. That he'd mentioned your name. I'm not a brave person, I know that. I just couldn't go . . . and tell you. I didn't remember, not really, until yesterday. But I've been hiding." He wiped his nose on the sleeve of his tie-dyed baseball shirt. "I'm not brave, like I said. It was like . . . if I said anything, it would happen all over again."

Oh Christ . . . I thought briefly about running away, but I couldn't move my legs. The truth was a poor second choice. "Chuck, I came here . . . because things have been happening. I'm afraid you were beat up because . . . I think Tony Markham is back."

I told him what had been going on. He stared at the squares of the afghan the whole time.

"I can't tell you how sorry I am, that you got dragged into this. I don't know why he—or whoever it was—chose you, but—"

"I do. You like me. That's why. If it was Professor Markham, well. He was never very nice, though sometimes he tried, I could tell. But he wasn't stupid. He knew this would make you sad. Angry."

The tears slid down my cheeks, fueled by an apparently inexhaustible supply of guilt and regret. "Chuck, I'm so sorry . . ."

"I know. I know you are. But you know, it's kinda my fault, too. He wouldn't've picked on me if he didn't think . . . he didn't think he could get away with it. I'm not very brave. He knew that." Chuck picked at the worn yarn. "I'm an easy mark."

His words cut me to the heart. I had no idea what to say next.

"Look, I'm okay. Robin—that's the girl who saved me—got there before anything worse happened." He flushed red. "I'm not going to die. I feel dumb, and I feel scared, and I feel kinda mad. I don't like it, but I'll survive. And you know, if it is Professor Markham—"

Even after all Tony had done, and might yet be responsible for, Chuck still used his title.

"—or anyone else, for that matter, you find them, okay? Whatever you're doing, don't you let me be the thing that stops you. Don't let them get away with that, promise me."

"Chuck, I—"

"Professor, promise me." He looked at me now, his face red and swollen from tears and the beating. I'd never heard him use the imperative before.

"I promise." I swallowed, rummaged in my pockets for a tissue, found none. I went into the kitchen, found some tissues, brought the box back for both of us. "Is there anything I can do for you? Do you need groceries, or anything?"

"Naw." He blew his nose, then blushed again. "Robin's coming over this afternoon. She said she'd bring some stuff."

"Robin sounds very nice," I said.

"I think she's great," he said simply, looking at the afghan again, blushing again like mad. "Robin is great."

Chuck said "Robin" the way other men had said Helen or Cleopatra.

He brightened a little. "You know, I'm just thinking . . . I wouldn't have met her, if it wasn't for . . . that guy. You never know what will come out of a situation, no matter how bad it is at the time. If he . . . if I . . . she and I would never have met. We would have walked along the path, never thinking about the other one." He smiled now, and I saw a little of the Chuck I was used to.

"Well, you let me know if you need anything," I said, getting up. "You take care of yourself."

"You take care of yourself, too. And you find whoever this is. Make sure they don't hurt anyone else."

I nodded and left. It was a heavy task he was charging me with, but I would take on an even heavier penance than that if I could just forget the alien hurt and anger in Chuck's eyes.

Chuck's place was near one of my favorite spots—the Caldwell Burial Ground—but I couldn't bring myself to stop and rest under the shade. The burial ground was, for my money, the best refuge on campus—away from my office, away from everyone, great headstones to look at, but there was too much room for reflection and I couldn't face that yet.

That evening, all hell broke loose. I dutifully overcame my reticence to tell Brian about Chuck, when he started telling me that he already knew.

I stared at him. "What? How can you—?"

"I didn't know it was him at first," Brian said slowly. He looked a bit dazed. "I've been getting alerts on my search engine at work, anything to do with you, Caldwell, Lawton. I read about the attack in the archives, but I didn't realize that it was Chuck. I didn't know his last name and the Caldwell paper, well, it was the town paper, not the college, so it said 'college employee.' Nothing about the anthropology department."

"You've been getting . . . alerts?"

"Yeah, I thought I'd keep my eyes open, look for anything that seemed suspicious. I'm glad you told me—"

"What, did you think I wouldn't?" I said sharply.

Brian gave me a startled look. "No, that's not it—"

"You're spying on me," I blurted, and immediately wished I could take it back.

"Wow. Emma, you're scaring me. I'm not spying on you."

"I didn't mean spying, I just meant . . . you're going to take this the wrong way."

Brian laughed, a sound with no humor in it. "I'm taking everything the wrong way, these days."

"It's just, I'm sorry, I didn't mean to bark at you. But . . . it just struck me wrong, when you said you were getting the alerts. Like someone else was . . . keeping tabs on me."

"Emma, it's not stalking, I'm looking out for you. I'm just concerned about you."

The look in Brian's eyes told me that it wasn't just my physical safety he was worried about.

* * *

Life doesn't stop because you're worried, can't sleep, or start at the sound of every siren, so the next day, I went out to do a bit of surveillance work at the Chandler site. I was there because I'd been invited to a blackmailing party as the guest of honor. I don't mind a spot of blackmail, now and then—I indulged in it myself, occasionally—but Bradley Chandler, director of the Stone Harbor Historical Association and cheapest man on the face of the planet, had threatened Meg's wedding.

Meg wanted to have her wedding on the site of the old eighteenth-century house overlooking the harbor and Bradley had said to me, her application in hand, that they were just too strapped for time and staff. Couldn't accommodate her request and meet the requirements that the state had put on him regarding archaeological research . . .

Which was crap, I knew, because the two weren't related, but he had the say-so over functions, and knew Meg had her heart set on it. Bray, as he was known, had a faint smile on his lips—a faint smile decorated with something green, which I hoped was spinach and not an alarming lapse in dental hygiene. We had a long history of locking horns over topics just like this. I was an archaeologist, so I cost him, or rather the historical society, money and time. I also had indicated that while he might be related to the Chandlers who'd built the house, he was not a direct descendant, and that nettled him. I'd caught him fooling around on his wife. I was clean, reverent, loyal . . . and he was a slob, mean, and a liar.

So I pointed out that I could do the afternoon's work by myself, gratis, if Meg got her day, with a "friends of the historical society discount," of, say, twenty percent. If anything of importance came up, I'd be back with a full crew, at the usual rates.

Bray twitched nervously as he tried to recall my reports about what might be located on that section of the property. He quickly realized it was a good bet, hemmed and hawed

and allowed that he might be able to see his way clear to fifteen percent.

And I allowed as that would be fine. Of course, I was taking a big risk, I'd pointed out, by wedging this last bit of
work into my schedule, I could put the finish dates behind on
a number of projects he'd asked me to do on other properties.
"The work at the Crane Farm, for example," I said, "after all
your hard work getting the permits from the city, the state,
lining up the contractors, the grand opening . . . I'd hate to
think that I would impede that by taking on this other work."
I looked him straight in the eye. "And I know you would
never dream of doing that work without an archaeologist."

"But . . . delay that project?" he said. "We can't, you
couldn't . . ." Bray twitched again, then his eyes narrowed. It
took a weasel to recognize a weasel's tricks, but he got the
message. "But it would be just one day . . ."

"One afternoon," I corrected. "Plus my time to do the artifacts and report."

"One afternoon isn't so much. And if it was understood . . .
between us . . . that this sort of arrangement . . . was just for
this once . . . maybe you could work it out?"

"Well . . . I could only do this kind of favor once. Just for
you." Damn straight; there was no way he was getting any
other freebies from me. This was a special deal.

And so I found myself outside on a gorgeous afternoon,
watching over the shoulders of the alarm installers. Every
once in a while, I'd stop them, and noted what was there
when I saw a bottle or sherd poking out of the ground, but
luckily, as I'd suspected, there were no features, no unmixed
stratigraphy. Under the grass mat, there was a little topsoil
that was probably put down in the sixties when the site was
turned into a tourist attraction, and then debris from the
widening of the road about the same time.

Once I stopped them; there appeared to be an assemblage, a cache, of artifact fragments clustered together. The

excavators, not thrilled with my presence, had soon learned that I wasn't automatically going to cause trouble, and were grateful for the twenty-minute break they got, on the clock, while I took a few quick measurements and a photo, just in case. It turned out to be a late-nineteenth-century flowerpot that had landed in a divot in the pathway alongside the house; the fragments on the bottom were smaller and closer together, those on top were larger and scattered, and some of them seemed to be broken in situ. I looked up and saw that we were almost directly under a window and envisioned the scene: A strong wind or a careless gesture knocked the pot off the windowsill, it fell beside the house on a narrow pathway between the house and the fence that delineated the street that wasn't often used at the time. Someone walked past—no, better yet, make it a kid skinny enough to squeeze through the narrow space, a game of hide and seek—and stepped on the larger surviving fragments, breaking them in place. The pot is left there because it wasn't in the way, wasn't noticeable, or perhaps it was left because it filled in a low space in the pathway.

I scraped away the soil around the shards with my trowel, enjoying the ringing noise of metal on rocky soil, the smell of the dirt, and satisfied myself that there was nothing else going on. I wrote down my notes, got the guys back to work, and we were finished an hour later. It was actually a lot of fun to be there by myself, doing the work myself, building my own stories from the evidence. I had no other demands on me except to do what I did best. The noise of the powered entrenching tool aside—and it was an earsplitting racket—just helped hide me in my own blissful little world, which was more precious than ever. Never doubt the benefits of denial.

It even had the benefit of annoying Claire Bellamy across the street, who'd been a thorn in my side before this. Bray had straightened her out—I had no idea how—and she no longer protested my every move on the site. When I saw her glowering at me, I waved to her, shrugged, and held my hand up to my ears, shaking my head. We'd be done soon enough and then she and her pampered dogs could return to their carefully considered lifestyles. The dogs, Monet and Matisse, were giant standard poodles, black as coal and possessed of sinister demeanors. I was pretty sure they had it out for me, though Bucky assured me that they were just big intelligent dogs with too little to keep them amused.

I finished up, and was surprised to see that the alarm guys were packing it in for the day. Pikers. I could have gone on for hours, even in an area as unpromising as this, the dirt smelled so good.

I was delighted to find that my stomach was growling. I was really hungry, for the first time in what felt like weeks. To hell with Brian's lectures about fast food: besides, the entire time we were in San Diego we were running from Jack in the Box to Rubio's, all in the name of recapturing his California junk-food fantasies. And his mother cooked like a dream, so this made even less sense to me.

I was hungry, and by God, I was going to celebrate that fact with fries and a Big Mac.

I snaked through the drive-through, got my order, and pulled over. Wondering briefly what the guy at the window would have said if I'd tried to order it "animal style" the way Brian did at In-N-Out, I opened the box the way that Indiana Jones might have opened the Ark, with awe and reverence. The smell almost made me weep—it was late enough in the day that they'd had to make the burger fresh, and the grease was still sizzling. I took a big bite, feeling the lettuce and sauce squish out the back of the sandwich and onto my jeans. I didn't care, grabbed a fistful of fries, scooped up the sauce, and jammed them in my mouth. Mmmm-mmm, I was humming along as I munched, and the old prayer came back to me: "Some would eat, and have no meat, and some can't eat that have it. But we have meat, and we can eat, and so the Lord be thanked." I swallowed a big sip of Coke and hiccupped, giggling to myself.

My cell phone rang. I glanced at the screen—so much more high tech than my home phones—and I saw a New Hampshire number I didn't recognize.

Huh. "Hello?"

No one answered.

"Hello? Someone there?"

Still nothing.

Just as I was going to end the call, I heard low laughter. A man's voice, I was willing to bet. The skin crawled along my back.

"Look, I don't know who this is, but the police are involved, they're looking for you, don't—"

I knew as soon as the words left my lips how inane I sounded. The laughter didn't stop, and cold, I finally found the "end call" button. I pressed the call log, found that the caller's name was withheld.

The sight of the food on my lap, the smell of the salt and grease, made my stomach contract. The thought of actually eating was now revolting. I bundled it up, got out of the car, and threw out the remainder, then rolled down all of the windows to get the smell out faster.

I had to give my old ex Duncan a call to find out how the weather was in New Hampshire and just how badly he'd taken the loss of the job he blamed me for.

I drove home in a haze, climbed to my office, my good mood blown. I found my ASAA phone directory and called Duncan.

"Hello?"

"Duncan, it's Emma Fielding."

There was a long pause. "Hello, Emma," he said cautiously.

"So just how big a grudge are you holding against me?"

"Nice to hear from you, too. What the hell's your problem now?"

"I want to know just how bad you're feeling against me. Because I didn't give you that letter. You didn't get the job."

"Damn, you think well of yourself. I got a raft of letters, from scholars who . . . how shall I put this? Have a lot more pull in the field than you do. I decided not to take the job because it wasn't a good fit."

That was a lie, I was sure of it. "Still. You don't like it when things don't go your way."

"Can you name one person who does like it when things don't go their way?"

"So what's the deal with you and Noreen McAllister? Why is she lurking around Caldwell College?"

"I have no idea what you're talking about. Ask Noreen. If you haven't got anything important to discuss—"

"Oh, trust me when I say this is important. You're not having an affair with her?"

"That is none of your damned business."

"Sounds like a 'yes' to me."

"As a matter of fact, it wasn't. I'm not, not that it's any of your business, either. What's this all about?"

"And where have you been all summer? Any little trips to Maine or Massachusetts I should know about?"

"I'm going to hang up now. You take care, Emma. And you can look under 'Psychotherapists' or 'Psychologists' in the yellow pages, okay?"

I hung up before he could. Well, that didn't go nearly as well as I'd hoped. Duncan sounded confused, surprised, a lot of things, but not like he'd been expecting my call. Not like he had something to hide.

He was good at concealment, though, there was no one who knew it better than I. I made a few calls to his department and found out he'd been away for days at a time. Couldn't rule him off the list, but I had nothing else to pin on him either. I clenched my hands, wishing there was something more I could do, anything, to stop feeling so powerless. So off balance. Crazed.

Downstairs, the kitchen screen door slammed; I couldn't hear it, but I recognized the vibration. After a couple of years,

I'd learned all the creaks, noises, and shudders of the old house and where they were. My computer beeped, and small screen popped up.

"I'm home," Brian IM'd.

"K, brd," I responded. Okay, I'll be right down.

"CCOS," he typed. "Caution, Cats on Stairs" was a joke with us, after having discovered the hard way that both cats played on the stairs. *"What dinner?"*

"Don't care," I typed back. *"Not hungry."*

Chapter 12

THE DAY OF MEG'S WEDDING THE SATURDAY BE-
fore Labor Day was gorgeous, sunny, and warm. We
were lucky to be down on the lawn overlooking the harbor at
the Chandler site. We got there early, about 9:30, ostensibly
to help Meg, who'd been on 'red alert' for the past week; I
wanted to keep an eye on things.

Brian and I had already argued about clothes once that
morning, when he'd announced that if he was going to suf-
fer in the heat with a noose and shoes, then I wasn't allowed
to go with dress pants and flats. Now I was wearing a floral
print silk dress, vaguely 1930s in appearance with its short
sleeves and narrow silhouette. My shoes, strappy sandals,
seemed to be made for sitting. I'd thought a pair of flat shoes
and trousers would be more serviceable if someone tried
something at the wedding, but Brian refused to go if I didn't
wear the dress I'd bought for the occasion.

"So why is it that you're not more worried about the
wedding?" I asked, finally. "Why are you taking it so lightly,
when you seem to be so anxious about everything else?"

"Because I'll be there," Brian said, as if that made all the sense in the world.

Maybe it did, for him, but it didn't reassure me all that much. I bit back a hundred logical retorts, and found my purse.

We got there to find Meg had beaten us, and she was in a tizzy. Her dress was exquisite, even more lovely than it had seemed in my office—now that she had the appropriate foundation garments, and stockings now covered the legs that had been unshaved and scratched from fieldwork. Her hair was its usual platinum, but the spikes had been tamed beneath a small headdress, a golden crown of laurel leaves with a short veil. Two stray locks found their way up through the leaves, and the effect was altogether charming. Although she'd taken out her eyebrow ring, her many earrings fluttered festively. Someone had pinned her down and got just enough makeup on her to accent her eyes and yet not make her look like a clown. Meg was stunning, but the effect was ruined by her high color and the dangerous look in her eyes.

"What the hell do you mean, no one's set up the seats?" Her fiancé, Neal, a good foot taller than she, stepped back under the impact of her words. "All that miserable bastard Bray had to do was to have the groundskeeper open up the shed and set up forty chairs! How hard is that?"

"It's not hard, I'm sure he's just late—" he began. Neal looked as though he was about to sweat through his plain black tuxedo, though more anxious about his volatile bride than his approaching vows. But he didn't look any happier in his tie than Brian did.

Meg wasn't having it. "Bull! It should have been ready an hour ago."

I couldn't help but agree; this seemed like the start of another nasty surprise.

Brian volunteered to check whether the shed was open.

"We'll get it sorted out," Dian said. She was in the sleeveless, drop-waist lilac bridesmaid dress, which suited her dark hair so that she looked even sultrier than she did ordinarily. More baggable than your average bridesmaid, even. Perhaps the corporate world agreed with her, and I realized that she was responsible for Meg's bachelorette party. I was curious as to what that had been like.

"Yeah, well . . ." Meg wheeled on her friend, and Dian stepped back, but Neal was already working on containment.

"Hey, Emma," he said quickly. He began to carefully rub Meg's shoulders. "Did you have any problems when you got hitched?"

"Well," I said, "not problems like this. Trust me, this will be a great story tomorrow, Meg, don't worry about it. But what did happen was my mother got a little crazed, possessed by the same angry, suburban demon that drives the competition for space in the *New York Times* wedding pages. I was about to choke her when my sister took things in hand. Bucky'd come prepared for just this emergency.

"Bucky told our Maternal Parent that she needed to look after herself and eat something. Didn't she have to pay attention to her blood sugar? Of course, Mother loved the attention, and scarfed down a brownie from the batch that Bucky'd so thoughtfully prepared."

It was working. Meg was starting to get some of her normal color back, and Neal was grinning. Dian looked as though she wouldn't bolt just yet.

"I'd thought of having a brownie too, until Bucky gave me a warning look and said something stupid about not wanting me to break out. What she didn't say, and what you've probably already guessed, was that there was a generous helping of hash in the mixture. Ma got so stoned she didn't know what to do with herself.

"We had to hide the rest of the brownies before the army of aunts showed up, and worse yet, Mother got the munchies: If she'd eaten all the brownies she wanted, we would've had to scrape her off the ceiling. I felt like a rat and could have killed Bucky, of course, but I will admit, it improved my life dramatically for the next several hours. It was honestly one of Mother's more pleasant moments. By the time the cere-mony was over, everyone remarked on how . . . composed . . . she was. Like a Zen garden stone.

"Bucky laughed her head off the whole time. Mother keeps pestering us for the recipe. I finally told her that we lost it. But every Christmas, every Thanksgiving, and at all the wakes and weddings, Bucky threatens to rediscover that recipe."

I checked Meg, who was breathing normally now, and her color was better. "See? It wouldn't be a wedding without a story."

"Right," she said, and she stuck her bouquet into Dian's hands. "But now I'm going to break into the shed and get the chairs myself."

"You can't do that, Meg!" I pleaded. "Your dress! The dirt is still loose where I was working."

"I'll take it off, then," she said, and began reaching for the hem to pull her gown over her head.

"No, wait! We'll take care of it," Dian said. "Don't be an idiot."

I might have been curious to hear Meg's retort, but I was suddenly wondering whether we were going to find the groundskeeper in the shed as well. . . .

Brian came around to the side. "The shed's locked up tight. But it's not a great lock. If anyone has a Swiss Army knife—?"

I immediately reached into my purse, and at the same time Neal and his best man, his brother Craig, searched their trouser pockets. All three of us simultaneously pulled out our knives.

Brian chivalrously took mine; he felt my hand shaking, and held it tight a moment. "Everything will be fine," he said. He opened the hacksaw blade. "Trust archaeologists to come armed to a wedding," he muttered, shaking his head.

"Meg, come sit in the car for a minute," I ordered. "I've got some water. Brian's going to indulge in a spot of B&E, then he, Craig, and I will set up the chairs. What time do your folks get here?"

"Everyone is supposed to arrive in forty-five minutes. Neal's folks are getting his grandmother and they'll be right along, too," Meg said a little dizzily. Neal patted her hand again, but he too looked a little dazed.

"Plenty of time," I reassured her. "Brian, could you . . . ?"

He leaned over and kissed me. "You take me to the best parties. None of the other husbands get to break into anything. C'mon, Craig."

I led Meg over to the Jetta and sat her down. She looked like she was going to pass out, so I tried a joke. "I'm kind of surprised you didn't whip out your knife too, Meg."

She leaned over, and for a minute, I thought she was going to put her head between her knees to stave off a faint. But then she lifted up her skirt and showed me a tiny white satin holster on her garter. "I just brought the small one with the corkscrew," she said. "I didn't think I'd need a hacksaw on my wedding day!" Her face began to crumple.

"And so you don't," I said. "We've got it under control."

I made sure she drank some water, then Brian came back. He was sweating and his face was the picture of consternation.

"What's wrong?" I stood up, believing the worst had come to pass.

"I'm sweating my ba—" He caught himself. "I'm very warm. The shed is open, now, the chairs are there. Em, would you hold my jacket?"

"I'll help you." Good; no dead groundskeeper.

"No, you won't. Not in that dress and shoes. You just cool your heels a minute, and we'll get it all set up in a jiffy."

It didn't take long to do so but the first guests—and the groundskeeper—began to show up as they finished. I was glad for the moment to collect myself after the excitement.

"Everything okay?" Brian was at my side.

"I'm fine," I said, though my heart refused to stop pounding. "Let's go get our seats."

* * *

After a short and remarkably pretty ceremony, Meg and Neal were married. We all smiled when the minister asked if anyone had any reason they shouldn't be married, and there were a few giggles when Meg turned and glowered, daring anyone to speak up. At one point during his vows, he seemed so determined to get it right that Neal began to stammer. He almost stomped his foot, in a gesture more like Meg's than his own, trying to get hold of himself. Meg stood on tiptoe and kissed him, whispered something in his ear that made him blush and smile. He had no trouble after that. When they were finally pronounced married, their kiss—Meg on tiptoe again, Neal stooping—elicited an "ah" from the guests.

I turned and saw that Brian was looking back at me, the two of us remembering our own wedding day. I leaned over and quietly kissed him on the cheek.

"I love you," I whispered.

He took my hand, and whispered back, "I love you, too. And you look really, incredibly hot in that dress!"

I laughed and felt my shoulders relax slightly.

People were milling about, drinking champagne while the pictures were taken, and I watched Meg, her four brothers—all taller than Meg and mercilessly bullied by her—and her father as they posed for the family shots. Although her father was in a tuxedo for the wedding, and through the years, Meg had referred to him variously as "the lieutenant," "Ghenghis," "the admiral," "Kaiser," and "the sarge," after a short conversation I was finally able to determine that he was probably properly called Colonel Garrity.

But I couldn't sit still or make polite conversation. I paced about, hoping that locked up chairs were the least of our worries. I scrutinized the guests carefully. My gaze lit on the treeline where we'd discovered a body, several years ago, but I saw nothing there. I knew there was no one in the house, after a quick circuit, and there was no one by the water. That left the road and the trees where someone could come in.

"Here," Brian said, handing me a glass of champagne. "Settle down, there, killer. You look like a guard dog running the perimeter."

I nodded. "Yeah, well. Don't forget, Meg was the one responsible for stopping Tony that night at the Point."

"Drink the wine, Em. Try to have a good time. I'm here, we're both keeping our eyes open, it's okay. I'm going over to see if Meg needs a glass of water or a snack to keep going."

"She'd probably prefer a beer," I called after him.

There was so much hubbub at the tree line on one side of the lawn, where the buffet was, that I went over to see if I could help. I found Fee, Fiona Prowse, there, run off her feet. She was so often the picture of the unflappable and competent accountant that I knew she was in trouble—one of her ringlets had escaped its lacquered fastness and stood up like a question mark over the rest of her helmet head. She looked like a character for Dr. Seuss that I had to stop myself from staring.

"Emma . . . ?" She wasn't greeting me, and not really asking what I wanted. She didn't trust me, though long ago, I'd kept secrets for her.

"What can I do to help, Fee?" I really didn't like her, but I would do almost anything to keep the wedding going smoothly. Once in charge of the books, she now also managed the Chandler house property. Something was bothering her, as she hadn't even gotten the groundskeeper there on time.

"The caterer. She's got several more trips. Just wait here to answer any questions she might have. And she's arrived late."

"Fine, no problem." As if I knew anything about the plans.

"Excuse me, I've got to make a few quick calls." And she was off, without another word.

I looked at the tables. Beautifully simple, ivory cloths with pale lilac plates that were the colors Meg chose for her "backup," as she called her bridesmaids, darker purple flowers in simple-to-the-point-of-starkness arrangements that suggested formality, kept from being flouncy or stuffy, and yet were gorgeous. Meg had succeeded in keeping her wedding from looking like what Bucky had once described as "an explosion at the potpourri factory."

There was one thing that didn't match, I noticed. One of the platters didn't match the others. Pretty enough, white china, but wrapped in plastic wrap and not the little mesh tents, or silver chafing dishes, or plastic containers that the caterer was using. Frowning, I went over to check it out.

I had just picked it up when I heard a sharp voice. "Can I help you?"

A harassed young African-American woman in immaculate chef's whites was behind me, setting down a large blue plastic insulated box.

"Uh, I was just . . ."

"You can't leave that here, I've already discussed the set up with Ms. Garrity, the bride. Perhaps you could keep it at your table; but I don't have enough space for guest's dishes." Her name tag said CHEF VICTORIA.

I shook my head. "It's not mine. I wanted to check it . . ." Shit! What the hell could I tell her? "I'm worried someone's trying to hurt the bride."

She looked at me, her face immobile, clearly assessing my sanity. "Oh?"

"Look, it sounds crazy, but . . ." I told her briefly about the situation at the site. No reason to go into elaborate detail. "I've been trying to keep an eye out for her. I just didn't want anything to spoil today. This didn't fit here, but it could be . . . I dunno. Aunt Minnie's Swedish meatballs or something. I just don't want anyone to eat it, until we know for sure."

She cast an expert eye over the plate. "It looks like phyllo to me. It might be Aunt Melina's spanikopita, but I don't want it here, you don't want it here. I'll stick it in the hot chest, and when someone squawks, I'll pull it out, say I was keeping it warm. But only if it looks like Aunt Melina, and not some head case."

"Thank you!" I didn't bother keeping the relief from my voice. "I know how crazy—"

"Don't worry about it." Chef Victoria didn't have time for thanks or debate. "Like I said, I don't want it here, and you've given me the perfect excuse to hide it. Besides, anyone gets sick at one of my jobs, you know prospective clients are not going to bother to remember that it was some stalker. I've got my sterling reputation to maintain."

I nodded. "Can I help you with anything? Fee said you were running a bit behind."

"Thank you, no. You'll understand if I say I'll get this done a lot faster without you getting in the way." Victoria picked up the odd platter and fixed me with a look. "And that Fee can say I was late all she wants, but I told her sixty times that I'd be here at ten-thirty for eleven-thirty. I was fifteen minutes early, and so were my assistants. And I'll say no more on that subject."

"I've . . . worked with Fee before. I understand."

Chef Victoria nodded. "I'll put this away, unload the rest of the food, and then adorn myself with my hat, so everyone will know who to thank for the amazing meal they're about to eat." She picked up the platter, and looked at it more closely. "Pity. It's a pretty pattern. German, I bet; my mom used to collect china. A little old-fashioned. Love the lilies of the valley."

I had just turned away but was arrested by her words. "Chef Victoria. Please be very careful with that plate, how you handle it. I don't think there is any Aunt Melina and I'd like to save it."

After a few hours, people began to clear out. The food was decimated, and yet the chef had managed to keep everything looking neat and presentable down to the last crumb. I noticed that she sent one of her assistants to the car for more business cards, they flew away so quickly.

Chef Victoria packaged up the leftovers beautifully, and Meg wouldn't need to cook for the next week. She saved the china plate for me.

I took it. "No Aunt Melina?"

"Nope. No Aunt Melina."

"Okay, thanks."

She looked at me, politely curious. "What are you going to do with it?"

I looked over to where Brian was talking with Neal; both had a bottle of beer. Brian was obviously giving Neal his patented "how-to-stay-married speech." There was the joke version: "learn to say, 'Anything you want, dear.'" Then there was the real list: don't go to bed angry, try to argue about what you're arguing about, trust the other person, keeping up fifty percent of the relation isn't nearly enough, etcetera. "I'm going to give it to a chemist I know," I said to her. "See if he can tell me anything about it."

She gave me a look that suggested that she still thought I had a few bats in the belfry. "Well. I hope you enjoyed the rest of the wedding."

"Oh, yes. Very nice." My stomach was in a knot, but now slowly unclenching. Meg and Neal were married, and I wouldn't tell them about the plate or my worries.

Victoria's mouth twitched. "If you find I'm going to be catering any other functions you attend this summer?"

"Yes?"

"Give me the head's up first, would you?" She was smiling ruefully, and I found I had to, too. "I'll want to keep an eye out for Aunt Melina."

"You got it."

"What's that?" Brian was looking at the plate of food I handed him when we got home. "Can I have some?"

"No! It showed up uninvited to the wedding. And no one claimed it. I want you to test it for me. Test it for poisons. So don't eat it."

He cocked his head. "What exactly do you want me to do with it?"

"Can't you test it, see if there are compounds in it that shouldn't be? I mean, take your favorite poisons and try them out. Or something?"

He asked, "Why would I want to torment a perfectly nice looking plate of spanikopita? Em, I didn't see anyone there who looked dangerous."

Trust a man to believe that he could sense evil from afar. "Because no one came to collect the plate afterward. Because Meg was the one to stop Tony—she shot him—and the wedding is too public, too good an opportunity to pass up, if he's looking for revenge." I looked him in the eye. "Because I very seldom ask you to do anything like this. And it's no more cautious than you've been on other occasions."

Brian's lips compressed and his eyes narrowed in thought. "Okay. There's a toy I'm quite desperate to use and I happen to be owed a favor by its keeper. But if it comes up negative, not poisonous, can I eat it then?"

I wrinkled my nose. "Who knows how long it was sitting in the sun? I wouldn't."

Brian smirked. "I'll feed them to Kam. That way, we'll find out for sure."

"Why—" But I knew why. Brian and Kam worked together, and the fact that Marty wasn't speaking to me probably affected their friendship as well as their working relationship. Brian was taking my side. "Sure. If Kam doesn't keel over, you can try one, too. Just make sure that you nuke them first. Kill off the biggest cooties."

Brian took the plate, but he didn't look happy. I didn't care, he said he'd do it, and he would. That was one of the things I loved about him.

Brian came home Tuesday night, a look of disbelief on his face. "I think we have a positive for ricin. I would have called you, but I asked Roddy to run the test again, just to make sure I wasn't doing something wrong. The mass spectrophotometer is his baby."

"Rice 'n' what?" I said. "Mass what?"

"Just ricin. It's derived from the waste of processing castor beans. A powerful poison. I remember reading that it was used on an umbrella tip to poison someone in London. And the mass spectrophotometer takes the sample you give it and determines the molecular weight of all the compounds in it. Then it tells you what the 'mother' was. In this case, it was ricin."

"So there's no chance it could have gotten into the food accidentally?" I was reaching, I knew.

"None. The symptoms show up in a matter of hours, and if you're not treated—well, there is no antidote, by the way— you can die within a couple of days."

"So no one got into it at the wedding," I said, half to my-self. "Thank God for that, at least."

Just then, Brian's shorts rang. He pulled his phone from his pocket and answered it. "Yeah? Hey. Seriously? Wow. Okay, thanks, man. Just put it someplace . . . oh. Good idea. Thanks again."

He hung up. "It was Roddy. He's confirmed it. Holy shit."

I sat down. "Yeah."

"Okay, well, first thing, we should call the cops."

"Yeah, I guess so. Which ones?"

"Hell, all of them. Stone Harbor first? I mean, that's where the stuff showed up. And you know Bader there, so that can't hurt."

"I suppose."

I called, and Bader was in. He greeted me in a friendly fashion. After he'd heard my story, he was concerned and then annoyed.

"You should have called me right away," he said gruffly. "You shouldn't go tampering with evidence like that."

"What evidence? I mean, we know now. And if someone had eaten it, I guess we would have found out quickly enough. But at the time, what was I supposed to do? Call you in to investigate a plate of food? There was no crime scene!"

"You might have brought it straight to me, if you were that worried," he insisted.

"Would you have believed me? And based on what evidence could you have brought it to the State Police crime lab? You know better than I how backed up and underfunded they are."

"Just let me talk to your husband," Bader said.

"Why?" I liked Bader, but he had an old-fashioned chauvinistic streak that occasionally rubbed me the wrong way. Like calling women girls, and that sort of thing.

"Don't get up on your high horse. He was the one who conducted the test, right?"

"Hang on." I handed the phone to Brian.

"Hello? Oh, yes, positive without a doubt. Or at least, so little doubt as to be . . . what? United Pharmaceuticals. In Cambridge. Well, I'm pretty sure it won't be disturbed. The whole thing, plate and the rest of the sample? It's been put into a storage freezer. Yep, very tightly wrapped and we marked it with tape that says "radioactive," so I don't think anyone will confuse it with their lunch. Just me, and my colleague. Emma and the chef, that's right. Yes, we have her card," Brian said, nodding at me, as I dug it out of my purse and waved it at him. "You'll contact her? Good."

There were a few more pauses, and I wished I'd put them on speaker phone. "No, it's directed toward Emma," Brian said. "Completely. No, we don't know who, but it's getting more and more serious all the time. I'm more than concerned. I'm scared out of my wits, actually."

I put my hand on his arm.

"I didn't catch that? Well, there was no body found, and there seem to be other clues that it's him . . . his style, if you like. He would be the most likely—Perry Taylor's in prison, isn't she? I think it's possible. Well, I used to think it was only improbable to impossible, so yes, I am actually moving to that conclusion. Yes, until a better suspect comes along, and Emma's been careful to work on ruling those . . . I think you should take it seriously, too."

My heart soared. Brian was talking about Tony.

"Yes, I know she's not the authorities, but it's only recently that we've had something more concrete. Yes. Yes, I will. Good night."

Brian hung up.

"Well?" I asked.

"He's pissed you didn't go straight to him, but we have to live with that. I'm going to give him the report—mine and Roddy's—the plate, all the names of the people who handled it. It seems that he thinks you've got a fan in Stuart Feldman, and he might be able to do something about getting a friend of his to look at the rest of the food—the sample."

"Okay. Well, thanks for sticking up for me." I felt myself choking up. "Thanks for bringing the stuff to the lab."

"Hey, what else am I here for?" He held me tight. "And it was fun." Brian pulled back, looking sick, though. I felt none too good myself.

"I'm going to call Dave Stannard, up in Maine," he said. "And then I'm going to be out on the porch for a while."

I thought briefly about protesting, but Brian was right. Everyone had to know.

I nodded. "I'll be right there."

"Don't be too long, Em, okay?"

I nodded again. I needed to think. I couldn't tell Meg, I couldn't ruin her wedding memories, especially since no one got hurt. I would tell her, though, to be even more careful than usual. Quasimodo the cat yowled at the door. I let him in, and watched him mow down some food while I got the bourbon out. Quasi finished in a hurry, and ran back over to the door, looking at me hopefully.

"No way, cat. You stay in whenever I catch you; there's coyotes out at night. Consider yourself caught."

Quasi growled; I poured my drink. Eventually he slunk off, sulking as obviously as any human. I went upstairs.

Tony knows everything about me, I thought. He knows I abhor bullies, and so that's why he went for Chuck. And Dora, I thought suddenly; for all her forceful personality, she has a lot to protect, and he found that out. He knows the painting meant something to me, and that was taken, possibly destroyed. He knows how I feel about the site, about my crews, about the artifacts. It wouldn't be hard for him to find out about Dora's parents—he might have been one of the few people to know, having been here as long as she—or Marty and Sophia or my parents. And Meg, there's all of that . . . And don't forget Michael—

I put the bottle down suddenly. How did he know about Michael Glasscock?

Michael had been to the house exactly once. Michael and I knew each other from a brief month of research at the Shrewsbury Library. While anyone could have read about the murders that left us alone in the house together—suspecting each other—there was nothing that would indicate that we'd kept in touch since. I couldn't even describe our relationship: Michael was dismissive and rude about my style of research, clinging as he claimed, to antiquated notions of material evidence. At the same time, he occasionally sent me references that were spot on for my work, and got me thinking down avenues I would never consider, but it always made my research better and more interesting. For my part, I asked him questions about the history of philosophy for the periods I studied, and maybe my "almost Neanderthal obsession with the mundane, the quotidian, and the material" inspired him in the same way. Not that he would have admitted it.

Brian was vaguely jealous of Michael. Despite the fact that I found him attractive, it had never been anything more than an amusing sort of crush, mostly based on how his brain appealed to me. Brian had said that was worse than mere physical attraction and teased me mercilessly about it. And Michael was notoriously attracted to anything with a double-X chromosome. Whoever sent that image knew that there had been a frisson between us.

But we never even spoke on the phone, aside from that call last week, and he never even sent me anything in the mail, so it couldn't be by rifling my college mailbox—

But my home mail was another story. That had been violated.

Michael never sent me anything there.

It has to be through email. And anyone with half a brain looking at even one of Michael's most innocent emails would have picked up on his obsession with sex and sensuality. It just came off him like a pheromone.

I called Michael, just to be sure he hadn't sent me anything through the post.

Michael was amused, naturally. "Nope. Not me. Why, did you get a naked picture of me?"

It really was tiring; how did men keep so constantly engaged by sex? I mean, it's fun, but I'm not thinking about it twenty-four-seven. It had its place, but it seemed Michael had more places than me. "I'm trying to find out how someone would know we've been in contact."

"And know enough to send tawdry and yet infinitely compelling pictures to me?" he said. "That is disquieting. No, I haven't sent you anything in the mail."

"So it's email. Someone must be getting into my email."

"You've got firewalls and software and shit, though, right?"

"Of course I do." I do now, anyway. "It could also be someone tampering with my machine at work."

"Good thing whoever it is didn't slash your credit record," Michael said.

"Right. Got that covered." However stupid I'd been about firewalls, I was very careful about my credit and had it protected, checked, several times a year. And Brian had double-checked as soon as people started getting presents that I didn't send; I figured my credit report was next. "Thanks Michael."

"Whatever, Auntie. Say, did you want to hear about what my friend the graphologist had to say about the letter?"

"You got it already?"

"Sure. The most interesting thing that happens to me all week, you think I'm going to sit on it?"

I let the potential double entendre slide. "What did she say?"

He paused dramatically. "It's a fake."

"Yeah? I could have told you that."

"No, you don't understand. Someone was trying to imitate your handwriting, as well as cover up their own."

"Right. That makes sense."

"But why not just type it? Add a signature? Wouldn't that make more sense?"

"Only if you think I'd type mash notes."

"Dear God in heaven. 'Mash notes?' " Michael sighed, disappointed in me again. "What century is that from?"

"I'm sorry, Michael. I haven't got your experience with pornographic literature. Or love notes, for that matter." Ouch, Emma, that might have been a little much. "I mean, well, what do you call it?"

"A solicitation? Invitation? Exhortation? Invocation? Sure as hell not a mash note."

"Whatever."

Michael was curious now. "So. Would you? Type them?"

"I'm not in the habit of—no." I sighed. "Short answer, no. Did she give you anything else?"

"Just that it was a good job, for an imperfect forgery. While it wasn't an exact copy of your handwriting, there was enough attention to detail to get things like the spacing and drops correct. There was one thing, however, that reminded her of your Tony's handwriting."

"What was that?"

"The distance from the margins. That seemed to be very like the sample you sent me. It is, however, significantly less than conclusive as to identity. But whoever it is, is strange about the past. Connected and disconnected all at once."

I couldn't help asking: I wondered what my writing said about me. "And mine?"

He didn't answer right away. "How old is the sample you sent?"

"Pretty recent. Earlier this summer, I think."

"You're much more interested in the future, right now. Looking to make a change, maybe? But you're agitated, something's up, is what she said."

"That's a surprise?" It sounded like nonsense to me. "I couldn't tell you."

"Thanks for trying. And you'll send those right back to me? I don't know which is safer. Send it to my house I guess. Request a signature, okay?"

"Okeydoke. Just as soon as Trish the Ink gets the outline of my tattoo done."

The doorbell chimed the next morning. Artie, I thought. I went downstairs with an odd mixture of triumph, dread, and reluctance: No one likes confrontation.

After I let him in, he glanced hopefully at the coffeepot. Thinking that I'd catch more flies with coffee than vinegar, I'd made a batch and now invited him to sit. Artie looked chuffed. Finally, I was starting to appreciate the way he deserved to be treated. I was only sorry I didn't think to get donuts for him.

"So. Artie," I started, after he'd settled in. "There have been some strange goings-on around here."

He stopped in mid-slurp. "Oh yeah? What kinda strange?"

"Someone's been into my mail. You haven't noticed anyone lurking around here, or down by the mailbox, have you?"

"Oh, no. No."

The answer came a little too fast for me. "See, I think someone stole some of my mail, and the problem is, they might have grabbed a few bills along with it. The phone company, the electric—I'm getting second notices and stuff." I kept it something he might be able to relate to. "Are you sure you haven't seen anyone?"

"Like I said. I didn't see anyone." He seemed much more confident now.

"Okay. Just checking." I took a sip of my coffee, not tasting it, trying to feign casualness. "Hey, last week and a half or so? You didn't happen to leave the house when I went out to run some errands, did you?"

He took a big swallow of coffee. "Why would I do that?"

Aha! "Maybe to get some more supplies," I said, trying to hide my impatience and my growing excitement. "It could happen to anyone as busy as you are. There's a hardware store, not five minutes away. It wouldn't have taken you long to run out, run back." Grab a cruller. Grab a dozen.

"Well. Let me think." He glanced away, drank noisily.

I gave him a few moments, smiling, wishing I could shake him.

"You know, now that you mention it, I might have needed some outlet plates. I might have run out and picked up a few of those. And—"

"What?" He'd stopped so suddenly, I knew he'd thought of something.

He proceeded nervously. "I thought it was nothing. I figured it was a neighbor, maybe. Leaving something in your box. I didn't see him take anything."

I felt my pulse speed up. "What did he look like?"

"I dunno. A guy. Medium height, medium build. Older, I guess, but not too old. I didn't see him take anything. He waved at me," he finished, as if that was significant.

"Oh. Well, that helps. It sounds like my neighbor," I lied. "I'll check with him, see if he's had any problems."

"And I wasn't gone all that long," Artie said.

"Well, you see, it helps. If you'd been working, you wouldn't have seen him, and then I wouldn't know to ask him."

It was weak, but more than enough of an excuse for Artie, who set about finishing his coffee and bustling about his work with a focus and efficiency that I hadn't seen before.

I went down to the post office and let them know about the

mailbox being rifled. I hadn't noticed anything else was missing, no, I explained as patiently as I could, but then, I hadn't known about Sophia's picture coming either, so I didn't know what else might have gone missing. I was concerned about recurrences.

They gave me the appropriate form to fill out, told me that the supervisor would be notified, and if anything else happened, it would go to the Post Master, then the Postal Inspector, if necessary, for investigation. Until then, I had a choice of doing nothing, renting a post office box, or getting a lock for the mailbox we had.

I figured since Tony had never really hit the same place more than once, he wouldn't be back, but wasn't going to take the chance and promised them I'd get a lock and give a key to my letter carrier. I'd wait until he started blowing up the mailboxes to apply for a post office box.

The next evening, I came down from my office to answer the doorbell: it was the overnight guy with the original letter and picture back from Michael. He must have had someone else—an assistant, an adoring undergraduate intern—do the label, because it was legible. I opened the envelope, and found another envelope, and a note.

I recalled that Michael's scrawl was nearly impossible to read, and I had to wonder what his friend had made of *his* writing, but perhaps out of courtesy to me, he'd typed his note. It read: "Auntie, here's the pic and the letter. My friend handled it carefully, with gloves (she's used to working with me), and as little as possible, so the cops shouldn't get anything else but my fingerprints on it. Sorry about that. Let me know when you catch this freak; I'm worried about me now. Michael." The signature was barely recognizable as such.

The graphologist was used to working with Michael? Was that some kind of euphemism? Or was she merely used to handling historical documents?

I found a pair of disposable latex gloves in the kitchen and opened the interior envelope carefully. When I pulled the image out, I turned away out of habit, but the thing's fascination and my own need to know what was going on overtook prudishness.

Michael was right; it was a good job. There was an egregiousness to the breasts, and too much perfection; even so, I thought, mine were better. But if my legs had been that long, I'd have given up archaeology for the stage, and there was a slight awkwardness to the neck where the image of my head had been attached. I didn't recognize the picture itself, but the hair was long, so it had to be from a while ago. Years, maybe. And why was my head back, eyes closed . . . I dislike having my picture taken, so I usually try to compose myself. This was a candid; I was laughing. But in this context, it looked like sexual ecstasy.

I put the picture aside and picked up the note, which Michael had been cautious enough to put in an acid-free document holder. I pulled it out, and read it. Again, he'd been correct; there were elements that one could argue were stylistically similar to mine—whoever had written this was familiar with my work—and there were certain quirks of punctuation and word use that were reminiscent of my writing. I seriously doubted, however, that if I'd written this note, I would have been quite so . . . rooted . . . in my academic persona.

And the porn wasn't anything like my personal fantasy life.

That cheered me up. Whoever was doing this might know a lot about me, might know that I favored certain words, but didn't know diddly about the real me, inside me. What was private—really private—was still safe.

I thought about giving Marty a call, telling her about this, and then realized that I couldn't. I still hadn't heard back from her. Ditto with Bucky. I actually thought about calling Michael back, but it wasn't really the kind of thing I could talk about with him.

Brian came in from work and glanced at the pile of papers. "What's that? Holy—!"

As his eyes widened, I resisted the urge to cover up the picture. After all, if several total or near strangers had already seen it, then who was I to hide it from Brian?

I handed him a pair of gloves. "This was sent to Michael Glasscock. You know, the guy from Shrewsbury a couple of years ago?"

He looked at the gloves, then shrugged and put them on. His eyes went straight back to the picture. "The one who came over, just as we got the news about Sophia being born? Yeah, I remember. We left him, he almost set fire to the house trying to cook a hotdog, and then he drank all the good bourbon. But why—?"

"The same reason someone would send flowers to your mother, meat to my father, and chocolates to my mother. Screw with me."

Brian looked thoughtful. "Yeah, but . . . why couldn't this all be from Michael?"

"Huh? Because it isn't, that's why."

"Hell, Em, the guy's a flake. Remember the first time I saw him? He was sleeping on the floor of the living room, in his raincoat. I mean, he's not normal. And you've always said he was a bit of a pervert."

"I said he was obsessed with women. Pervert is different."

"Okay, tell me the difference."

"Brian, will you stop peeing on my parade? It wasn't Michael. He's living with Sasha—"

"How do you know?"

"He told me."

Brian let that hang between us for a while.

"He wouldn't do something like this," I repeated, but then I remembered what Michael'd said about stalking women years ago . . . he was the outlier in all these occurrences, after all. And what if he'd sent the image to himself as a matter of indirection?

Brian shrugged. "Why not? You told me he was spending all his time looking at nude images in the library. I wouldn't cross him off your list so easily."

I tried to find the reasons. "I'm not his type. I'm too . . . ordinary. And besides, he'd be way more obvious. He's not the sort to do something . . . as coy as this."

"I still think you're giving him too much credit. It's a possibility, isn't it?

"Fine. I know Michael better than you, that should count for something. And I can call up and talk to Sasha. Find out if he's actually with her."

"Like living with someone would prevent him from doing this." He picked up the cellophane envelope. "Why all the shrouds? Covers? A bit like a striptease, isn't it?"

I looked at him; it was not the sort of thing he'd come up with on his own.

"Hey, I took English in college," he said defensively. "I know how those guys think. All layers and revealing and stuff."

"He put it in the envelopes so that there wouldn't be any more fingerprints."

"Any more? So his are on there? Emma"—he looked at me doubtfully—"look, you are going to give this stuff to the cops, right?"

"I want to, but I suddenly wondered . . . who? I mean, what jurisdiction?"

"Maybe you should leave that up to them. I bet Bader would be willing to hold on to it, until we sort this out."

"Probably."

"You're embarrassed to show this to them, aren't you?"

"Aren't you?" I answered. I could feel my face going red.

Brian shrugged. "I don't like it. But I know it isn't you, and I'm not going to keep evidence from them just because I'm embarrassed."

"Maybe." I was still mad at him for trying to blame Michael. It just wasn't Michael's style, any more than that letter was mine. And yet, I could hardly fault him for trying to find a ready solution to this.

Brian picked up the letter and read it. I watched interest and curiosity cross his face, and finally he frowned and put it down. "It doesn't sound like you."

"I didn't think so." That was something, at least. I needed to feel close to someone, I needed to know that Brian still was there, that he still knew me, no matter what was going on. What ever problems there might be between us, our relationship was only strained, not broken.

"I don't know. If you really felt this way about someone, you'd send them something . . . Shakespeare. And you'd only do it if whoever was going to get it knew just exactly how much passion that meant for you. It wouldn't matter if they got the poem or the reference, or whatever, it would matter that they knew you knew." He looked at the letter, then straight at me. "You'd save the hot stuff for the bedroom."

I leaned over and kissed him hard. "Yes. Exactly."

I spent the next afternoon dropping off the materials at the Stone Harbor police department. Bader's face didn't change much when I told him what was in the envelope, but it was the fixedness of his expression that told me he was disturbed. After, I returned home and went up to my office. Tried to get into my office, anyway: I realized that the end-of-season clutter had merged disastrously with the new semester's piles of papers and files. If I did nothing else today, I would have to clean a path to my computer, maybe put some of the summer's work back in the barn.

After putting the drying screens aside, I rearranged the books and papers into what could arguably be called more-organized piles. At least I could move freely through the room after a few hours of sorting, and had a good idea where everything was. I brought the screens, now empty of the artifacts I'd cleaned, down to the barn for storage.

I opened the padlock, and pulled the door open. When we'd first bought the place, I was nearly certain that the barn would have to come down, but had soon learned that it wasn't in as bad shape as its appearance suggested. Most of the older barns in New England seem to be standing up through memory only. The smell of old dirt and rotting wood and oil—it had been made into a garage after it had housed animals—hit me, and I thought about how nice and cool it would have been here, before it was closed up as a garage. Not so now. It was stifling.

I flipped the light switch on and set the screens off to the side. As I was turning around to get the next load, I realized that the tool bench was also due for a sorting out, cluttered with the safety stuff Brian had for using power tools, a pile of boxes of fasteners—ah, the hand vac I needed. As I went over to get it, I noticed an extension cord was plugged into the outlet behind the bench.

I frowned. It was black; we only used orange. Easier to see.

The cord ran up to the loft. Since every odd occurrence was now suspect, I climbed the stairs to the loft—and then went back downstairs to get a flashlight. The lights were only on the first level.

On my way back up the stairs, I noticed that there was a fresh crack in the wood of the stairs. I hadn't heard a crack going up the first time. This was fresh, not filled in with dirt or dust. Someone had been up here, someone heavier than me. I didn't think Brian had been in the barn in some time.

The extension cord snaked up a beam; it was nearly invisible. I traced its path with the light, and realized that there was a small bulge in the supporting beam. I had never seen this before. I went over to inspect it.

It was a camera. Pointed out the window. Aimed at the house.

I shuddered, then pulled out my cell phone. I pressed one of my speed dial numbers—I was getting to be a very technical girl. "Hi, it's me," I said, knowing Joel had caller ID. "I found something. How soon can you be over?"

"I'll leave right away," Joel said. "It'll be a couple of hours. Don't touch anything."

"No problem," I said, and hung up. I called Bader, left a message saying what I'd found and when Joel would be over, and said I would wait to hear back from him. Then I called Brian and left a message for him, trying to be as reassuring as I could.

I got a call back from Bader, about two hours later. "Don't touch anything. I'll be over with one of my people. What time will your guy be there?"

I told him.

"Good; we'll be there when he gets there. Don't touch anything."

Despite what everyone seemed to think, I had no desire to touch anything. As excited as I was by this discovery, I was also creeped out beyond words. After a few minutes of trying to guess what could be seen through the lens, I went back into the house and tried to work. I spent the next half hour pacing, and running to the window every time I heard a car.

Tony, you son of a bitch, I thought. You were just too damn clever for your own good. If you'd stayed at the surface level, with the obvious stuff, you would have gotten away with it. But you had to get complicated. And that's what will finally give you away.

Bader and a uniformed officer showed up a few moments before Joel did. I made the introductions, and then Joel and the uniformed cop spoke to each other. I am proud of my command of English, am reasonably fluent in French, have a smattering of Latin, and because of Brian's influence, about six words of Spanish. I had no idea what they were saying to each other, after several minutes of conversation, and, to judge by his face, neither did Bader. I got the impression that they were trading credentials, feeling each other out, and eventually both were satisfied they were speaking the same language. At least they were; I could tell that Bader was no more informed than I.

"Here's the plan," the uniformed officer said. "We're going to take the camera and the extension cord. We'll send someone over for prints later. But we're going to have a look at whatever the camera's been seeing, too."

"You remember, there's been nothing transmitted from the camera through the network since we encrypted the wireless network," Joel said to me. "About two weeks now."

The uniform put on some gloves, messed with some cables, and then plugged in a notebook computer to the camera. He typed a bit, and then an image came up. Surreally, I now could see two versions of the side yard of the house and the driveway. I watched fascinated as a car went down the street. Another one followed, and I shivered as I watched Brian's truck pull into the driveway. Whoever had set this up could see our comings and goings easily. They could also see into the kitchen, back bedroom, and into the dining room.

I thanked heaven that I was still scrupulous about pulling the blinds, even though there were no neighbors to pry. Sometimes being uptight is its own reward.

After a moment, I said, "Can we, I don't know . . . trace this back to whoever was looking at it? Can we find out where he is?"

The uniformed cop and Joel both shook their heads. "No, it's set to an address on the web. There's no access log, so you can't get at the address that way."

Brian joined us as the police were taking everything down and bagging it. He looked so alarmed that Bader stepped in immediately.

"This is very good," the detective said. "A tremendous break. We might be able to learn something from the equipment here, and we might get lucky and get some prints when our guys come by. In any case, you've really done some serious damage to this jerk. Good work, Emma."

After they left, Brian and I ordered takeout, and I tried to foster a celebratory feeling. The best I could do was that scrubbed and virtuous feeling you get from cleaning or paying taxes. Not fun, in and of itself, but satisfying. Something accomplished. The more I thought about it, the more I was uneasy and reassured at the same time: We'd removed a dangerous snake from the house.

I even had the good grace to tell Brian that he'd been on the right track. He was gracious enough not to say "I told you so."

Maybe Tony's getting desperate, getting sloppy, I thought, as I threw out the sushi containers. Maybe this means he'll show his hand sooner rather than later.

The next day, Saturday, I had an evening class with Nolan for the first time in several weeks. He'd gone on vacation just after we had. Going to a regular class after so long was good, felt normal, and I embraced it wholeheartedly.

As I walked through the parking lot, I realized that I simply hate early fall. The acorns are starting to fall and make a racket and a mess, the weather is hot and humid, then cool, and you're always dressed wrong. At least with spring, it's like something's struggling to become; with the end of summer, it's like something's in its death throes and can't just get down to it. I hate indecisiveness in people; in seasons it's worse. The ominousness, the portentiousness of it all—birds behaving differently, the leaves getting brittle but not yet turning color—might as well be three-headed cows and babies born speaking Latin backward, as far as I'm concerned. I'm itchy for something concrete to happen, even while I'm sweating and trying to get my lesson plans in order.

The crickets were rasping like a fingernail against a comb, and there were patches of burnt-out color on the trees. I realized that I felt twitchy, like I was at the starting gate, conditioned by years of getting ready for the first day of school. It never goes away, that anticipation. . . .

Brian told me that feeling comes from the light changing and the days getting shorter, and I should take a nap or something. I was living on naps, these days, now that I was always waking up so damned early, and trust him to find the chemical reason for my anticipation of the school year. He also said that I might be projecting. I could believe that.

Just fifty minutes later, nothing was farther from my mind. Somehow, Johanna'd done it again. I was pinned to the mat, and Johanna was sitting on top of me, and she'd managed to hold me down—somehow—simply by keeping my own left arm across my neck and tucking the wrist behind my head. I couldn't get out. I tried bucking, but I was laughing too hard: Johanna had gotten me into this hold before and now she was laughing too, giving me a noogie, just to show off how much better at grappling she was than I.

"If you two ladies are done playing and chatting here, perhaps we could save the rest of the coffee klatch for later and move on with the rest of the class?" Nolan was standing over us both, almost frowning, which meant trouble.

"This isn't a coffee klatch!" I said, breathing hard. "Get off me, you cow!"

Johanna gave me another set of noogies, just for good measure, and jumped up lightly. "Me, cow? You're the one who always gets trussed up, Bessie."

I got up, and pretended to stumble, then threw a round kick at her. Johanna scooted back, only just in time. Under Nolan's impassive—and somehow, at the same time, disapproving—gaze, we got back to our knees, touched hands, then started another bout of grappling.

This time, instead of my usual few moments of feinting and sizing her up, I immediately faked a shot high to her shoulder, then tackled her at the waist. She went back, with me on top of her, and I got into the mount, sitting on her chest. We were both too tired to do much of anything—it was the very end of the class—but I did know that Johanna had a weakness for the very dangerous backdoor escape. I pretended to fumble, giving her the indication that I was going to try for side control, and gave her the hint of an opening that I knew she was looking for. She rolled over and tried to scuttle out backward between my legs, but this time I was

ready for her. Instead of following through with the side
mount, I waited until she was just about to move, and I got
my hooks in. Now she was trapped on her stomach with me
on her back, and my feet hooked under her legs. It was about
the worst position you could be in. Even worse than being
pinned down with your own arm and given noogies.

"Moo for me, Jo," I said.

She couldn't moo; she was laughing too hard, which
bounced me around, but only pressed her into the mat harder.

"Time! Line it up!" Nolan shouted to the class, studiously
ignoring us.

We hustled off the floor, into the lineup with the other four
students, and bowed out for the day. While the others packed
up their pads and gear, I caught Nolan heading back to his
office. "Got a minute?"

"Just one. Shoot."

"That hold that Jo always gets me in? How the hell do you
get out of it?"

Nolan frowned again. "You can't really; you have to act
on it as soon as you feel her intent. Anticipate it, and don't
get into it in the first place. Don't give her the opening."

"Easier said than done," I muttered.

"That's why I'm here, Red. To beat your bad habits out of
you. You've already got the instinct. You're starting to set Johanna up, exploiting her bad habits; you got her good because
you just wanted to beat her badly enough. You didn't stop to
think. And don't I keep telling you? Fighting is like sex or
chess: once you get in the groove, you're better off not over-
thinking it. But not too shoddy, tonight, Red. Not too shoddy."

I was almost wiggling, I was so pleased with his praise.
"Thanks, Nolan."

He grinned a wolf's grin. "All you have to do now is improve yourself."

"Oh, great. Very helpful, thanks. See you Thursday."

"Thursday it is, Red."

I ignored his use of my hated nickname—Nolan not only
could isolate your physical weaknesses, he could also

pinpoint your emotional Achilles heel as well—and went out onto the floor to collect my towel, water, and gear. I met Jo on the way out.

Just then a gaggle of students from the aerobics class burst into the hall by the door to the gym.

"Man, is Sheila tough or what? I thought she was going to set her Lycra on fire!"

"She's been pushing us really hard lately," another agreed. "I'll be feeling this tomorrow."

Jo and I exchanged a glance, smiled to ourselves. Yes, the aerobic class looked like they'd had a good workout, but if they'd been training with Nolan, they'd be puddles of paté by now.

"Catch you Thursday?" we said at the same time, and then nodded in unison.

I stopped for a drink of water before I hit the parking lot. The evening air was warm heavy with humidity, yet still fresher than the sweaty, air-conditioned gym. The light was starting to fade finally from the sky, and the damned crickets were at it already. Still. I hate crickets; they always seem to be telling me how late it is.

I'd almost reached my car, parked beneath one of the lampposts, when I heard someone call my name. I turned; it was Nolan.

I furrowed my brow. Seeing Nolan outside the gym seemed wrong, somehow, like seeing Superman at the mall picking out tights.

"Dr. Fielding! There's a call, they said it was urgent"—he trotted over to me—"I'm glad I caught you. He said it was Brian, that he—" Then he suddenly stopped, frowned. "Why did they call me? Why not your cell phone?"

"I don't know—what about Brian?" I asked.

That's when the first shot rang out.

Chapter 13

NOLAN SHOVED ME HARD, BACKWARD.

Time slowed down. The light from the lamp dimmed, narrowed. It seemed that I could count the instants it took me to fall. I tried to fling my arms out to break my fall, but the pavement came rushing up all too fast.

Another shot followed the first.

"Get down!" Nolan shouted as he threw himself on top of me.

I couldn't believe how hot it was outside. The sweat was pouring down me in rivers, it felt like, and my head and back hurt like hell, but was fading to numbness.

All I could hear were the damned crickets. A door slamming somewhere in the distance. The squeal of tires.

Maybe it was another trick of time, but Nolan was taking a long time to get off me.

"The car . . . we should try to get cover," I could hear myself saying from a very long way off.

Nolan didn't say anything I could understand. The sweat continued to pour off me in torrents. I thought I saw his eyes flutter, but it was so dark. Had I imagined it? Could he see me?

"Someone's out there, we should . . ." I shook him. He didn't move. A dead weight.

"Shit! Nolan . . . Nolan!" I thought I heard a low groan, but it might have been me. I shoved harder, now squirming to get out from underneath him. "Nolan, Nolan, come on, man! You gotta wake up . . ."

He stirred, this time.

"What was that, Nolan?"

". . . nothing at the post office . . ."

"I don't understand! What?"

". . . hurts like the devil . . ."

Someone screamed. Nearby. It wasn't Nolan. I didn't think it was me—

"Holy Mother of God!" It was a woman, one from the aerobics class. Her mouth was hanging open. She dropped her gym bag. "What . . . what?"

The look of horror on her face woke me up, somehow. "You need . . . get back inside! Someone's shooting out here! Call the cops, call an ambulance!"

She stood there, shaking her head, staring at us, at all the blood.

Nolan groaned, a horrible noise that sounded nothing like him.

"Go *now*!" I screamed. "Call an ambulance! Move!"

She backed up a few steps, then finally turned and ran. Her hysterical cries stopped at the door to the gym, where I heard other voices rise in concern and fear.

Good; that would keep the rest of them inside.

"Okay, Nolan, I don't know whose blood this is, but I'm moving and you're not doing so hot, so we're going to guess that it's you, okay?" I felt his body move off my legs, with a sick, lifeless sort of roll. My stomach heaved. I tore open my bag, grabbed one of my shin pads, and stuffed it under his head. I looked at him, there was blood everywhere. Most of it seemed to be on his right arm and chest. Damn it, near way too many arteries.

"Nolan? Nolan? If you can answer me, I wish you would. Can you talk to me? I can't see too good, but I'm going to try to slow down some of this bleeding, if I can!"

He muttered something, but I couldn't make it out. I had to act.

Oh God, where do I start? Upper body first, more organs there. Blood soaked his sweatshirt, torso, and sleeves, blood was spattered on his face. My fingers kept slipping; I was coated, too. I pulled out my workout towel and pressed it where I saw the most blood on his chest. The white terrycloth blossomed, instantly turning reddish black in the odd orange light of the streetlamps. I took off my T-shirt, and pressed that down on top of the towel. It too was soaked through in a heartbeat. I kept pressure on it while I tried to think. My sweatshirt was in my bag, buried down the bottom, saved from early spring. I grabbed that, used that next. Nothing seemed to stem the flow of blood.

"Nolan, I don't know what else to do, I don't have anything that will help . . ."

He wasn't even moaning anymore.

The aspirin, antacids, and bandaids I kept in the car were laughably useless. "I'll try to call someone, I think that woman was too scared, maybe she didn't—"

But I heard sirens in the distance, and for once, prayed they were for me. They grew louder, until I could see the strobe of red and blue lights on the road that ran alongside the gym parking lot.

"Okay, help's here, Nolan, so you only have to hang in there a little longer. They'll take care of you, I promise, I'll make them. Just hang in there, just keep . . . breathing, keep breathing, okay?"

I know that I kept babbling, telling him about the progress of the emergency vehicles, anything I could think of that might give him something to hang on to, something besides the pain, the fear he must be feeling.

It also kept me from facing the fact that I hadn't seen Nolan's chest rise since the first sound of the sirens. In the near dark, I couldn't for the life of me remember anything of long-ago CPR classes. Should I try using heart compressions, or would that only exacerbate his wounds? Break his ribs? Damn it, I'm *not* helpless, I'm better than this!

Without letting up the pressure on his chest, I tried to feel for a heartbeat, then tried for a pulse, but couldn't feel anything with my numbed and trembling fingers. If I tried mouth-to-mouth, would that cause more problems than it solved?

At that point, I became aware that there were men, police, EMTs, pressing around me, asking me questions.

"What happened? Are you hurt? How long ago was he shot? Did you see who did it?"

I seemed to be losing track of reality. I couldn't untangle the questions that seemed to come from every side at once. It took too great an effort of will to pick one and address it, so I settled for summarizing what I knew and saying it as clearly as possible. That helped me focus a little, trying to get my story out.

"I don't think I'm hurt," I said. Things were happening too fast, so I held on to the questions as a lifeline. "I mean, I don't think I was shot, but there's an awful lot of blood, and my neck hurts a little. And my head. Where I hit it. I don't know if it's mine. The blood, I mean. I don't think so."

I did as I was asked, I could handle that. Told the EMT I knew my name, the date, when he asked. They asked me questions about Nolan, and whether he had any medical issues I was aware of. I was ashamed to realize that I didn't even know if Nolan was his first or last name. I noticed that the medic attending me had a large mole on his cheek, and that it lent him a kind of raffish charm, like he was wearing one of those seventeenth-century patches. Firm and incredibly gentle hands probed at the back of my head. I winced, but it didn't feel to me like anything more than the effects of skull landing on asphalt. Not great, but not as bad as could be. Not as bad as—

"Where is he going?" I asked. The ambulance with Nolan was pulling away. I tried to get up. "I should go with him."

The same hands that probed my skull held my shoulders down. "You'll be there, soon enough. He's in good hands. You have to help us, here, now."

Well, shit. Even dazed as I was, I could tell when I was being managed. But he wasn't wrong.

I went in the other ambulance. I remember bright lights, lots of questions, and feeling like the ambulance was going almost as fast as my thoughts were.

"Do you have any idea of what could have happened?" he asked again; maybe he was trying to keep me from passing out. I didn't feel faint, but I did feel a thousand miles away, glad someone else was driving. I had to work to focus on a face; the darkness was real now, and the light in the interior of the ambulance made it even eerier.

Then we were at the hospital: more people asking me if I knew my name, my mother's maiden name, then questions about my medical history. Then forms and more forms. I asked everyone who came to talk or clean me up or poke me or check my eyes or hand me another piece of paper to fill out whether Nolan was all right and got vague answers that were increasingly alarming as time went on: At last, one of the nurses told me it was very serious, he was in surgery, and did I know his next of kin . . . I cursed that I didn't know, told her to try at the gym. Brian wasn't home, wouldn't answer his phone on the road.

More sitting in the waiting room. And then a cop was talking to me. I vaguely recognized him as the guy who'd taken my statement after I'd nearly been run off the road: Franco. Even as I struggled to tell the story again, I began to feel the impact of it all and had to shove aside the denial that persisted.

My eyes flicked over to a movement outside the window. I'd been staring, trying to pull myself together when I saw the face again. "Oh my God, it's Tony!" I said. There was that same evil grin I'd seen at the airport. He vanished, as soon as he'd appeared. "The one I told you about—you have to . . . I have to go get him! He's right there!" I tried to get up, but Sergeant Franco held me down.

"Whoa, hang on there! You're not going anywh—"

"But I think the guy who shot—I just saw him, who I think it was!"

"The shooter? Where?"

"Out there! I just saw him!"

He took off, and came back, a moment later, shaking his head. "There was no one out there. Are you sure you just didn't see a reflection?"

"No," I said. "He was out there. I know, I saw him. . . ." Finally, I was able to tell Franco what I thought had happened.

At least he'd been familiar with my story, and was convinced that I wasn't making this up, imagining it, or anything else. I started to cry, feeling besieged by so much I couldn't control. Franco talked with one of the nurses and then came back, serious: Nolan had been shot in the chest, had lost a lot of blood, was in surgery. He called Brian for me—I hadn't thought to leave a message on the machine—and I found an old T-shirt in my bag to change into.

As soon as Brian came into the room, I started crying again, nearly hysterical, trying to get to him. The look of horror on his face made me wonder what I looked like *before* I was cleaned up.

They wouldn't tell me anything but that Nolan was in danger and they were working on him. Then they finally persuaded me to go home.

I couldn't do much over the weekend besides sit in my home office and stare. Nolan was still in very bad shape: Franco had told me he heard the bullet had collapsed Nolan's lung, and was lodged near his spinal cord. They weren't certain that he was going to make it, and if he did, if he'd ever be the same again. He was partially paralyzed now.

The outside world seemed like too much to handle, but I couldn't stand the way the pills the doctors gave me made me feel either. I couldn't bear to leave my house. On Monday, classes started, and I called in, probably delighting my undergraduates and confusing my graduate students by having Meg hand them their syllabi before dismissing them. I emailed or called Brian about ten times in the day, eagerly watching the IM screen to see if he signed on; that way, I could see that he was at work and all right. I know he was doing the same.

The semester beginning was almost more than I could bear to think about. I couldn't watch television or listen to the radio for fear I'd hear more about the shooting. I watched DVDs about factual CSI cases, not so much to feed my avocational interest, but more, it felt, to inoculate me against the idea of unexplained death.

Even the mailbox seemed an awfully long way away from the house now.

Jo called me Monday night, asked me how I was doing. "We've been really worried about you."

"I've been better," I said, then realized how churlish I sounded. "Sorry. Who's we?"

"The rest of the class. Look, I can't imagine how you're feeling right now, but we've been calling around, and it seems that the consensus is that we're going to keep meeting for our classes. Until, you know. Until Nolan gets back."

If Nolan ever gets back, I felt like saying. "I think that's fine. But I don't know how I feel about it. I'm thinking of taking a break, that is. I feel awful about what happened, and I don't think I can face everyone."

There was a long pause at the other end. "Em, it's not like you were responsible or anything, you know. If there was anything more that could have been done, we all know you would have. From what I hear from the aerobiqueens, you did everything just right, got someone to call the ambulance, stayed with him . . ."

I couldn't tell Jo what I knew and hated myself for, that the bullets *were* for Nolan, because of me. Why else had there been the false phone message? He'd been shot because of his connection with me. She didn't know the whole story, and I wasn't going to tell her now. Too many people thought I was nutty as it was. "Maybe."

"Sure. Look, no pressure, okay? You've been through a lot. But you know working out will make you feel better, and the advanced people will help the newbies. And, well, you know we're there for you."

I felt my eyes fill up at "newbies"—it was a word that she'd gotten from Nolan. There she went again, laying a surprise move on me. But hell, my eyes filled seeing the cats playing, these days. "Okay, I'll give it a try," I said, already half planning to forget all about it. "Regular meeting times? Classes and drop-ins?"

"Yep, we already squared it with the gym management. See you then." She hung up before I could change my mind.

Between Brian pushing me—out of a kind of desperation at seeing me so lost—and my own niggling guilt that I'd told Jo I would show up, I actually went. I was a little late when I showed up. I'm almost never late, but I knew I was dragging my feet and why. Maybe they wouldn't ask me, but I would tell them all what happened the night that Nolan got shot, just once. Then the telephone game that was rumor would take the story, but at least they would have heard it from the source, just once. So while I wasn't eager to push myself, it was possible they had news of how Nolan was doing.

By the time I made it down the hall, I could hear them warming up. Someone brought in a radio, which was a good idea; Nolan never let us have a radio, but it would be a good distraction and might improve morale. As I drew nearer, I could hear feet pounding mats as people warmed up. I stopped at the doorway, to see what was going on, and my jaw dropped. Then my workout bag hit the floor. In the middle of the sweating ring of students, puffing their way through what looked to be about six hundred jumping jacks, was the golden, the demigodling Mr. Temple.

My heart leapt, even as I gaped.

"Ah, g'day, Daniel-san! I was wondering whether you were going to join us at all. Don't stand there playing the diva, no one's going to roll the red carpet out for you here. In fact, since you're so sloppy as to miss nearly three minutes of my excellent warm-up exercises, you may give me thirty and thirty, if you'd be so kind."

Whatever else I might feel that I'd brought on the class, there was no denying that Mr. Temple seemed to lay it on just a bit thicker because I was there, his special pet. He kept announcing that he'd begun to put me on the right track, and so I would set an example for the rest of the class. He pushed us hard, and I got a couple of dirty looks, but he pushed me hardest of all, in the capacity of exemplar.

For the rest of the class, we were all on the verge of collapse. Despite that, some of the guys, and Johanna, looked like they'd just discovered their new hero. Surprisingly, Temple stopped the class early, within ten minutes of when we would usually let out.

I didn't dare look at the clock to confirm this anomaly, already having given Mr. Temple too many of the "juiciest" when I'd fallen behind. I couldn't wring anything else out of my poor, beaten body. It was almost as if he had something against me, and I almost thanked him for it: It was the first time I hadn't thought about my problems in ages. Something tore in my shoulder, once, when he threw me, but I was so pumped with adrenaline that I didn't feel it fully until we'd stopped.

"Now, I will repeat what I said at the beginning of class for the benefit of stragglers, layabouts, and our diva, Daniel-San, over there. I will be standing in for Nolan while he is recuperating. I do not say substitute, nor do I intend to replace him, as I know the old bastard, while giving the due respect to a great warrior and brother-in-arms, is milking his recovery for all it is worth, pinching the nurses, demanding sponge baths, and stealing extra pudding."

I could see nothing to joke about and I found my anger rising. At the same time, I marveled at how quickly Temple had gotten here, and he'd left his family and classes behind in what must have been the wink of an eye to do it. That got him something, in my books. I was thankful as hell that he was here, but not if he kept teasing about Nolan.

"With that in mind, I will take the opportunity to mold you in my own shining image. I will work you hard and you will be piteously grateful, giving me all you have in return. You will leave it all on the mat, and if I suspect that you are holding out on me, I will make sure it is the second thing I report to Nolan. The first being that I will tell him that I have taken the liberty of upgrading his cable television while he was away. Is that understood?"

"YES, SIR!" I was surprised to hear the class bellow. The man naturally elicited it, though.

"Until Thursday, then. With the exception of Daniel-san, you are all free to go forth, and sin as much as you can get away with."

We bowed out. I grabbed my towel and followed Temple into Nolan's office. I was grateful to the point of tears that he did not sit in Nolan's chair behind the desk, but sat on the desk itself. He did, however, offer me water from Nolan's stock in the little fridge.

"No doubt you are delighted to see me. I give you leave to express your pleasure—no? Perhaps just curious as to my presence. That I will grant you. I came when I heard that Nolan was in hospital. But I also decided that I could profitably spend my time keeping up his classes, keeping myself gorgeous and in condition, and perhaps, keeping an eye on you. Clearly, you're attracting some serious trouble."

"Um," was all I could manage.

"I don't expect thanks, not from you, Emma. Old Nolan would do the same for me, it's understood. But if my worries are justified, then you will, perhaps, give me the benefit of an extra two hours of your company a week, for private sessions. Perhaps your husband would join us."

I looked up quickly. "How did you know Brian is here, too?"

"Nolan keeps quite accurate notes on his students, including the family relationships. Elementary, Daniel-san."

"Oh. I don't know about Brian . . . he's pretty busy at work, right now." I could feel my face, already hot from the workout, go another shade red. I didn't want Brian out of the house any more than necessary.

Temple looked at me sharply, but I wouldn't say anything else. "Very well. I will discuss that when he comes into class tonight, should he chose to do so. Now then, what does your schedule allow, in terms of more fun and frolicks with Yours Truly?"

"Well, the semester's just started, so I'm actually also going to be very busy the next week or so—"

"Of course. So we'd better make them first thing in the morning, and perhaps the hour class with the others? Surely you can manage that?"

"Um, not really, no."

He smiled hugely. "Splendid, I thought so."

What was with this guy pushing so hard? "No, seriously. My schedule is pure madness for the next six weeks. I can't possibly add more on to it now." Big points for me, I thought, for standing up to him.

Temple cocked his head, looking very serious. "I think you can manage one extra class, can't you?"

"No, I really can't." There it was, polite but firm.

Except it didn't take. We went around the block a few more times until I finally agreed to give him an extra hour a week. I should have known I was doomed from the first: Who was going to win an argument with a mountain? Except maybe Mindy. And God, how I hate early mornings . . . not that I'd been waiting for the dawn chorus to wake me up lately.

Time for a change of topic before he realized that if I didn't sleep, there were about six hours a night I could train, too. "Mr. Temple? Have you seen Nolan? Do you know how he is?"

His face darkened. "They're letting no one but family see him—"

I had no idea Nolan had any family at all.

"—but I did find out that his condition is most grave. He lost a good deal of blood. I know of six men who are waiting for me to call and tell me that I've found the bastard that's done this. Then, there will be no need for any further authority involvement."

I chewed that over, the particularity of that very specific number, the fact that Temple could speak so casually and so convincingly of murder, for that was what was in his eyes. All I could do was nod, and I felt myself getting ready to cry again.

His expression turned to alarm. "Now! None of that!"

I felt his hands on my shoulders; Temple gave me a shake. Then he shoved a hanky into my hand. I blew my nose gratefully.

"Sorry."

"Now, now, you're not going to scare me with a bit of waterworks. I've got a wife and children, you think I've never seen tears before? Ha! Old Nolan's tough as a root, he'll be just fine."

"I hope so. It's my fault he's hurt in the first place," I said.

Though we weren't on the mats, I'd finally managed to stun Temple. I told him how Nolan came to be outside with me the night he was shot. He listened so carefully, that I told him the rest of the story as well.

"Hmmm. It's quite possible that it is your Mr. Tony Markham who is responsible, in which case, he's made a very serious mistake." He chewed it over a bit more. "It is, however, equally possible that it has nothing at all to do with you. It could be a random event, as there are a great many evil and demented bastards out there in the world. It is also possible that it is someone from Nolan's past—about which I will tell you no more—who is responsible. If that's the case, then I'm sorry that you were there to see it. In any case, our six friends will also be making themselves busy in the weeks to come. You must tell me everything again."

I did. He surprised me, taking down notes as I spoke. I wouldn't have thought that he would believe me, care, or be so methodical about it all.

"Three things," he said, when I'd finished.

I nodded.

"First, you really need to consider what you've told me about when you've seen this Tony person. It seems to me that while you are a sharp cookie, at least when you're not on the mats. All of your sightings have been when you were exhausted and half asleep—in the airport—or when you had just had bad news—about your little friend Chuck—and when you were with old Nolan at the hospital."

I nodded, shrugging. I didn't like hearing what he said, and didn't believe it, but had to consider it.

"Second. You know from class about being on your guard. I don't need to tell you how important that is now. You can't afford to feel comfortable, anywhere."

I shrugged. That wasn't even an issue.

"Next thing. Very important."

I leaned in to hear it.

"Make sure, for God's sake, you are on time when you come in tomorrow."

Chapter 14

I SLEPT WELL THAT NIGHT, AND AFTER CLASS THE next morning, I felt so good after I showered that I realized that I was going to blow off schoolwork and indulge in the radical activity of doing some grocery shopping. We were down to gulag food—coffee but no milk, bread crusts with no butter, and canned emergency rations—and needed some fresh supplies ASAP. I felt good enough to leave the house again.

Halfway down the street, I was singing to whatever song was playing on the radio. It felt good to be silly for a change, it felt good to be able to do something proactive about the situation, no matter how slight. An extra class, a little time to myself where I wasn't obsessing, it could only do me good.

Then I nearly drove off the road with my next thought.

Artie's absence had allowed someone to get into the unlocked house, but how had that someone gotten into the barn? The lock was still in place when I checked with Joel, and there were two copies—one on my chain, one on the spare rack on the way out of the house.

The keys.

I pulled over and rushed into CaféNation, and sure enough, the keys I'd seen before were still there, but now they were on a shelf behind the counter. The bright red metal of the carabiner caught my eye instantly, and the twinkle of the charm stood out among the white porcelain mugs. I whipped my head around, looking for Tina. She wasn't there.

"Shit!"

At that moment, one of the kids, Isabel, came out from the back. "It's okay, Emma. I'll get your coffee now. Remain calm, take deep breaths." Her smile faded as she realized I wasn't just jonesing.

"Sorry. It's not that, Isabel. I was looking for Tina, is she around? It's kind of important."

"She's off today. Can I help?"

"It's . . . it's going to sound strange, but can I . . . you remember the keys that were lost—the ones back there? Well, is it all right if I take them? I think I know who they might belong to."

Isabel frowned for a minute as she considered. The little dumbbell in her eyebrow moved as well, an added emphasis. "I guess so," she said as she handed them to me. "I mean, Tina knows you, right? And no one's been in to pick them up for a long while. And we know where you live anyway," she joked.

"I'm afraid you're not the only ones," I said.

"Sorry?"

"No, I'm sorry, I'm just . . . I'll bring them right back, if my theory doesn't pan out, okay?"

"Sure. Maybe give me a call if you find out, okay? Just to keep us in the loop?"

"Absolutely. I have to run."

I went back out to my car, feeling pretty stupid, but also fairly sure I was on the right track. I paused before I hit the unlock button, and decided to follow upon my paranoid feeling. Getting down on my hands and knees, I looked under the car for anything that shouldn't have been there. While this might have been par for the course for some of my colleagues who worked in more dangerous parts of the world, I wasn't sure what a car bomb would look like. Of course, I'd just driven, but just on the off chance that it was something in the key that triggered it . . . well, just better to work with the paranoia.

I didn't notice anything unusual, nothing new or shiny or clean that might have been the tip-off, so I got back up, and dusted myself off. I'd half convinced myself that I was really losing my mind, just as everyone kept telling me I was, but I stepped off a ways and made sure there was no one else around before I pressed the button.

I heard a faint click.

My car was now unlocked. I was sure that I'd locked it before I went into the coffee shop. I always locked it.

I tried locking the car, with the remote that I'd found in the coffee shop.

It locked. The alarm armed.

I walked around the car, ascertaining that it was in fact mine. There was my WELL-BEHAVED WOMEN SELDOM MAKE HISTORY bumper sticker and my sticker supporting the Democratic presidential ticket. In the backseat was a shovel and milk crate full of artifacts to study at home. In the front seat was my collection of empty water bottles.

I took out my keys, held one against its counterpart on the carabiner: There was no mistaking this. Somehow, the key to my car—or a copy of it—was left at CaféNation. The coffee shop I stopped by at least five times a week, where they knew my orders by heart. A key to my car, on a key chain that I'd been automatically drawn to, wanted to handle and play with from the first moment I'd seen it.

I now had no doubt that the rest of the keys would fit the locks to my house.

The charm was another matter. I didn't go for good luck pieces, I didn't naturally gravitate to Irish emblems, though there were those in my family who made more of the Irish part of our heritage than I did. That was the only thing that was inconsistent at the moment.

I examined the charm again, and was struck by the same impressions that I had the first time I handled it. The enamel was dark green and beautifully made, the gold showed no scratches, no signs of wear at all, and the stone at the center of the leaves was probably a real, cut diamond. Brand new.

I turned it over and saw that there were initials on three of the leaves: "EJF."

My initials.

Someone had the keys to my car. Had the keys to the house. Might not know the alarm codes, but had, at one point, most likely been inside the house.

Sometime later, my shovel scraped hard against a rock; the screech of metal on the rock jarred me. I looked around: I was in a shadowy, wooded area. The smell of pine needles, sap, and fresh dirt—a new note in the musty perfume of the woods—filled the still air. Just beyond the blade of the shovel I saw a hole in the ground, nearly filled; a small, scattered pile of dirt was beside it. I was sweating hard in spite of the shade and it felt like I'd been at work for a while. My hands were blistering—apparently I hadn't been using good form—and there was dirt jammed deep under my nails. I looked down and saw my trowel stuck into the ground like a dagger. I wasn't exactly certain where I was or how I'd gotten there. I recalled the visit to the coffee shop. I had driven here, I don't know how. Muscle memory or instinct or dumb good luck got me there. I didn't really remember anything. Hardly knew where I was.

A moment later and I recognized that I was beneath the trees at the far corner of our property. If I stretched, I could just make out the back of the barn, and I was far enough in that I couldn't see or be seen from the house or street. A chill took me as I began to re-excavate the hole I had been filling. The soil was still soft and so the work was easy. I still had to work half bent over to avoid the low branches. Cedars and pines that looked so soft to the touch jabbed and scratched my head and arms.

The hole got smaller as I went down, but at least I was no longer constrained by the lattice of roots knotted under the earth; I'd cut through them the first time. When it got so that I couldn't move dirt with the shovel, I threw that aside and pulled out the trowel. That got me another few inches, the hole narrowing even more quickly now. My shirt stuck to me, broken twigs and leaves hung on to my shirt, and more dirt wedged under my fingernails.

I found the keys from the coffee shop, just where I'd buried them, and dusted them off as best I could. Then I refilled the hole, scattering the duff of dead leaves and pine needles over the top. It was almost as though I'd never been there at all.

The car was in the driveway, I was relieved to see. After I replaced the tools in the garage, I went into the house. I didn't bother locking the door; there didn't seem to be a point. I dropped the carabiner and keys onto the counter, then went upstairs. I stripped down and got into the shower. I don't know how long I was in there, but after a while I realized that I could barely breathe for the steam and my skin had gone bright red and pruney. I got out and pulled on some shorts and a jog-bra, then sat in my office.

I sat for a long time before I realized that I'd forgotten to turn on the fans. I was sweating again. I drank a whole bottle of tepid water, and then looked for another one.

The charm was a present, I understood that now. Tony'd been sending tokens or expensive presents to everyone—flowers, chocolates, photos—and now gold jewelry for me. The shamrock wasn't my taste, but I thought that was just a good guess. What really bothered me was that he knew how much I'd like the carabiner.

Does the fact that I realized what Tony was doing, that this was a gift, mean something? Did it mean that I was starting to think like him? Or was I just so weirded out that I was reading too much into things? How could I tell what was real anymore?

I didn't want to think that I was right. I didn't want to think like Tony. I didn't want to do things and then not remember them. That was crazy.

I shivered and felt myself break out into a sweat again.

Brian came home shortly after that. One look at my face, and he was at my side.

"What is it?"

I told him about the key chain and the car. I showed him the charm.

"Okay, this is bad," he said. "But nothing's happened to you?"

I shivered, shook my head.

"That's something." He looked at the key ring more closely. "Why is there so much dirt on them? Maybe that's a clue—"

"No. It's not."

He looked at me sharply. "Why not?"

"I . . . I dropped them." I couldn't tell Brian about the time I'd lost. "My hands were shaking . . . after I tried the keys on my car. And we can forget about fingerprints, too; everyone at CaféNation will have handled them by now. What do we do?" My hands were still trembling, I felt like I had flu.

"Call the locksmith, call the cops. Check the house."

I nodded numbly, my arms wrapped around myself. Nolan, the keys, it felt like I couldn't even think straight, couldn't keep a thought in my head long enough to act on it.

Brian made the calls. He found me a glass of water, and then sat down and waited with me. Suddenly, he looked up.

"The spare keys!"

I looked up; the rack by the back door where we kept the spare keys seemed to be much the same as ever. Brian rushed over in excitement, though.

"Look, they've been rearranged!" He picked through the keys, put them back the way that our system required. "They've been moved so that you can't tell a couple have been taken! That's how he got into the barn when it was pad-locked! There's no valet key for the car! It's okay!"

"What do you mean, it's okay?" I felt more exposed than ever. "My God, Brian! Tony's got a copy of our keys!"

"Right, but he only had time enough to grab a couple, re-arrange them so we wouldn't notice right away, and maybe that's when he grabbed the mail with Sophia's picture on the way out. Because we've used the alarm every other time, we know he hasn't been into the house since then. So if Alfie—"

"Artie."

"—whatever—wasn't gone for too long, that was the only time he could have gotten into the house!"

I slumped forward in the chair. "I guess I don't see why that makes it okay."

"It means that it wasn't magic, how Tony or whoever got in here. And I'm happy to move one more step toward de-mystifying all of this. It's logical, and we can contain it. We also know that it isn't any worse than changing the locks, getting someone to check out the car."

I wasn't so sure. If nothing else, I knew I'd be cleaning the whole house as soon as I could, just to wipe away the taint of someone having been in there.

The locksmith came, and didn't overcharge us too badly, considering. The police came, and took a statement, took the key chain, and I gave them a copy of the rest of the file I'd been compiling about what had been going on.

I didn't sleep a wink that night and every noise seemed to be cause for fear. Sometime around dawn, I drifted off, only to wake up to the alarm clock a few minutes later. "I'm sleeping in," I mumbled. "I'll go in later."

"I'm calling in sick," Brian announced from the other side of the bed.

"Why?" I sat up. "What's wrong? Do you have a fever?"

"Nope. I'm fine. I'm going to stay home and we're going to fart around today and pretend we're normal. It'll be the best thing for you."

"Your deadline—"

"Can wait a day. I'll work late or bring something home with me."

"Are you sure?"

"Yes. Why, don't you want me here?"

"Let me get another three hours of sleep and I'll show you how much."

We did virtually nothing that day. Well, to be fair, we cleaned, did laundry, went food shopping, and went out for lunch and breakfast—I had pancakes at both and not only did I eat most of it, I started picking at Brian's french fries as well. For some reason, pretending to be normal helped a lot. Fake it until you make it.

The next day, Brian left for work, and I sat in my home office because it went against every fiber in my being to leave the Funny Farm. Now it was Brian who pointed out that there was no way we should let anyone get in the way of our lives more than they already were. We'd done all we could to remove access to the house, and we'd probably even done it in time.

I might as well go to work, I reasoned, at last: It didn't help much that I still felt haunted, even at home. And it felt like everywhere I went there was some reminder that I was being harrowed. Work, home, the coffee shop . . . I realized that I was avoiding places I usually went, trying to stay holed up, out of danger, always on the alert. At home, every time the phone rang, I jumped; the doorbell, when the letter carrier showed up with a package for me, almost sent me to the moon. I caught Minnie staring at the closet and it took me a good five minutes of listening for noises before getting the poker and opening the door. Quasi came shooting out, howling indignantly about having been shut in. Nothing could just be what it was, it was all freighted with the promise of doom.

But when I got to school, I found I stumbled through my new lectures and moved through the familiar ones like a zombie. It seemed as though my arduous workouts with Temple were the only thing that gave me an hour's precious respite.

It was a crappy way to live. I knew that I'd been avoiding a lot of things lately, deliberately not going to my favorite places, lest they be next on the chopping block. Brian was right, I *was* avoiding life. So I gave myself a goal, that afternoon, after work, to go to the liquor store to get some beer, then drop off the books I'd promised Raylene almost three weeks ago.

Was this what it felt like when you were losing your mind?

It took a long time to get myself together, changed, bag, keys. It took a physical effort to will myself to do something so simple, and I almost decided to postpone it for the next day, on my way to work.

But that was nuts; I shook myself. It was simple. A six pack. A quick stop by the restaurant to drop off the books. There was nothing sinister, nothing overwhelming about any of that, but faced with the prospect, it still took me about a half hour of dawdling before I got into the car.

I waited too long to pull onto Lawton's main drag—too busy searching for the fake police car that had chased me, despite the fact I knew it was gone—and someone honked at me. It wasn't an impatient honk, just a little tap of the horn, a woof, to let me know I should stop woolgathering, but the adrenaline almost launched me into orbit.

Take a pill, Em, I told myself. Maybe it had come to that. . . .

I pulled into the Yacht Club's parking lot, which was empty. That made me try to remember what day it was—I kept losing track of time in the past weeks—but I knew that it was Friday. Something must be wrong; Lawton Yacht Club was one of the most popular places around and should be just gearing up this time of a weekend night. The closed sign was visible from the edge of the parking lot, but I figured I'd just try the back door, and if no one was in, leave the books for the kids there with a note.

The door opened even as I raised my hand to knock. Tiny Raylene was pale, her eyes wide.

"Emma . . . how did you know?"

"What do you mean? Know what? I just came over to drop off the books I told you about. For the kids. What's going on?"

She shook her head, her long black hair was knotted in a big braid. "I was just about to call you, tell you to come over."

"Raylene, what's wrong?"

"I'm telling people that we had a problem with the electric, we're closed tonight."

"Telling people?"

She hugged herself, and looked away. "Do you trust me? Trust Erik?"

"Uh. Yeah, I do." And the funny thing was, I did trust them, despite our slight acquaintance. We knew them from the bar, of course, and we'd gone out on their boat with them and other guests a couple of times. They weren't our best friends—it was too soon for that—but my instincts told me that they were okay.

She nodded. "I need you to go down to the docks, meet Erik. Something's . . . happened. Happening. I think between the two of you, we'll get some answers."

The skin of my scalp prickled. Oh God, no. "Okay. Can you tell me what it is?"

She hesitated before she said, "It's serious."

I swallowed. "I get that. Where's Erik? Is he okay?"

"Everyone's fine, as far as I know. There was a man here. He came in the back and attacked me—no, I'm okay! The kids are fine, and so is Erik. But Emma, he had a picture of your house and one of the bar with him. His license said his name was Tony Markham."

"What!"

"Do you know the name?"

"Raylene, he's the guy who's been . . . I think he shot my friend, Nolan! Is he here?"

Her face was a blank. "No, Erik has him. Down at the boat."

"Why on earth—?"

Still, Raylene's face gave nothing away. "You need to see Erik. Take our truck, it's out back, and no one will think anything of it if they see it going down to the harbor. We're always going out to the boat."

"Right." Then I frowned. "What did Erik drive?"

"He . . . he took another car." She nodded, tight lipped, and I knew she wouldn't say anything more.

"I'll take the truck."

Raylene nodded, turned, and led me through the dining room, out through the kitchen, to a back hallway. She handed me the keys to the truck, and handed me a coat, too. Probably one of Erik's, as it was too big, but one of Raylene's wouldn't have fit me in a million years. "Gonna be cold out on the water."

"I'm going out on the water?"

"Yes. Emma, please hurry. Erik will tell you everything." She opened the back door, anxious to have me on my way.

I hesitated again, shrugged and nodded, pulled on the coat, and rolled up the sleeves and got into the truck. It took me a minute to rearrange the mirrors and find the lights, but I was down at the harbor five minutes later. My heart was pounding fit to burst out of my chest. I was at a loss to explain what was going on, and Raylene's strange orders truly scared me, but if there was any chance that Tony was there . . .

Erik was down there, as advertised, and he looked like grim death. Erik is medium height, and doesn't look like anything special, but something about his eyes is hard and watchful and I get the impression that hitting him would be like punching a pallet of cement blocks. Close-cropped hair that made me think he'd never gotten over the habit from the navy, and a blurry tattoo on his arm that might also be a souvenir of those years. He has a hint of a mustache and chin whiskers that are never quite shaved, never fully grown in, and makes him look youthful. But there's a hardness to his face that speaks of experience. He walks with a rolling gait, whether from some injury or too many years on deck, at sea, I don't know.

Usually he's in the background of things, quiet, happy to let Raylene run the show with the customers. Once, however, some drunk mouthed off when she told him she was calling a cab. Things escalated and he smashed a glass. Erik came out of nowhere. The guy was outside before anyone could move to help Erik, and people who were there swear that the next noise they heard was the guy's head bouncing off the outside wall of the bar. When they came back in, Erik frog-marched the drunk up to the bar, where he stammered an apology to Raylene, and then asked her to call an ambulance. Erik made him wait outside so that Raylene didn't have to clean up anything else besides the glass.

I learned from that incident that Erik's nickname, "the Red," came not from his hair color, his politics, or his bank account.

It was his temper. Quiet or no, no one screwed around with Erik twice.

He extended his hand to me; it was rough, knotted, and strong. "Emma. Thanks for coming so quick."

"I just showed up at the restaurant, Raylene said she was going to call. What is all this?"

He shook his head. "Wait until we get out a ways."

We went down to his dinghy. After I hopped in, he cast off, and we were off. Erik is one of the smoothest, strongest rowers I know, and we cut across the water swiftly, more quietly than I could have imagined. The lights from the docks diminished as we moved out toward his boat, *Belle Jeanne-Marie,* and we were nearly in darkness.

"Now?"

"Noise carries too easily. Let's get under way."

We tied up, and I hopped onto the deck of the cabin cruiser. Erik flicked on the running lights, and got us under power. We motored out a ways beyond the breakwater, and up the coast a little bit. Then he cut the power and we were nearly in silence. The coast above Lawton is sparsely populated and most folks would have been watching television about now, not looking at us, had they been there to see us. Pity; if I had that view, in one of those houses, I would be staring out the window, myself.

"I've got someone below," Erik began. "I think he's trouble."

"What? He's in trouble?"

"No, Em. Trouble for *us*. You see, he came to the bar tonight. Looking for us. Looking for trouble. He threatened Raylene." That last statement that sounded like a jury's sentence to me.

And yet . . . "You didn't call the cops? Why is he out here?"

"He's out here because I think he has some information you might be able to use. I think he's part of the trouble we've been having around here recently."

"What?"

"You said that someone's been following you, stalking you? Making trouble for you and yours?"

"Yes." I felt a bitter taste in my mouth, one that came from feeling like I was being mocked. "Tony Markham."

"Well, I think he's a part of it."

My eyes suddenly filled and my throat closed up. Erik actually believed me about Tony. It was a moment before I could speak. "How do you know?"

"I turned his pockets out. He had pictures. He had your address." Erik flicked another switch on the console—the faint lights reflected up on his face—and then looked directly at me. "And a few other things. Like I said, trouble. I wanted you here when I found out exactly what kind."

"Jesus, Erik."

He shrugged. "I don't think the Man has anything to do with it. But there's this, too."

He showed me a thin leather wallet.

"Erik?" My throat closed up again, for an entirely different reason this time.

"We can go through all of the stuff in it later. For now, I think I've got your Tony Markham down below. Don't worry. He's trussed up tighter than my Aunt Gert in her Sunday girdle."

I found myself dizzy, and I held on to the table until the world stopped spinning. Then I found myself turning around, looking for something I couldn't put a name to.

Frustrated, I turned to Erik. "I feel like I need . . . something. Something to have in my hands."

Erik laughed, and it scared me. "Like a piece of pipe?"

I nodded, relieved to have identified what it was that was driving me. "I guess. Silly, huh?"

"Not at all." Erik leaned over, but he didn't bring out a chunk of lead pipe. He pulled out a shotgun. "Perfectly natural urge."

I stared at it.

"Shall we?"

He led the way down to the cabin, and paused before the door. "Ready? Only . . . just so's you know. There might be some blood. I had to hit him a couple of times to get him compliant."

I nodded, not smiling, thinking of how Tony could be. "Perfectly natural urge."

I thought I saw wolf's teeth by the moonlight, but I'm sure it was too dark to see whether Erik was really smiling. He opened the door.

We stepped in, turned on a light, and while I waited for my eyes to adjust, I heard a moan, somewhere ahead of me in the cabin.

"Hey, butthead," Erik said, striding into the cabin. "Wake up. Time for answers."

I saw a man stretched out on the bunk, feet bound together with duct tape, his hands raised above his head and secured to the wall with a rope looped through a tiedown. Another moan, and Erik turned him over.

It wasn't Tony at all.

Chapter 15

IT'S NOT HIM," I SAID. I COULDN'T STOP STARING AT the guy. He was about the right build and coloring—well, coloring last time I thought I saw Tony close up, at any rate—but he seemed too old. Not that I could be sure about his age, the guy wasn't looking his best. His face was gray, where it wasn't streaked with dried blood, a piece of gray duct tape slapped haphazardly across most of his mouth, and his nose probably hadn't started out the day at that odd angle—I remembered a quote: *his nose is executed and his fire's out.*

I shook myself. I didn't have the luxury of retreating into Shakespeare. "Who are you? Why did you go into the bar? Why do you have my address?"

The guy tried to sit up, as well as he could with no free arms to support himself and his feet stretched out in front of him. He just glared at me, his breathing ragged because his mouth was nearly sealed shut and his nose wasn't working properly.

Holy snappers. "Erik, I've seen him before! He was working at Caldwell!" It took some effort, what with all the blood and all, to see the resemblance. I told him about seeing "Tony" while I was in the lab, our chance meeting in Duffy's office.

"That so? Well, that makes sense, and I'll tell you why," Erik said. "This one . . . he came into the back of the kitchen." He pulled out several shells and began loading them into the shotgun. The man's eyes followed every precise movement.

"He walked in, looked around, saw it was just Raylene, just walked up and slapped her a couple of times. She's clever, my woman, she grabbed a knife and cut at him, but he slapped the knife out of her hand, too. That's when I came in. I was in the walk-in. I soon put a stop to it. Wasted a good bottle of Riesling on him."

There was no trace of sarcasm in Erik's voice. He put the last shell into the shotgun. "You've got a lot to answer for, mister. Bad enough you dared touch my wife, but what if one of my kids came downstairs and saw that?" He turned back to me. "Ray stopped me before . . . well, we needed to find out what he knows. Got the duct tape and we emptied his pockets. And this is what I found."

He spread out the wallet and its meager contents on the table. The license was from Florida, and was indeed made out to Tony Markham. I frowned: Tony's first name was Anthony. This couldn't be a coincidence, though. There was a credit card, too, in the same name. Then I found the license and Caldwell ID with the name "E. Fishbeck" on them. There were also two pictures. One was of the Lawton Yacht Club, the other was of the Funny Farm.

I felt the world swim around me, and I clutched at the side of the table to keep from keeling over.

"Don't worry," Erik said quickly. "Don't worry. I was careful to only touch the corners and edges. When we hand the wallet over to the police, we'll ask them to dust for other fingerprints."

I had the sense that he was speaking to my panic rather than concerns about fingerprints. Why was he thinking

about fingerprints anyway? "When we hand the *wallet* over."
I repeated.

"Don't know if our friend here is going to make it as far as
that." Erik reached over and yanked the tape off the man's
mouth. I flinched and the guy screamed. Then he started
cursing, and Erik reached over and backhanded him hard in
the face. In spite of all I'd seen so far, my mouth fell open in
shock.

"Stop that, there's a lady present. Or have you forgotten
that you're not the only one who knows how to hit people?
My Raylene's a nice girl, a good mother, she stopped me
from . . . And she was right: What if the kids had come
down?"

He leaned into the guy, and I could see him trying to back
away from Erik as much as his bonds would allow. "But I
could have gone all night long." He paused. "Still could,
Ray's not here. You don't mind, do you, Emma?"

I shrugged. "Whatever. I'd rather get our answers," I said,
hoping like hell that Erik was just talking. He had me convinced at any rate.

"Let's start with that and see where we go from there.
What's your name? Your real name."

"Tony . . . Tony Markham," the guy said.

"I don't believe you," Erik said. "I've been tending bar far
too long not to recognize a fake license, no matter how good
it is. I'm betting the name on the Caldwell ID is fake, too."

I'd seen the license and thought it genuine. How was Erik
so sure?

He turned to me. "Emma, what do you do when you don't
believe people?"

I leaned against the cabin wall and crossed my arms. I
didn't say anything for fear of ruining whatever plan Erik
had, or betraying my own fear of this guy, this situation. I
hoped I looked tougher than I felt.

"Right," Erik said. "We increase the desire to reply."

He raised the shotgun up, sighted on the guy's chest, then
drew a bead down his body. He lingered with the shotgun

aimed at the guy's crotch, shook his head briefly, annoyed with the cliché of it, then paused at the kneecap.

"A lot of people like the kneecap for this sort of thing, Em," Erik said, as if he was discussing the best way of carving a turkey. "But I think too many things can go wrong. It's too close to the femoral artery. And with all the medical advances, these days, with our aging and yet more physically active population, it's not as much of an issue as it used to be. Besides the pain, of course, which is excruciating. Myself, I like to think longer term. An ankle. Lots of fiddly little bones in the foot, ligaments, tendons, lots more difficult to fix up, if that's still an option."

It was then that I noticed that the guy was barefoot. I couldn't help but feel the cold metal of the shotgun barrel as it pressed against his ankle. He jerked back too, and when Erik racked a round into the chamber, "Tony" began to scream again, this time for someone to come help him.

I almost stepped forward, convinced that Erik was going to do it, but then he glanced at me and the question Raylene had asked came back to me: Do you trust us, Em? I owed it to Erik to give him the credit of faking all this before I spoke up.

He had ten more seconds, I decided.

"Scream your head off if you like," Erik said, "but if I'm far enough off the coast for the shotgun blast not to be an issue, you can be sure that I'm not going to sweat your little noises." He turned slightly to me, nodded, winked suddenly.

That's when I settled against the wall again, confident that Erik was bluffing. We hadn't traveled that far, but the guy, tied up in the cabin, probably didn't know that, and more than that, he didn't know we'd hugged the coast rather than heading straight out to open water. With the door closed, no one would hear him, but the shotgun was another story. And Erik, if he used the shotgun, would not only blow off the guy's foot, he'd open a hole in the hull.

Relief flowed over me. I tried not to let it show too much.

"I . . . shit . . . my name isn't Tony . . . it really is Ernie Fishbeck. Damn! A guy hired me to do a couple of jobs for him." The words were practically tripping over themselves, he was so eager to get them out.

"Tell me," I said. "Tell me about this guy. Tell me what jobs."

"He told me . . . he wanted a couple of people paid back. Mess up a restaurant, make sure the owners had some trouble they wouldn't forget. Stake out a house, figure out the best way in and out. Watch a guy, find out his movements."

"What guy?" I said, a chill crawling down my spine.

"The guy with that house. There's another picture . . . in my shirt, in the pocket."

Erik reached over and fished it out carefully. He examined it, looked at me, paused, then handed it to me.

The image was grainy and out of focus, as well as smeared with Ernie's blood. It was Brian. It was taken while we were in Hawaii, because he was grinning, showing off the rash he had on his belly from surfing. But the angle was off; it was different from the picture we had at home.

Someone had been watching us while we were on vacation.

As unreal as the rest of the evening had been, a cold numbness rushed into my joints now. My peripheral vision vanished and I could only see the filthy, broken face in front of me.

"Who told you to do these things?" I said. "Where is he, how do you contact him? How long have you been following us around?"

"Fuck off." Ernie was smirking. In spite of the beating Erik had given him in the restaurant, the shotgun pointed at him, the son of a bitch still had it in him to be amused by me.

I grabbed him by the shirt. "Tell me, goddamn it!"

"Emma." Erik's voice was low.

"He needs to tell me—"

I didn't realize I'd raised my hand to hit Ernie until I couldn't move it: Erik had clamped his hand around my wrist. He was fast, he was strong, but he hadn't hurt me.

"Emma. I have another idea." He waited until I nodded, and then released me. "I don't want to spend all night here, and neither do you. Let's end this now. Go over to the other cabin. In the locker. There's a spare anchor there. Bring it here. And some rope."

The smirk was gone from Ernie's face now. "What are you going to do?"

Erik shrugged. "You won't talk, you're no good to us."

"You can't . . . you're not going to throw me overboard!"

"Why not?"

"I'll drown!"

"You break into my home and place of business, lay hands on my wife, and you think I'm going to let you go? You're out of your mind, mate. Furthermore—" He leaned over and began to whisper into Ernie's ear; the other man blanched under the mask of blood.

I left. I was grateful to Erik for giving me a task to focus on. When I got to the cabin, I found the anchor and rope, but I also realized I was still clutching the picture of Brian in my hand. I looked at it for a moment, carefully smoothed it out, and put it into my pocket, then picked up the stuff Erik had asked for.

On my way out, I paused. Another object beckoned to me. I reached out, drew my hand back, then finally picked it up and stuck it through my belt.

By the time I got back to the cabin, Ernie was sobbing quietly on the bunk.

"Good job," Erik said. "Now there's got to be a certain order of operations here, and we should make sure we know what we're doing before we get into the middle of it. Don't want to find out we've done it backwards. I don't want to untie him from the bunk until we've got the anchor around his ankles. But of course, that will make carrying him that much harder."

Then Erik looked up at me. "Emma, we don't need a hammer. The anchor will be plenty heavy enough."

"It's not for weight," I said. "He'll sink better with a few holes knocked into him first. Let the gases escape."

"No! No, no . . ." Ernie, who had been sobbing quietly, made a sound that was a half-choked whisper, half mewling. "I'll tell you whatever you want! Please, please don't!"

"Emma?"

"If he's convinced you at the end that he's told us everything . . . we can discuss it then. Otherwise . . ." I turned to look at what was on the bunk, and swallowed. "I don't much care if we knock the holes in him before or after he's dead."

Erik nodded. "The lady's a clever one, Ernie. She's righteously angry, she's inventive, and she's got a hammer. If I were you? I'd talk. And quick."

"There's . . . there's this bar," he began. "We only ever meet there."

And at that point, I realized that Tony was doing what he'd always done: gotten weaker men than himself to do his work for him. Whether it was charisma or creditable threats or blackmail or whatever, Tony had always preferred being removed by one or two degrees of separation. After all, he'd tried it with me.

"Back up," I said. "Who's 'we'?"

"A guy, only ever called himself Billy to me. About my height, my weight, age." He frowned and I realized that he was figuring it out as well.

The story went on along like that. Met him outside the Salvation Army. Got Ernie the IDs, a job at Caldwell, told him how to fill out the forms the right way, told him how to answer the questions about, "you know, the stuff in my past."

I didn't even ask about that. "And sometimes . . . he'd borrow your uniform? Your keys and ID?"

"How did you know? He said he was trying to impress a lady, that he had a job. Not that he ever seemed short of cash. He'd ask me to buy things for him, using the fake license, the credit cards."

"When do you have your next meeting with him?"

"I don't; I haven't seen him, not for a while. He always leaves me a note. I always have to give the note back to him at the meeting. He's squirrelly about that; once I didn't do it, I thought he was gonna flip his lid."

Deniability, I thought. No fingerprints, no note, no nothing. Smart.

"What did he say about these 'jobs' you mention? Why would you do things like that?"

"Hey, I owed the guy. And these folks, Billy said they were keeping him from seeing his kids. You don't do that to a guy, and what with the courts these days . . ."

His sudden, hot response told me that Ernie had kids that he wasn't allowed to see. Tony had found what buttons to push.

"What do you think?" Erik asked me.

"I'm not convinced that he's telling me everything. I'd like to find this 'Billy.' "

The shotgun came up again, and Ernie shied away as far as he could, screaming.

Erik looked at me and shrugged. I nodded.

"Let's bring her out to open water," he suggested.

He went up and, despite what he said, got us under way back into port. After making sure that Ernie wasn't going anywhere, I joined him up on the bridge. I paused, he glanced at me, and suddenly he frowned, grabbed my shoulders, and pulled me over to the side of the boat. I threw up over the side, even before I knew it was coming.

"Good girl, you're okay, you're okay. . . ." He said it in that way that guys have of saying "it's okay" when it's really not, but they don't want to believe it.

"—and I always appreciate a guest who can make it to the side in time." He waited until I nodded I was okay—wasn't going to go overboard, was done being sick—and he turned back to the wheel, made a slight adjustment to our course. "You did real good back there. Kept your head. The hammer was a nice touch." He groped for a word. "Dramatic."

I shrugged. I wasn't at all convinced that it was a dramatic impulse that made me pick it up. Suddenly, it was there under my hand and I was picking it up before I knew why I wanted it. But when I realized that I had it, I still brought it up to the cabin with me. The thought sent me to the side again, but I was done being sick for the moment. It scared the hell out of me, I thought as the damp sea air saturated my clothes in spite of the jacket. What was I turning into?

When we'd gotten in, tied up, and locked the gun in his truck, Erik called the police. It was just a few moments before they were there and I took the time to be seized by a fresh set of nervous shakes.

Erik and I went over our story—I couldn't believe I was going to lie to the police and said so. Erik reminded me that I was telling the truth, just a highly abbreviated version: Erik caught the guy on his boat, explaining why his truck was there as well as the car that the guy drove. He and I were there looking for a necklace I'd lost on our last trip out; I was frantic when I'd found I'd lost it. We surprised the stranger, there was a scuffle, and we tied him up.

When Ernie saw the cops, he immediately started screaming again, but in a different pitch, saying that we were going to kill him, that we were torturing him . . .

Erik took my hand and squeezed it. I could feel my teeth grinding together, I was trying so hard to keep my mouth shut.

I knew the cop who came, Officer Lovell, because I'd met him during the to-do out at the Chandler house a couple years back. He stared at Ernie in amazement.

"You're gonna have to do a little better than that, mister. Erik Reynolds is a business owner, got kids in the Sunday school here. Hell, I eat at his place once or twice a month, special night out for me and my wife. He always looks after us. And Mrs. . . . . er, Professor Fielding, everyone knows her."

I looked up, startled. Who the hell knew me?

"She does these programs about archaeology and history and stuff here at the schools for the kids, does some of her archaeology work, right here in town. And she's a teacher, up someplace in Maine, there. Very respectable person."

Respectable was news to me. I'd always thought of myself as politely invisible at best.

"So you're going to have to come up with a better story than that they were torturing you out on a boat, threatening your life and all."

"Officer Lovell. I admit, I had the shotgun, but it was never loaded. I just wanted to make sure the guy wasn't going to try anything." Erik asked permission and then showed Lovell that the shotgun was indeed unloaded; he must have removed the shells about the same time he locked the gun back up in his truck. "I didn't want him to get any ideas about rushing us . . . and with Emma here . . ." he trailed off, shrugging, obviously playing the knight protecting the damsel in distress.

"You got your paperwork?"

I felt my stomach turn over as Erik dug out the license and ID. Torture was exactly what we'd done, even if there had been no actual violence beyond the slap that I'd seen. Just the threat of it had been enough, and I was sickened by what I had said, what I had been playing at. I looked over and Erik was nodding sorrowfully, as if he was shocked and hurt by the crazy allegations against us. I don't know how he did it; I felt the urge to confess the truth, that it was largely as Ernie had said just then. I stuck my hand in my pocket and turned away, a whisker away from admitting everything. . . .

Then I felt the picture of Brian jab me under the fingernail. A sharp pain, and cold anger flooded me. He had threatened Brian, and that negated everything else.

Didn't it?

I spoke aloud, maybe trying to convince myself. "Look, whatever he might have tried to do tonight—which was bad enough—whatever he was planning to do, he also knows the guy who I think shot Nolan, down at the gym."

I thought I saw a flash of determination on Erik's face, really the first look of true emotion I'd seen since he'd mentioned Raylene and the kids. But it was very dark and I was very tired.

The questioning seemed to go on forever, but Lovell assured me that they would find out as much as they could, and finally took Ernie away. That's when I started feeling sick again, my body rebelling at this new self-knowledge. And still, part of me gloried in it, the stepping outside of the bounds, the violence of it, and the realization that I didn't crumble in the face of it.

Nolan and Temple would be proud of me, I thought with horror. I must be losing my mind.

Erik put his hand on my shoulder: I jumped. "Whoa, there. Why don't you come back to the place with me. We can check on Raylene and the little ones, have a drink."

"I better get home and make sure everything's okay there," I said. "Thanks anyway, Erik." I almost apologized to him for the way I was, the way I'd been on the boat. Then I remembered that not only had Erik instigated things, he'd played along with it and more than surpassed me. I don't know what he said to the guy while I was away. What could make a man crumble like that? Erik looked like a stranger to me now, and I wondered why he was so good at this sort of thing . . . don't be coy, Emma. Interrogation is not "this sort of thing."

"Brian is home, isn't he?" Erik said. "Not on one of his trips?"

"No, he's home. Just working late a lot lately. Project will be over soon. He's working late to avoid actually traveling, doing phone meetings instead."

"Okay, how about this? We'll go back to your place, make sure everything's fine, batten down the hatches. Then you'll come back, and we'll talk about what's going on, get rip-roaring pissed. Raylene will give you a lift home. And I'll tell you my special hangover remedy for the morning. What do you say?"

Not a word about why he and Raylene might be involved in this. Not a single syllable about the fact that it was their acquaintance with me that had endangered his wife, threatened his family and his business. After the way that Marty and Dora had asked me to stay away—and rightly, as much as I hated to admit it—Erik was willing to take me closer into the heart of his family. I could barely look at him.

And yet, the thought of spending even a few hours alone in the house, even with the cats, even with a phone call to Brian, was repugnant. I couldn't face it. Again, weakness. Not so different from the amoral weakness I'd just been rejoicing in. What was right? Was I weak to be afraid of being alone or weak to embrace violence to solve a problem?

All I knew was that I was running out of ways to deal with this all on my own. "Thank you, Erik. I think I will, if you don't mind."

"Good. Settled then."

Easy for him to say.

We drove back to the house; I checked the alarm, the doors, counted the cats by rattling the food dish.

I called Brian's office; he'd already left, so I talked Erik into staying and having a drink, rather than going back. I didn't want to call Brian's cell, he'd drive off the road when he heard the news. And I decided I didn't want him to come home to find the house empty.

He glanced at his watch. "Just one quick one. I'll call Raylene and let her know."

He called, and I found the whiskey and a couple of glasses. "You want ice?"

Erik scowled at me like I should know better. I did, but wasn't the sort to impose my religious beliefs on others. I slid a glass toward him, and he picked it up, glanced at the color appreciatively, and tilted it toward me.

"Getting the bad guys."

I raised my eyebrows at him, frowned, clinked. The burn at the back of my throat was exactly what I needed; the smoke and peat took me away for just a moment . . .

Not far enough. Not long enough.

We drank in silence. Finally, Erik cleared his thoat, looked away, embarrassed. "You know, you did real good tonight. You kept your head."

"Yeah. Thanks."

"Look, I know your type, I know what you're like—"

"My type?"

"You know what I mean. Girls." He shrugged. "Women. You keep your head in a situation, maybe, but you worry, pick over every little thing afterwards. I'm telling you: Don't worry."

I tried very hard not to slam my glass as I set it down. "Erik, what we did tonight . . ."

He waved his hand. "What I did. You didn't do nothing. Didn't lie, didn't hurt anyone."

"You know that's not true. I'm every bit as involved—"

"That's the worrying I'm talking about. Look, if there was a coyote taking your sheep, you wouldn't just sit there, would you?"

"This is different. What I did tonight, it really scares me. It's like . . . I don't actually remember picking up the hammer, but I know damn well that it didn't magically fly into my hand, you know what I mean? Something in me saw it and took it for a very specific purpose. I don't know how far I would have gone to get Ernie to tell us anything."

The sound of crickets filled the kitchen while Erik considered. "You kept yourself pretty cool. You didn't rush me, you didn't try and do anything yourself."

But there was this feeling, I thought, this feeling that I'd been reduced to a predator myself. I wasn't sure how upset I was by it, either, not once I remembered Brian's picture. For a minute there, back on the boat, I really hated how weak I was, that I felt constrained when dealing with Ernie. And then, I saw the hammer, and when I took it, I knew it wasn't for dramatic effect.

I took another sip of whiskey, and began to wonder what I was capable of. If Ernie hadn't talked, would I have gone further?

I said to Erik, "I guess . . . I think of myself as a pretty decent person—" I cut myself off when I heard how patronizing that sounded.

Oddly, Erik wasn't angry. "I'm not a decent person? I shouldn't protect my family?" He swirled the whiskey around in the bottom of the glass and glanced at me.

"No, no, of course you should. And I should too, I know, it's just . . . I guess I'm surprised by how fast I . . . by how . . . shallow everything is." I groped for the words. "Civilization, no, culture . . . doesn't seem to really go that deep." I shrugged and swallowed. "Maybe not as deep as I thought, in me, anyway."

"Guess it depends on what your culture is," Erik said. "Lotta folks would say that guy got off easy."

"Maybe I think we should have just handed him over to the police."

Now Erik was annoyed. "That's exactly what we did. I don't understand your problem, Emma. I don't like what we did either, I don't go out of my way to get into shit like that, but if it comes to me, to my home, my family, I'll do that and a hell of a lot more. Bet your last dollar on it."

"I know," I said, and sighed. "I also know that if we hadn't . . . waited before we called the cops, we might not have had as much to find the real Tony with." I looked up at him. "Thank you, Erik. I can't tell you how grateful I am to you for that—"

He scowled again. "Don't be grateful; it'll just fester. We found ourselves in a jam, we helped ourselves out of it, that's all. Cooperation, if you don't want to think of it as teamwork."

"No, it was teamwork. Look. I'm in it as much as you, I accept that and I'll deal with it, you don't have ever to worry about that."

He nodded and shrugged. "Like I said, don't worry. It's not worth it."

It was my turn to be impatient. "Okay, okay, and just so we're clear, I'm in it more, because it was my fault that the son of a bitch was there at all, and I can't tell you how sorry I am for that—"

"Don't be sorry, just fix the situation."

"For God's sake, Erik—!" Suddenly I had to laugh. "Okay, what am I allowed to be? Not sorry, not grateful, not worried?"

"Be happy." He grinned roguishly, and finished his drink. The smile stayed on his face, but left his eyes. "Just be ready, too."

Brian came home a few minutes after Erik left; I poured him a whiskey and decided I needed another finger or two for myself. I told him that everything was okay, that the police had the guy, told him what had happened. After his initial shock, Brian sort of hunched back in his chair, one arm across his chest, the other arm tight into him, fist against his lips. I told him about the discussion with Erik, how I didn't like what Erik was saying but couldn't deny that he was right about some things. To me, that seemed almost as important as the evening's events.

Brian loosened up enough to shrug. "Any animal will try to protect its mate," he said.

"You know, that really bothers me. What is it with guys and animal analogies?" It didn't matter that I'd been struck by the same thought earlier.

"Well, what do you think we are, Em? Monkeys with car keys."

I rolled my eyes. "It's not that simple."

"Sure, it is."

I shook my head. "The important thing is that we try to be more than that. It's important to me, anyway."

"Absolutely, but you shouldn't underestimate the urge to stay alive, to protect what's yours. It's not always a bad thing."

But what if you go there and you don't come back? I asked myself. Something in me had found the anger I felt on the boat exhilarating. It was so vastly different from what I was used to, what I thought I knew about myself, that it scared me almost as much as anything that had happened so far.

"Where did Erik learn to do all that stuff anyway?" I asked aloud.

"Who knows? We don't know much about him and Raylene before they got here. Maybe he just had a rough past."

"I don't want to be comfortable thinking like Erik." I hunched up on my chair, hugging my knees. "I like him, but it's too close to the edge of somewhere I don't want to go."

Brian thought a minute, nodded, then reached for my hand with both of his. "If there was anything I could have done to prevent you having to go through that, I would have. As it was, I wasn't there, and I hate that. We couldn't have predicted it. But you did great, and more than that, you got us one more step toward ending all of this. Finding out who's behind this. We know someone is out there, and you and Erik got us that much closer to finding him. I'm so proud of you."

I reached for him. "I'm . . . I was really scared."

He took my hand. "I know. I would have been, too. I'm scared now, but I think we're almost through this. It's a really good break. C'mere."

As he hugged me, we rocked back and forth on the chair, and I was a little comforted. At the same time, I was still troubled by what I'd seen in myself that night, and couldn't decide whether something I had cherished had been taken away or I was just blessed with an unwanted degree of self-awareness.

Chapter 16

CONCENTRATION CAME A LITTLE EASIER THE NEXT day, Saturday, and after calling Raylene to make sure she was okay, I went to campus to catch up on some work. Denial, mixed with a slight degree of relief that at least one of the octopus's tentacles was cut off, made a potent mixture, and I spent the morning actually finishing up the work on the Chandler house survey. Things had to be getting better, I kept telling myself, and maybe I let a little part of myself believe it.

I took my lunch and my book and headed for my sanctuary. After I'd taken the job at Caldwell College five years ago, it had taken me a while to realize that my office wasn't the sanctuary—even with the door shut and a DO NOT DISTURB sign hanging—and neither was the lab or the library. You were still in circulation there, so to speak, and so I'd found refuge a ways off campus. Now that the college— the museum and the department—had been subject to such violation, I needed my gravestone more than usual. Unlike after seeing Chuck, I now felt like I could afford to go.

At the edge of campus, the old center of Caldwell, Maine began, and like so many New England towns settled a couple hundred years ago, there was a town green and a town hall, with an old white clapboarded church nearby. In this case, the old white clapboarded church had burnt down and was replaced in the 1890s by a stone church, which looked a bit gloomy when it was leafless winter, but was cheered by flowering trees in spring and summer and positively glorious when the leaves changed in fall.

Better still, to my purposes, it was usually empty, especially at this time of day. The trees drooped with their leaves—willows from the nineteenth century and oaks from long before that—and I sought out my gravestone in the oldest part of the cemetery.

"Belinda Aamons, beloved wife, Jan'y 12, 1730. 'Many a woman shows how capable she is, but you excel them all,'" was on my gravestone, as I thought of it. Not that I'd ever lean against it while I was eating, but I always pulled up a space along the stone wall that was directly opposite. Old enough to be interesting, no tree roots to make me uncomfortable, and yet shielded from the entrance of the burial ground by other stones and trees, this was my favorite spot. Belinda's stone was all alone—no sign anywhere of Mr. Aamons, who'd thought enough of his wife to erect an expensive engraved stone for her—and I could watch the birds looking for worms, I could watch the street traffic and the low apartment houses on the other side if I wanted, or I could read my book. "The grave is a fine and private place," even if there was no one here I wanted to embrace. I just wanted my lunch and my solitude, for the moment. Maybe someday, the solitude of the graveyard would be enough for me. . . . It occurred to me that when you've lost everything else, you've still got the graveyard. It was an oddly comforting thought.

Morbidity, Emma. It's unbecoming in you, and since you're incapable of writing good poetry, let's have a stop to it.

It wasn't all that morbid, I reasoned, just stock in trade for archaeologists, who, at least on a practical level, are more conversant with the rituals of death than most people. I'd participated in more than one discussion where friends picked out their choice of final celebration. The argument over burial in a Viking ship versus being set to sea in a burning boat—both with appropriate grave goods—was a time-honored one, as was the choice of what would go on a headstone: an abbreviated curriculum vitae in Latin? An imitation of an American Puritan skull and crossbones with hourglass? Instructions on how to access and use the solar-powered CD-ROM that was sealed in the casket, which would provide details of the deceased's life? I myself was still undecided. Politically, I approved of cremation, but part of me wanted to leave something behind for future generations of researchers. A small stone, a few grave goods . . . just thinking how much fun that would be for someone down the road made me grin.

The sun-warmed stone wall was comforting, and I felt it easing my shoulder, still sore from its abuse by Mr. Temple, who seemed to take a little too much glee in beating his lessons into me. Never get on his bad side, I thought, realizing how easily, how badly he could hurt me if he wanted to. Brian was trying to be patient about how I was dealing with things, but he couldn't understand my willingness to go to Temple's class. "You have such a hard time leaving the house, I suppose I should be glad, but Em, why let that big monster beat the crap out of you?" But my classes with Temple were the one place where I didn't have time to worry about any of this.

I tried reading, but couldn't focus, and caught myself scanning the same paragraph three times over before I realized it wasn't worth it. Maybe just a quick doze, and then I'd head back to campus and try to catch up on my work. Push what was going on around me away, first with a little me-time, then throwing myself into work.

Thank God this is still here, I thought, drowsily. It seems like everything else has been tampered with, spoiled in some way . . . my house, my coffee place, my campus, my bar . . .

I jolted awake, but caught myself before I moved too much. I made myself pick up the book again, and this time, didn't bother trying to read.

Why was this one place not touched? I wondered. If Tony—or whoever—knew so much about me, then why wasn't this place vandalized or robbed or set afire or any number of other wretched options? Why was this left to me, when everything else was being taken away, more and more aggressively?

I kept looking at the book, trying to remember to turn a page every once and a while, move my head appropriately. My thoughts raced along lines that had nothing to do with the novel I was pretending to read.

A couple of ideas occurred at once. It was a controlled sample, perhaps, one place left to compare with the others that had been violated . . .

Maybe it was being saved, for an especially bad moment. To have this place spoiled would be terrible, not only for me but the community as well.

Maybe it was like a game preserve, where I could be observed in what might be "normal" circumstances. Or perhaps my classes were, nothing had happened there . . . yet.

But where would the observer be? I wondered, looking around. Probably not in the church, as the windows didn't afford a good view with their small, colored panes. Two busy roads on other sides, and that left . . .

The apartment buildings, the off-campus student ghetto. I always thought it would be cool to live there, overlooking the cemetery, and would have when Brian and I had our commuting marriage, but the on-campus housing for faculty was so much cheaper if less interesting . . .

Turn the page, Emma, and try not to look like you're having an epiphany.

If I wanted to live some place anonymous, I would pick those apartments. It could also be that if there was someone over there watching me, it would behoove him to keep things quiet near his lair. Don't shit where you eat, Grandpa Oscar would have said.

I was trembling in the warm sunlight now, all drowsiness gone. I couldn't go investigate immediately, but I would have to soon. I needed to think first. There were four three-story buildings that were rental properties—that meant twelve apartments—and I was going to have to check out every one of them. But not at the moment, not when I was sitting right here . . . but why not? If anyone bolted, I'd be able to see them easily enough . . .

I sat and thought until I figured out every aspect of my plan: There were fire escapes on the backs of the buildings, but they were rusted metal and they'd make a hell of a racket if anyone tried to get out that way. I couldn't do anything about that, but I could listen for the noise and be prepared. Otherwise, the windows on the ground floor were the only other ways out, and even those would require a sizable jump to the ground. Go in, look at the mailboxes, note any that looked likely, and—then what? Call the cops? Try and get in? I'd figure it out when I got there, I decided, suddenly impatient.

I stretched out, then jammed my book into my bag. I was as restrained as I could manage, walking at a normal pace, as if I was done with my break and heading back to campus. I had to assume I was being watched and was self-conscious: What did my normal walk look like—fast or slow? Did I keep my eyes on the ground or did I look around? Walking had never seemed so complicated a task.

I walked past the street with the apartments, so that it would look like I was heading straight back to school. I circled the next block, and started at the last building in the row. I got into the lobby, and checked the mailboxes: I was pretty sure that the ones with multiple names on them were students—some of these were festooned with stickers and flowers, making it obvious—and I figured that the landlord would expect only one label for one tenant. I knew exactly how nosy and attentive to every change of detail they were from my own days as a student renter.

There was nothing that stood out as obvious, so I moved on to the next building. As I stepped up to the foyer, the inside door swung open, and a gaggle of giggling females came pouring out: It was too nice a day for normal people to stay inside. I pressed up against the side of the vestibule, to let them by, but the door had a security hinge and swung shut almost immediately: There was no chance of getting in that way. The mailboxes were equally unhelpful, but there was one with a single name on it—I kept in mind to check that one if nothing else showed up.

The third building I struck pay dirt. Two of the mailboxes had two or three names, the third had just one. On a smudged piece of paper, I could make out just the first and last initials of the name: E and F.

Ernie Fishbeck. I had my man. Our Ernie, the one that was now unhappily the guest of Detective Bader and the rest of the Stone Harbor Police didn't live here; he had given them a local Massachusetts address. Tony Markham had used his identity to find himself a lair near campus.

I was staring at the label, trying to convince myself that I was on the right track and that I needed to decide what to do next when the door opened. I stepped back, hoping to sneak in as whoever it was left, when I realized no one was coming out. An older woman, maybe in her late sixties, came bustling out and planted herself in front of the door, blocking me. She wore a Caldwell sweatshirt over black leggings and had a bandanna kerchief tied over her short hair. She had a broom in one hand and an unlit cigarette in the other.

"Can I help you?" she demanded. It wasn't an offer so much as a challenge, the dragon at the gate.

"Uh . . . I'm not sure," I said. I decided that it was best to come out with a bit of the truth. "I'm trying to find someone, who might live here. Someone who has been . . . harassing me, hurting people." I pointed to the mailbox. "I'm pretty sure that's his name. My name is Emma Fielding, and I work at the college. I hope you can help me."

She fidgeted uncertainly, not sure whether to believe me. I pulled out my license and my Caldwell ID card. "Just so you know I'm not trying to pull anything. Can you at least tell me if there is an older man, who lives here alone? I can't read the label on the mailbox; that can't be any kind of breach of security or trust, can it? Is it Ernie Fishbeck on the label?"

It took her another minute to decide. "I manage all four of the buildings along here, hell, I own them, too. I usually only rent to girls, and I look after them. My girls are the best-looking and the smartest on campus."

I got the impression that she said that to all of the renters and their parents, if they were undergraduates, as if that would convince them that this was practically a convent they'd be installing their daughters in. My heart began to sink, when she continued.

"But yes, it's just one gentleman in this building. I wouldn't ordinarily, but both of the other places in this building are rented to couples, and I thought no one would get up to any funny business. Name he gave me was Ernie Fishbeck."

I tried not to get my hopes up, but I could feel my heart racing anyway. "How old is he? What does he look like?"

"He's older, but you know? I don't want to tell you any more. No offense, sweetie, you look like a nice girl to me. But I gotta look out for my tenants."

"Look, I'll tell you what I think the guy looks like, and maybe, if you recognize him, we can go from there, okay?"

She shrugged. "I ain't saying anything. You can talk all you want."

I gave her my description, and her eyes went wide. "And maybe," I concluded, "he hasn't been living here all that long? Maybe just renting month to month?"

"I ain't saying." But she sounded less sure of herself now.

I seized on that uncertainty. "How about we call the Cald-well police? There's been a couple of crimes on campus, and if we could nail this guy . . . a security guard was killed, over in the college art museum. I just want to make sure no one else gets hurt."

She hesitated, and I knew that the landlady didn't want to be held liable for anything. "We can do that," she said finally.

"Maybe you could ask them to come up quietly? I wouldn't want anyone to run away, or start shooting or whatever."

Now she looked truly alarmed, rather than suspicious of me. "Definitely gonna call the cops." She stuck her cigarette behind her ear, propped her broom up against the corner, and pulled an expensive cell phone out of the pocket of her sweatshirt.

"Who's this?" she said, as soon as there was a connection. "Good. Bill, it's Helen Clarke, down on Park Street. Yeah. Look, I got someone here, says she thinks she's found someone who might have had something to do with the murder at the college, recently . . . yeah, security guard, that's what she said. That was in the paper, right? Jeez, what you see, these days, huh. Now, I'm not going to let her look around without one of you guys . . . yeah. That's it. And, Bill? I don't think he's in, but maybe you could park on the other side of the street, or—what? Right, I'm at number seven, right now, park in front of number three, so we don't tip anyone off, okay? Good boy. Thank you much." She hung up and glared at me. "Well, they'll be here in a few minutes. You might as well come in, wait in the hall with me, so you're not sticking out there either."

I accepted gratefully, barely able to speak I was so nervous. The thought that I might be able to put this behind me . . . that this might be over today . . . was making me dizzy. The landlady pretended to sweep and dust the lobby—a hallway, really—but kept casting suspicious glances in my direction. I realized I couldn't feel my hands anymore, that the floor seemed to have vanished from beneath my feet.

* * *

I looked at my watch: two-fifteen. The cops might be here in
five minutes. Three more, to take my story. An instant to
climb the stairs and open the door . . . wouldn't even have to
break it down, the landlady has a key . . . it could be done,
all but the shouting, by two-thirty. Even before my lunch
break is over . . .

The rap on the door came ten minutes later; it took an effort to recall the first time I'd looked at my watch. The in-
stances between then and now were numerous and futile:
nothing stuck in my head. Ten minutes is fine, I'll be a little
late getting back from lunch, I've got no appointments, no
meetings the rest of the day . . .

The officer looked like he was in his fifties, and not well
preserved at that. He was crew cut and grizzled and weatherbeaten, paunchy and irritable. He took my information and
then my story, and to my credit, I told it beautifully. I could
tell—it felt as though I was watching myself do it—and I'm
my own harshest critic. My voice was level, my words clear
and to the point, my story succinct, all a thousand miles
away from where I felt I stood. The cop's disbelief wavered;
he looked to Helen, who, bless her, did not refute any of my
points, even nodded in a few places, and I loved her from the
bottom of her worn-out tennis shoes to the dandruff on the
shoulders of her red sweatshirt.

Officer Paunchy—I could not for the life of me fix the
name on his tag in my mind—called back to the Campus
Safety Office, asked questions, about the museum, Dora,
the painting, the death of the security guard. His eyebrows
raised, until he caught my hopeful look, and he scowled
again, turning away.

It was two-thirty-five by the time he turned and said, "Well,
I'll go up and check it out." He jerked his head at Helen, who
pulled out her keys and mounted the stairs. I moved to follow.

"You stay down here. Out of the way. Don't leave, either."

"But—"

"Stay down here. Don't leave. Got it?"

"Yes," I said. "I'll stay here. I won't leave."

He frowned, decided that I would do as he said, and then preceded Helen up the stairs.

I did move, I went to the back of the hallway, past the first-floor apartment entrance, and in the back there was another door—probably to the basement—and a small window. From there I could see the fire escape, the backyard, and the cemetery. I was struck by how nice a day it was, and I could see the oak trees better from this angle. I stood there, waiting, keeping an eye on the fire escape.

I could follow the footsteps of the two people up the stairs, a short way down the hallway. A brisk rap on the door, sharply spoken if indistinct words as the officer demanded entry. Silence, then a shuffling of steps: Helen was unlocking the door.

Barely aware of the warm sunlight on my face, I tensed, waiting for what had to come next. A shout, a scuffle, a shot . . .

There was a scream.

I pelted down the hallway, skidding on the well-worn tiles. I stumbled up the stairs, straining to identify what was going on.

The door was still open, and what I saw stopped me cold just inside the room.

A body swung gently back and forth, suspended from an old-fashioned lighting fixture in the center of the room, breaking the beams of light that filtered in between the slats of the Venetian blinds. It was wearing a Caldwell College Physical Plant uniform. A note was pinned to the front of the shirt.

It was Tony. I knew it.

A thrill ran through me, mingled shock, relief, and something that felt exactly the same as the moment I held my first book in my hands, the day I realized I wanted a second date with the guy who'd rescued me at the library, reading the letter that assured me of a full scholarship to . . .

Something was wrong. The cop was scowling, and the landlady wasn't screaming. He was angry, she agape with disbelief. I looked again, more closely this time.

It was a dummy. Carefully, even lovingly, constructed so that the weight looked right, there were no unnatural bulges, even a wig had been pinned onto the head, which now looked like a pillow case to me. Latex gloves had been fashioned into hands, and the boots had been fastened to the inside of the trousers.

Before she could be stopped, Helen touched the dummy, sending it spinning slowly. I could see a second piece of paper pinned to the back. As my eyes adjusted, I could read the note on the front, just two words, I saw now.

Too late.

I stepped around to the back, and stopped it with the merest brush of my fingertips against the shirt. There was a note there, too.

Tell me, where is fancy bred?

I felt my mouth go dry.

"What the hell does that mean?" Helen demanded. "And look, the stupid idiot misspelled 'bread.'"

"It's not . . . not that kind of 'bread,' " I said. "It's a note for me."

"Why should it have anything to do with you?" the cop demanded. "Where do you see your name on this?"

"For one thing, it's a quote from *The Merchant of Venice.* People know I'm big into Shakespeare. For another thing"— I pointed to the paper on which both notes were written— "these are shooting-range targets, one on the heart, one on the head. The next line goes, 'or in the heart or in the head.' A friend of mine was shot recently." I swallowed. "Most people agree that the rhyme in the poem directly references lead. As in, lead in the heart, lead in the head."

"Kinda out there," the cop muttered.

"There's something else." I pointed to the feet, slowly swaying, a pendulum running out of momentum. While the rest of the clothing was worn but clean, the only thing that

was unusual in any was the dirt on the bottoms of the boots.
I recognized it immediately, as it was the same color as I
often had on my own. I could even tell you the specific clas-
sification I had assigned it with the Munsell book, the color-
coded chart that archaeologists, geologists, and the like use
to describe soil colors: 10YR3/4, dark yellowish brown.

It was just a guess of course, the color was ubiquitous in
New England, but I was willing to bet any money that the
soil on the shoes would be identified to match that at the
Funny Farm.

The thing was, nothing about the room or its contents was illegal. The rent had been paid through the end of the month,
on a month-by-month basis, always with a bank check. The
room was spotless—literally. It had been wiped down of
every kind of print.

The only other piece of paper in the room was the third
shooting target on the window on the far side of the room. A
hole was cut through the bull's-eye, and looking through it, I
saw a great view of the cemetery, and the tree under which I
usually sat.

I went back to my office. It took me a long time to realize
I was just sitting there, with the door locked, and that I could
do that just as easily at home. I sorted out the papers on my
desk, making neat piles that meant nothing, and left my
backpack on the couch. I took my pocketbook and carefully
locked the door behind me.

I was too late because Tony had been on campus, watching me, waiting for the moment I might figure out where he
was. He would never go back there again, and I was willing
to bet that there were any number of similar lairs elsewhere.
He had used several fake IDs, but had used Ernie's near
Caldwell, confusing the trail with just enough true information. The cops showed Helen a copy of the picture of Ernie,
and she believed it was the man she'd rented the apartment
to, but wasn't completely sure. When she saw a picture of

Tony—I'd taken to carrying one around with me—she was positive.

Tony wasn't afraid to show his face around campus. He'd colored his hair, and he looked a little more rugged, less well-fed than he had when he'd been there last, but that was four years ago. No one was looking for him there. I wondered if the fact that he was unafraid to be seen meant that he was getting eager and sloppy, or whether it was just that he was no longer worried about people knowing that he might be back.

Neither thought made me very happy.

I was some ways down the off-ramp for the wrong exit before I realized that I wasn't heading home. I was heading to the Point. Not so far from the College, but I wondered what I was going to do when I got there. I guessed I'd find out.

An hour later, I pulled onto the historic site's parking lot, killed the engine, and got out immediately. I vaguely registered the insistent dinging of the sensor that indicated I'd left the keys in the ignition and the door open. Oh well.

The grass needed to be cut again, and it was still damp from the last good thunderstorm; grass seeds stuck to my jeans and my shoes slipped on the slick weeds. My ankles were damp and tickled by the taller, tougher stalks that had survived the last mowing. As I moved, bees varied their course from mine, mosquitoes swarmed, sensing fresh meat, and crickets leapt out soundlessly ahead of me, as if they were torch-boys running ahead of a coach. The air was humid and soon my shirt was stuck to me; I was aware of sweat beading on my upper lip and running down the back of my scalp. There was no wind. If there were noises beyond the pounding in my ears or the insects, I didn't hear them.

I ignored the excavation units that had been so interesting to me—what was it, a week ago? A month ago? I could barely tell what day it was anymore, anyway—and headed straight for the fence. I stepped up on the bottom rail, swung my leg over, and sat on the top rail. I looked down at the water, a few meters below me, and couldn't hear the waves for the roaring in my ears.

All it would take is a simple straightening of my legs . . .

Don't be an ass. It's far too short a fall, not nearly bad enough to do any serious damage.

Maybe not here. But think about it: It would be over. There would be no more fear, no more pain, no more worry. No more twitching every time you hear a creak in the house, no more jumping when the phone rings.

I'm not even—

People—your friends, your family—would be safe. They'd be left alone.

I don't think it works like that. It's just not as easy as that.

I stared at the horizon, a washed-out whitish gray over slate seas, the sun a cool white disc that occasionally gleamed through the shreds of clouds. The air was warm and damp . . . I started with that . . .

It took me a few moments of hard work, but at last I was able to feel my hands gripping the rail I sat on, could feel the rough-hewn wood under my palms. Another two minutes of concentration, and I could feel my feet, heels hooked over the bottom rail. A breeze, faint as a whisper, moved, and my cheek itched. My shirt was soaking, and I could feel the fabric pull and slide against my shoulders when I shrugged.

The feeling of cold numbness, the tingling adrenaline crawl that wouldn't leave my arms and chest, was still there, but I could feel my body again. I willed it to remain solidly in my possession. Ignore the shivers, ignore the numbness, I thought, don't let it take over completely . . .

A throat cleared behind me.

I lurched forward in surprise, but felt a hand grab the back of my shirt.

"Whoa, there! You okay?" It was Sheriff Stannard.

"Holy mother of . . . damn it, Dave!" Dave Stannard tried to shove me over? Get a grip, Emma, he was pulling you back. "You scared the shit out of me."

"I am sorry, Emma. I tried calling to you, back up in the field, but you were a million miles away—"

I swallowed, tried not to look as guilty as I felt.

"—and I swear, I made as much noise as wet grass will allow, but you didn't hear me. Better now?"

I nodded, and he slowly released my shirt.

"Want a hand getting down from there?"

I didn't really need a hand, but I took the one he offered anyway. The ground beneath my feet felt . . . real. Felt good.

"Don't need to go for a swim today, all you have to do is hang outside for a minute. Might as well grow gills, this time of year."

"Yeah," I said, wrinkling my nose. "Ugh."

"I keep telling the park rangers that this is completely the wrong kind of fence to have here, for exactly this reason. People climb up on it, sit down to get the view." He shrugged. "If they're dumb enough to climb up there and fall off, bust a leg, well, that's their business."

"I'm sorry. Sometimes I feel like I have the run of this place . . . I mean . . ."

"I know what you mean. Lots of your history here. Not just work, not just family." Pauline wasn't family, not in the strict sense, but Dave knew that.

I nodded. "I was just thinking."

"Lots to think about?" When I didn't answer right away, he said, "Your husband Brian's been keeping me posted. I was hoping it was just a fluke, the bones you and Meg found out here."

"No, it's Tony Markham all right."

"So Brian said. I'm still . . ."

He waited. I shrugged again. I wasn't ready to tell anyone what had happened earlier this afternoon. Not yet.

"Well, just take care," Dave said finally. "No sense in wasting all that history, is there? Who'd sort it all out for us?"

"It's getting chilly out here," I said.

"Fall's coming. But you're shivering."

"I've got a fleece in the car."

"I'll walk you up there, then."

There was no arguing with him, and I was done thinking.

Besides, Dave had asked the question I needed to complete my thoughts. If I wasn't here, who'd sort it all out? I couldn't leave that up to just anyone.

When I got home, Brian ran out to the driveway, waving his arms around like a crazy man.

"They found him! They found his body!"

I got out of the car. "What? Who?"

"They've found Tony's body. You don't need to worry that he's come back."

Chapter 17

SAY THAT AGAIN." I LEANED AGAINST THE CAR, not sure which Tony he might be talking about, not daring to believe him.

"Look, I know there's a long way to go before the case is completely closed"—Brian's eyes were wide open, a smile on his face—"but it really looks like Tony Markham is dead. They found his body."

"How long ago?"

"I just got a call now—"

"No, I mean how long ago did he die?"

Brian frowned. "I don't get what you mean."

"Knowing that tells me whether he died five years ago and someone else is responsible for all the crap that's been going on around here. Or it tells me he died last week, and we might really be through it."

Brian nodded. "I don't know exactly, but they kind of gave the impression that it was more recently than not. We'll have to wait for a full report."

I nodded impatiently; of the two of us, I wanted to be the judge. "Tell me what they told you."

"A man's body, fished it out of the water near Stone Harbor." Brian swallowed. "It had been in the water a while. It . . . well, it was kind of a mess . . . the skin . . . actually—"

My renewed anxiety pushed aside an image of what water and marine life will do to a human body; the books I'd been reading for fun—mostly about forensic techniques and crime scene processing—were all too clear on the subject. But the fact that there was skin left at all suggested that it hadn't been in the water very long, probably less than a couple of weeks, I guessed. "But then how can they tell it's Tony?"

"A male, the right age, the right build, the right kind of clothes—what's left of them anyway. You know, good quality, not too showy—"

"Yeah, I could find six guys like that down the coffee shop at lunchtime," I snapped. "Doesn't make them Tony. What about teeth? What about fingerprints?"

"No teeth. No fingerprints, either."

"None of those things? Not even teeth? They should have survived, even if the soft tissues didn't."

"Apparently, this guy's hands were . . . removed. Probably cut off before he was dumped in the water." Brian swallowed, looked queasy.

"Cut off? As opposed to what? Shark attack?"

He shrugged. "Yeah, I guess so."

"Okay, what about teeth?"

"No teeth. His head was cut off as well. Somebody really didn't like this guy."

"Are you joking? Brian, this sounds like they've found a body and want to call it Tony; it's all so terribly convenient." I didn't want to give up, not yet. "What about blood type, DNA, that sort of thing?"

"Right, they're doing it," Brian assured me. "I guess they have to find Tony's old medical reports, or a relative or something, and that's going to take time, on top of a full-blown autopsy."

"And maybe they'll look for fingerprints then?"

"Em, I said there were no hands."

"Not his fingerprints. The killer's. They might be able to find something from that, something left on the . . ." I slumped down in my seat, shook my head. "Brian, what in the name of God makes them at all sure that it's Tony?"

Apparently some measure of peace of mind was keeping Brian calmer than I. "I know we need to wait, I just think this is a real hopeful turn. But there's a couple of things that I'm hanging on to. For one thing, the fact he was shot is significant. We know that he—whoever has been hassling us—was consorting with some pretty shady characters. Getting a head chopped off . . . well, it's not inconsistent."

Not inconsistent? Not good enough. I bit my tongue, just nodded for Brian to go on.

"Then there's the rope that was tying his guy up. The fibers matched a brand that's made in the United States, and is used for marine equipment. Sold locally."

We lived on the coast; I couldn't get excited about that. "What else?"

Brian broke out into a smile. "The most important thing was a coin."

"A coin?"

"A coin, found stuffed in one of the shoes." Brian paused, closed his eyes to help remember. "A gold coin, a guinea, he called it. Is that right? From the 1750s. The sort of thing that you'd find on a ship . . . that had gone down before the Revolution."

"Like the one that Tony was looting back at Penitence Point," I said slowly.

"Right. I never thought I'd be so glad to find out someone was dead." He grabbed my hands and tried to dance around, but I wouldn't move. "What's wrong?"

I shook my head. "It's too perfect."

Brian had a dangerous look in his eye; he really didn't want to be gainsaid in this. "Too perfect, how? It's pretty good to me."

How could I explain that after trying to convince Brian and the rest of the world that Tony was back, that I didn't think this was him? Bad vibes aren't quantifiable and aren't very convincing.

"I think someone wants us to believe it's Tony. I think there was a lot of care taken to ruin all the identifying body parts—head and hands removed, all the quickest identifiable elements dumped in water. It's classic. Then really damning evidence, something that is too perfect, is planted. And it's the kind of evidence that doesn't deteriorate in water."

Brian was working really hard to keep his patience. "Right, okay, I said they need to do the autopsy. Try to get some DNA. Absolutely. But until then . . . would it be so bad if we could imagine Tony is dead?"

"It's just like every soap opera and monster movie you've ever seen, Bri. You don't believe he's dead until you see the guy in the casket, with fingerprints, teeth and dental work, all intact. Or DNA or something more than evidence that could be planted on a conveniently mangled corpse."

Brian nodded, but I could tell he was stubbornly hanging on to the hope that this was Tony. "Your dummy in the apartment and this . . . these are the first tangible evidence that Tony's involved. And now we've got a corpse, right physical look, right location, lots of clues lead to Tony. It's a real good start."

I put my hand on my hip. "I think the body's being served up to us on a silver platter."

Brian was quiet for a very long time. "Well, when the autopsy is done, you'll have all the proof you want. Blood types, broken bones, that sort of thing. In the meantime, I bet the attacks will come to an end. I'm betting this is over." He paused. "I would really love for this to be over."

I sighed. "Me too. But it may take a long time for the autopsy to get done. Crime labs are wicked backed up these days."

"Well, until then, we'll just have to wait and see."

I called Sergeant Franco myself and they confirmed everything Brian had reported to me. They were "cautiously optimistic" that they had Tony. They said the location where the body was found suggested it wasn't too far from the place that Ernie said that he met Tony for his instructions. In fact, they'd used the news of Tony's body being discovered to try and get more from Ernie. While he seemed uneasy with the news—somehow Tony was able to convince his pawns that he cared about them—he didn't give out any new information. In fact, he became even more reticent than before. Maybe he knew more of Tony's plans than he was letting on, or maybe he just didn't know all that much to begin with. It would take about a week to get the report from the autopsy, if we were lucky. Longer, probably, for Tony's medical history, and what we really needed for conclusive evidence was a DNA sample from a close relative, and I'd never heard Tony mention family; they'd have to work through university records . . .

Not one untoward thing happened the next day, or the day after that. No spooky presents, no strange cars following me, I didn't even get cut off in the parking lot at school. No one died near me.

I even won ten bucks on a lottery ticket I bought on impulse.

Maybe my luck is turning, I thought. Maybe I can take this as a sign.

A week passed. Nothing happened still. Cautiously, I tried on the thought that Tony was gone, that the siege was at an end. That I was free.

It still came back to me that if I were Tony, I'd orchestrate just this kind of thing to get someone to let her guard down. But I didn't want to think like Tony. Didn't want to think that he was anything but fish food.

Trying not to think of it was almost as good as actually believing it. Brian helped, he told me how he had been wrong when he'd said it had been Duncan or Michael or even Ryan, that it had been Tony, and now Tony was gone. A couple of times he got a little too insistent, but I let it go. It wasn't quite I-told-you-so, on either of our parts. We began to smile at each other again, pat each other in passing, for no good reason, just like we used to.

Nolan was going to live. He was still in bad shape, but there was reason for hope.

My short-term memory came back. One day the phone rang, and I was merely surprised and annoyed, not startled to death. It was a telemarketer, and I told him in the nicest way possible to take my name off the list, to have a good day. I was proud of myself.

I tried drinking a beer because I felt like a beer. I did it without wondering if I was trying to blot something out, as I had the weeks before. I drank it only because drinking a cold beer with a burger on a hot day is a good thing. I stopped scrutinizing myself for every potential indication that I was losing my mind.

It was Tony, and now he's gone. He won't be back. I practiced saying it to myself every once and a while. It was like having an onerous task that had been hanging over my head like the sword of Damocles suddenly removed.

If I'm still wired, it's because it's close to the anniversary of the night out at the Point, all those years ago . . .

Late one afternoon, about a week after the body was found, I realized that I hadn't recently checked the computer files for pictures, the way that Joel had told me.

I did it now, if only to remove the useless ones from the hard drive and reclaim some of my memory. All of them were pretty boring, shots of the front of the house and the side, probably triggered by birds and squirrels where there weren't clear pictures of me and Brian going in or out. The last one, however, was dark and blurry. The only thing clear about it was that there was a human form there. Something the size of a Sasquatch with fair hair lurking outside my door. About three days ago, three in the morning.

I thought quickly. It was faint, and there were no details, but it was definitely human, definitely male, and looked way too much like Temple for me to be completely comfortable.

Whoever it was, was big, at least as big as the guy who attacked Chuck. There were a lot of big guys in the world. None of them had any business wandering outside of my house late at night.

Wait a minute—if the people at the hospital weren't letting non-family know about Nolan, how did Temple know to come to Massachusetts, to take over his class?

God, it couldn't be . . . could it?

I thought for a moment, my skin crawling as my mind raced:

How did he know to come? How did he find out Nolan was shot?

Chuck had been attacked weeks ago . . . I had just assumed that Temple arrived after Nolan was shot . . .

He knows all my weaknesses, all my bad habits . . .

Had Nolan ever actually mentioned Temple by name? He'd said he'd had a friend in California, that I should visit the school, but mightn't that have been Mr. Anderson? All I could remember was that Nolan had given me an address and telephone number.

Why did he come?

He could kill me with his bare hands . . .

The first time I spoke to him on the phone, he was talking to someone who wanted money from him. My God, he was arguing with his wife about money when we saw them in the restaurant that night.

He warned me never to feel too comfortable . . .

Tony loved indirection, separating himself from the dirty work. Temple had gotten here alarmingly fast—was he working for Tony?

He didn't seem to be the brain dead sort that Tony favored . . .

I stared at the image awhile, wondering what to do. I had just decided to call California, try to wring some information out of someone at the dojo when I noticed that the IM screen showed that Brian had logged off from work some time ago. He'd be home soon. Not soon enough to quell my suddenly jangling nerves.

The icon suddenly went on; Brian was downstairs. I was never so grateful for his lead-footed driving.

You home? I typed.

Yep, came back the reply.

Long day?

NTB. Not too bad.

K,brd, I typed. Okay, be right down.

TTYL.

I frowned. Why would he write *talk to you later* and not *ccos,* "caution, cats on stairs," as he usually did?

I typed, *k.* Then I thought about it and typed: *Dinner-E1'sP?* Evil one's pizza for dinner?

A long wait, then, *whatever.*

Now that was just plain wrong. Brian would never defer to me about pizza, especially not when it came to the evil, addictive sauce that Mario's Pizza was famous for. I sat for a moment, wondering whether Brian was really okay, whether he wasn't more burnt out than I thought.

Something was up.

The lights went out.

Damn Artie. I'd asked him to take care of the problem where the printer surged when the fridge did . . . Wasn't that problem with the electricity supposed to be taken care of before today?

"Brian?" I called out from my desk.

There was no answer. I felt the all too familiar rush of adrenaline and prayed that it was just one more innocent situation that would be explained away in a moment . . .

A soft, rhythmic noise from downstairs . . . more a vibration than a noise . . .

"Brian?" I said, much more softly, and heard my voice crack.

Nothing.

I looked outside. His pickup wasn't in the driveway. Through the open window, too high to be an exit, I could hear the muffled pounding. I picked up my phone. No dial tone, no nothing.

The hairs on the back of my neck were standing up. A softer noise, barely a noise, much closer . . . I recognized it was Minnie, almost invisible, a shadow in the mottled dark of the house. She was inching toward the door and stairs slowly, tail not even twitching, hesitating the way she does when she's stalking or unsure of something.

I had to get downstairs. If something was up—I could either get my cell or hit the panic button on the alarm. I wasn't going down there unarmed. I thought for a moment, wishing I hadn't moved the tools down to the barn, then grabbed a dumbbell that I kept by my desk. Not perfect, not a lot of range, but a lot of wallop.

I scooped the cat up, went down the stairs softly, and glanced in the bedroom. A great lump was in the center of the white bedspread: Quasi was taking a last nap before trying to escape outside for the night. I dumped Minnie in there, shut the door on them both.

My cell phone was charging downstairs by the back door.

The rhythmic pounding continued downstairs, louder than when I was in my office. It stopped for a moment, then started up again, farther off.

I was at the bottom of the stairs now, avoiding the ones that I knew creaked the most. Then I saw the quick sweep of a flashlight beam, heard quiet footsteps.

Right. Out the front door, and no detours, Em—

The sound of a flashlight clicking off. The footsteps had stopped, too.

I thought I heard heavy breathing, as if whoever it was had run a quick race. Perhaps it was anticipation.

My heart stopped dead. I wasn't sure that my mind wasn't playing tricks on me, when it came again, after a pause, as if someone had swallowed.

I went to the front door, unlocked it, and tugged, quietly. It wouldn't budge. I pulled harder, I could feel that I'd slid the deadbolt back, but the door still stayed shut. I yanked with all my might, but it was wrong, wrong . . . the door never stuck like this. I pulled. *Why* wouldn't it *open*—

And then there was the voice.

"Emma? Is that you?"

It was him.

"I've been waiting."

It was Tony Markham.

Chapter 18

I SWALLOWED, TRIED TO KEEP MY KNEES FROM BUCK-ling, and I leaned against the doorknob for support. In the dark, it was too easy to believe that I was asleep. Having so nearly convinced myself that the nightmare was actually over, to have it unfolding in front of me now was almost too much to take.

"Four years, I've been waiting. It's time."

A sound, a foot edging along the uneven boards of the hallway near the back door. I knew where he was.

There was no light now. Did he know where I was? He seemed to be moving this way . . . had moved into the dining room.

"You have to understand, it's over now."

A chill swept over me. It was like the years were stripped away and I was back on the Point—the cold, the voice that swept away every bit of my strength.

I pushed—willed—myself away from the door and edged into the kitchen, over to the counter, as quietly as I could. I was barefoot, and could feel the grit on the floor, but made almost no noise. The voice was still coming from the dining room. That meant that he could either come through the living room or back out the other dining room door into the kitchen. I looked over to the back door, a mile away, my only hope. A small pool of light came in from the outside, the street light at the end of the driveway, illuminating the wedge under the door. Two, three wedges. Maybe more.

I'd never get them all out before he got to me.

The cellar door was blocked with Artie's tools and boxes. I'd never get through it all in time, not without giving myself away.

"It's time for an accounting."

I felt a wave of dizziness and nausea wash over me but, somehow, that helped. Fighting off illness reminded me that I had some control over myself still, I wasn't done yet. I stepped another foot closer to the counter. Another step closer to the block full of expensive German knives I gave Brian last Christmas . . .

I set the dumbbell down and slid out the biggest carving knife I could, the faint thrill of metal on metal barely reached my ears. Rejected the serrated one, despite the fact it would make a wound that was difficult to heal. I wanted all the edge, and all the distance I could get, to keep between us . . .

I had the knife. I would step back toward the front hall and the living room, and I would wait behind the wall. And when Tony Markham got close enough I would slash it down and across his face. Even if I didn't get an eye, the blood and pain would be enough to distract him, and if I was very lucky, I would get a second chance and go this time for the throat, digging in, slashing out as hard, as raggedly as I could . . .

" 'You're thinking of something my dear, and that makes you forget to talk,' " came the voice again, Alice's Duchess. "Here's the deal, Emma. My dear Emma. You're a clever girl, you're planning what you're going to do. You're resourceful and you're tough. And you're fucked to a fare-thee-well. I've been planning this for a very long time. You don't have any time left."

I stepped backward, one step, two, and then heard a shuffle—he was moving. Which way, the kitchen or the dining room? A bump and an exhalation; he was definitely midway through the dining room now, had knocked into the boxes that were there. It's my dining room, of course you can't dine in it. All the stuff for the kitchen was in there.

I was by the doorway, stumbled a little, got behind the wall, waited. My heart was pounding, my hands were so sweaty I could barely tell I was holding the knife. My hand brushed the wall and my trembling fingers skipped off it. I tried to compose myself, find that ready stance, but it felt like a sham. All my training, and I couldn't pull it together.

"You're still thinking too much. It's a problem for you. You should have acted long before this. As a result it's too late. You're done for."

He's just trying to freak me out, I thought, even as I knew he was echoing my own thoughts. He'll come by here, he's going that way around, and I'll get him, I'll end this, I swear . . . My breathing grew heavier and heavier as I readied myself . . .

I am going to end this. Another minute, and it will be over, I can wait a minute, stand here calm and quiet for a minute and then ten seconds more and it will be *over* and he will be *done,* and I am going to end this *now.*

Just saying it gave me resolve.

Wait patiently, I told myself, another moment, keep breathing . . .

And suddenly, he was there, but on the right hand side of me. He'd come around back through the dining room and the kitchen to the hall and it all went to hell right then.

I screamed, stepped forward, swung out, slashing. I was off balance, I'd been ready to go to the other side, but I caught *something* . . .

A grunt. And then I felt the knife ripped out of my hand, heard it clatter to the floor, skitter away from me. What—

"—the *fuck*?" At nearly the same time, something hard caught me upside the head; I saw stars, couldn't figure out where I was. Falling. I hit the ground, almost broke my fall, but only then feeling the pain in my ear, my jaw.

"I don't like you with knives, Emma!"

I heard the words, that voice, distantly, it was like the ocean was roaring inside my head. I felt the step coming toward me and I rolled away. Tried to kick, and only succeeded in entangling his foot with mine as he tried to stomp on me. I shoved a little harder, felt him stumble back. I struggled to my feet, moving away.

The voice hadn't stopped. "—you wanted to use a knife before, Billy's knife, at the Point, and it was a cheap little trick, and it didn't *work,* you never had a *chance.*"

The hall stand . . . I'd backed into the stand, that meant that the umbrellas were right behind me. I grabbed the biggest thing there. Oscar's walking stick.

I stepped in, jabbed as hard as I could at a little lower than my own shoulder height, what might have been Tony's sternum, the widest part, the biggest target. He grabbed at the stick, I wrenched it away, followed him as he moved into the living room. I swung at his head. The stick got caught in the standing lamp behind the chair, and that's when the gun went off.

I screamed at the noise, flinched convulsively, let go of the stick, but felt nothing. Not yet. The flashlight came on then, blinding me.

"You look very stupid, standing there, holding your hands up like that. You should know, better than anyone."

His voice was different then, different from the way it had been a second ago. What was it?

I had to keep him talking. I licked my lips, raised my hand against the light. "I should know—?"

"You should know better . . . I don't want to hurt you."

Still blinking at the powerful beam, I tried to follow his voice. "I find that hard to believe." There was a noise, on the flashlight, and I realized that he was wearing the chainsaw glove that Brian had had in the barn with the other safety equipment. It had deflected my knife.

"Of course not. You're more than unusually dense, at times, and that's why you don't understand. I'm trying to teach you something."

"What's that?"

"I'm trying to teach you your limits."

I said nothing. The flashlight wavered, briefly, and I heard the glove hit the floor. Though my eyes were adjusting to the room that was indirectly lit by the flashlight, they didn't refocus fast enough to catch a glimpse of Tony. His voice was the way it was before . . . what was it? Something about the knife . . . His voice was stronger than it had been before . . . Tony was in my house . . .

"I'm going to take the very best care of you, Emma. You're going to be well and fit and sane for as long as I can manage it, because that way you will learn." He sounded so confident, so strong.

The rest of the room resolved itself now, and I could orient myself. It was like staring into the sun, though, with the flashlight in my face, but I knew the gun was still there. Too far away for me to do anything, *maybe* too far away for him to nail that first shot.

"No, we're going to get the lights back on. Then we're going to sit down and have a glass of wine."

"Huh?" I had a better sense of where he was now, and I tried not to look headlong into the light, trying to see what I could in its penumbra.

He continued patiently. "Then we're going to call my friend outside the house."

"There's no one out there," I said instantly, a force of habit. Damn it, Emma, shut up and think! The knife, the knife . . . what is it about the knife that made him different?

"No, I assure you there is. Please, do as I say. Clasp your hands in front of you. Back up, three steps only. Turn your head to the side—no more than that! And you should see him. The big blond fellow out there is working for me."

I couldn't see much. But I could see a very large form, a man, waiting by the side of the porch.

He seemed as big as a house. It looked like he might be the size of a Temple.

"Step back this way again, please. Keep your hands in front of you, where I can see them."

"We call your friend," I said. "And you don't shoot me." I tried to imply that I still failed to see anything so bad about this.

"We don't call him yet," Tony said. "You are amazingly stupid sometimes."

And there was that change in his voice again . . . he was frustrated. The knife . . . I had almost had the chance to use one on him that night at the Point. My kitchen knife reminded him . . . and now it reminded me.

That was something . . . something I could use. "When do we call him, Tony?"

"We call him when Brian comes home. My friend out there is very talented. He claims to have worked for the government at one point, but I think that's a lie. Still, you never know. His talents are hard to come by—at least in conjunction with his remarkable ability and peculiar lack of conscience—and I can't imagine anyone in a position to need them would be very picky about his other disquieting traits."

"Yeah, whatever," I said, as deliberately insolent as I could manage. This was the test.

"You'll be laughing out the other side of your mouth in an hour, and for a long time after that!" There was that note again, the one that said that Tony didn't believe he would be challenged. Couldn't conceive it. It was when he felt least in control, that his voice changed. That control had very little to do with the gun. He had gone way off the deep end.

"You might have . . . interrupted me, once, but that was a fluke, a situation that had to do more with your luck than my plan." He caught himself, tried to settle down. "And still, for all of that I got away, and have been watching you ever since."

I couldn't help myself: I shivered.

He nodded then, faintly satisfied. "We'll listen on the phone. I'll be very interested to see what you'll try to do to stop Brian's screams."

I felt the world swimming in front of my eyes and felt my stomach clench.

"What will you do, what *won't* you do, eventually, to let Brian die? Imagine a place where that would be the very best you could offer him. I believe you'll find the edge of your sanity and leap, to save him."

He let me think about it. God help me, I found myself imagining things unthinkable.

"My friend is a thug, but he has a delicate subtlety when the conditions are right. It could be weeks. Months, even."

My mouth was so dry I could barely form the words. "What's . . . why?"

"You're much more limited than you might think, and I'm going to show you that. You might have gotten inflated ideas about yourself, having interrupted me before—and it was no more than an interruption. No more than that, and if I'd taken a bit more time, tempered my enthusiasm for the project just a little, even that wouldn't have happened.

"Your mind, your will, your body. Not much at all. You've got luck, perhaps a kind of . . . cunning . . . that has a sort of virtue to it, so I won't believe you easily. I'll have to be very sure, know that you're not just faking the knowledge to stop the lesson. I think I'll be able to tell when you've truly learned. And then we'll be done. Then you'll know that I've won."

"You've won already, Tony." I didn't know if I could convince him, but I had to try. "Brian and I . . . we're having troubles. My friends are hurt, one close to death. I can't sleep, I can't eat, I can't concentrate—the people at the college think I'm losing my mind. I don't know what more proof you want. You got away, with the gold. You avoided the international authorities. You came back, and still didn't get caught, even after all you've done. And at every turn, you've bested me. I don't know how better to let you know: You've truly won."

He spoke sadly. "Emma, there's a difference between knowing something, and owning it. I need to believe that you've owned it. Then we'll be done."

I felt myself burst into tears. It wasn't hard; it wasn't an act. But it was also good cover.

He let me sob, watched the tears flow and my nose run and kept the gun on me with an understanding patience that worried me.

This was about control, just like Temple had said back in California. So now I understood I had several choices, any one of which had to happen in the next two minutes or so.

I could hope Brian wouldn't come home, but that wasn't likely. And it still didn't get me out of this.

I could hope that in a fight outside, Brian would win. Also unlikely, if what Tony said was true.

Assuming that I couldn't beat Tony, I could hope that Tony would screw up and kill me first. That would break his control, he wouldn't have me to torment, and that was what this was all about.

Unappealing as well, but it would have to do. I'd either beat Tony or make him kill me. And I had to do it soon.

I tried to wipe my face on my shirt, and sank to one knee. My hands were still clasped in front of me, as he'd commanded, but now I raised them, as if pleading.

"Don't do this! You can't do this! I'll do whatever you want, I swear, only leave Brian out of it. I'll leave with you, I'll go anywhere, do anything, only don't do this to me! Don't hurt Brian!"

"Sshh, shhh. It's all right. This is going to happen, Emma. You should accept this. You're going to learn from this."

"You can't, you can't do this! You won't get away with it—!"

I deliberately used challenging words. The frown appeared again, the pitch of his voice changed back to the almost querulous insistence. "I am getting away with it. This is going to happen—"

I charged him then.

From my half crouch, I tackled him, ran straight for his hips.

The gun went off, then.

The lights went on, then.

The noise was unbelievable. I felt heat up my back, neck, but surprisingly little pain.

We went down. The flashlight landed with a hard crack, the light out of my eyes, at last. I was on top of Tony now, and spots popped in front of my eyes, but that wasn't important just yet. Didn't need to see him to get in close, get control, isolate his gun, arms, legs, teeth.

He tried to push me away, slammed his fist into my face even as I slid up his chest and, with both my hands, pinned his gun hand to the floor. He shouldn't have tried to push me away, he should have tried to hold me close so my attacks wouldn't have so much momentum. We grappled, and I kept trying to move up, get my knees under his armpits, to hold him in the mount. Tony threw wild punches, then tried to get my hands off his pinned wrist.

I glanced up and saw his face for the first time in four years.

He'd changed the color of his hair again—dark in Chicago, it was now back to what I assumed was his natural gray-white. Maybe that meant something to him. The beard was gone too; and his face was lined more than the tan skin weatherbeaten, nearly toughened into leather. He was older, but he was stronger, too: He'd had a goal, after all. But it was the sharpness of his eyes that was so recognizable, and more than determination, an inhuman focus terrified me, brought me all the way back to Penitence Point, reminding me how helpless I felt then. The shock of those memories was sharp and fresh and suddenly I could feel the cold saltwater and desperation leaching the strength from me all over again.

Sweat glistened on Tony's face and I saw the scar I'd left on his forehead. I'd hurt him then. I was stronger now, too. I renewed my efforts.

Outside, a man screamed. It was a terrible sound.

Inside me, something died.

Tony hesitated, for an instant. I slammed his fist to the ground. His fingers opened, and I couldn't grab the gun but could I shove it away from us.

He roared at the loss and writhed beneath me, trying to shove my face away. Keeping my left hand on him, I leaned with my right forearm against his throat. The feel of his struggles under me, as I leaned all my weight on his throat, was beyond satisfying.

Tony turned red, but he was still resisting too much. He grabbed at my hair, but it was too short now for him to hold on hard enough and I brought my head low enough for a couple of head butts.

That brought blood.

I leaned down, my right forearm crushing his throat, pushing his head back against the floor—too high, but I couldn't reposition myself. I could feel his breath against my ear, hear the guttural noises he made as he fought, or maybe that was an illusion, the gun's report still ringing in my ears. I could feel the heat of his body beneath mine, felt his heart pounding next to mine. And every time he moved, I countered it, and if that didn't work, I dug around in my bag of tricks for something else.

His fingers in my face hurt like hell, but I had more tricks than I thought. He was not, was *not,* going to get away with this.

He bucked, a desperate move, a reaction, unplanned, actually got me up off him a moment, but I'm not a small woman. I've always been tall, reasonably fit, but now thirty pounds heavier with more muscle than the last time we fought. There was nothing but lean and mean on me. I landed back on him, hard on his breast bone, and I heard the breath whoosh from his lungs. I posted, one leg out, to keep him from bucking me off entirely, but kept all my weight on top of him.

Nolan was right: Fighting is just like chess and sex.

It was only me and Tony, now, in the whole world.

There was no thinking now, all the hesitation that I ever felt in training, that reluctance to hurt my sparring partner, had evaporated as soon as I'd heard that scream. No hesitation, no thinking, no future.

A tiny part of me remarked quite distantly: It was pleasant, in its way, the not-thinking, the no-future . . .

Enough. Work first.

His arm was freed, now, after trying to get me off the top of him, and he tried to shove at me. It was a weak push, he was probably tiring, he wasn't a young man and I'd done some damage.

I tried sliding my right leg up, just a little, to reach the gun, but that was a mistake. Tony grabbed my elbow, pulled my arm mostly off his neck, which probably hurt him like hell and didn't do my elbow any favors either, slamming into the floor like that. I landed almost on his face, but he was too busy trying to breathe to think about biting me.

His hand slipped and mine shot up. I didn't bother going for the throat, this time, but the face.

I didn't reach the eyes—he grabbed my arm again before I could get that far—but I sunk my fingernails into the flesh of his cheek and, as he pulled down, I *raked* . . .

Tony screamed. An ugly noise. Pleasing.

Maybe it was the pain or the sight of his own blood that inspired him, but he finally did what he should have done all along. My balance was off, with my left arm stretched so far out, and he shoved his hand under my right armpit and pushed so that I was forced to roll to the left.

I brought my knee up straight away, aiming right for his groin, but he'd done almost the same thing, and I smashed my knee right into his. The bones met at exactly the wrong angle, and pain shot up my leg. I screamed.

It shocked me and I hesitated, trying to get my bearings, trying to see through the tears. Better to get up than stay down, not when you can't see what you're going to do next, not when you can't see where he is . . .

Tony was standing, but facing the wrong direction. I think he realized for the first time that the lights had come on, and he grabbed the gun. That gave me the extra second I needed to stumble to my feet. I tried to step toward him, but the pain in my knee was blinding.

Tony turned, brought the gun up. It shook, but I could tell by his eyes that he wasn't lost yet.

I brought my hands up, half to distract him, half to get them in front of me for what was going to happen next.

But I had no idea what was going to happen. If he shot, he could still miss, I reasoned. He'd probably get a few shots off before I got to him, and one was bound to hit me . . .

In the kitchen, the cellar door opened with a crash, its crappy, rusting hinge shrieking an announcement. It scattered Artie's tools and the kitchen chairs all over the place.

Tony turned to see what it was.

It was Brian. Coming out of the basement. Fear and wonder on his face. A pry bar in his hands.

Tony raised the gun, pointed it at Brian.

And that was it.

Something clicked inside me.

I don't remember what happened, not really. I don't know when I started to move, couldn't have told you what was going to happen if you'd asked me. I don't remember looking anywhere but at Brian, but I must have: All I remember was his face. I couldn't have just put my hand out, found a weapon instantly under my fingers. I don't remember feeling the desperate pain in my knee, I don't remember the ringing in my ears.

All I do remember is Brian staring, a horrified look on his face, at Tony and then me. I remember total silence, save for the metal mechanical noises of the gun as Tony prepared to fire, but it couldn't have happened that way, could it? There had to have been breathing, screams, footsteps, something. But I don't remember anything like that.

This must have been what happened: I picked up the heavy black rubber electrical cord for the new washer and dryer. Nearly an inch thick, bent in half to a length of about two feet, and neatly tied with white plastic ties, it fit my hand perfectly. One thing I do remember now is the weight of it, now, how all that lovely, copper wiring gave it the perfect heft.

It came into my hand. I pulled my arm back and swung it like a mace. Its chunky skull-shaped plug arced through the air, and landed heavily on the side of Tony's head.

I heard a crack.

Too bad, I thought: The four stubby prongs were facing outward. Next time, then.

Tony dropped like a sack of potatoes. Straight to the floor, do not pass go, do not collect $200.

I raised my hand again. Brought the heavy cord up and lined it up with the back of Tony's unmoving head—

"Emma! What the hell—?"

Brian was still there, the crowbar in his hand. Suddenly all the pain that I'd remembered having came shooting back, invading my bones and muscles, and I wished for the silence, the numbness I'd felt before.

The second blow went awry, across Tony's back, before I dropped the cord and staggered toward Brian. I stopped, remembering, and turned. I found the gun, made sure that it was fast, and replaced the safety. I put it into the drawer, automatically imagining Sophia coming over and finding it.

"Don't touch that! You could get hurt!"

I looked at Brian, and frowned: stupid.

"Are you okay?" His face was sweaty, dirty, but not a scratch on it—

Beloved.

And then the realization that he was safe, that he was whole, that nothing I'd been thinking had come to pass, that it wasn't going to happen flooded me. The disbelief that follows waking from a nightmare, that none of it was real, took my breath away.

Hysterics. There wasn't enough breath in me to feed my aching body, fuel my tears, talk, and keep life going, but thank God for autonomic muscles. We clutched at each other, repeated sentences back at each other.

I looked down and there was dirt and blood all over his hands, his knees. I realized the blood had been there before I'd hurled myself at him.

"What happened? There's a man, outside—was it him? The scream—what did he *do* to you?"

"Shhh, it's okay. Temple has—"

My chest constricted. "Oh, Jesus, Brian, how did you ever get away from *him*? Did you kill him?"

"What? No, Emma, he helped me. He got the—"

"No, he was working for Tony, the big blond guy, he got here so fast—he was on the video! Where is he now?" I looked around wildly.

Brian held on to me, tried to keep my tenuous grasp on reality together by physically holding me. "Video? Joel's video? No, he wasn't—yes, maybe he was on the video, but he was here, keeping an eye on us. He was the one who took care of that someone outside—I came home and found them fighting. He yelled for me to get to you. It was the other guy who screamed." He looked down at his torn-up hands, as if seeing them for the first time. "The doors were jammed, I couldn't get in. I went in through the bulkhead, to the basement."

"No key?" The key was usually on the rack with the spares. It was there now.

"No key. Crowbar. No lock now, either."

A crash in the dining room. We looked: Tony was up, covered in blood. He shoved the air-conditioner out of the window. Before I could move, he threw himself out down to the driveway.

Brian and I untangled ourselves, stumbled toward the window. I shoved myself through, got hung up on a ragged piece of torn-out windowsill. Brian was smarter, went for the back door, pulled the wedges out, found the locks.

"Derek! Temple! He's getting away!" I screamed. I pulled myself back through the window and tried to tear the snagged fabric off the splintered wood. No luck—then it gave. "Temple!"

There was no sight of him. No sign of the stranger Tony claimed was waiting for us outside.

I heard a gargantuan bellow down the street, saw Brian run down the driveway. I tore out the back door, took the steps two at a time, and hit the gravel before I remembered I was barefoot, knee screaming. I didn't care, there was no way Tony was going to get away from me.

Headlights were coming down the street toward us. I could hear sirens now, but the car coming toward me was no cop car. Derek was down the street, where the car had come from, now charging back after it.

Tony shot out from behind the old oak tree to our right. Headed for the car—he was going to get away.

Brian and I started after him, but the car didn't slow down.

Tony ran in front of the car and seemed to pause.

The car never slowed down. Plowed right into him, and then over him. Dragged him a bit, before something—a shirttail? A finger?—gave and Tony's body fell away behind. Something—shock, perhaps, or a chunk of Tony getting wrapped around the axel, I hoped—made the car veer. It almost cleared the ditch, but instead, slammed into the far side of it.

I watched as the back of the car flipped up, nearly made it to ninety degrees, before gravity claimed it and the rear end fell back down, leaving the car upright. Whoever was inside had probably experienced a full-body chiropractic adjustment but didn't go through the windshield when the car slammed into the ditch.

I reached out for Brian, waited for Temple to join us. He didn't stop, but went straight through to the driver's side of the car. He tried to open it, couldn't do it, slammed himself against the window. That only made him bellow the louder.

"Derek! The door—don't worry about it! The cops will be here in a second, they'll get him out!"

"The police are on the way, man!" Brian shouted. "You'll hurt yourself!"

"I don't give a toss about the police! The malignant bastard tried to knife me!" He groped around on the ground, found a stone, and smashed the window open.

The cops arrived just as Mr. Temple succeeded in pulling a very large man through a very small car window.

Chapter 19

I SPENT A LOT OF TIME AT THE HOSPITAL AFTER that. It's not like they could let me into ICU to see Tony, and of all the people there—cops, detectives, doctors—I didn't think he'd want to see me. I went all the same. Brian wasn't sure it was a good idea, but I couldn't see any way around it. Tony was still out of it, attached to all those tubes anyway. I had to do something, so I sat in the waiting room when I finished with school for the day. I tried to figure out what I would say to him, when I finally got the chance, that seemed to be the most important thing, so I stopped pretending to do work and brought a notebook with me and wrote.

At first my journal was completely random, like I was just trying to make the whole thing make sense—or go away completely. An exorcism or an imposition of order? Both and neither, page after page it came and it all boiled down to a few troubling and enlightening thoughts.

Against what seemed all logic to me, I felt guilty. Oddly, it wasn't over the fact that I had tried to kill Tony, but that he had come back for me. If I'd been smart enough or strong enough, I could have prevented the terrible things he'd done to everyone around me, couldn't I? If I hadn't provoked him somehow—what was I, to deserve such rage?—in the first place, it wouldn't have been an issue. It went against every fiber in my being, and yet the guilt remained and I could make no sense of it.

And I felt rage that even hurting Tony didn't dissipate. Part of it was the realization that he would never understand my anger, would always see it misplaced, with the skewed logic of insanity. I would never be able to show him how wrong he was, how much he deserved to be punished for what he did, and that injustice ate at me. I would always be the villain, to him.

Part of it too, was that he had succeeded: He'd made me see what I was capable of. I'd gone to bad places, places I never wanted to visit again. Tony had told me once, a long time ago, that we were the same. Maybe he meant that everyone is capable of going into the dark; he ran to it, embraced it, and then showed me I wasn't immune to it either.

As much as that scared me, I knew I'd do it all again, if I had to. If anyone tried to hurt me or my family—the one I was born into, or the one I chose—I'd drop civility in a heartbeat. As illogical as my guilt was, that thought cheered me, because the final thing that Tony taught me was that I left the dark of my own free will.

My writing helped to sort out what had happened that night. The police came, signaled by the alarm company that the phone lines had been cut. They had been delayed, however, by the two fiery car wrecks that happened to occur at the far ends of town. It seemed that Tony had more than just this pair of accomplices, but they faded into the woodwork, and Tony wasn't talking. Cut off the head . . .

Finally, about a week later, it was over. The nurses came out and told me, when Tony finally died. No one claimed his body. The nurses wouldn't stretch the rules enough for me to go in and see him, so that was it. He'd never hear what I had to say now, not the questions, not my explanations. Not my apologies. Now I had nowhere to put my guilt in all this, much as I knew logically, I didn't deserve it.

It took me a long time to stop crying. No one kicked me out of the hospital. The cop who was there seemed to understand that I needed to know for sure Tony was gone, and asked sympathetically if someone could come and pick me up. I had already decided that I was going to pull it together on my own, and get home under my own steam, if nothing else. It's all about the small triumphs, for me, right now. Hey, if it's small or nothing, I'll take small and be thankful for it. For now.

The sun was down by the time I got home. The lights were on in the house—I think Brian still prefers to burn the electricity rather than have the shadows too close these days— and seeing that brightness helped a little. Like a good deed in a naughty world . . . maybe there was something to *Merchant,* anyway. I'd have to reread it again. I knew there were some truly dark places inside me, and I needed to start lighting those single candles. Marty had given me the name of a good shrink—it was no surprise; she always knew the best of everything—when we'd gone out for margaritas and reconciliation. I'd already made my first appointment with her.

I decided to keep my journal, and not throw it out right away. I've got a lot of work to do with it.

After I got done washing my face, I found Brian in the kitchen, eating leftovers and reading a copy of *Rolling Stone.* I can't stand the hipper-than-thou prose, but hey, music was his thing, and if it made him happy, more power to him. He looked up, and I guess it only took one glance at my face to realize that Tony was gone for good.

Brian came over and hugged me, tight as he could. He patted my head, and I kind of missed having long hair then, because it was so nice to have him stroke it all the way down my back when I felt this bad.

"It's not you, it's not your fault," he said over and over, and I hated hearing it again, true as it was.

"I'll get through it," I said, finally, when I stopped crying. I hadn't even realized that I had started again. Must have been some place between the sink and the stairs. Then again, I didn't even remember much of the drive home. All I really remembered was trying to drive carefully, at the same time, rushing home, to the only place that seemed to help when I had to have these thoughts. School was good, I could work to banish stray thoughts there, but if I had to think about this, it had to be here. It was easiest to bear my thoughts here.

"I'll get through it," I said again, and pulled away, gently.

If I start right now, I thought, I can clear my head by bedtime. Fake it until you make it. Pretend to be normal enough, or well, work at it hard enough, and some of it is bound to rub off. Soon.

Soon enough.

A little more than a week after Tony died, I was back at the gym. Nolan wasn't up to full speed yet, but pushing himself through recovery at what I thought was a hazardous pace. He was doing well enough to oversee my lesson this week, well enough to sit on the sidelines and add a brow beating to Mr. Temple's when I screwed up. But I'd tagged Temple once, even working around my knee, so when the bruise comes up where he hit me back, I'll wear it as a badge of pride.

I made the same mistake again, and Nolan gave me another dose of sarcasm that imprinted the correct move on my brain and muscles. Nolan's got Temple calling me Red, now, so I'll have to take that, too, for another week until Temple goes back. Between the two of them, it would be a hard week, but I nodded and took the criticism, and tried not to smile, thinking how good a day it was.

After I'd packed up my gear I saw Temple and Nolan talking to Erik Reynolds in Nolan's office. I slowed and stared as I walked past, then, outside, dawdled near his truck, waiting for Erik to come out.

"Hey, Erik. You know Mr. Temple? And Nolan?"

"Hey, Emma. Yep."

I tilted my head, glaring at him for his stupid answer, but he just smiled and unlocked the truck, opened it and rolled down the window. "I mean, how do you know them?"

"Oh. Well, Derek likes to eat." He got into the truck and shut the door. "And Nolan lives around here."

"Yeah, but that doesn't—" I began impatiently. Suddenly, I realized I had a lot of questions for Erik, like how he'd handled himself on the boat, for starters.

Erik smiled again. "Em, I could tell you. But then I'd have to kill you."

He said the words exactly the same exaggerated way everyone else does when they're goofing around. I looked into his eyes and saw no threat there, but it struck me that he was wondering whether I'd push the issue.

"Maybe another time."

"Another time, then." He winked, and pulled away.

At home, my jog-bra hit the floor with a plastic clatter. Startled, Minnie bolted out from under the bed with a scrabble of claws on the hardwood floor. The one thing in the world that I hadn't learned to fight is a sweaty athletic bra made even more rigid with breast protectors; the hooks in the back made escape considerably easier. I was surprised that my sweatpants didn't make nearly as much noise, and the knee brace and groin protection went next, with not so much as a clunk as a soft thud. I'd already taken out my mouth guard, put it in the pile of things to be washed, along with my sweaty handwraps, in which Minnie was already rolling, happily grokking the smell in the yards of black cotton. I hit the shower, feeling energetic and pumped and tired all at once. Although I knew that as soon as the water hit me, I would be done for the day, I thought about my moves at the gym and fancied that I could have gone another half hour. I knew it was the endorphins talking, but I felt great.

I turned on the radio and waited to hear the pre-game for the Red Sox as I got into the shower. They were doing amazing things this summer, and I allowed myself to fantasize that they would defeat the Yankee's Evil Empire in time for my birthday in October. A pennant would make a hell of a thirty-fifth birthday present. Hell, why stop there? Why not wish for the Series?

It could happen. Everything in the world is possible.

I went downstairs to find the answering machine light was on. It was Stuart Feldman. My first forensic science class starts next semester. It would mean late nights, long hours, massive juggling, and the possibility of some seriously scary stuff.

I couldn't wait.